"DON'T ASK MORE OF ME THAN I CAN GIVE...."

Like burning coals, Arif's eyes glinted darkly at Holly, but the hand that traced her lips was gentle.

Her mouth tingled deliciously; still, she had to speak. "I can't be satisfied with half measures," she whispered.

"You want the primrose path?" he taunted. Then his lips crushed hers in a kiss that blotted out all reason. Lifting his head, he murmured with rare tenderness, "If you were my Turkish wife I would christen you Melahat—beauty."

Never had Holly desired so deeply, but her aching vulnerability had blinded her to the harsh reality of their situation. "If!" she cried. "Always if—if you loved me, if I were your wife.... What can you give me beyond those meaningless phrases?"

"Nothing at all," was his inevitable response.

And though her heart protested, she knew it was true.

AND NOW...

SUPERROMANCES

Worldwide Library is proud to present a
sensational new series of modern love stories—
SUPERROMANCES

Written by masters of the genre, these longer,
sensuous and dramatic novels are truly in keeping
with today's changing life-styles. Full of intriguing
conflicts, the heartaches and delights of true love,
SUPERROMANCES are absorbing stories—
satisfying and sophisticated reading that lovers
of romance fiction have long been waiting for.

SUPERROMANCES
Contemporary love stories for the woman of today!

CASEY DOUGLAS

INFIDEL OF LOVE

A SUPERROMANCE FROM
WORLDWIDE

TORONTO · LONDON · NEW YORK · SYDNEY

Published, July 1982

First printing May 1982

ISBN 0-373-70025-3

Printed in U.S.A.

CHAPTER ONE

HOLLY TOUCHED HER SPURS to the mare's chestnut flanks. At this subtle command Mandarin Lady's ears quivered against her flaxen mane and she leaped into a canter, her hooves drumming sharply on the frosty ground. Holly worked the reins lightly in her gloved hands, so intent on the surge and movement of the swiftly cantering mare beneath her that the gray stone walls of the low château were nothing but a blur glimpsed through the leafless elms.

After five minutes of hard riding, her own honey-blond hair had worked free from its practical bun so that its long silken strands seemed to blend in with those of the mare as Holly leaned down to whisper, "Good girl! If you ride like that tomorrow, the race will be ours."

Horse and rider retraced their steps more slowly now along the dirt path separating the bare manicured lawns of Malmaison Château outside Paris from the wilder stretches of terrain where the international competition would be ridden the following morning. Holly gently pulled back on the reins as they approached the centuries-old stone-and-timber stables that had once housed the mounts of Napoleon and his empress, Josephine.

Holly's relaxed mood was shattered, however, as they approached the corner of an outlying tumble-down shack and the mare without warning reared up, nearly throwing her from the saddle. Pulling in swiftly at the reins of the nervously whinnying animal, who still pranced and lunged against the bit, Holly was at last able to risk a glance around to the source of the mare's disturbance. Her taut gaze was met by the bold laughing eyes of a man who sat easily in his saddle atop a black stallion despite the animal's excitement at sight of the mare.

Mandarin Lady swerved and shied before her curvetting admirer. Through all her nervous prancing the mare's eyes were fixed on the stallion, who lifted his head high and flexed haughtily as if to proclaim his dominance. Amid the turbulence of the plunging horses, Holly's practiced eyes took in the stallion's straining muscles, his fine sweep of shoulder and erect carriage. Her gaze traveled upward once again, and for a moment it seemed that all the fire and fettle exhibited in the rearing stallion was but an extension of the wild-eyed rogue who held his reins.

Caught off guard by her inquisitive stare, the rider relaxed his steellike grip on the reins and the stallion surged forward. Instantly the man had his powerful animal in check once more, but not before Mandarin Lady, in a state of fearful excitement at his advance, had backed up against the shack and kicked through the low timbers.

Angered now as she caught the jagged sound of wood against the mare's unprotected leg, Holly addressed the man as bitingly as her limited French would allow. "You have no business riding such a horse, *monsieur*, if you don't have the ability to control him."

To her surprise she saw his lips, partially hidden by a full black mustache, curve upward in a smile. "But you're mistaken, *mademoiselle*," he rejoined in flawless French. "It's the mare who is quite uncontrollable. I've never seen a female flirt quite so shamelessly before. She prances and minces like a chorus girl."

Holly's green eyes darkened angrily at this gibe, but she did not bother to reply as she flung her leg across the mare's back and slid to the ground. Pulling the leather glove from her right hand, she ran her fingers gently upward along the hind leg over the hock.

"I don't think she's injured, *mademoiselle*."

Startled, Holly whirled around to face the man. Somehow she hadn't expected him to dismount. She had sensed an arrogance of bearing about him, a careless offhanded manner of dealing with women that should have made him gallop away from the amusing little scene with the laughter still twisting the full lips beneath his mustache. Yet there he stood before her. Holly watched in silence as he, too, ran a practiced hand from pastern to hock. His fingers were long and supple, the backs of his hands dark, deeply veined and work scarred.

"No, I don't think there's any danger. Luckily, the wood is half-rotted and so moist that there are no sharp edges to catch the leg tendons." He stood up straight and grinned. "You have no need to worry that her feminine grace will be hampered."

Riled by his implication that it was the mare who somehow was at fault, Holly drew herself up to her full five feet nine inches, intending to fix him with a disdainful eye. Once ashamed of her rather imposing height, Holly had outgrown her tomboy coltishness and learned to carry herself as regally as a queen. She had found, too, that her stature could be a subtle tool in bringing people around to her own way of thinking.

With this man who stood before her, however, it was she who was forced to crane her neck upward to regard him. He was a full five inches taller than Holly, his own commanding stature proof that the energy and character she had felt flowing between the man and his steed had not been an illusion. Even as he stood relaxed before her, his riding crop held negligently in his gloved hand, Holly felt strength and a rugged sense of power emanating from him. He would be a formidable rival in competition, she thought involuntarily.

Nettled then at having allowed herself to feel intimidated by the man, Holly raised her chin even higher as she regarded him. "I hope you ride a gelding in tomorrow's race, *monsieur*. With his wayward appetites, that stallion will be a menace to everyone on the field."

The man's laughter was surprisingly low and suggestive. "Why should I deny pleasures to my mounts that I myself take full advantage of?" He reached up and ran his hands slowly down Mandarin Lady's gleaming chestnut flanks, his keen eye not missing the subtle blush that spread across Holly's attractive features, already rosy from the cold morning air. "Besides," he added with cool arrogance, "I can control Sinjon absolutely."

Holly glanced across at the black stallion he called Sinjon, tethered now to a tree and calmly awaiting the return of his master. "That's what I so admire about European men," she retorted dryly, "their humility."

His dark eyes flashed at her. "Is that the trait that brings *you* to the European competition, *mademoiselle*—humility?"

Holly felt a smile tugging at her lips as she replied. "Touché, *monsieur*."

He flashed a grin in return, his eyes taking in more slowly the tall blond woman standing before him, from the frayed woolen pullover and faded jeans tucked into the tops of her muddy riding boots to the silken mass of fair windblown hair framing her face. "You are Norwegian?" he ventured at last.

Traces of the old tomboy grin lit up her features as she laughed up into his eyes. "Heavens, no! There may be a little Nordic blood coursing through my veins, but I'm American born and bred."

"Ah." The single spoken syllable was accompanied by another quick penetrating look, as though he couldn't quite connect her aristocratic fine-boned features with her down-at-heels working clothes. When he spoke again it was not in French but in faultless English that had a slight British intonation to it. "So the rich young American women find a new outlet for their energies," he ventured once again.

"We aren't all rich," Holly replied pointedly. "Mandarin Lady is owned by a Virginian woman who's backing me on the continental circuit. I make my living by winning purses...through my own riding abilities."

"I see." His eyes rested a moment on the frayed sleeves of her pullover. "No idle rich girl's sport for you."

"Precisely." Holly's voice was edged with hauteur, and her cool green eyes met his observant black gaze with the reckless challenge of two adversaries meeting on the field of battle.

He regarded her for another long moment, as though he had never met a woman quite like her before. "You're a professional, then," he remarked at last, although it was as much a question as a statement. "I have to admit that when I first heard about this competition with both men and women riders, I was quite skeptical. Now I see that I may find it something of a...challenge, after all."

Holly watched him as he ran his hand lightly across the mare's back, then gently rubbed her long nose with its blaze of white. His eyes seemed to judge the animal at a moment's glance, yet she sensed, too, a genuine love for horses in his capable touch. "Are you a professional competitor?" Holly asked, her eyes taking in his impeccable khaki jodhpurs, black sweater and highly polished black boots.

He met her gaze directly. "It's a convenient pastime for me."

"You don't take it seriously, then?"

"On the contrary. The circuit is quite important to me," he replied with a sardonic smile.

Regarding him intently, Holly noticed with surprise that in repose his sculpted Mediterranean features had an almost Asiatic cast to them. His cheekbones were set at a slight angle beneath heavily browed black eyes that hinted at untapped depths, and she guessed that his natural skin tone beneath the deep reddish bronze of his tan was dark olive. For the first time she was curious about his nationality, but it was too late to ask. He had already walked over to his spirited stallion and was untying the reins from the low tree branch when Holly called out impetuously, "I intend to win tomorrow!"

He turned and his dark eyes regarded her intently a moment. Then he threw back his head and laughed, a virile sound that brimmed with rich amusement. "Tell that to Sinjon," he replied, cocking his head at the stallion behind him. And with the easy grace of a man born to the saddle, he swung himself up onto the horse's back and rode down the path.

Staring after him, Holly was reminded of an ancient bas-relief she'd once seen that depicted Assyrian warriors on horseback riding into battle as if they were wolves coming down upon a fold of sheep. She shivered slightly in the crisp morning air at the strange comparison that had leaped unbidden to her mind. Never before had she met anyone like the arrogant dark-eyed horseman, as untamed as a wild mustang on the American plain. She sensed danger somehow in that wildness, a throbbing undercurrent of potent masculinity that had reared up openly between stallion and mare and was echoed more subtly between the man and herself. She felt her senses curiously alert and tense as she remounted the patiently waiting mare.

After a long leisurely pace around and around the yard, which served to cool down both animal and rider, Holly dismounted once again and led Mandarin Lady into the long low stable that had been newly refurbished for the meet. Grooms and trainers bustled back and forth among the rows of stalls, which bore the familiar smells of worn leather and hay. The muffled sound of stamping hooves echoed along the earthen corridor as they passed. Holly was curious to meet the other riders against whom she would be competing, but she had been the first at Malmaison that morning and no others had yet arrived. . . except for the master of Sinjon.

Her wandering train of thought was broken as a familiar rasping voice drawled from Mandarin Lady's stall, "There you are! I thought you two might've got lost on your mornin' workout."

"No chance, Rusty!" Holly grinned down at the diminutive trainer who stood waiting with curry comb and dandy brush in hand. "We had a terrific run."

"I always said Mandi-girl is dependable as the mornin' sun," he drawled, using his affectionate nickname for the proud mare. He delved into the pockets of his worn jacket and brought out a handful of carrots, which the animal nibbled at daintily from his hand. Rusty clucked and whispered soothingly to Mandarin Lady as he loosened her girth and removed the light saddle.

Watching the two together, Holly smiled to herself. Rusty Wilkins was a Wyoming-born man who had begun his horse-riding career as a cowpoke roustabout on the Western cattle plains before leaving to try his luck as a jockey in thoroughbred racing. He'd retired after a respectable career on the racing circuit and had since devoted himself to training. Despite her long association with the ex-jockey, she never ceased to be amused by the contrast between his lazy drawling speech and the quick-eyed taut manner born of his lightning-quick rider's reflexes.

As he glanced up from his grooming chores, Rusty happened to catch her eye. "What're you starin' at, gal?" the trainer growled, although his eyes were affectionate. He'd worked with Holly for six years and had watched her blossom from an ungainly coltish fifteen-year-old into a superb rider and a beautiful woman, though she still hadn't come to realize the latter fact. He scowled suddenly.

Holly laughed over at him as she reached down into the supply box amid the saddle soap and metal polish to retrieve a hoof pick. "And what are you looking so angry about?" she teased.

"Aw, nothin'," he grumped. "I was just thinking of Winthrop, that lamebrained ex-fiancé of yours, trying to keep you from riding."

Holly became serious as she shot the trainer a warning glance. "Look, Rusty, you know we had an agreement not to bring up Stan anymore," she said quietly.

"I know," the old trainer persisted stubbornly. "But I was just thinking it was the smartest move you ever made to break off with that—"

"Rusty!" she interrupted warningly.

"All right, all right," he conceded. "I'm only hoping you'll use as much good hard sense in getting our Mandi-girl over them fences tomorrow."

Relieved to have the conversation diverted to another topic, Holly caught it up eagerly. "What do you think? Have you walked the course yet, Rusty? I'm afraid it's a difficult one."

The trainer shook his gray head, which retained traces of fiery red hair. Rusty was not one to mince words. "It'll be the toughest you've ever ridden." He waited to let the words sink in, pleased to see that she didn't flinch. If he had schooled the girl in one thing in the past six years, it was to be a hard-boiled realist. She knew her limitations as well as her strengths, and that pleased him. Honesty and courage were as important in the rider as they were in the horse, especially now that she was entering the ranks with her new professional status.

"But you think we've got a good chance?" she asked, her green eyes flashing in the dim stall.

"'Course I do," he replied at once. "Otherwise why d'you think we bothered to cross that danged ocean?"

Holly laughed, her good spirits restored. "Have you seen any of the other competitors yet?"

"Not to talk to, but I got a list of their names out in the minivan. It'll be a real international show all right. Lots of South American and English riders, some from Japan, Australia, Turkey and Denmark. Not too many from the Communist countries, though I think there might be one Russian girl ridin'."

Holly thought then of the dark-eyed rider and his spirited stallion whom she and Mandarin Lady had encountered on the deserted path. "Did you happen to see the mustached man with his black mount?" she asked casually.

"Yep," the grizzled ex-jockey replied laconically. "That one's all bone and strength, fine shoulders and carriage. Frankly I ain't ever seen such a potential for power."

"Are you describing the man or the horse?" Holly teased, although her heart sank a little at Rusty's unflinchingly honest assessment of the magnificent black stallion.

Rusty looked up with narrowed eyes at her question. "Well, I'm describing both, I reckon. The rider looked as if his mother had foaled him in the saddle and weaned him on mare's milk, just like those wild Mongols in the history books."

"I had the same impression," Holly replied broodingly to the trainer's half-jocular words.

"Never mind now," Rusty put in quickly. "Our Mandi-girl's got the spirit and courage to meet that bold black devil as an equal on the riding course." He reached up and scratched the mare between her ears, while she in turn nuzzled his arm affectionately. Rusty turned back to Holly. "Now, why don't you put that hoof pick in your hand to work digging out anything she's picked up on her run, while I go out and check the feed? I don't trust this European feed nohow...not enough oils," he muttered half to himself as he opened the stall and headed toward the minivan parked at the far end of the stable yard.

After Rusty had gone, Holly lifted the mare's right rear hoof and set to work with the pick, her mind only half on the task before her. Her thoughts roamed once again to Sinjon's master with his flashing black eyes and arrogant confident grin. She recalled with a twinge of guilt her own air of bravado in informing him that she was a professional rider. Holly hadn't added that this was to be her first professional competition and that the Virginian who owned Mandarin Lady had not exactly hired her. The woman, Jean Sims, was Holly's aunt. Her air of false bravado, however, did not take away from her stated intent to win the race, or at the very least to place among the top finishers. It meant more to Holly than anything else in the world to be successful on the riding circuit. *That black-eyed equestrian and his superb stallion be damned,* she thought with a return of spirit.

Her uncomfortable musings were interrupted by a low discreet cough from outside the stall. She dropped the mare's hoof and wheeled around. "Alec... Alec Wright! What on earth are you doing here?" she cried in delight, letting herself quickly out of the stall and throwing her arms around the man. Then she drew back, realizing rather belatedly that her dusty riding clothes would leave their mark on the exquisitely tailored dark wool suit. The man was as elegant and impeccable in his personal grooming as he was in his diplomatic dealings.

Alec smiled at her with an expression that combined affection and amusement. "How are you, Hortense, my dear?"

She shook her head petulantly. "Don't call me by

that dreadful name, Uncle Alec!'' she cried, reverting automatically to her childhood pet name for the beloved man who'd been a close friend of her family for twenty years. "I'm just plain Holly now... Holly MacKnight!''

Alec smiled understandingly at the spirited young woman who stood before him. She had been christened Hortense MacKnight Holliford after her maternal grandmother and had lived with the burdensome name for fifteen years. It was Rusty Wilkins who'd begun by calling her Holliford, which was finally shortened to Holly. It was a short step from that to adopting Holly MacKnight as her name when she'd begun riding in competition several years earlier. Alec Wright knew it was a symbolic act of rebellion against all that the Holliford name stood for. Even as he regarded her now, he saw the pleasure in her sparkling eyes dimmed slightly by suspicion.

"Did dad send you here to check up on me, Uncle Alec?'' she asked quietly.

He continued to regard the girl affectionately. "Not at all, child. I was sent here by the justice department to do some diplomatic troubleshooting in the Middle East. Since I have a few days in Paris I thought I'd look up my favorite girl.''

She leaned over and kissed his cheek. "Thanks, Uncle Alec. You're sweet.'' As they slowly strolled together out of the dim stables into the pale sunshine of a December morning, she turned to him again. "Do you have an engagement this evening?''

"No, I don't, Holly. Shall we meet for dinner?'' he inquired with a smile.

"Actually I'd be very appreciative if you'd be my

escort to the Horsemen's Ball, which the British Embassy is hosting this evening. Old Rusty wouldn't set foot on a dance floor on a bet. Besides,'' she added with a rueful shake of her head, ''even if he did go we'd look more like a crazy Mutt-and-Jeff routine.''

"I see what you mean,'' Alec chortled as he watched the short-statured ex-jockey approach them.

"How're you, sir?'' Rusty began, putting out a hand to the diplomat, who seemed to tower above him.

While the two men spoke to each other, Holly's attention was caught by a crescendoing thunder of hooves and she turned to watch as Sinjon and his master rode into the yard. The stallion's neck was flecked with foam and his nostrils were dilated from the excitement and exertion of the run. Beyond Sinjon's rearing head, his master's face perspired despite the morning chill, the sweat imparting a silken sheen to his dark sun-bronzed features. Watching them, once again Holly felt a curious sense of apprehension and quickening of her pulse. She saw the slight smile on his lips and unaccountably felt the color rising in her cheeks as he nodded curtly in her direction. He was gone then, disappearing beyond the outlying stable buildings, and she returned her attention with an effort to the two men who stood before her.

"Good. It's settled, then,'' Rusty was saying.

Holly regarded him blankly.

"You're going to ride back into Paris with Mr. Wright so that you don't have to hang around here waiting for me to finish up my chores,'' Rusty explained.

"Oh, how nice," she replied faintly, not at all certain now that she even wanted to leave the château grounds. "But really, it would be no trouble for me to take the Malmaison bus later to the Métro station."

"Nonsense, child," Alec replied firmly, steering her in the direction of his rented blue sedan. "No sense in your wasting two hours on the bus and subway when we can be in the heart of Paris within thirty minutes."

After guiding the car onto the busy highway, Alec turned to Holly and asked, "How does the situation really stand with your parents? When I broached the subject in Philadelphia with James, he became extremely annoyed."

"Yes. Dad can be very unpleasant when he sets his mind to it," she replied ironically. "Things have been positively grim since I broke off with Stan. Mother and dad have threatened to disown me... as if I care a damn about the Holliford millions! Aunt Jean has given me this chance to prove myself professionally on Mandarin Lady. That means much, much more to me than being a wealthy—and bored—socialite."

"You and young Winthrop quarreled?" Alec asked quietly, his sympathy tinged with curiosity.

"I suppose it was I who picked the quarrel as an excuse. We simply weren't right for each other," Holly explained, her eyes staring past the tidy French villages and barren winter fields as she recalled her last conversation with Stan Winthrop. Their parting had been as dry and passionless as their six-month engagement, although he had conceded to being "perturbed" at her thoughtless disruption of his future plans. She laughed bitterly to herself. The engagement, orchestrated as a perfect alliance between the two scions of Philadelphia high society, had been yet another futile effort on the Hollifords' part to force their daughter into a more proper role. But Holly had rebelled in the end, using her twenty-first birthday as the opportune time to break off with Stan and sign up for the European events.

At twenty-one she felt herself to be her own woman at last, free of the wealth and strictures of her parents' society. After a lifetime of being fawned over as the daughter of James and Alice Holliford, she found it wonderfully refreshing now to be a Ms. Nobody, prepared to succeed or fail entirely on her own abilities and character. She couldn't put the feeling into words for Alec. Despite his kindly sympathy, he, too, was bound by the upper levels of society in which he moved. Unlike Holly, however, Alec loved that kind of world. It was his milieu, much as the dangerous and exciting world of the horse arena had become Holly's. She sighed and glanced over at the gray-haired diplomat. "It's so hard to explain," she said at last.

They had reached the outskirts of the city, its familiar landmarks of the Eiffel Tower and the crowded hills of Montmartre standing out among the gleaming high-rise office buildings of the new Parisian skyline.

"Where are you staying?" Alec asked her as he directed the car onto Avenue Marceau, one of the city's principal arteries feeding into the Arc de Triomphe.

"It's a little place called the Bonaparte, on Rue Bonaparte just off Boulevard St. Germain," Holly explained, and fifteen minutes later Alec had brought the car to a stop on the narrow tree-lined street. She saw his brow contract a little as he took in the old-fashioned stone facade of the hotel. "Don't say a word, Uncle Alec," she warned with a teasing smile, "or you'll sound like mother. The Hôtel Bonaparte may be a relic from the last century, but it's quaint, comfortable and cheap. Besides, it's all that I can afford now that they've cut off my allowance."

"Perhaps I can help," Alec began, reaching into his suit pocket for his billfold.

"No, please!" Holly's arm shot out immediately, her eyes managing to express laughter and genuine alarm at the same time. "That wasn't a complaint; it was a boast. You don't quite fully understand yet, do you, dear Alec? I love being poor! It makes me all the more determined to succeed on my own."

Alec leaned over and kissed her cheek. "If you insist, child," he replied uncertainly. "Shall I fetch you around eight, then?"

"Perfect," Holly agreed as she stepped out onto the sidewalk. "And thanks for the lift."

After bathing away the morning's grime, Holly donned warm walking clothes and left the faded chic of the Bonaparte's high-ceilinged lobby for the near-by Quai Voltaire, which skirted the Seine. She loved the profusion of art galleries, studios and open-air booksellers' stalls that lined the street between the Pont des Arts and the Pont du Carrousel. Holly walked quickly to ward off the bitterly chill wind that blew across the river, and she buried her hands more deeply into the pockets of her parka.

The pale sunshine that had managed to break through the winter cloud cover over the fields of Malmaison had not reached the city limits of Paris, so that the afternoon was gray and gloomy. Holly stopped a moment at the wall and glanced down at the wide stone walkways that paralleled the river's edge. They were deserted except for an occasional *clochard*, or bum, who sat hunched beneath the arches of the bridge. In the middle of the Seine a flat barge was overtaken by a fishing trawler, and she watched as the fishermen waved jauntily to the crewmen on the slow-moving freight barge.

Holly breathed in the chill invigorating air, willing her mind to be clear and calm. Her surprise encounter with Alec Wright had served to dredge up all the old arguments and turmoil she had hoped to forget. Despite his kindness to her, Alec was a part of the Holliford world, which she had no wish to rejoin. She forced her thoughts back to the morning ride and to Mandarin Lady's performance across the open fields, mentally ticking off the mare's good and bad points on the workout.

But even these thoughts were stymied as her rebellious mind thrust into vision the dark rider who had teased and somehow challenged her, man to woman, on the wooded path. She saw his strong-boned face before her with unbidden clarity, the full sensual lower lip framed by a black mustache and his equally black eyes, which had seemed to flash as easily in anger as in laughter. Once again she felt the strange quickening in her blood, and she wondered if he would be present that night at the embassy ball.

THE WIDE EMBASSY FOYER was awash in prismatic colors reflected off the crystal lobes of the chandelier, which quivered each time the heavy mahogany doors were opened to admit another guest. As Holly waited with nervous impatience to be introduced—her hand clasped reassuringly in the crook of Alec's elbow— she happened to catch her own reflection in a long gilt-framed mirror opposite her. The bias-cut skirt she wore was a shimmering vista of silken blue green plaid broken only by the elegant line of a black velvet belt around her slim waist. A thin gold chain with a teardrop diamond pendant shone against her throat, drawing the eye to the full contours of her breasts beneath the bare-cut bodice. As she swung her head in confused delight at the reflected vision, which bore no traces of the gawky tomboyish image she'd carried within for so long, Holly saw the diamond studs sparkling in her earlobes through the dark burnished gold of her hair.

Her bemused contemplation before the mirror was broken as Alec smoothly drew her forward to the ballroom entrance and she was introduced to the British ambassador and his wife. A flash of royal blue caught the corner of her eye, and she turned to stare into a familiar bold black gaze. "Miss Mac-Knight, I should like you to meet Captain Arif Hakal, who will represent Turkey in the competition tomorrow."

The ambassador's formal introduction already seemed a distant echo as she felt herself being pulled with breathtaking suddenness onto the dance floor by the captain in dress uniform. She cast a helpless little glance over her shoulder in Alec's direction, but the American, already engrossed in conversation with the British diplomat, who was an acquaintance of many years' standing, didn't seem even to have noticed that his young companion had been dragged away so summarily by another man.

Alec Wright was forgotten then as she felt Arif's hand slip around her waist and he led her into the slow cadence of a waltz. For a brief panic-stricken moment Holly thought she would not remember the hated boarding-school dance instruction that had been forced upon her in the eighth grade, but surprisingly she felt herself falling into the three-step rhythm as her partner wheeled her with effortless grace around the gradually filling room.

Holly felt his eyes upon her face and she glanced up into a gaze that seemed to hold her with an air of cool, almost insolent possession. Nettled by his easy assured arrogance, she addressed him with frosty detachment. "Is it Turkish custom to take something without asking the owner's permission first?"

His full lips parted in a grin, revealing teeth milky white against the lush blackness of his mustache. "Not Turkish custom, Miss MacKnight, but mine alone. Besides," he added, his dark eyes narrowing to unreadable slits, "what I want is usually offered before I have to ask."

She felt his arm tighten against her back as he drew

her more closely against him. With unexpected force she became aware of his lean body, hard, muscular and supple from long hours in the saddle. She sensed a poised tenseness within him, as though he were holding back the urge to leap beyond the civilized cadence of the dance music. The feral tension within him washed over Holly, and she found herself unwillingly responding to it with quickened heartbeat and a curious warmth that spread along her limbs.

Arif's glance slid to the other dancers in the ballroom, his eyes sharp as black diamonds as they surveyed the whirling crowd with a lazy yet somehow hungry detachment. Once again Holly was reminded of the image that had come to her on the Malmaison path: a lean wolf among the sheep. She stared up at him so intently that he was forced to recall his attention to the woman in his arms.

He caught her questioning look and deflected it with a smile. "You're as light and graceful as the filly you ride," he murmured.

Beyond the smooth flattery, however, Holly detected a subtle note of wariness, almost as though he feared she'd glimpsed too closely into his soul. The sensation was gone in an instant. She read nothing more in his bold expression than the same teasing challenge to her femininity with which he'd regarded her that morning.

"Perhaps so, but I'm not nearly as flirtatious as Mandarin Lady," Holly commented dryly.

He grinned appreciatively at her coolly ironic retort. "I'm forced to concede the truth in that. The similarity between mistress and mount goes only so far. Sinjon, however, is like his owner in every respect—he desires to be master of all he sees.'' Arif's eyes moved slowly along her bare shoulders before dropping to her breasts, the soft creaminess of their full high contours just evident beyond the curve of her bodice.

The molten passion in his dark gaze seemed to ignite a smothered flame deep within her. Suddenly she was aware of his strong supple fingers against the small of her back, kneading her skin through the thin silky fabric and pushing her even more closely toward him until her breasts were crushed against his unyielding chest. Instinctively she pulled away and straightened her back, as if the lofty hauteur of her bearing were a protective veil shielding her against depths that were better left unexplored.

Although he relaxed his hold in response to her tacit withdrawal, his flashing eyes still pursued her relentlessly. ''Yes,'' he murmured in a voice that was low and deceptively soft. ''Sinjon knows exactly what he wants. . . as do I.''

Holly struggled to keep her breathing even and regular, fearful, too, that her racing pulse would betray the seething emotions he had aroused in her. When she spoke at last, her tone was cool, light and faintly mocking. ''Stallions are capricious. No doubt it was nothing more than a passing fancy on Sinjon's part.''

Once again, when he spoke, Arif's voice was so low that she was forced to lean closer to catch the words over the music and the laughing conversation of the other dancers. ''Perhaps. Still, I find it a tragedy to see the animal's burning desire destined to go unfulfilled."

Alarmed at the turn of the conversation, Holly rather abruptly changed the subject. "Are you still active in the military, Captain Hakal?" she inquired, the words sounding ludicrously stilted even to her own ears.

"No, I am not, Miss MacKnight," he replied with such a studied air of decorum that Holly knew he was mocking her own formality. "After I graduated from the University of Liverpool I served in the Turkish Army for nine years. Though I've officially retired from the military, I still compete under its aegis."

"You were in England, then, for four years?" Holly asked, cocking her head with genuine interest. "I thought I detected a faint British accent."

He smiled briefly. "Yes. I studied equine management and science. Of course, I competed whenever I could—the Royal International Horse Show, the hunterchase at Fontwell in Sussex, Harwood Hall. . . . Riding is my passion; or rather," he amended with a flash of dark fire in his eyes, "it is one of my passions."

Holly ignored this last sally as she reflected on what he'd just told her. She guessed him to be thirty-four or thirty-five. She noticed then the flecks of gray in his thick mass of dark hair, like tracings of steel on black velvet. He truly was a seasoned professional on the riding circuit, but she refused to be daunted by the knowledge. It only strengthened her resolve to win on the following morning.

Feeling his eyes fixed inquiringly on her face, she

addressed him once again. "You make it sound as though these competitions mean everything to you, yet this morning at Malmaison you told me the circuit was merely a convenient pastime."

"Did I say that?" His fierce gaze lost its cutting edge for an instant. Holly felt the wide powerful shoulder beneath her hand shrug almost imperceptibly. Arif glanced restlessly about the ballroom once more before continuing. "I suppose what I meant is that I've been a playboy long enough and must settle down. Actually, what I'm seeking is a wife."

Holly looked up, startled at such a bald pronouncement. The somberness was gone from his eyes so that she could not be certain now whether he had been serious. Without her realizing it, the string orchestra had slipped into another melody, and Arif whirled her adroitly through the surging crowd.

He drew her closely to him and she relaxed a little against his chest. "You know, Holly MacKnight," he whispered down to her with a caressive laugh, "you're a rare woman. Beautiful and feminine, yet strong. I can hold you in my arms like this without fear of crushing you. I could envision a woman like you beside me—long limbed, mettlesome and proud. And I'd be willing to wager that if a man cared to, he would find an enkindling spark of passion beneath that cool facade."

Holly stared up at him, her green eyes with their flecks of amber seeming to capture and deepen the pinpoints of light scattered by the flickering candelabra. She hoped her face did not betray the flush of excitement she felt inside at the words no man had ever spoken to her before. "Thank you, captain, but I'm not interested in marriage," she replied in a tone that she hoped was crisp and dry. "I've just recently broken off an engagement."

To her surprise Arif threw back his head and laughed, an explosive sound charged with energy and passion. "A pity for the man. You were too much woman for him, perhaps?" His eyes were as caressing as his words had been earlier, but there was laughter still in his voice when he spoke to her again. "But you misunderstood the meaning of what I said. You are quite beautiful, Holly, but you don't suit my...requirements. I was making no offer of marriage. Like the capricious stallion, I can only offer you the passing pleasures of my bed."

She went white at these words. "How very generous of you, captain," she replied icily, the arctic coldness of her voice reflected in eyes as hard as greenstone. "But I'm not interested in being any man's mistress."

Arif grinned, his nostrils flared like those of his excited stallion. He seemed totally unabashed by her curt rejection. "More's the pity, Holly. You seem to have been molded for my arms."

"Save your sweet blandishments for a woman who may be more susceptible to them than I," she retorted haughtily.

His eyes flashed with dark fire at that. "As you wish, *mam'selle*."

Without another word he deposited her at Alec's side with a curt bow, then disappeared into the crowd.

"You seem to be enjoying yourself, Hort—or rather, Holly," Alec remarked with a pleasant smile.

"Yes, quite," she replied tautly, her eyes following Arif's dark head and massive shoulders, which seemed to tower over the crowd.

"Who is that arresting-looking young captain who asked you to dance?"

"Arif Hakal. Rusty thinks he'll be the competitor to beat tomorrow."

Alec shook his head. "I wouldn't doubt it. The Turks are superb horsemen."

Thereafter Holly danced a few times with Alec. He would have been a more attentive escort, but Holly insisted that he continue his reminiscing with the British ambassador, which both men seemed to be enjoying thoroughly. She was spared the humiliation of being a total wallflower, however, by being invited to dance by two men who appeared undaunted by her height. The first was an earnest, rather gangling young Briton whom she couldn't possibly imagine to be collected enough to ride in the grueling event. The second was an affable strapping Dane with a rather unfortunate propensity for trampling on her toes. After that Holly decided to give up the pretense of socializing and went to stand at Alec's side, a smile fixed in position on her face.

From time to time her gaze traveled over the colorful swirling crowd, green eyes drawn against their will to the tall rugged form of the black-eyed captain. He seemed to have found a most willing partner in a beautiful auburn-haired woman as petite and curvaceous as Holly was tall and slim. Holly despised Arif

Hakal for his arrogant proposition, as though he'd taken it for granted that she would willingly tumble into his bed. Nevertheless, she felt an unreasoning pang of jealousy as he leaned down more closely to hear some witticism his partner was whispering up to him.

Staring after the darkly handsome profile, Holly realized that her first intuition had been unerring: Arif Hakal was a man accustomed to using—and discarding—women as they suited his needs. Hadn't he even described his search for a wife in terms of a woman who could meet his requirements? She felt the anger swelling up within her once again. Yet even as her nettled pride rose fiercely at the remembered insult, she felt an undercurrent of desire budding within. Uncontrollaby she felt it rising to meet his magnetic sensuality, as overwhelming even in memory as it had been when he'd held her in his arms on the dance floor. With her strong will she steeled herself to beat down the alarming feelings, and she even hoped that Arif would approach once more so that she might coldly rebuff him. He did not stray to her side again, however, nor did he even glance in her direction.

In the end it was with a tremendous feeling of relief that Holly saw the dimming of the candelabra that signaled the close of the evening festivities, and she donned her wrap with such alacrity that she and Alec were the first guests to have their car brought around by the valet. As they were settled in the front seat of the sedan, Alec turned to his young companion. "You seem keyed up," he observed with his usual keen sense of perception. "Are you worried about tomorrow's race?"

"Yes," Holly lied. She hadn't thought about the race at all except in terms of a one-on-one battle with the arrogant Turkish captain who was so damnably confident in his mastery over both horses and women.

"How about a nightcap at Montmartre, then?" Alec inquired solicitously. "A thimbleful of cognac might help to relax you so that you can sleep well before the competition."

Holly shot him a grateful smile. "That sounds delightful." As Alec wheeled the car along the wide deserted boulevards to the steep crowded back lanes of the picturesque hilltop quarter, she asked casually, "Who was the auburn-haired woman at the embassy?"

"Stunning creature, wasn't she?" Alec replied. "The ambassador pointed her out to me. Her name is Geneviève Lamine. She is half French and half Tunisian. Her father is a steel magnate. She's a pampered young aristocrat. The family owns a stableful of horses at Rambouillet."

"I see."

Alec took his eyes off the twisting cobblestone lane they were climbing to glance over at Holly. "Do you think the Frenchwoman will be a formidable rival?"

Holly smiled bitterly at the unintended irony of his words before replying, "That's difficult to say."

Alec parked the sedan and the two strolled along the lane fronting Sacre Coeur basilica, which sat like a graceful white sentinel above the jumbled rooftops of the city. Far beneath the cold starry dome of winter sky, the lights of Paris lay scattered before them as if they'd been flung down by the negligent hand of a bored goddess. In the distance she could just pick out the dark gleam of the Seine as it divided and flowed around Notre Dame on its ancient island.

A few minutes later she and Alec were seated at a small marble-topped table in a nearly deserted bistro, grateful for the amber-colored cognac that warmed them against the chill of the night. As she glanced over at the beloved familiar features, Holly seemed to notice for the first time the long careworn lines cut into the handsome planes of his face. His eyes held a distant expression.

Feeling her gaze upon him, Alec looked up. "You know, my dear, I still have the feeling that you think I'm judging you harshly for having run away from Philadelphia and the life your parents had mapped out for you. But I'm not. I've never told this to anyone before, but when I was in Paris after the war as a bustling young attaché, I met a woman. She was an Italian artist, a refugee from the Mussolini regime, and quite beautiful. We fell in love, and I desperately wanted to marry her. But my father learned of the liaison and exerted pressure on me to end the relationship, insisting that such a tie could only hamper me in my diplomatic career. Against my heart, I followed that judgment."

"Uncle Alec, how terribly sad!"

He smiled tiredly at the vivid young woman before him. "It's much too late for regrets on my part, dear. The simple moral of my tale is that I hope you'll follow your own heart and not bow down to what the rest of the world demands of you."

Holly reached across the table and touched his hand. "Thank you, Uncle Alec. I'll remember that."

CHAPTER TWO

LIKE SPONTANEOUS COMBUSTION, excitement seemed to flare up in the barren pastoral fields of Malmaison. It spread from the crowds, gathered on hillocks and car tops to witness the grueling four-mile circuit, to the horses circling and prancing with arched necks in the paddock. The sun struggled to emerge from the frieze of wind-driven clouds that overhung the course like a heavy mantle.

Holly sat quietly in the saddle, willing her tense hands to relax on the reins, while Mandarin Lady stood with ears pricked as if she were straining to catch a distant sound. The proud thoroughbred was alert and poised, yet aware of the tension and anxiety in her mistress, which was communicated downward by the pressure of Holly's thighs against her chestnut coat.

Holly thought back to the bitterly cold hour at dawn when she had walked the course step by step with the imperturbable Rusty. The blackthorn hedges and five-foot post and rails over which she would have to school the mare had loomed with frightening immensity. Rusty had talked softly along the entire route, pointing out each dip and hollow and indicating the best takeoff for each fence.

She had quailed inwardly at the thought of the thirty-fence course that would be run at a punishing six hundred and fifty yards per minute. "Rusty, I'm frightened," she'd confessed at last in a taut whisper.

"That's good," the trainer had shot back. "Use the fear. It'll give you that extra edge of awareness. Just remember what I told you. Stick to the inside. The fences may be a tad higher, but Mandi-girl can handle 'em. It'll save you precious yards in the end."

Now Holly glanced around, her wide-open gaze taking in the bright panoply of silks representing two dozen international farms as if they were miniature medieval kingdoms. With a restless hand she smoothed the magenta-and-golden silks of the Sims' Virginia farm. Then her eyes found the dark gallant profile of Sinjon, his master bedecked in the crimson and white of the Turkish state. Arif's gaze seemed directed inward with intense concentration, and Holly could almost feel the tautness and strain emanating from within him. Somehow the thought gave her heart. She knew then that tension and fear did not belong to her alone.

The excitement in the air seemed to grow and swell, fed by the bustle of grooms making last-minute adjustments to bridles and girths and hurried consultations between riders and trainers. Prancing and swerving as if their hooves danced on hot coals, the horses were ready to leap into battle.

Rusty reached up and gave a final tug on the hand-sewn bridle. "Go for it, gals!" he whooped with barely controlled excitement.

They were at the starting line, the mounts jockeying for position in the milling, plunging lineup. Arif caught sight of Holly and broke his concentration to throw her a dazzling grin. "Your filly is gorgeous," he called over to her as his eyes took in the meticulously plaited locks of the mare's golden mane and tail. "But beauty is as beauty does. *Bonne chance, mademoiselle.*"

Annoyed at his dismissing tone, Holly inclined her head stiffly. "Good luck to you, *mon capitain.*"

Their brittle repartee was swallowed up by the sound of the starting gun, and Holly had no thoughts then but for the awesome course ahead of her. With hands light but firm on the reins, she kept the mare well back from the thundering herd. Mandarin Lady took the first jump like a seasoned pro, extending superbly and meeting the drop with ease. Then Holly was swept up into the pistonlike rhythm of her mount's stride and they took fence after fence with cool aplomb, gradually gaining ground as Holly religiously kept the mare to the inside edge of the course.

At the sixth obstacle, the vast blackthorn hedge that had caused such trembling in Holly's heart, she saw three horses go down. Riders were thrown helter-skelter while following steeds crashed into the imposing barrier. With stomach churning fearfully, Holly urged Mandarin Lady on. Her heart swelled with pride as the mare soared over the hedge and through the colorful melee of fallen jockeys and wild-eyed horses as if they were no more than a scattering of autumn leaves.

The course grew trickier as the track became

plowed and uneven from the crushing pressure of a hundred hooves. Riderless mounts, impossible to second-guess, veered and stumbled along without knowing where to run. Still Holly and the mare continued to gain ground. Glancing ahead she saw ten competitors racing against time and one another, schooling head and head over the jumps. At their fore, Holly caught a glimpse of brilliant scarlet against rippling black muscle, and the sight seemed to impel her forward like a goad.

It was nearly two-thirds over, twenty hurdles breached with ten left to go, but the brutal pace was demanding its toll. Holly felt the breath torn from her in painful gasps; still she managed to keep a steady firm pressure on Mandarin Lady. The animals, too, were approaching exhaustion: it was evident in their lowered heads and white-foamed sides. Holly and the mare had nearly reached the tails of the forerunners at the twenty-fifth fence when a bay gelding stumbled and fell, breaking the strides of the two mounts that rode on either side of it. One crashed full force into the heavy barrier, catapulting its rider into the muddy turf, while the other, a brown Arabian, soared over with legs asprawl.

Holly, following closely behind, was congratulating herself once more on the neat manner in which Mandarin Lady had sidestepped the confusion at the fence when midway through the jump she stared down in horror at the Arabian sprawled precisely where her own mare should be landing in the next second. The moment seemed to be frozen in stop motion as fear rose and pounded in her ears. Then in the same instant she felt Mandarin Lady execute a precise flying change and touch down not more than two inches from the unfortunate Arabian's head.

Adrenaline was surging in her blood as she flicked the mare's side lightly with her crop while crooning encouragement over her finely groomed head. There were but two competitors before her now, a gallant-looking gray Hanoverian and the black Sinjon. Holly pressed her spurs into the chestnut flanks and they surged past the gray, leaving no rider before them but the bold-eyed Turk. At the twenty-ninth fence Holly and her mount had nearly reached them, just a half stride behind as the double brush-and-wire obstacle was negotiated. Excited with this neck-and-neck schooling over the fence, Mandarin Lady surged forward so that she was even with the stallion. Holly felt more than saw the flickering glance of surprise cast in her direction by Arif.

At the thirtieth and final barrier the mounts took the fence at the same moment, as if they were partners in a wildly choreographed ballet. Seconds later, the beautiful mare and the fierce stallion thundered to the finish line as the surflike roar of the crowds gathered in a screaming crescendo that drowned out the clink of metal, the thundering hooves and the gasping agonized breaths of the competitors.

It was over then. Once past the finish, Holly drew in on the reins until the mare slowed to a trot. She slumped exhaustedly over Mandarin Lady's neck, which was hot and wet after the long punishing race. Crowds of shouting people surged onto the track, news photographers and well-wishers fighting for elbow space against the grooms and track officials as they all sought to reach the chestnut filly and the black stallion. Exhausted and emotionally spent, Holly did not glance up until she heard Rusty's familiar rasping drawl in her ear. "You ran like champs! I'm proud of you."

"Did...we...win?" Holly managed to ask between gasps of breath.

"Don't know yet," he replied, excitement threatening to burst through the laconic drawl. "They're already calling this the horse event of the year. Can you believe it, gal? A photo finish! Just as if this'd been a flat race on a quarter track!" He slapped his thigh in amazement.

A hush fell over the milling crowd as the track officials whistled shrilly for attention. But the call was simply to announce formally the third-place finisher, Lieutenant Tatiana Bulgakov, who rode the gray Hanoverian gelding called Kazan. Disappointed that the photo-finish results had not yet been received, the onlookers raised their voices once more in a loud speculative murmur.

"That Russian gal rode like a real trooper," Rusty observed approvingly.

Holly glanced over at the solemn dark-haired equestrienne, who seemed as lithe and small as a gymnast against the deep girth of her mount. Her attention was drawn back again as the official whistle shrilled piercingly once more.

"The winners are," the official barked out, "in first place Captain Arif Hakal, representing the Republic of Turkey, and in second place Mademoiselle Holly MacKnight, representing Sims' Meadows in the state of Virginia, U.S.A.''

It was over, the stark pronouncement somehow anticlimactic after the dramatic surging course of the race's final seconds. Holly had dismounted and begun to lead Mandarin Lady to the cool-down paddock when Arif broke through the pressing crowd to stand before her. ''You raced well, *mam'selle*,'' he began, his eyes brimming with excitement.

''Not well enough, captain,'' she answered shortly, tossing a length of blond hair over her shoulder, as she turned and led the mare away without a backward glance. She refused to concede to him the triumph of the moment.

Holly should have been delighted with her near victory. Indeed, the second-place purse of five thousand francs would ensure that she, Rusty and the mare could compete long into the spring events without having to worry about running short of funds. If the victor had been anyone other than Arif Hakal, the bitterness of defeat would not have tasted so strongly in her mouth. She had yearned to best him in the competition, but the arrogant Turk and his handsome stallion had proven themselves superior. He was a man accustomed to winning, and Holly had wanted to change that. The memory of Arif's arrogant offer of his bed, as if no woman would even think to refuse him, still rankled in her mind.

Slowly she walked the mare around the paddock, vowing to beat the dark-eyed captain on his own turf. That, she knew, might prove most difficult. The next scheduled site of the cross-country circuit was Istanbul, Arif's home soil.

Holly led the mare into her stall, her thoughts flashing ahead to the long train trip before them. The International Horsemen's Guild, which was sponsoring the meet, had arranged a special train to transport the competitors to Istanbul along the route made famous by the old Orient Express. How could she possibly avoid Arif Hakal for sixty hours on the train, she worried. She knew he would flaunt his victory in her face at every possible opportunity.

As if in tune with her agitated thoughts, Holly's hand scraped so roughly along the mare's still-wet flanks that Mandarin Lady turned to regard her inquiringly. "Sorry, my girl," Holly whispered contritely as she finished the grooming chore with rather more gentle hands. Finally she wrapped the protective bandages around the mare's legs and leaned back against the wooden stall. "We shall beat him in the end, Mandi-girl, one way or another; I promise you that. Our feminine pride demands no less."

THERE WAS NOTHING BUT CONFUSION at the Gare de l'Est, Paris's easternmost disembarkation point for rail lines heading into the heart of the European continent. The clamoring rhythmic chug of engines reverberated along the entire length of the platform as trains arrived and departed, and blue sparks flashed in the cold, rapidly falling dusk where steel met steel on the polished tracks. At the far end of the station Holly could just make out the lettering, *Transport Chevaux de France*, on the trucks backed up to the end train cars, and she knew that the horses were being loaded for the long trek to Istanbul. She glanced restlessly over the milling crowds, hoping to catch sight of her trainer's grizzled sandy-colored head. Holly soon realized that the task was a hopeless one, however, and she headed for the iron steps of the coach that matched the number on her ticket.

She was just setting her makeup bag out on the washstand of the narrow train compartment when there came a tentative knocking at the door. Opening it, she found herself staring down at a dark-eyed woman.

"Forgive me, miss," the woman began stiffly, her excellent English tinged with a definite foreign intonation, "but the conductor has assigned me to this car at the last moment."

Holly recognized her then as the Russian equestrienne who had placed third in the morning competition. "Oh, hello. Please come in. I had thought it an extravagance for them to have assigned one passenger to this twinberthed compartment," Holly smiled, eager to put the woman at ease. "You're Lieutenant Bugla... Bulka—"

"Bulgakov," she corrected, her mouth drawn in a thin line. "And you are Miss MacKnight. You ran a splendid race."

"Thanks, but so did you," Holly replied with a laugh.

"Not so well as I had hoped."

Holly saw the tightening along her jawline, heard the words that seemed a curious echo of her own feelings after she'd learned that Arif had beaten her by a nose, and she realized that each rider must have his own compelling reasons for wanting to win.

"I'm sorry to trouble you," the Russian lieutenant

went on rolling her *r*'s slightly as she spoke. "I know that Americans are accustomed to space and luxury, and I would have requested a *couchette* with a comrade of my country if there had been one. It was not meant that I take the overland trip to Istanbul, but my trainer was recalled to Moscow. So now I am here to watch over Kazan."

Holly let pass the remark about luxury-loving Americans. She sat down on the bunk and regarded the Russian curiously. The woman was not nearly as young as she had first imagined. There were dark circles under her eyes, and her coarse black hair was drawn back severely from the sharp planes of her face. It was Lieutenant Bulgakov's petite frame, as lithe and muscular as a boy's, that had given the first illusion of youth. Holly guessed that she must be in her mid-thirties. "So you were going to fly to Turkey for the next phase of the competition?" she asked conversationally.

"Yes. There would have been no point in my idling away two days on the train that could have been spent working out on the Selimiye track."

A teasing light flared in Holly's expressive eyes. "You were going to get the jump on the rest of us riders, then?"

Lieutenant Bulgakov raised herself stiffly, and Holly saw the first spark of emotion in the woman's eyes: it was anger. "My only goal is to achieve the utmost I can. It is not my fault that the rest of the competitors chose to travel by train."

"I was only joking," Holly retorted quickly, her own temper threatening to flare.

An uncomfortable silence followed, which was broken unexpectedly as the car lurched forward. Holly jumped up and peered out the window. "We're on our way!" She stared out at the lights of the offices and apartment buildings, which began to blur together beyond the station as the train picked up speed. Holly turned away from the window and switched on the light above the washstand. She felt the Russian's gaze intent upon her as she brushed a smoky gray green shadow over her eyelids, then touched the tips of her long lashes with mascara. Holly quickly finished her toilette with a light sweeping of blusher across her cheekbones and a slicker of peach gloss on her lips. Turning to the severe lieutenant, she held out the makeup kit. "Would you like to try some?"

Lieutenant Bulgakov drew back as if she'd been offered poison. "No, thank you. I have no time for such—" she searched her mind a moment for the proper word "—for such fripperies."

Before another awkward silence could ensue, Holly said quickly, "I'm going to join my trainer for dinner. Would you like to come along?" She had added that last as a polite formality, fully expecting the lieutenant to refuse. It was to her great surprise that Holly saw her nod stiffly in assent. It had not occurred to her that her new roommate, beyond the forbidding manner and harsh expression, might be quite lonely.

After a few wrong turns and finally being directed in the right direction by a pleasant conductor, the two women located the dining car. Holly immediately spotted the trainer, seated at one end of a long table set with six place settings. "Rusty Wilkins, I swear you're ruled by your stomach," Holly addressed him with mock severity.

He grinned up at her, his spoon poised above the bowl of steaming soup before him. "I can't deny it!"

After the introductions had been made between the tiny Russian lieutenant and the American trainer, Rusty observed, "That's a plucky surefooted steed you're riding, miss. I've always had a liking for the Hanoverians."

At this praise of Kazan, Lieutenant Bulgakov's eyes softened somewhat. "Thank you. He is a good horse."

A few minutes later Holly looked up from the menu the white-jacketed waiter had placed in her hands and saw that the Russian's gaze was directed toward the far end of the car. Feeling Holly's inquisitive eyes upon her, she turned to her companion with a taut smile that was almost a grimace. "You wonder what I am staring at?" The lieutenant cocked her head subtly to the rear right-hand corner of the car. "That man is—how do you say it in English—a tail. He follows me everywhere."

Shocked, Holly glanced swiftly at the burly but otherwise nondescript man who sat alone at a table, reading a newspaper as he ate. "He's to protect you?" she asked in disbelief.

The Russian's answering laugh was brittle. "To keep me from doing anything...foolish." The woman's sharp brown eyes moved then to the opposite side of the car. "Not only that, but I see another of his ilk."

Holly followed her gaze once more and regarded the second man, in his own way as nondescript as the first. He glanced down quickly at his cup when he saw the two women looking at him.

The Russian spoke again, lowering her voice instinctively. "I've never seen that one before, yet I know his kind all the same. Take my word, Miss MacKnight, he's another tail."

"Please call me Holly," the American replied automatically, feeling rather unsettled by her companion's strange conversation.

"And you must call me Tatiana," the Russian replied with rather dampening formality.

"That's a lovely name!" Holly said brightly, eager to put the conversation on a lighter track.

"Thank you. My father chose it. As a professor of Russian literature, he was a fervent admirer of the great Tolstoy. That author, too, had a daughter called Tatiana."

"Your parents live in Moscow?" Holly asked with interest.

"No. They are dead," Tatiana replied in a curiously flat voice.

Holly was beginning to despair that her conversation with the Russian woman could ever get beyond the stage of stiff awkwardness when she was spared the need of replying by the arrival of two newcomers to the table. Holly's glance took in a pair of finely muscled thighs clad in tight gray breeches, then moved upward to the gray-and-black plaid shirt

opened at the collar, revealing a springy tangle of
black hair. Her gaze continued inevitably up along
the powerful masculine frame, at last meeting the
flash of black eyes that simmered with vitality and
subtle unspoken questions. But Holly refused to meet
Arif's stare, instead allowing her eyes to roam to his
companion in a revealing cocktail gown, her hand
clutching possessively at his arm. Holly recognized
her at once as Geneviève Lamine, the pouting young
heiress who had monopolized Arif's attentions at the
embassy.

Arif was addressing the Russian seated beside
Holly. "You ran a good race, lieutenant."

"Thank you, captain," Tatiana replied formally.
"Congratulations on your victory."

"May we join you for dinner?" Arif asked in the
low voice that was becoming so familiar to Holly.

She said nothing, although her silence went unno-
ticed as Rusty and Tatiana immediately urged the
captain and his companion to sit down.

Without another thought for the three women,
Arif turned to Rusty and engaged him in a lengthy
technical discussion about horses and the pros and
cons of various feeds.

Geneviève's sultry amber eyes flickered across the
table at Holly and Tatiana. "I suppose I should feel
privileged to be seated at the winners' table," she
observed in a bored voice. "You were quite the talk
of the stables this morning after the race, Mademoiselle MacKnight. I must say you displayed amazing
form for all your...lankiness."

Before replying Holly regarded the rosy swell of

bosom in the low-cut gown that left little to the imagination, and the long coral nails that had probably never been soiled by the actual day-to-day care of a horse. "It's obvious that you ride strictly for your own amusement, since you don't seem to care whether you even finish the course, let alone place among the top finalists."

Geneviève was silenced momentarily by this none-too-veiled reference to the fact that her mount, Bijou, had been one of the first to go down. She allowed her eyes to flicker contemptuously around the dining car, then spoke again as if Holly had never addressed her. "You would think that since the guild went to all the trouble to hire a special transport train, at least they could have obtained the old Train Bleu of the Orient Express. Then we could have traveled in the sumptuous surroundings of damask and velvet, rather than having to make do with such stark utilitarianism." She uttered the word as if it were a disease.

"If the thought repels you so, why didn't you fly on ahead rather than subjecting yourself to the. . . tortures of a long overland trip." Holly's words, spoken with such a studied air of innocence, were belied by the flashing intent of her eyes, which lingered meaningfully on the plump manicured hand still clutching Arif's sleeve so possessively.

The Tunisian heiress smiled slightly, revealing a row of pointed catlike teeth. "I regard it as an adventure, *vous comprenez*. There is so little of that in my life anymore. Besides, I am in no great rush to reach Istanbul. It is the Bombay of Europe, noisy and dirty," Geneviève remarked, her dainty features shadowed by an expression of disgust.

"But it was also a center of civilization for a thousand years," Holly countered. "When your ancestors were nothing but a rowdy tumble of robber barons fighting it out among themselves, the Ottomans were forging vast empires and producing great mathematicians and scholars," she elaborated with as much spirited conviction as if she were a foremost Turkic scholar. Actually she hadn't known the facts that she was so glibly reciting to the Tunisian woman for more than a few hours herself. During her pleasant victory/farewell lunch with Alec earlier in the day, he'd gone off on one of his erudite ramblings through history. Holly had perked up her ears when his talk roved to Istanbul, little knowing that she'd be using the information as conversational ammunition against the detestable Geneviève. "Anyway," Holly went on, enjoying herself thoroughly, "surely you have enough imagination to picture the city as it once was."

Geneviève had made a deprecating moue with her lips and was about to retort with a disparaging remark of her own when their acid clash of wits was interrupted by the sound of cutlery as the waiter spooned steaming vegetables onto the plates and handed them around.

Holly ate quickly, glancing up once to find Arif's eyes upon her. She could have sworn she detected a subtle sparkle of laughter above the arrogantly tilted cheekbones, but then his gaze had slid to the other women at the table. In his flickering indulgent gaze

Holly imagined a sultan regarding with imperious disdain the squabbling members of his harem; her blood simmered angrily at the thought. Had he overheard the waspish interchange between herself and Geneviève?

Tatiana had engaged Arif in conversation then, so Holly was able to get her trainer's attention for a moment. She leaned across the table. "Rusty, why don't you stay here and enjoy your after-dinner brandy with Captain Hakal, if you like. I'll check on Mandigirl to see that she's set for the night."

"Thanks, Holly. You're a good gal. I haven't had much time for man-to-man talk since we crossed the Atlantic."

She smiled at him, then stood up and inclined her head at the others around the table before moving down the aisle of the dining car. Passing the last table on the left, she was reminded of Tatiana's words about the man whom she suspected of being another bodyguard. She stared down at him curiously, but he did not glance up. Holly felt a stab of pity for the Russian woman, whose life apparently was not her own. She shivered at the thought of someone watching over her every move, reporting back to some higher authority, preventing her from doing anything "foolish." What had Tatiana meant by that, she wondered.

A half hour later Holly sauntered down the length of the train, swinging a bag of carrots in her hand, a treat for the near-victorious mare. As she approached the livestock cars, which had been divided into stalls for the horses, the temperature within the train grew appreciably warmer. She realized immediately that the guild was taking extra precautions to protect the valuable competition animals against drafts and the possibility of contracting influenza, a virus to which they could be highly vulnerable. As the warmth increased, she loosened the top buttons of her soft green velour shirt.

A vigorous snort from one of the stalls caught her attention, and she stared into the fierce eyes of Sinjon. "I should have guessed!" Holly laughed, reaching into her bag to retrieve a handful of carrots, which the stallion gobbled greedily. "You ran superbly, bold Sinjon; I'll concede that to you, though I'd never admit it to your insufferable master." She patted him on the nose, then continued along the line of stalls.

In Mandarin Lady's box she checked the feed and water supply before kneeling down in the straw to remove the protective bandages and briskly massage the mare's legs from knee to coronet. She thought she felt a slight swelling above the right rear hock, but she couldn't be certain. Expertly replacing the bandages, she made a mental note to point out the possible swelling to Rusty in the morning.

As she let herself out of the stall, Holly drew a sharp breath. Arif Hakal stood before her, lounging against the door of a neighboring stall with hands thrust in the pockets of his tight breeches and one polished boot crossed over the other.

"Did you follow me?" Holly asked, her voice slightly breathless from the start he'd given her.

"Did you want me to?" he countered, his eyes roving with interest down the elegant length of her legs in tan cords.

She ignored the teasing provocativeness of his words. "What are you doing here?"

He shrugged slightly, the muscles along his shoulders seeming to swell and ripple with the casual Mediterranean gesture. "The same as you. I came to check on my mount. He's restive in his box. Despite the length of a train car, the faint scent of the mare still arouses him."

"A pity he makes himself so uncomfortable for no reason. She's completely indifferent to him."

A spark of laughter seemed to leap from his eyes to his lips, giving the lie to her airily spoken words. Holly would have brushed past him then to return to her own compartment but for the fact that he had sat down on the plank bench adjoining the box door and extended his long booted leg across the aisle to the window ledge, effectively blocking her exit.

Thoroughly exasperated by his manner and annoyed with herself at the rush of tingling sensation his closeness had aroused in her, Holly put her hands on her hips and would have ordered him rudely to move. But it was he who spoke first, twisting his torso slightly forward and leaning an elbow on his thigh so he could stare up into her seething green eyes. "I'm curious," he began conversationally, ignoring her anger. "Why did you defend Istanbul to Geneviève?"

Holly regarded him in startled silence, taken aback by the unexpected question. To her chagrin she felt the telltale color rising in her cheeks as it became apparent to her that he'd overheard the women's barbed exchange over dinner. When she replied at last it was in a wry, almost bemused tone. "I don't know why I defended the city. I've never even been there. I suppose it was her attitude that annoyed me. If instead of criticizing Istanbul she'd chosen to assert that the moon is made up of nothing but lunar rock and soil, I'd probably have insisted she was wrong and defended the 'green cheese' theory."

Holly was startled by the explosive shout of laughter that erupted from Arif's lips. "Do you dislike her so much?" he asked after a moment, his eyes still flashing with mirth.

"We're from different worlds," Holly parried, "so I don't think we're destined to see eye-to-eye about anything. I don't know her well enough to dislike her."

"Liar." The word was spoken so softly it was almost a whisper. "I've not lived thirty-four years without having learned something about women. They read one another immediately. I think you're jealous of her."

"How ridiculous," she answered rather too hotly.

When Arif spoke again it was almost as if he were addressing himself. "Yes, the rich and beautiful Geneviève flaunts her charms as though she were on display at Les Halles meat market."

"Yet I don't see you going out of your way to avoid her." Holly could have bitten her tongue even as the catty words were spoken.

Arif's sharp hunter's eyes were full upon her. "Not jealous, eh?" He stood up with slow easy grace and faced her, his lean muscled bulk seeming to fill the narrow aisle. "You, Holly, on the other hand, are shy and subtle as a newly awakened filly, wearing your womanliness like an alluring veil." His eyes traveled to her unbuttoned shirt, open from the slim column of her throat to the shadowed hollow of her breasts, where a tiny black mole served to catch his eye and draw it downward. When he spoke again his voice was a silken caress. "I find your innocence an irresistible challenge."

He stood so close to her now that she felt his breath, fiery sweet as warmed brandy, on her face. She lifted her arms to brush past, but he caught her elbows and drew her to him until her hands were pinned against his chest. She felt his palms, rough and strong through the soft fabric of her blouse, as they gripped her.

Imprisoned against his chest, her heart beat wildly, out of control, as if it were a frightened starling caught in an iron mesh and pinioned helpless before its captor. She gazed upward past the molten fire in his eyes to the slow rhythmic pulse point in his temple. Arif was utterly in control as he bent his face toward hers. His lips parted, allowing strong white teeth to catch her lower lip and prize open a passageway for his inquisitive tongue. Her own teeth were clamped as tight as a castle drawbridge, only to part a moment later in a soft moaning sigh as he turned her around until she was crushed against the outer wall of the train car. She twined her fingers in the curling black mat of his chest while his own hands played a slow sensuous duet along her torso to the subtly rounded swell of her hips.

As her mouth parted in unspeakable delight, his kiss became more explorative and she felt her stomach and hips molded to his own, igniting a sweet aching fire within her.

A neighing sound, faint and distant as though from a far-off mountain peak, broke into the hypnotic rhythm of their embrace. They drew apart as a strong light shone into the dim livestock car where the connecting door between the coaches had been thrown open. Arif stood back, slowly fastening the buttons of his shirt that Holly's pinioned hands had unknowingly loosened as she'd struggled against him, her anger drowned in unlooked-for passion.

"I was mistaken about your icy facade," he whispered slowly as footsteps echoed down the aisle in their direction. His eyes were taunting and edged with a faintly cruel light. "You're as wanton as a brood mare ripe for mounting by a sire."

"How dare you insinuate that I...." But Holly's strangled reply was cut off by the crisp staccato sound of booted footsteps at Arif's back.

He turned then and she heard his voice—pleasant, unconcerned and smooth as velvet—as he wished good-evening to the newcomer. Holly just caught the drawling reply of her trainer, Rusty: "Evenin' to you, cap'n."

Arif had brushed past him and was halfway down the car when he turned around again. "By the way, Mr. Wilkins, I'll go through my research folder for that comparative study on feed grains that we discussed over dinner, and I'll get it to you tomorrow."

"Thanks. I'd be mighty obliged," Rusty called in return before turning around to greet Holly, not noticing the rigid angry set to her shoulders. "Now there's a nice boy," he observed approvingly. "Smart as a whip and as respectful to me as if I were his own father—even though he could toss me over his shoulder with one hand if he had a mind to."

The trainer's chuckle grated on Holly's raw nerve endings. "He's hardly a boy, Rusty," she retorted.

His sharp eyes played over her features. "So you noticed that, gal?" he asked laconically, not expecting an answer as he opened the box door to give a good-night pat to the mare and check her blankets.

Ten minutes later Holly let herself into her own compartment as quietly as possible. The lights were off and the practical single-minded Lieutenant Bulgakov was already in bed. Holly eased into the lower bunk, but sleep eluded her. She thought back sickeningly to her melting acquiescence in Arif's arms. He had played her as a bored musician might run his fingers over the keys of his instrument, with practiced ease, certain of the response he would elicit. Less than twelve hours earlier she had vowed to beat him at his own game, yet her own treacherous body had made her a malleable plaything in his arms.

CHAPTER THREE

HOLLY STARED OUT THE TRAIN WINDOW, her breath misting the cold glass until it seemed she viewed the Austrian countryside through a damp white fog. The express had rolled across the Austro-German frontier and through Salzburg a few hours earlier as the sun had risen behind its hilltop citadel. The eleventh-century fortress loomed like a vast silent guardian over the cobbled lanes of the sleeping town.

Now Holly raised her hand to the glass and rubbed a small porthole at eye level. Beyond the ancient city that had been founded by the Celts and later incorporated into the Roman Empire, the sky had grown increasingly bleak and gray. A freezing slantwise rain had begun to fall, so that even through the cleared circle of windowpane Holly could see little of the breathtaking mountain panoramas for which central Austria was famous. Still she continued to gaze out at the wet veiled landscape, her senses lulled by the rhythmic clacking of the wheels against the eastward-reaching tracks.

She had slept restlessly the previous night and had finally risen just before dawn, letting herself out of the compartment as quietly as possible and making her way to the dark deserted dining car, where a

sleepy-eyed conductor had roused himself to fetch
her a cup of tea and plate of toast. Holly had eaten
the Spartan breakfast in absolute solitude, the vague
annoyance at her restless night transformed into
silent pleasure as the white-frosted rooftops of Salzburg had come into view, rising to either side of the
darkly glistening Salzach River.

After breakfasting she'd strolled the entire length
of the train, eager for any exercise that would keep
her lithe form from tightening up over two days of
inactivity aboard the Istanbul-bound express. Finally
she'd checked on Mandarin Lady, satisfying herself
that the mare at least had passed a comfortable night,
before returning to the berth she shared with the Russian lieutenant. Tatiana had risen during Holly's
absence and presumably gone to breakfast. Restless
still, Holly had begun to leaf through the magazines
and English-language newspapers she'd brought
along to ease the tedium of the sixty-hour trip. But
she had given that up after a while and gone to stand
before the window, where she remained gazing out,
despite the dreariness of the sleet-shrouded vista.

She willed her thoughts away from Arif Hakal and
her humiliation in his arms the previous night, refusing to admit to herself that her sleeplessness had risen
precisely from the warring emotions of passion and
passionate hatred that he'd roused within her. She
squeezed her eyes shut at the memory, feeling her
cheek hot and flushed against the misted pane, but
the gesture only served to conjure up his vision with
even greater clarity. Again Holly felt the hot pressure
of his mouth upon hers, felt the deep black silkiness

of his mustache as it grazed her cheek in a soft sensual brush stroke.

The bittersweet torture of the remembrance was broken as she heard the doorknob rattle at her back and she turned to see Tatiana Bulgakov entering the compartment, her tiny ninety-five-pound frame radiating health and the cold freshness of the outdoors.

"What did you do this morning—jump off the train and jog alongside for a few miles?" Holly inquired in a lighthearted tone that she hoped would mask her confused half-angry musings before the window.

"No," the lieutenant replied seriously. "After breakfast I walked briskly for thirty minutes, then opened one of the corridor windows and put my head out. The train heat is not good for the stamina," she added, sniffing the closed air of their compartment with a disapproving air. "I see that your face is quite flushed."

Holly raised her hand to her cheek in response to her companion's sharp-eyed observation but said nothing, so that after a moment Tatiana addressed her again. "You breakfasted earlier?"

Holly nodded absentmindedly. "I had some toast and tea before anyone else was up."

"What kind of food is that for an athlete?" Tatiana replied, her disapproval even more apparent. "You will grow weak without protein."

At these words Holly turned to regard the Russian competitor, marveling silently at the strength of will that seemed never to waver. Tatiana seemed less a woman to her than a finely tuned machine, and she found herself growing curious about the Russian's background. Holly moved away from the window and sat down upon her own bunk, plumping up the bed pillows against the wall behind her head and curling her slim legs underneath her. "The military is your career?" she asked tentatively, worried that the woman might think her guilty of prying.

But Tatiana surprised her once again by perching stiffly on the edge of Holly's bunk and smiling wryly. It was the first gesture of friendship, however faint, on Tatiana's part since she and Holly had been thrown together as roommates. "Yes," she replied at last, "the military is my life, although it is so not because of my love of the Soviet Army but because of my love of horses." She gave a rueful little shake of her head. "My mother and father could not understand. They wished their daughter to be an intellectual like themselves. Yet look where it got them. . . ."

Tatiana's bemused monologue was interrupted by a sharp rap on the compartment door, which caused Holly to leap up like a startled gazelle. She felt the illogical pounding of her heart as she stood before the unopened door, half fearing and half hoping that it was Arif come to ask her forgiveness for his deliberate toying with her the evening before. But it was only the conductor who stood in the corridor, offering a pot of tea. Holly took the tray and set it down on the foldout table before the window, the clattering spoons betraying the tremble in her hands. Even as she'd flung open the door she'd realized the hopeless naiveté of expecting any sort of apology from the arrogant horseman whose sexual dominance over women was an amusing game to be played and won, his prize the melting surrender of his vanquished competitor in bed. Seething at the thought of how easily he had brought her to the brink of passion, Holly set a cup upon its saucer with unnecessary force.

"Is something wrong?" Tatiana asked curiously. "You looked as though you expected to open the door to the devil himself."

Holly forced a smile to her lips as she handed the Russian woman a cup of tea. "Not at all," she lied convincingly.

Tatiana sipped the fragrant brew gratefully. "The one custom I miss when I am traveling outside my homeland is the Russian samovar always filled with hot water for tea."

The quiet observation served to recall Holly's attention to the conversation that had been interrupted by the conductor's knock. She sat down once more on the corner of the bed with her graceful fingers locked around the white cup. "You said your parents didn't understand?" Holly prompted gently. "Yet they didn't try to stop you."

"They did attempt to but soon realized it was hopeless. I despised academics and did poorly in most of my subjects. My parents had no choice but to acquiesce when I decided to join the Soviet Army. No university would have admitted me. My officers recognized the potential of my horsemanship and groomed me for international competition. I was a Russian team member in four Olympics," Tatiana told her proudly.

Holly bit back the question that had half formed on her lips. She had been about to ask why Tatiana wasn't in training with her teammates for the upcoming Olympics but had discerned the answer for herself almost immediately: the lieutenant's age was undoubtedly a factor.

Although Holly hadn't uttered a word, the sharply observant Russian seemed to have divined her unspoken question. "I am relegated to these secondary circuits because they think me past my prime." The deceptive calmness of her words was belied by the tense whitening of her knuckles around the empty teacup in her hands.

"Yet they must think you're an important competitor if they've assigned two bodyguards to you."

Tatiana glanced up sharply. "You misunderstood me last evening at dinner. I merely pointed out that there were two guards in the dining car. I do not believe that the second one was assigned to watch me. Ordinarily I would have assumed that it was his duty to guard another of my Iron Curtain comrades, but I am the only one competing on this circuit." She shrugged her shoulders. "His presence is a mystery to me. The only thing I am certain of is that he is indeed a watchdog."

Holly was intrigued by the woman's acuteness of observation. "But why do you have to be tailed at all?" she asked finally, although she thought she had already figured out the answer to that question, as well.

Tatiana sighed before replying, her eyes tired and cynical beneath their thick dark brows, which were contracted in a frown. "There are two reasons. The first is to prevent any 'embarrassment' to the Soviet state. There have been so many defections in recent years—a jet pilot, chess players, ballerinas, ice skaters—that they do not wish the Western world to witness any more escapes from their perfect utopia," she explained, her voice imbued with brittle irony. "The second reason is that they fear I may have been tainted... by my parents."

"Your parents?" Holly echoed in perplexity.

"Yes. Both my mother and father were active in the human-rights movement, demanding more freedom for Russian intellectuals to speak and write without censure. Eventually they were sent into exile into Siberia."

"And died there?" Holly asked in a hushed voice, remembering Tatiana's curiously flat voice the evening before when she'd informed her over dinner that her parents were dead.

"Yes. There was no overt torture, so to speak. But my mother, who was a prominent physicist at the university, became despondent at being separated from her life's work, and her health had never been good. She died shortly before her five-year term of exile was over. My father, too, became despondent and died a year later, a broken and unhappy man."

"I'm so sorry," Holly whispered.

Tatiana shrugged sadly. "That is in the past. It is over." She turned around to face Holly more directly. "Now that I have told you the dull story of my life, it is your turn to tell me about yourself."

Holly reached behind her shoulder and retrieved a

bed pillow, which she tossed in Tatiana's direction. "There isn't much to tell," she replied, shrugging her shoulders in unconscious mimicry of the Russian woman's gesture, "but you might as well get comfortable." She watched as Tatiana scooted back to lean against the wall, neatly crossing her tiny black-slippered feet. The sense of precision and strength that emanated from her diminutive form reminded Holly curiously of her own trainer, Rusty. She sighed before beginning to speak, choosing her words with care as she embarked on a heavily abridged version of her own life.

"I became an equestrienne against my parents' wishes, the same as you did, although it took me until the age of twenty-one to rebel completely. From the time I was ten until this past summer I felt as if I lived a dual existence. I went to school and lived with my parents in Philadelphia, but summers and other holidays were always spent at Sims' Meadows. Riding came to mean more to me than anything, especially after Rusty Wilkins was hired on as trainer and took me under his wing. I pretty much ran away from home after my family tried to push me into an arranged marriage."

"But your parents did not attempt to stop you?" It was Tatiana's turn to express her curiosity. "I thought the rich were very powerful in America and could accomplish anything they wanted."

Holly sat up a little straighter at these unexpected words. "Rich? Why do you say that? The only money I have to my name is the five-thousand-franc purse I won at Malmaison," she replied in a tone that was at once rebellious and self-righteous.

Tatiana inclined her head stiffly. "Forgive me. Perhaps I assumed too much, but everything about you—the ease and certainty with which you deal with waiters and porters, your very manner of walking with grace and confidence as if the rest of the world should step aside—"

"I'm like that?" Holly broke in with a startled expression.

"Yes," the Russian insisted. "It wasn't just your manner, of course, that made me assume you were rich. It was the little things, as well—the fineness of your boots and watch and the exquisite trappings of the mare."

Holly shifted uncomfortably against her pillow at the thought of the patient and thorough scrutiny to which the tiny Russian lieutenant had subjected her.

The conversation was broken off as Tatiana glanced down at her own plain but sturdy watch. "Well, we have passed the morning in a most interesting manner. It is nearly lunchtime already. Shall we walk in the direction of the dining car?"

Holly uncurled her long limbs and got up from the narrow bed. "I don't think I will. Would you mind having the conductor send me down a sandwich and a glass of milk?"

Tatiana watched in silence as the tall slim American girl moved toward the washstand. "It seems to me there is someone whom you wish to avoid today."

Holly began to brush her hair with rather unwonted vigor. "Don't be silly."

After Tatiana had let herself out of the compart-

ment, Holly sighed. Her large green eyes stared back
in exasperation from the mirrored reflection. She had
the growing suspicion that she would be able to keep
very few secrets from the keen-eyed Russian woman.

THE COLD GRAYNESS of the short winter's day deepened swiftly into night as the express train rolled eastward, slowing down only as it reached the outskirts
of Vienna. Although it was once resplendent as the
turn-of-the-century capital of the Austro-Hungarian
Empire, nothing remained of that grandeur but the
weatherworn facades of its elaborate rococo buildings. Still, Holly had heard that the city with its opera
and vast palaces was quite charming, and she was disappointed that the train had to continue inexorably
eastward. At the Yugoslav border there was a brief
stop to check visas and take on additional cars, then
the express picked up speed once again over the freezing barren terrain, bound for Zagreb, Belgrade and
the Bulgarian frontier.

The thought of the sights and cultures she was missing by being confined to the narrow world of twenty
train coaches made Holly restless. She flicked on the
light above the mirror and regarded herself critically
before deciding that the long claustrophobic day had
made her somewhat wan and tired-looking. She was
just beginning to apply a little makeup when Tatiana
returned from dinner and climbed into the upper bunk
with a book in hand. Once again she felt the Russian
woman's dark eyes intently scrutinizing her.

"Did you happen to see my trainer while you were
out?" Holly asked at last.

"He was at the opposite end of the dining car from me and looked to be in deep conversation with a Japanese trainer."

"That Rusty can be tight-lipped as a clam," Holly laughed in reply, "but he's an animated conversationalist where horses are concerned—always wanting to hear the latest techniques and advances that others are using. In all fairness, though, I have to say he's exceptionally generous with his own fund of experience."

"I have noticed that," Tatiana replied. "He gave me some excellent pointers on my Kazan. I look up to your trainer."

"You're one of the few who can," Holly shot back, grinning at her own pun. When she saw the puzzled expression on Tatiana's face she added, "I meant that as a joke. At five feet two, Rusty's a pretty short individual, but he stands a good two inches over you—so you literally *have* to look up to him."

"Oh," the serious-eyed lieutenant replied blankly.

Holly shook her head in exasperation as she opened the door of the compartment, wondering if all Russians were as humorless as her roommate appeared to be. "By the way," she called over her shoulder, "I've left my makeup bag out in case you want to experiment with the powders and brushes."

She just caught a glimpse of Tatiana jumping down from her berth as Holly shut the door firmly behind her and made her way along the dimly lit corridors, intent on finding Rusty's compartment but not certain of its exact location. She was just glancing down at the number her trainer had scribbled on the back of an old hotel bill for her when a door opened, flooding the corridor with warm lamplight. She moved toward the light. "Pardon the intrusion," Holly began, "but I wonder if you know where I'd find the compartment of the American trainer Rusty Wilkins?"

A dark head glanced around the door and she found herself staring up into Arif Hakal's liquid dark gaze, his eyes brimming with laughter, curiosity and not a little mischief. "Holly MacKnight! We missed you today in the dining car. I'd been looking forward to hearing you and Geneviève sharpening your wits at each other's expense and unsheathing your claws like a pair of she-cats."

Holly drew back swiftly, as if she'd confronted a caged wolf who refused to be daunted by the artificial barrier thrown up to keep him at bay. Then, realizing the cowardice of her retreat toward the dim sanctuary of the corridor, she sought to mask it by regarding him with a cool haughty stare before replying. "Are you always such an arrogant and condescending bastard, captain?"

His eyes mocked her pretense of brittle sophistication. "After last night," he retorted slowly, placing deliberate emphasis on each word, "I'd expected you to come rubbing your back against my leg and begging to be petted like my sister's pet kitten, Ayesha."

She would have moved quickly down the corridor and away from his hated presence, but before she could do so he spoke again, his words edged with a cool impersonality that held her in check. "Since you're heading in Rusty Wilkins's direction, would you mind passing along the research materials he asked for last night? I haven't had a chance to speak to him today." He regarded her a moment. "Step in out of the corridor draft, if you like, while I find the papers."

Wary but reluctant to show cowardliness yet again, Holly walked into the compartment behind him. His back was to her as he riffled through a thick sheaf of papers, so that she was able to glance around the berth with unabashed curiosity. She was startled at how the plain compartment had become overlaid with the Turkish horseman's personality in so short a time, as if unconsciously he sought to create his own private world. A navy greatcoat hung on a wall peg, beneath which stood two pairs of polished boots, while a nearby shelf was piled high with books on equine science. Even the very air seemed imbued with his personality, Holly thought as she caught the scent of leather and wool, their harsh out-of-doors quality undercut by the subtle gingery sharpness of cardamom. Her eyes traveled to the washstand with its chipped shaving mug and well-worn brush, and to the table at the foot of the bed where he'd thrown a red silk handkerchief over the shade to soften the harsh white glare. She leaned down curiously to examine a small string of jade beads that seemed to have been tossed casually on the table, but her eye was caught by a small framed photograph that had been propped with evident care against the lamp base.

"Here they are at last," Arif spoke at her back, his voice still cool. "Tell him to read the grain study at his leisure, and if he finds it to be of value we can have copies made once we arrive in Istanbul.''

Holly turned to face him, and as she did so she was struck again by the faint Oriental cast of his features in the reddish glow of lamplight. As she stared up at Arif, she recalled something else that Alec Wright had observed in passing about Turkey. He'd told her that the country straddled the European and Asian continents, its actual physical geography echoed in the Turkish culture itself, which was neither wholly Western nor wholly Oriental but a curious blending of both. As Holly took in Arif Hakal's black Mediterranean eyes and exotically tilted cheekbones, she felt instinctively that within him there was a subtle warring between two worlds, one modern and one ancient. For the first time since she'd met the rugged horseman, Holly glimpsed beyond the arrogantly sexual male animal—to which her own blood had leaped so impetuously—to see the complexity of the man himself. Against her will, she found herself fascinated.

Holly had taken the framed photograph in her hands to examine it more closely and held it now before her. ''Are these your parents?'' she asked, her head tilted questioningly so that a length of fair hair tumbled forward over her shoulders.

He came toward her, the papers in his hand momentarily forgotten. ''Yes. I like having their faces before me when I'm traveling outside of Turkey.'' Arif leaned closer so that Holly caught the rugged spiciness of his scent and felt the treacherous quickening in her blood. He lifted his hand then, but it was only to point out the open compound behind the vigorous gray-haired couple in the foreground. "This is our ranch, on the Anatolian plateau just east of Erzurum. We call the site Riadja. It is my parents' pride and passion and has come to be mine, as well," he explained with almost boyish eagerness.

"You raise horses?" Holly looked up at him over her shoulder.

"Yes. Polo ponies mainly, although we want to begin a new breed ranch that will carry on the traditions of Eskishehir. That is where the imperial black horses of the sultans were bred for a hundred years. Sinjon is of that lineage, and he's sired a foal who will have reached eight months come January...."

His eager words trailed away and Holly was startled by the brooding light that crept into his energetic gaze. "Riadja must be a great source of satisfaction to you," she prompted.

But his mood of buoyant pride had been quenched inexplicably. He shrugged in a careless offhanded manner. "A man cannot subsist on his dreams." When next he looked at her, Arif's eyes held the familiar teasing glint. "Now I have shown you my parents, you must show me yours."

Holly shook her head. "I don't carry a photograph of them. Unlike you, captain, I'm attempting to forget rather than remember."

"Ah, yes, I'd almost forgotten the classic dilemma you were fleeing from. The parents wish their beautiful daughter to marry a rich man whom she does not—cannot—love. Am I right?" The low harmonious texture of his voice was in sharp contrast to the knife-edged sarcasm underlying his words.

Holly wondered fleetingly if he really considered her beautiful or if his observation was nothing but a sarcastic embellishment to his remarks. The idle thought was gone, however, as Arif turned away from her and began to pace slowly the narrow length of the compartment between window and door. Once again she was reminded of the controlled ferocity of a wild animal trapped within a cage. His dark gaze was as hard as obsidian.

"Unlike you, *mam'selle*," he mimicked her tone, "I am not permitted the luxury of rebellion. You Americans are aggressively self-indulgent."

She bridled at his criticism. "We're not trapped by decrepit customs out of the past," Holly shot back, her eyes traveling inadvertently to the beads before the framed photograph.

Arif sensed the meaning behind her gaze and bent to pick up the finely crafted stones. "They are *tesbih*—prayer beads. I carry them out of respect for my father, who is devout in his religion," he said quietly.

Holly flushed. "They are quite beautiful. I did not mean to insult—"

To her surprise Arif interrupted with a laugh. "I see that our truce was destined to be a short-lived one after all. Let's try again, shall we? I'll forgive you if you'll forgive me."

Holly nodded reluctantly.

"Good; it's agreed, then," he said with a mischievous air as he stopped before her and gripped her arms lightly above the elbows, propelling her backward to the edge of the bunk.

Holly stiffened and was ready to bolt, but the laughing Turk merely set her on the edge before reaching beneath the bed to retrieve a small brass-bound trunk. He opened the lid and drew out a bottle of clear liquid and two shot glasses. "We should drink to our fruitful cross-cultural exchange."

"What is it?" Holly asked doubtfully, poised still on the bed's edge with the wary intentness of a bird on an unsteady branch.

"Raki," he explained with a grin as he poured the liquid into the glasses. "It is the fiery spirit of the Turkish soul."

Still kneeling beside the open trunk, he drank his portion neat, then watched in amusement as she sipped carefully at her glass. Arif laughed outright at Holly's futile attempt to suppress the coughing gasp that bubbled to her lips after she'd swallowed the throat-burning brandy with its aftertaste of licorice. "You are so terribly innocent, Holly, that you will need a strong protector in Istanbul."

Holly stood up and carried her thimble-sized glass to the window. "You're speaking nonsensically, captain."

He came to stand beside her. "Am I?" he asked softly, the low yet powerful timbre of his voice like storm waves striking against a distant shore.

She did not reply, but turned her head to stare out into the darkness. The freezing sleet that had dogged the train across Austria had been transformed now into heavy wet snowflakes whirling downward to mantle the brown frozen Yugoslav earth. Suddenly Holly had the feeling that she was adrift on a vast ocean with no other companion but the man who stood before her. The moment stretched into minutes, enveloping them in a strangely intimate stillness that each was reluctant to break. Holly turned away from the darkness finally and raised the glass in an awkward toast. "Thanks for the drink, but I really must be going...."

The rest of her sentence was swallowed up in a great rending screech of brakes. There was a terrific jolt that sent her headlong into Arif's arms, while the *raki* splashed them both from eyelash to chin. His hand shot around Holly's waist to steady her as the train came to a grinding halt in the middle of the bleak empty plain.

"What could've happened?" Holly began.

Even though the train had stopped and there was no further danger of their being pitched crazily around the compartment, Arif had not relaxed his grip on her waist. As he turned to peer out into the white-veiled night, Holly was intensely aware of her breast where it pressed against his powerful bicep.

To her surprise, a great burst of laughter erupted from his throat. "What is it?" she asked, thoroughly perplexed.

"Look for yourself."

Holly pressed her nose against the cold windowpane. Beyond the heavy swirl of snow the train stretched out in the distance like an iridescent serpent, its skin surface marked by small square rectangles of light. To her amazement Holly saw in the distance the shawled figure of a woman who evidently had descended from the stopped express and was now trudging slowly across the flat white barrenness of plain, arms heavily laden with two bags. "But where on earth can she be going? She'll freeze!"

Arif's brooding stillness, which Holly sensed was only the fleeting expression of some darkness within him, had gone, and in its place was the familiar animallike vitality. "You don't understand, do you, Holly MacKnight?" he laughed still. "You are an innocent in more ways than one. The woman is a Yugoslav peasant. I've no doubt it was she who pulled the emergency cord, bringing the train to screech dead in its tracks."

"But that's a serious crime!"

Arif flung his head arrogantly in the direction of the frozen plain. "Tell that to her. No doubt she was one of the passengers who boarded near the frontier, eager to return home to cottage and family after marketing her crop of cabbages and buying needed supplies. She chose the simplest, fastest route even if it meant a bit of inconvenience for the rest of us."

"You have to admit it was irresponsible!" Holly protested.

"To whom? To all of us, whom I'm sure she regards as rich foreigners, traveling in warm comfort across her country? We mean nothing to her." He laughed at Holly's stubborn look of disapproval. "I admire these people of the soil. They're strong and hardworking. You will see the same in Turkish peasants." He broke off his spirited half-angry defense to grin once again. "Their lives may be tough and grim but the Turks know how to dance. You know the *göbek*, Holly?"

She smiled now, too. "The what?"

"*Göbek*—you foreigners call it belly dancing." Arif stood back from her and gave a practice undulation of his stomach.

Holly laughed irresistibly. "I had no idea you were a man of such multifaceted talents. Did you make your living that way before joining the military?" she teased.

"So you *can* laugh and joke, Holly. I'm glad," Arif rejoined, his eyes playing over her features with interest. "But the *göbek* must be taken seriously. We Turks learn it as kids hanging around the bazaar; it's an amusing pastime, like shooting marbles. But the professional women dancers raise it to the level of an art on the stage. It is not easy."

Holly shook her head, still laughing at his antics. "I'm sure it's not."

"Look—I'll show you!" Arif said impetuously, reaching down to pull his tan sweater over his head so that he stood bare chested before her in the red lamplight.

Holly stared at him as he stood totally unselfconscious in his nakedness as an animal might have: unaware of the powerful vitality emanating from within, yet, paradoxically, supremely confident in it. His wide shoulders rose above the crisp mat of black hair that could not quite conceal the tensile fabric of muscle banding his chest and hard flat stomach.

Arif reached out and took Holly's hand, placing it high on his abdomen. "You see, it starts here, pushing downward from the diaphragm," he explained.

Only half-aware of his patient instruction, she

stared in fascination at her fair hand against the naked maleness of him. His skin was warm and dark, yet faintly burnished with the reddish gold patina of antique copper. Then with a curious sense of excitement and expectancy she felt the rippling undulations as his torso came to life beneath her fingers.

He was speaking again. "You understand? The muscle control starts here. Once you know that, it is not so difficult. Now you must try it."

Before she realized what he was doing, Arif's hands had imprisoned her slender waist once again and were pushing up the soft cashmere of her pullover to expose an elegant length of torso. The touch of his fingers against her warm bare flesh sent an exquisite shock wave pulsating through her, and almost immediately she steeled herself against it.

Still casting himself in the role of instructor, Arif was as yet unaware of the sensual flood his fingers had so innocently released. "Holly," he complained, "you're stiff as a corral post. The first step in the *göbek* is to relax."

He glanced up into her eyes and caught their expression—open, vulnerable, half fearful and half desiring. A flame seemed to leap the narrow chasm between them, igniting the dry explosive tinder of their passion as if a firestorm raged about them.

Strong supple fingers that a moment before had taught the workings of muscle and sinew now moved languorously in a more subtle instruction. They trailed lightly up her sides and down again until one fingertip reached out tantalizingly to explore the swelling curve of breast beneath the lacy sheerness of her bra.

She drew back from the unexpected intimacy of his touch and her eyes flew open, their green depths a subtle mirror of the conflicting emotions raging within her heart. A dark wave of womanly fear and wariness struggled against the totally unfamiliar onrush of passion that his fingers had awakened.

"No, I must go," she whispered hurriedly, half twisting out of his grasp.

But his hard fingers held her. "Holly, I would never hurt you," he replied in a low husky whisper of his own, the words rippling over her senses like a hidden riptide drawing a helpless swimmer beyond safe depths. "You are too lovely, too innocent."

She shook her head slowly, her wavering gaze caught and held by the black fire burning in his eyes. "Maybe you're right after all, Arif. If I am as you describe me, then you yourself can only be. . . ."

The smoldering flame of passion in his eyes mingled now with the sparkle of laughter. "Then I can only be what?" he demanded.

"Dangerous." Her swift reply was spoken in a voice at once soft yet deadly serious.

The laughter in his eyes spilled downward to his full lips and erupted in an amused growl that filled the silent compartment. "I'm a man, Holly Mac-Knight, not a wild animal. I will not devour you... unless that is your wish."

Her heart thudded agonizingly in her breast as his eyes did what his lips swore he would not. His gaze raked her like a hot wind, imprisoning her with its sweet intensity. Arif bent his head toward her once again and his mouth brushed the silky hotness of her cheeks. Then his lips parted so that his tongue might probe the corner of her mouth, perhaps seeking the last vestiges of fiery sweet brandy that remained there.

Holly felt as if she had tumbled into a field of wild fennel, the rough and aromatic stalks entwining her in bittersweet captivity. She struggled against him, fighting the dark magnetism of his advance yet feeling herself drawn irresistibly by it. She felt his lips moving inexorably downward, tongue flicking at an earlobe before his mouth brushed the surging fullness of her breasts beneath the soft wool of her sweater. Holly gasped, the harsh intake of breath an expression of shock not only at the audacious liberties his lips and tongue took so arrogantly, but at her own mounting desire, which threatened to melt her resistance.

Heedless of her strangled cry of protest, Arif pulled her backward with rough mastery and eased himself down on the edge of the bunk. Now his mouth was marking an incandescent and tantalizingly slow arc along her supple torso, traveling upward to the rounded contours of her swelling breasts, which his practiced fingers had freed from their lacy bonds. His lips parted to trace a feathery circular pattern around the dark aureole of her nipple.

Yet even as her brain screamed inwardly at his wanton invasion, her treacherous body spoke a subtle yet unmistakable surrender. The pink tip of her nipple rose tautly as he caught it between his teeth in a light caressive nibble.

"Arif, no," she whispered agonizingly. "You must not—"

"Holly, you are *güzel*...beautiful." His voice was hoarse with passion yet surprisingly gentle. "I want to love you fully."

Alarmed at how far the rising tide of passion had carried her, Holly nevertheless felt herself poised on the brink of some nameless abyss.

The charged intimacy of the moment was shattered by a crack of impatient knuckles on Arif's compartment door. A moment later Geneviève Lamine's mellifluous voice called through the thin panels, "Arif, darling, it's I. Have you forgotten our date to have an after-dinner drink in the train lounge?"

"*Mon Dieu!* I had forgotten." Arif rose swiftly from the bed, pushing Holly gently but firmly before him until she stood behind the door. Holly barely had time to straighten her disarranged apparel before the door was opened, and she saw Arif cast a charming smile across the threshold. *Bonsoir, ma chérie.* I was just on my way."

Holly gritted her teeth in silent anger as she heard the insinuating purr on the woman's lips. "Ooh-la-la, such a handsome chest! Why don't we just stay here for that drink?"

Before Arif could block her entry, Geneviève had slipped past him into the warm chamber. The seductive smile died on her lips as she caught sight of her American rival behind the door.

Holly raised her head and inclined it slightly in a curt gesture of greeting. "Good evening, Geneviève."

"Miss MacKnight had just dropped by to pick up an article for her trainer," Arif interposed smoothly as he leaned down to retrieve the forgotten papers from the table.

"I see," Geneviève replied. Her amber cat's eyes flicked from Arif's half-naked form to the tousled bunk and silk-shaded lamp, then back again to Holly, whose coolly composed features were betrayed by the carmine flush of spent passion and growing mortification.

Geneviève stamped her high-heeled foot angrily. "Arif, how could you behave so sordidly with the *Americaine* at the same time you're speaking marriage to me?"

He cast an apologetic grin over his shoulder as he shepherded the seething young heiress out of the warm compartment and into the corridor. As Holly let herself out, she heard their voices echoing back to her along the narrow passageway. Geneviève's high pettish tone was met with a soothing reply that Holly could not help overhearing. "Never mind, my love. There is no comparison between what I feel for her and what I feel for you."

Holly stumbled blindly down the corridor in the direction of her coach, tears of rage and humiliation choking her throat. She stopped a moment in the connecting passageway between cars, allowing the onrush of bitingly cold wind and the sharp clank and sway of the hurtling express to drown her agonized feelings. *Scoundrel,* she screamed inwardly, feeling like a bit of rag that has been soiled and discarded.

Arif had sensed her tremulous vulnerability and

had taken advantage of it to satisfy his passions. He had sought a tawdry affair with her while talking lifetime commitment to another! More than humiliation, Holly felt a sense of deep and bitter hurt. Although she could not deny the overpowering sexual attraction between them, which seemed to propel her into his embrace against all reason, Holly had thought she sensed something deeper growing between them that evening: a fleeting moment of shared words and laughter that bespoke an undercurrent of communion of caring. Nor could Holly deny that Arif Hakal had affected her in a way no man had ever done. How could desire and loathing grow so inextricably entwined on the same branch? She longed to lash out at Arif, to hurt and degrade him, to punish him as his callous behavior had wounded and humiliated her.

Holly hurried down the empty corridor, eager for the numbing solitude of her own berth. She did not notice the tall, pale but otherwise nondescript man at the far end of the corridor who watched with no discernible flicker of curiosity as she finally pushed open the door of her own dark compartment and disappeared within.

HOLLY WAKENED THE NEXT MORNING to a curiously still world. There was no rhythmic clacking of wheels against steel tracks to lull her back to sleep. Everything had been silenced by the winter storm that had dogged them throughout the long night, at last enmeshing the train in its icy bonds. From her compartment window she saw the Bulgarian plains stretching away to the distant horizon beneath a thick mantle of white.

When five minutes later she stepped out into the corridor, Holly was surprised to find it crowded with passengers who were talking and gesticulating animatedly in half a dozen languages. The thought of being snowbound had served to bind the international group with a lively new sense of camaraderie after the word had spread with lightning rapidity. The severe weather conditions, combined with a derailment a hundred miles ahead outside of Bulgaria's capital, Sofia, would leave them stranded for at least ten hours.

Holly's restive mind immediately leaped ahead to thought of Mandarin Lady in her stall. The mare had been more than thirty hours now without exercise, the latest trip delay pushing the anticipated arrival in Istanbul even further in the future. Holly's concern for her mount was echoed in the comments of the riders and trainers milling excitedly along the narrow length of train aisle, and within an hour permission had been obtained from the engineer to allow the animals to be let out of the stalls and exercised in the snowy fields beyond the tracks.

Holly found Rusty Wilkins already at work in the mare's box. "Good morning, stranger!" she greeted him as she opened the door and let herself into the warm hay-strewn stall. "I feel as though I haven't seen you in days."

The trainer's muffled response came back to her from the opposite side of Mandarin Lady. "I haven't had such a chance to pick first-rate horse minds since the hunters' meet in West Virginia last spring.''

Holly went to the front of the stall and patted the mare's nose before scrambling across the feed box to join Rusty where he stood with one shoulder pressed against a chestnut flank, leaning down to examine a rear leg. ''I thought I detected a little swelling the other night,'' she began, a trace of worry in her voice. ''Do you think I'm just imagining things, Rusty?''

''Nope. I was just wondering the same thing myself,'' the trainer confirmed. ''Let's get her saddled and out of here and see how she does in a canter through all that snow.''

Outside the sheltering warmth of the stranded train, the air had a brittle sharpness to it. It had stopped snowing for the time being, although the low gray clouds seemed prepared to continue their wintry onslaught over the flat terrain.

Mandarin Lady whinnied with excitement as her mistress swung up lightly into the saddle and urged her into a slow trot. They rode the entire length of the express, gently working out the muscles and tendons that had become cramped from prolonged inactivity. By the time mare and rider had retraced their path through the powdery white snowdrifts, all the mounts had descended the wooden ramp and were going through their paces. The rhythmic chink of metal stirrups and bits was interspersed with bursts of laughter echoing sharply in the crystalline air, and to Holly's mind the milling horses and riders took on the aspect of a medieval winter circus come to town to entertain the snowbound peasants.

Her musings were broken as she caught the familiar low resonance of Arif's voice, raised a pitch higher now with laughing exuberance as he sought to organize some sort of impromptu polo match in a narrow field adjoining the tracks. With the air of one accustomed to issuing commands and seeing them obeyed, he had chosen two teams of five riders each when he caught sight of Holly and her mare standing apart at the field's edge, half-hidden by a copse of bare willows. He rode swiftly in her direction and drew Sinjon up before them. The stallion's nostrils were dilated widely with the thrill of having escaped the confining stall to ride freely in the bitterly cold air, and his white breath curled upward to mingle with that of his master.

"We are going to play *cirit*, Turkish polo. Will you join my team, Holly? You can display your competitive form once again," Arif teased.

"No, thank you, captain," she replied. Her eyes were like greenbrier, hard and edged around with prickly anger. "I'm not interested in your kind of play."

He sensed her meaning immediately. "What do you want of me?" he asked with mocking arrogance. "An apology? Last night you were like a breath of summer, while today you chide me like a wife. I thought American women enjoyed casual affairs on the run...to prove their newfound equality."

"Not this woman, captain. I don't enjoy being trampled by your boots. Talking marriage to Geneviève while—"

"Why bring her up?" Arif exploded angrily. "My

relationship with her is none of your concern. As you yourself observed, Holly, you and Geneviève are from two different worlds.''

Holly blinked back the tears that threatened to well up. ''Yes, captain, I know,'' she retorted, her voice a bitter whisper. ''You made that quite plain last night in the corridor.''

Her bitterness was drowned by the impatient shouts of Arif's waiting teammates, eager to begin the sport. He wheeled away and cantered into the field to join them, with no further thought of the prideful woman who remained behind, staring after him with wrathful eyes.

Holly schooled herself to contain the seething emotion born of a wounded angry ego, and she spent the subsequent hours exercising Mandarin Lady under Rusty's watchful gaze. She tried to ignore the lively game in progress beyond the bare willows, but her eyes were drawn inevitably to the trampled snowy field, curiosity gradually overcoming her fomenting anger. She saw that the sport was more like jousting than English polo, since the riders did not hit a ball down the field with a mallet but instead tossed short wooden sticks at the opposing team members.

It was no surprise to see Arif dominating the play with his daredevil riding and lightning-quick control of the stallion. Once again he had dropped the polished European veneer and was the wild horseman of the steppes, playing to win at the traditional winter sport born in the eastern Turkish highlands where the country shared ancient borders with Persia and Russia.

The thought made Holly realize that Arif Hakal indeed was nearly home, the victorious warrior returning. He had conquered on the riding field and elsewhere, Holly reflected, her cheeks blazing at remembered intimacies and the horrifying ease with which she'd succumbed to his dark sensuality. She yearned to teach him a lesson somehow and to return his cool deceit in double measure.

Long after the horses had reboarded and the train had resumed its journey across the snowy landscape, Holly mulled over her silent vow, little dreaming that the arrogant captain himself would provide the means for her swift and sweet revenge.

CHAPTER FOUR

A DECREPIT PLOW had cleared the narrow-gauge tracks after midnight, and the once snowbound express was rolling again in rhythmic clacking motion across southern Bulgaria. It had roared through the ancient capital of Sofia hours before, the cityscape a blur of Eastern Orthodox church domes and brilliant red banners draped over building fronts in celebration of some Communist holiday. Now the terrain beyond the narrow world of the train tracks revealed once again a stark desolation. To the north rose the white forbidding peaks of the Balkan Mountains, while stretching away to the south was the vast Thracian plain.

The brief interlude outside the stopped train, when the jangle of stirrups and the drumming of hooves had mingled with the riders' excited cries, seemed days rather than mere hours distant. Holly had not spoken to Arif again after their short angry confrontation before the polo match. The rigorous fast-paced game had ended in victory for Arif's team, and both victors and vanquished had celebrated later in the dining car with rounds of German beer and *raki*. Holly had stubbornly avoided the celebration, taking her cup of hot chocolate to a table at the far end of the car and staring out beyond the cold windowpane to the trampled snowy field where the riders had engaged in their impromptu competition. Rusty and Tatiana had joined her a few minutes later, and they quickly had become immersed in an animated three-way conversation about the prospects for the upcoming equestrian event in Istanbul. Holly had been grateful for the conversational diversion, though her gaze had returned again and again to the churned flat field with its provoking reminders of Arif's cool dominance. The anger had continued to foment within, even as twilight deepened over the wintry terrain.

It was late morning now. The express had gradually picked up speed across the flat Bulgarian plain, and they were but one hour from the Turkish frontier, with Istanbul almost another six hours beyond that. Holly stretched restlessly before the window in her own compartment, eager for the confining journey to be at an end. She felt as though she had been on the train for ages, that she had made a crossing into new emotional frontiers more exotic and unsettling than the Eastern European terrain beyond the window. Instinctively she knew that she had been right to think of Arif in terms of danger, a threat to her all-too-vulnerable emotions. In retrospect she felt nothing but gratitude toward the coquettishly feline Geneviève. It was her timely knock that had freed Holly from the bonds of Arif's dangerously seductive charm, and it was his soothing reply to the heiress's petulant outrage that had made Holly realize the truth about the arrogant Turk: he was a man accustomed to taking what he wanted without giving anything in return. Her bitterly philosophic musings were interrupted by a rap on the door and she moved away from the window to answer it.

A portly conductor in a navy blue jacket and cap looked up at her. "Good day, miss," he began politely. "Just a reminder that once we cross into Turkey, all the passengers will be required to descend from the train with their baggage for the customs check."

"Yes, thank you," Holly replied. "I'll be ready."

After he had gone she pulled her suitcases from beneath the bunk and began to pack in a quick methodical manner. Unlike Tatiana, whose neat cloth bags had been packed and set in the corridor some hours before, Holly had put off the irksome task until the last moment. It was with a rueful grin that she compared herself to the highly efficient, organized Russian woman, well accustomed to the discipline and authority of army life.

As she rearranged her clothing in neat compact folds, a flash of orange caught her eye. She pulled out the bright second-place ribbon and smoothed its rumpled satin corners. She retrieved a small notebook from her overnight bag and slid the ribbon between its stiff covers before tucking it back into the suitcase. The little bit of ribbon was a sharp reminder of what she had nearly achieved at Malmaison and what she hoped to achieve on the remainder of the riding circuit. She willed her thoughts away from the memory of Arif Hakal's powerful muscular form astride Sinjon in his moment of victory.

Before continuing her packing chores, Holly

stooped down to glance under the bunk for any last
stray article—a forgotten shoe or lost earring. What
she found instead was another bit of vibrant ribbon,
this one a brilliant purple. Turning it over, she realized that it was Tatiana's third-place trophy from
the Parisian competition. Had it fallen behind the
bed, or had it been tossed there in disdain? Somehow
Holly rather suspected it had been deliberately cast
aside. The diminutive strong-willed Russian lieutenant wanted no reminder of almost victory. For her
the stakes were too high.

Holly's musings were interrupted yet again by a
knock at her compartment door and she flung it open
distractedly, half expecting to see the neatly uniformed conductor armed with customs form and in-
structions this time. She did indeed stand face to face
with a uniform: long muscular legs encased in khaki
gabardine, and wide powerful shoulders that seemed
even more imposing in the short battle-green jacket.
Reluctantly Holly lifted her eyes to the face of the
man whose virile arrogant form seemed to fill the
doorway. His handsome, rather angular features
were grave, and the sensuous lips beneath his thick
black mustache were unsmiling. "Good morning,
Holly," Arif addressed her, his dark gaze roving
speculatively over her surprised features.

Holly quelled the stab of physical pleasure that his
liquid gaze elicited from her unarmored senses, and
she inclined her head stiffly. "Captain," she greeted
him in return. Her lithe form confronted his rugged
masculine presence with stubborn grace. She refused
to budge one step from the doorway, refused to ac-

knowledge the slow treacherous onrush of sensual attraction that his proximity aroused. The exotic subtleness of his spicy scent mingling with wool and harsh Turkish tobacco wafted into her cabin—a quiet invasion that she found impossible to ignore. "Have you forgotten something?" she asked ironically, remembering all too vividly her foolish surrender in his arms two nights before. She vowed to keep her own tiny patch of territory at her back inviolate.

Sensing the purpose of her protective stance, Arif grinned mischievously. "Not at all, Holly," he replied in a low amused voice. "I simply came to give you these books. There's one on the imperial stallions and another on the Turkish Riding Academy in Ankara. I think they'll offer some new insights."

Reluctantly Holly accepted the books from his outstretched hand. She turned away from him and dropped Tatiana's ribbon on the bedside table before slipping the volumes into her bulging overnight bag. "Shouldn't these have gone to Geneviève?" Holly inquired with deceptive sweetness as she stood up to regard her visitor levelly. "As far as I can tell, she's the rider who needs all the help she can get."

Arif's laughter erupted in short staccato bursts like machine-gun fire. "My God, Holly, you are a prideful woman! Will you continue to punish me for the rest of the circuit?" he demanded playfully. "I think we both understand Geneviève. She's more interested in the romance and mystique of the international circuit than in the riding itself."

Holly shrugged indifferently, refusing to share Arif's deep amusement. *Geneviève is interested in the mystique of one particular horseman,* she thought, immediately chiding herself for the inward show of jealousy. She vowed not to give any further ammunition to the laughing Turk's already ample ego.

She resumed her packing, steadfastly ignoring his presence. Amused rather than annoyed by her deliberate snub, Arif leaned against the door frame and crossed one polished black boot over the other as he watched her work. Then he noticed the frayed purple ribbon on the table and leaned down to pick it up. "Lieutenant Bulgakov has forgotten her Malmaison trophy," he remarked.

Holly looked up at him. "I think it wasn't forgotten, captain, but discarded. That must be a meaningless ribbon for an equestrienne who's competed in four Olympics. Tatiana is accustomed to winning."

Arif wandered casually to her side, and Holly—without being consciously aware of it—took a step backward in self-protection.

Sensing her retreat, Arif grinned once again. Without warning, his dark supple fingers shot out and gripped her chin, forcing her to look up at him. "And what about you, Holly?" he demanded. "Do you still intend to best me?"

She bridled at the teasing arrogance in his face, and her own expressive eyes narrowed. Their lambent green depths were like those of a silky Russian Blue cat—bright, watchful, intent. "That's the Muslim custom, isn't it, captain? An eye for an eye, " she snapped, at the same time wrenching her chin free from his steel grip.

Arif exploded with laughter once again, and he

gave her a mocking bow before retreating from the cabin.

Holly slammed the compartment door after him and finished her packing in a haphazard fashion, so that lacy bits of lingerie and the tie of her cream-colored silk riding shirt fluttered untidily at the edges of her bulging suitcase. Mindless of her thoroughly unprofessional packing job, she set the cases in the train aisle outside the door and flung her heavy over-night bag over her shoulder. She refused to admit to herself that Arif Hakal's unexpected visit had un-nerved her. How could she continue to face him on the riding circuit when his mere physical presence had such a devastating impact on her? She drew a deep determined breath and made her way swiftly down the crowded aisle toward the lounge car.

The wide burgundy-carpeted compartment was deserted at the noon hour but for the swarthy waiter behind the bar who stood drying glasses with the bottom edge of his clean white apron. She ordered a glass of sparkling water with a twist of lime and carried it to one of the deeply padded Art Deco chairs in navy velvet that faced one another companionably across the carpeted aisle. After a moment she remembered the books Arif had brought to her cabin, and she drew out the slender volume on imperial breeds. She opened it at random and pushed aside a thick envelope that evidently had been used as a book-mark. The entire two-page color spread was devoted to a dark mare of magnificent conformation. Her jet coloring combined with her great depth of body and length of quarter brought Sinjon to mind, and Holly thought that she could easily have been the black stallion's dam.

Holly had made a mental note to ask the captain if she had guessed correctly when her attention was caught by the unusual bulk of the envelope, which she'd casually pushed into her lap as she studied the photographs in the book. Since it was not sealed, she didn't resist the impulse to peek inside. To her astonishment she saw that it was full of five-hundred-franc notes. She surmised immediately that the money was Arif's winnings from the Malmaison race. As she closed the book on its little treasure trove, Holly smiled in wry amusement at the image of Arif's frantic dismay when he came to realize he'd misplaced the large sum of money.

Her thoughts were drawn away from her amused speculations by the suddenly animated voice of the bartender. "Turkiye!" he called excitedly, gesturing beyond the snowy plain to the small guard stations marking the bleak fontier. She just caught a glimpse of the grim-faced soldier's salute as the speeding express rolled into the ancient country that straddled two continents.

Hurriedly she stuffed her belongings back into the canvas bag and made her way to the connecting platform between the lounge and sleeping cars. The frigid wind whipped about her mercilessly, but a weak ray of sunshine had somehow managed to pierce the heavy mantle of winter storm clouds. Although her eyes watered from the lashing cold, she kept them fixed on the flat eastern horizon.

Several long minutes passed, but her vigilance was

at last rewarded by an incredible sight. She felt her blood pounding with a strange excitement as her eyes made out the outline of four minarets in the distance, like silvery fingers of ice piercing the wintry sky. The train seemed to pick up speed over the rolling plateau, and a few minutes later a series of tiled domes bubbled into view beneath the graceful pencil-thin towers. A thrill of pleasure and of fear raced along her veins as her eyes took in the exotic skyscape of mosques and minarets.

This was Arif Hakal's world, a totally new and strange land she had never known. It was she who was the interloper, an inexperienced outsider who had vowed to match wits and skill with the dark lean wolf of the steppes on his own terrain. Holly shrugged off her darkly romantic fantasies and made her way swiftly toward the warm shelter of the train's interior.

Fifteen minutes later the express rumbled into the Edirne station. Holly descended the two narrow iron steps to the railway platform, half carrying and half dragging her heavy bags. Despite her awkward load, her senses were still infused with the same sense of excitement she'd felt upon first seeing the minarets rising out of the gray brown plain. Beyond the station she caught a glimpse of narrow cobbled lanes overhung with wooden balconies, while above the twisting streets the rounded dome of yet another mosque cast its profile against the pale sky. She had picked up her bags to resume her awkward difficult trek toward the customs building when she suddenly felt a hand slipping beneath her fingers to take the heavier suitcase from her arms, and her startled gaze flew upward to meet Arif's dark laughing eyes.

"What do you think of Turkey so far, *mademoiselle*?" he inquired teasingly as he shifted his own canvas duffel bag effortlessly to his powerful shoulder.

"Rather overwhelming for a woman who was bred on American soil and never ventured farther east than Atlantic City," Holly laughed in return. Her eyes traveled once more toward the magnificent dome above the tangle of medieval streets.

"That is the Selimiye Camii, a mosque built more than four hundred years ago for the sultan Selim," Arif answered her unspoken question. "I wish we had time to tour the city. Believe me, it still lives up to its fabled reputation as the gateway of the East."

His lips parted once more in an engaging grin, and Holly suddenly found herself regretting the fact that there was not enough time to stroll through the shops and bazaar of the ancient town with Arif as her guide.

They entered the drafty cavernous customs building, and Arif casually threw down his duffel bag on the long conveyorlike table before hoisting his companion's heavier suitcases next to his.

The customs officer's small black eyes flicked in Holly's direction, assessing her tall blond good looks as if she were a precious gem being imported into the country. He took Arif's passport and flashed a gold-toothed grin at his countryman. "Welcome home, captain," he said in heavily accented English for the American woman's benefit. "We heard of your victory in the Parisian competition. Congratulations!"

"Did you expect less of a fellow Turk?" Arif grinned in return. "If we claim ancestry with the Mongols out of the East, then we should be able to guide a stallion between our knees, right?"

The official raised his heavy brows in a mournful expression. "Ah, yes. But the days of empire and flashing steeds are gone. We compete for prize winnings rather than national honor, is that not so?"

Despite Arif's answering shrug of indifference, Holly felt his subtle tensing. And she watched curiously as the official went through his bag with methodical purpose.

The customs officer looked up at last. "No gems or other precious booty to declare, captain?" he inquired mildly.

"None," Arif assented. "You know as well as I that an officer's pay allows little for such baubles."

The man turned to Holly, and his gold tooth flashed dully as he grinned once again. He lightly fingered the bits of lace protruding from her untidily packed bags, causing Holly to blush, but he did not bother to open them. After a cursory examination of her passport, he indicated she was free to go.

"That's all there is to it?" Holly asked in some confusion.

The official bowed, smiling once again. "You are a tourist, miss. It is only Turkish citizens whose bags must be examined rigorously."

"I see," Holly replied as she shifted the burden of her heavy canvas tote bag from one shoulder to the other. But as she did so the bag slipped from her fingers and fell onto the table. Wallet, hairbrush and books spilled outward. Almost at once it seemed as if three pairs of eyes were fixed on the edge of the thick envelope that had slid from between the pages of the slender volume on horses.

The official casually picked up the envelope and examined its contents. Expertly he flicked the bills between thumb and forefinger, tabulating the amount in silence. He glanced up after a moment and smiled. "Ten thousand francs. It looks as though you're ready to have a good time in Istanbul."

Holly looked up swiftly in Arif's direction, her uncertain gaze met and held by his darkly defiant, arrogant expression. With a sudden flash of understanding, she realized what he had meant to do. She had laughed at him for so foolishly misplacing his winnings when all the while he had known exactly where the envelope was. Her cheeks flushed angrily at the thought that he had intended to use her once again. Fleetingly she recalled their acid interchange in her train compartment that morning: "Do you still intend to best me?" And her quick retort: "An eye for an eye...."

A sparkle of vengeance flashed in Holly's emerald eyes when she turned to address the customs official. "Actually, that isn't my money at all. It belongs to Captain Hakal, who won it in Paris. He must have left the envelope in that book by mistake."

"In that case," the official replied with a jovial laugh, his gold tooth glittering mischievously, "we had better declare this. He will have to pay a tax on it," he remarked smoothly, drawing out several five-hundred-franc notes from the envelope. He peeled off one of the bills and thrust it into Holly's jacket pocket. "Your honesty is appreciated," he said ironically as he tucked the remaining notes into his breast pocket before handing the rather thinner envelope to its rightful owner.

Arif flashed her a look of anger as he pocketed the funds. In return she shot him a defiant smile of victory, eager to let him know that she had bested him in a clever hand of revenge. But it was a hollow victory. As she trudged alone back to the waiting train, Holly squirmed inwardly with embarrassment, secretly horrified at the barbarous exchange of money. She had hoped to make Arif look the fool, but in actuality it had been she and the unctuously smiling customs officer who appeared greedy. Holly felt cheapened by the incident, but it was over and done with. Her eyes anxiously surveyed the milling crowd for Arif's tall imposing figure, but he, too, had vanished.

The last leg of the journey into Istanbul seemed interminable. Holly stared with unseeing eyes past the neat patchwork fields and occasional thatched cottages dusted with snow, her fingers idly twirling a teaspoon. She had eaten very little of the light supper served in the dining car, and her attention to the lively conversation around the tables was only fitful. At the far end of the car, Arif sat with Geneviève Lamine and the other members of the French riding team. For one brief moment the captain's dark eyes had blazed into Holly's over the length of the car, but just as swiftly his gaze had flicked away disinterestedly. Her stomach had tightened into a hard knot at Arif's dismissing indifferent expression.

Perhaps it's for the best after all, Holly mused quietly. The depth of her attraction to the enigmatic captain had frightened and overwhelmed her. No man had ever made her feel as Arif Hakal had done. For all his selfish arrogance, he was the most passionate and fascinating individual she had ever met. He had touched her life in a maddening yet magical way, and the thought that he might not do so again left her feeling oddly cold and empty.

With a will she turned her thoughts back toward the laughing group around the table and their joking references to cabin fever. As she joined in the laughter, Holly leaned forward and caught a glimpse of Tatiana three chairs over from her. The petite Russian lieutenant seemed pensive and withdrawn, her eyes flickering darkly toward the rear of the car. Holly followed her gaze, shivering slightly when she realized that Tatiana was regarding her burly nondescript bodyguard. As she studied the darkly thoughtful Russian woman, Holly recalled the third-place ribbon that had been left behind in their shared train compartment. For the first time she found herself wondering nervously what would become of the quiet intense equestrienne.

At long last the twinkling lights of Istanbul's suburbs rose out of the rolling plain in the deepening twilight, and the express rumbled through the quaint outlying stations. A blur of factories and well-lit apartment blocks marked their entrance into the city proper. Within five minutes the express rounded Seraglio Point, and the roar of its diesel engines echoed off the ocher walls rising to the left of the nar-

row railway tracks. Someone announced that the
walls contained the celebrated courtyards and harems
of Topkapi Palace.

Holly regarded the massive stone ramparts with a
little more interest, but they quickly vanished from
sight as the train chugged into the turreted and cren-
ellated Istanbul railway station. Situated in the
Sirkeci, the old quarter of the vinegar makers, the
Turkish Gothic station seemed a fugitive from a
long-dead era. Holly half expected to see beggars and
cats and suspicious-looking men with fedoras pulled
down low over their eyes lounging on the entrance
steps, but she realized with a curious feeling of letdown that Istanbul's fabled reputation for intrigue
was long past.

As she descended from the train for the last time,
Holly paused for a moment on the polished iron step.
The station was abuzz with people, most of them
stocky men in ill-fitting overcoats with their raw-
boned hands clutching battered suitcases bound with
rope. The men were en route to the more prosperous
countries of northern Europe—Switzerland, France
and Germany—where they would work in factories
and restaurants, saving enough money until they
could return to their Turkish homeland to buy land
or a business of their own.

Glancing over the busy terminal, Holly's heart
beat a little more quickly as she caught sight of Arif
Hakal's commanding figure striding purposefully
through the milling peasants. With his bronzed com-
plexion and exotically tilted cheekbones he seemed an
intrinsic part of the northward-bound crowd around

him. Yet at the same time his arrogant purposeful stride set him apart.

Holly had begun to wonder which world—East or West—was wholly his when she saw him bend down and swoop up a darkly beautiful petite woman into his arms. Holly's heart twisted painfully at the sight, wondering at her own naiveté in not expecting that the handsome captain would have a lovely country-woman eagerly awaiting his return. With a sigh she descended the last step to the concrete platform.

A moment later she heard her name called out and she whirled to face her short laconic trainer. "Here you are, Holly. Thank God you're five foot nine, blond and tower over these Turkish folks; otherwise I'd have despaired of ever findin' you in this mad-house." He jerked a finger over his shoulder. "I got us a porter, too. *Hamal*, or some such word, they call themselves. Let's get a move on. I'm lookin' forward to sleepin' in a real bed for a change!"

Holly grinned affectionately at her trainer. She had realized long ago that his gruffness was all for show; Rusty Wilkins was one of the most equable good-hearted men she'd ever known, and she was particularly grateful at the moment for the grum-bling jokes and complaints that immediately served to lighten her mood. "Well, how do you think I feel?" she replied in a bantering tone. "I bet I'd have a hard time finding you at a pygmy conven-tion. Too bad you no longer have a flaming beacon of red hair!"

Rusty glared up at her pugnaciously, his blue eyes sharp with laughter. "Maybe I'll get me a wig."

Holly threw back her head and laughed. "You'd make a terrific Raggedy Andy, you know!"

Their banter was interrupted as Tatiana Bulgakov came to a stop beside them on the crowded platform and extended her hand forthrightly to the slender blond American who towered above her. "You have been a good traveling companion, Holly MacKnight. I am certain that we will see each other again at the end of the week for the horse trials." She next turned to Rusty. "And thank you, Mr. Wilkins, for your advice about Kazan."

Rusty took her outstretched hand sheepishly. "You bet, lieutenant. Anytime!"

She was about to turn away when Holly said impulsively, "Wait a minute, Tatiana! Why don't you come to our hotel with us and have a drink? We aren't stayng at the Hilton or Sheraton like some of the others, but I'm sure the Pera Palas is comfortable at least. When we made the reservations in Paris, the travel agent told us the hotel had a certain 'quaint old-fashioned charm.' Heaven only knows what that means," Holly added laughingly.

Tatiana's dark heavy brows came together in a slight frown of concentration. "I...I do not know. A representative of the Soviet Consulate was supposed to meet me." She stood up on tiptoe on her tiny black-slippered feet and looked around the station.

Rusty grinned impishly. "Maybe he forgot."

To her astonishment, Holly watched the dour lieutenant grin impetuously in return. The happy expression softened her small sharp features so that she

seemed almost pretty. "Very well," Tatiana announced quietly, as if she'd come to a sudden decision. "I shall accompany you to your hotel. We shall
give my tail a run for his money at least, eh?" She
cast a swift disdainful look over her shoulder.

Once again Holly felt a stab of pity for the lonely
guarded woman whose life was not her own, but the
feeling was dispelled as the trio ran quickly to find a
taxi. Ten minutes later their driver, who manipulated
his vehicle with the aggressive ferocity of his warrior
ancestors, careered left onto the Mesrutiyet Caddesi
and deposited them abruptly at number ninety-eight.

As Holly and Tatiana stood waiting for the creaking elevator to descend through its central ironwork
shaft, the American girl reflected that the once opulent hotel was indeed charming. A white marble staircase climbed upward in a series of landings decorated
with enormous potted palms and ferns, and Holly
tried to imagine the place in its heyday during the last
years of the Ottoman Empire. She imagined elegant
women in clingy gowns descending the wide stairway
to the ballroom, and the tinkle of champagne glasses
and trilled piano chords floating out into the mirrored lobby.

Her idle reverie was interrupted as Tatiana whispered up to her, "Such bourgeois decadence."

"Yes, but don't you prefer it to drabness?" Holly
replied with a laugh, noticing the Russian woman's
expressive brows drawn together consideringly at
that unexpected observation.

Holly found her room on the fourth floor to be
equally charming. It was a large high-ceilinged affair

with faded rose wallpaper and a suite of dark polished mahogany. She freed the latch on the wooden
shutters covering the balcony doors and stared in
delight at the twinkling lights cascading over the
city's seven hills. Impulsively she pulled open the
doors but was met with a blast of icy wind blowing
inland from the Bosporus Strait, the narrow band of
water separating Europe and Asia. Both Holly and
Tatiana were leaning against the multipaned door to
close out the fierce wintry onslaught when Rusty
knocked energetically and entered a moment later
bearing an ornate brass tray. There was a cold beer
for himself and a pot of steaming smoky tea for the
two women.

After pouring the tea, Holly kicked off her shoes
and sank down upon the gold bedspread. "Oh, God,
this is heavenly," she sighed. "This is the first time in
three days that I've been able to stretch out completely."

Rusty eased down onto a curved-leg chair opposite
Tatiana, who sat demurely, warming her fingers
around the china cup. "Yeah, it'd be heaven all right
if I just had a Coors or a Lone Star beer," the crusty
old trainer conceded.

"You cowboys are all alike!" Holly teased.
"Haven't you ever heard the expression, 'When in
Rome...'?"

"If you're referrin' to that *raki* stuff, well, look
out," he drawled in mock horror. "It'd raise hairs on
my chest that I didn't even know I had."

Tatiana's dark serious eyes darted from one to the
other during this exchange.

Holly noticed her confusion and quickly apologized. "You'll have to bear with our teasing ways, Tatiana."

"No, no," the woman demurred. "I was enjoying your repartee, although I must confess that I did not understand much of it. But it is a nice thing for me to see a trainer and rider getting along together so well. There is no tension."

"Wait'll you see me schoolin' her and Mandi-girl over a course," Rusty growled. "Tension! By God, you'll see fireworks!"

"Rusty used to be a redhead!" Holly explained with a laugh. "His hair may have grayed a little, but unfortunately his temper is as fiery as it's always been."

The easygoing conversation was interrupted by a sharp forceful knock on the door. Tatiana replaced her teacup in its saucer with equally clattering force as Holly rose from the bed and hurried to answer it. A heavy-jowled man in a dark suit stood in the doorway.

"I am Viktor Kerensky, a representative of the Soviet Consulate in Istanbul," he began by way of introduction, his harsh uncompromising gray eyes boring into Holly. "I believe you are harboring one of our citizens."

"I wouldn't say 'harboring' is quite the word, Mr. Kerensky," Holly observed dryly, stepping aside so that he might enter the room. "My trainer, Rusty Wilkins, and I invited Lieutenant Bulgakov to our hotel for a cup of tea, since there was no one at the station to meet her this evening." Holly's tone conveyed the slightest sense of reproach, a subtle method of putting a man in his place that she had learned instinctively from years of observing her own imperious mother use it to withering effect.

Serenely she ignored the man's baleful glare as she turned back to Tatiana. The Russian woman had risen from her chair and stood with head and shoulders painfully erect, her hands clenched in white-knuckled fists at her sides. Kerensky uttered a few sharp words to her, and swiftly she moved across the room in his direction.

"Good night," she said stiffly to Holly, "and thank you for the tea."

"Wait a second," Holly said impulsively. She went over to her overnight bag and pulled out the small leather makeup case that held the essentials of eye shadows, blushers, lipsticks and brushes. She held it out to Tatiana. "Please, I want you to have it."

Tatiana shook her head. "No, truly, I couldn't."

"Please," Holly insisted, and the Russian woman took the soft pouch from her hands.

A moment later the door closed soundlessly behind the retreating figures of the two Russians.

"Whew," Rusty breathed at last, breaking the almost palpable tension that had crept into the room. "I wasn't expecting that."

"Do...do you think she'll be punished, Rusty?" she asked, her gaze troubled.

The trainer stood up and stretched. "Who knows? I'll tell you one thing," he observed practically. "They won't do anything until she's had a chance to prove herself in the competition later in the week."

As he made his way to the door, he stopped and patted her arm affectionately. "Now don't go worryin' about it. I have a feelin' that's one little lady who can take care of herself."

A few minutes later Holly slipped out of her clothes and climbed wearily into the wide bed. Despite her exhaustion sleep eluded her. Her thoughts whirled in a crazy quilt of images, returning again and again to the troubled expression in Tatiana's eyes as she had left Holly's room. The Russian woman's gaze had brought to mind another pair of eyes like winter sable. During the long overland trip, Holly had felt the full spectrum of Arif's compelling dark gaze—arrogant, playful, incredibly sensual or filled with disdain. She tossed restlessly as she recalled the tawdry little scene at the customs station. *He deserved that and more,* Holly told herself angrily before drifting off at last into a troubled sleep.

CHAPTER FIVE

THE SPACIOUS BATHROOM in the old-fashioned hotel had white porcelain fittings and thick white Turkish towels draped over heated rails. Holly stretched out in the enormous tub and luxuriated in the steamy perfumed mist rising from the water as she soaked away three days' worth of grime. She refused to let her mind rove beyond the delightful relaxation of the hot bath; forbade her thoughts from returning to the troubled images of the preceding night.

The long and exhausting train trip across Europe had depleted her emotionally, as well. She was eager to return to the demanding physical work of the horse arena. Perhaps a hard pounding workout over the flats at a full gallop would help to blot out the unsettling images of Arif Hakal that rose unbidden in her mind.

Holly lifted the washcloth and wrung it out over her shoulders, feeling the hot droplets of moisture coursing downward slowly between the creamy white mounds of her breasts. She became intensely aware of her pink nipples teased by the liquid warmth of the water's surface, so curiously like Arif's warm sensual fingers. Once again she disciplined her thoughts, reluctantly quelling the memory of his electrifying touch and the frightening ease with which he could inflame her. She stood up and climbed out of the tub, drying herself vigorously before the fitful warmth of the hissing radiator.

Room service would arrive any minute with the pot of tea she'd ordered a half hour ago, Holly realized as she toweled her wet hair and combed out the long honey-gold strands. She belted her rose velour bathrobe loosely about her waist and padded barefoot into the bedroom. When she opened the wooden shutters, a stream of pale gray light filtered into the room. Istanbul and the Bosporus beyond were shrouded in mist. *Perhaps it still is a city of mystery,* she reflected ruefully.

A moment later there was a sharp efficient rap on the door, and she hurried across the room to open it. Holly was shocked to find herself staring up into the bronzed face of Arif Hakal, who seemed to carry with him the harsh invigorating chill of winter. He wore a tawny suede jacket, its wool collar lining drawn up against the springy jet black thickness of his hair. She felt her heart beating a little quicker at his unexpected appearance and wondered if he had come to declare a truce, as he had done once before, laughingly, in his train compartment. A slow flush rose upward from her neck as she recalled the outcome of that encounter.

When she addressed him at last, her tone was light yet edged with a faint undercurrent of vulnerability. "Arif. Somehow I didn't expect to see you at my door this morning."

His gaze flickered over her head into the room,

and her flush deepened as she recalled the scattered lingerie and rumpled bed, the perfumed mist that pervaded the room from her bath. Arif's grave eyes, revealing nothing, returned to her face. "Nor did I, Holly. The Turkish Army Riding Academy arranged for us to host the foreign riders this week, and I have been assigned to be your guide to the city," he explained, his lips twisting in a tight sardonic grin.

"I see." Her eyes flashed dark as greenwood. "Tell me, captain, why didn't you just use your considerable persuasive powers to trade me for someone more to your liking?" she retorted, her sarcastic inquiry a veil to mask the vague disappointment she felt at realizing that his visit was merely one of formal politeness.

His facial muscles tightened at this gibe, so that the harsh angularity of his features grew more pronounced. It was undeniably the face of a very strong and willful man. "It is my duty to escort you, pure and simple...though I would not expect you to understand that," his low voice grated with unexpected anger.

Stung to the quick by the implied criticism in his words, she flung back at him, "If this duty is such a painful one, I think I'd prefer to forget the whole thing. I'm quite capable of finding my own way around Istanbul!"

"This is not Philadelphia, Holly, and you are very, very young. If something were to happen to you, I would bear the full responsibility."

Her eyes flashed dangerously at this arrant display of male superiority. "I haven't the least intention of spending a day with you under those terms. Goodbye, captain." She made a move to shut the door, but one powerful forearm easily forced it open again.

Arif came into the room and leaned against the door with his hands behind his back. Holly heard the unmistakable click of the brass key turning in its lock, and she retreated a few steps.

When Arif spoke again, there was an undercurrent of brittle amusement in his attractive voice. "I have no intention of shirking my duty, Holly MacKnight. I'm a patient man. I'll wait right here until you decide to change your mind. And if you don't... well, as you yourself admitted, Holly, my persuasive powers can be considerable."

Haughtily she drew herself up to her full height, though in her bare feet she was still forced to crane her neck upward to flash angry eyes at her taunter. "Very well, captain. You win again. I'll meet you downstairs in the lobby."

A feral grin played about his lips at this victory, although his eyes were hard. "By the way," he added as he opened the door, "please wear something suitable. We'll be visiting a few mosques. Turkish women no longer wear the black *charshafs* and veils that covered them from head to toe; still, there is a tradition of propriety." His words were belied by the flashing gaze that raked over her, lingering on the shadowed outline of her breasts and her slender hips beneath the clinging robe.

Holly stared back defiantly, resisting the urge to clutch the robe protectively up around her throat. After the door had closed behind his back, she swore angrily between gritted teeth, "Damn you, Arif Hakal!"

There was no trace of anger in her face a half hour later, however, when she emerged from the creaking antique elevator. Arif turned from the open doorway to meet her, and as he did so his eyes narrowed in surprise. Holly smiled inwardly at his reaction. She had carefully chosen her apparel with an eye to chic elegance, grateful that her practical aunt had insisted she pack a well-rounded wardrobe for the European circuit. She had paired a slim green wool skirt and a gray silk blouse delicately patterned in green and black with a pair of tall gray leather boots. Then she had gathered up her thick blond hair into a French twist that swept deeply over her forehead from a side part. A pair of delicate gold knot earrings shone against her earlobes, and she carried a simple black wool wraparound coat over her arm.

"Perhaps I was wrong after all," Arif observed in his low sensual voice. "Suddenly you seem more a sophisticated woman than a wide-eyed innocent girl. I could see you more easily on Fifth Avenue or London's Mayfair than on the busy sidewalks of Istiklal Caddesi."

Had Holly just imagined the fleeting touch of regret in his voice? She looked up at him curiously, but he had taken her arm and already was hailing a cab from the narrow curb.

Istanbul's daytime traffic was rather more daunting than its nighttime counterpart, Holly decided as the taxi hurtled along the twisting cobbled lanes and shadowy alleys roofed over with leafless vines and creepers. After a few more minutes she decided that it was downright terrifying and shut her eyes fatalistically, expecting at any moment to hear the rending crash of metal and the moans of the injured.

"You might get a better view of the sights if you opened those lovely green eyes of yours," Arif remarked in undisguised amusement.

Her brown lashes fluttered upward and she regarded him levelly. "Where are we going, anyway?" she asked.

"Don't you enjoy surprises, Holly?" he replied with a wry grin.

She turned to look out the window and soon became engrossed in the changing scenes before her. She gasped in astonishment as her eyes took in the struggling figure of a porter, his upper body bent forward nearly parallel to the street as he carried a small sofa on his back.

Arif's gaze followed hers and he observed quietly, "The *hamals* are incredibly strong. I have seen them carrying pianos and a whole load of bicycles. They are truly the workhorses of Istanbul."

A few minutes later the cab skirted a large busy square where a group of shoeshine men sat before their elaborately worked brass boxes like lords of their domains. Then a gaggle of rosy-cheeked schoolchildren in black pinafores and white Peter Pan collars ran by, and Holly laughed in delight at such a whimsical turn-of-the-century scene.

Suddenly she felt Arif's fingers on her chin as he gently turned her face toward him. "Your laughter is beautiful, Holly. It seems to bubble up from so deep within. You should laugh more often."

Taken aback by this unexpected compliment, Holly

regarded her companion curiously once again, but she was spared the need to reply as the taxi drew to a sudden screeching halt and deposited its passengers at the foot of a low bridge whose far side was still concealed by white mist. Even at that early-morning hour the pavement was aswarm with jostling crowds and impatiently tooting cars and trams.

Holly felt the pontoon bridge swaying slightly beneath her feet as Arif took her arm with a grin and led her toward a wooden stairway. "This is the Galata," he explained, "one of the busiest bridges in the world. But more surprising, there is another little city concealed beneath it."

Scurrying commuters jostled their elbows as Arif and Holly paused at the bottom of the staircase. Holly's eyes widened as she took in the dozens of tiny restaurants, newsstands and booths selling everything from whole fried fish wrapped in paper squares to bazaar trinkets and pistachio nuts. She saw that several ferryboats were docked at the east-side berth and quickly realized that the boats were the principal reason for the hundreds of people hurrying downward into the bowels of the old bridge.

Ten minutes later the two of them stood side by side at the rails of one of the old steamers as it nosed away from the berth and threaded a passage through the scores of fishing boats and quaint *kayiks* with their half-moon gunwales that jockeyed for space in the busy inlet of the Bosporus.

The mist gradually began to lift as the ferryboat set a steady course along the northern shore of the winding water route. Holly drank in the cold sea air with delight. "I feel as though I'm on a voyage of discovery," she laughed at last, cocking her head with a questioning look at her companion. "*Now* are you going to tell me what our destination is?"

Arif grinned, as well. "This inlet is the Haliç. In English it's called the Golden Horn. I suppose some romantic Westerner dubbed it that a few hundred years ago. Our destination is Eyüp, about a half hour from here."

"The Golden Horn." Holly savored the words on her lips. "It *is* a terribly romantic name for a waterway."

"The shores of the Haliç used to be lined with palaces, pleasure kiosks and imperial gardens, but these days it isn't quite so idyllic," Arif replied as his gaze roved over the far shore.

Although thin scarves of mist still clung to the hilltops and the clefts of the valleys between, the white veil had lifted from the shoreline to reveal a workaday profile of factories, coal heaps and marine repair yards.

"I see what you mean," Holly answered ruefully as her gaze followed his.

Arif seemed to read the fleeting pang of regret for lost beauty in her words. "I'm seeing a wholly new side to you today, Holly MacKnight—first the smart city sophisticate and now the dreamy-eyed romantic. All of a sudden it seems this outing may be a voyage of discovery for me, as well." Although the words were spoken teasingly, his dark eyes flashed with an indefinable half-questioning look.

Holly sought to meet his gaze, to read the hidden

meaning behind it, but swiftly he had looked away.

A moment later Arif spoke again, in a cool controlled voice that bore no traces of his light teasing manner of a moment ago. "I myself am a hard-eyed realist rather than a romantic. The fabric of dreams is very different from the needs and demands of our everyday lives. You know, the romantics complain about the new ugliness along the Haliç, but not me. I see the ugly factories as proof of a stronger economy for the country." He shrugged. "Maybe if I had been born and raised here in the city I would feel differently. But then we are a pretty insular people. If you ask a Turk where he is from he will name not his country but the region in which he was born. He will say he is a man of the Black Sea or Lake Van, or like myself, a man of Kars."

Holly's eyes played with new interest over his intent, darkly handsome features. She sensed that his talk of hard-eyed realists had less to do with the pollution of the Haliç shoreline than with some conflict within himself. Once more she felt that she'd had a fleeting glimpse beyond his arrogant self-confident facade, and she yearned to know more about him. "The town you mentioned as your home," she began tentatively. "That's far to the east of here, isn't it? Beyond Erzurum?"

"Yes, that's right. You have a good memory." The reply was abrupt, curt, as if he wished to forestall further questions. His eyes, too, were hooded and seemed filled with a brooding light.

Holly knew instinctively that he had no wish to talk about himself, and that he realized the things he'd said already had somehow revealed more to her than he intended.

Once more when he spoke he had reverted to the cool tour-guide role, and for the moment Holly had to be content with that. Very quickly she became intrigued with his knowledgeable and colorful descriptions of the Turkish past and the succession of eastern Roman emperors, Seljuk pashas and Ottoman sultans who had ruled ancient Byzantium and Constantinople before it had become modern-day Istanbul.

Holly was surprised when a few minutes later the ferryboat bumped up gently to the dock at Eyüp. Arif lightly placed his hand across her back to half turn her and direct her gaze toward the town, but she was less aware of the quaint profile of the village than of the warmth and unconscious strength he exuded. She longed to lean back for a moment in the shelter of his arms, but she knew it was impossible. His presence was a command, a duty that had nothing at all to do with desiring or caring. Nevertheless, she felt a thrill of pleasure when he took her hand to help her over the rough cobbles as she stepped off the boat.

"You should have worn low shoes for walking," he chided her.

In her soft leather boots with their three-inch heels, Holly found that her eyes were nearly at a level with his wide jaw and she needed only to flick them upward slightly to meet his reproving gaze with sparkling green intensity. "I prefer being on an equal footing with you, captain," she shot back.

Arif grinned unexpectedly at the dual-edged meaning of her words. "In the short time that I've known you, Holly, I've felt the full brunt of your damnable pride and will. I can see why you haven't met your match in a man...."

She lifted her fine-boned chin in an attitude of pert defiance, willing him to complete the sentence. *Until now.* The unspoken words floated in the cold air between them, swallowed up in the warm breath of mist that had escaped from their lips to rise and mingle above their heads.

Once again the fleeting moment of shared understanding, the sensation of having been on the brink of some deeper communication, had gone. They climbed the winding lanes of the old village in silence, admiring the wooden buildings with their beautiful fretwork balconies leaning dangerously over the narrow streets.

"The town used to be famous for its toy shops," he told her after a while.

"And now?" she asked curiously.

For answer he led her over the breast of a hill and down another narrow lane that widened before an incredibly lovely white mosque. "This is the tomb of Eyüp. He was the standard-bearer of the prophet Muhammad, and so his burial site is a beloved pilgrimage goal for many Muslims," Arif explained. He led her through a wide courtyard to a smaller white-walled enclosure decorated with intricately designed glazed tiles in reds, yellows and blues.

Beneath the enormous tree growing in the center of the smaller courtyard wound a silent line of worshipers. Arif pointed above the heads of the queued Muslims to a small brass latticework opening in the wall. "It's called the Window of Help. All of these people have come to pray before it and beg a favor at the tomb. You can see how they rub their fingers on the grille to take away some of the blessings with them. The line before the tomb is endless," Arif explained in a low undertone as he led her beneath an archway toward the entrance of the mosque.

"Thank you for bringing me here, Arif," she said at last. "I think it's given me a deeper understanding of Islam. Your countrymen are incredibly devout."

"It's a devotion born of centuries," Arif rejoined, his black eyes intense. "In the past it was the *jihad*, the holy wars, that led to the expansion of the Turkish empire. But then," he added teasingly, "I expect you know a lot about that. I seem to recall a stinging little lecture you delivered to Geneviève in the dining car of the train several days ago."

Holly's lips parted in a pretty smile. Not even the mention of the preening Tunisian heiress could disrupt her serene mood. "That was purely a bluff!" she explained. "All of this is quite new...and fascinating to me."

"Good. I'm delighted to hear you say that, because there's more on the agenda. Come on." He took her arm as they left the mosque enclosure and followed a pathway to the right along the walls. Eventually it led to an old, ill-kempt cemetery. They slowly climbed the weed-strewn paths among the drunkenly leaning tombstones, and Holly loosened her coat as the surprisingly bright winter sun evaporated the last wisps of morning fog.

When they finally reached the summit of the hill, Holly gasped in astonishment. "Arif!" she cried, her voice as high as a child's with excitement. "Why didn't you prepare me for what to expect? This must be one of the most stupendous views in the world!"

The tapered thrust of a thousand minarets pierced the fairylike cityscape of softly rounded domes in the distance. As a counterpoint to the graceful towers was the tangle of streets merging and dividing in the countless silver rivulets across Istanbul's seven hills.

Arif grinned at her pleasure. "The view is all the more wonderful when you come upon it unexpectedly like this, I think."

Later, as they sat on the glass-walled terrace of an old café, sipping tea from small glasses set in brass holders, Holly continued to marvel at the view.

"But you see, too, that the ancient minareted skyline is blocked here and there by modern high-rise buildings," Arif pointed out, his gaze riveted, as well, on the profile of the dynamic two-thousand-year-old city spread out before them in the distance. "Istanbul has always seen the cosmopolitan clash of cultures. In the past it was Armenians, Venetians, Greeks and other Europeans in their little quarters of the city. Now it is more simply the clash of East versus West, old against new. You see a real example of it in the gaping holes that have been cut into the medieval walls of the old city to make way for broad avenues leading to the airport."

Holly turned away from the magical cityscape to

regard her companion. "Arif, where do you fit into that clash of cultures?" she asked suddenly, aware yet again that she had broken their tacit agreement not to touch on personal matters.

He turned swiftly to regard her, eyes narrowed to dark slits. She would never know whether he meant to give her an explanation or a reprimand because their own taut little clash of eyes and wills was interrupted by a young boy whose appealingly innocent eyes were belied by his quick streetwise air.

"Take your picture, miss," the boy wheedled, holding up an ancient battered Polaroid camera. "Only twenty *kurus*."

Before she could reply, Arif muttered something impatiently to him in Turkish and waved his hand as if to shoo him away. Undaunted by this rebuff, however, the boy cast a slow sidelong glance in Holly's direction before uttering a voluble tirade of his own in Turkish.

At the boy's words, Arif threw his head back and exploded with laughter.

"Would you mind telling me what's going on?" Holly demanded as her green eyes regarded the two of them in perplexity.

Arif bit his lower lip as if to forestall further laughter. "After I told the little squirt to get lost, he took a long look at you and asked me whether you were a Circassian or a Western movie queen. 'Either way,' he told me, 'you'd better get a picture of yourself with her or none of your friends will believe it when you tell them the story after she's gone.'"

"The kid's got taste," Holly laughed.

Arif's eyes played over her features slowly. "Yes, I suppose he has." He made a quick gesture to the boy then and impulsively lifted Holly's hand from the table, entwining their fingers. "Snap away, *kapici*!" he commanded. "We'll record this historic meeting of East and West for posterity."

Half a minute later, after the photo had been developed and the boy paid, Arif handed it over carelessly to Holly. "Here, a little souvenir of your visit to Turkey."

Holly stared down at the sharp black-and-white photograph. Arif's full lower lip jutted out arrogantly beneath the black mustache, while his eyes gleamed with a mock ferocity edged with silent laughter. By contrast, Holly's aristocratic fine-boned features were half in profile, eyes downcast almost demurely. In the background was the blurred outline of the thatched-roof café. Holly found something quaintly old-fashioned about the photograph, as if it had been snapped half a century rather than half a minute ago. When she looked up again, she found Arif's eyes upon her.

"Do you like my little gift?" he demanded, a suspicion of laughter still evident in his eyes.

"I've seen rather enough of your features today without needing a photo to boot," she retorted dryly. Nevertheless, she carefully tucked it into the pocket of her coat.

Later, as they walked down the hill to the ferryboat, Holly asked, "What is a Circassian?"

Arif's harmonious laughter rang out over the gray tombstones. "I was wondering how long it would take you to ask that. They're a tribe of people who live in the Black Sea area. Their women were fair and prized for their beauty, and in the past many of them were sold into slavery in Turkey.''

Holly's eyes flashed at that. ''I'm glad times have changed since then.''

''What! You don't think it would have been appealing to have a virile Turkish warlord for your master?'' he teased.

''If I were there against my will, I'd have made his life miserable,'' Holly shot back, her eyes dark as polished jade.

''Allah be praised! What a blond spitfire of a woman you have thrown in my path!'' Arif's rich laughter echoed down the hill toward the narrow inlet of sea.

THE REMAINDER OF THE AFTERNOON was a kaleidoscopic whirl of Iznik tiles and Arabic calligraphy, marble courtyards with fountains and gem-encrusted daggers.

Arif and Holly strolled through the grounds of Topkapi Palace, whose fortresslike walls skirted the train tracks leading to the old station. To Holly it seemed less a castle than a richly emblazoned collection of halls scattered among courtyards and clipped rose gardens.

Her ears pricked with interest as they passed by a guide who informed his tour group that some of the sultans in their seven centuries of rule had kept a retinue of five thousand, which included the harem girls, eunuchs, guards, servants and three hundred cooks in ten kitchens.

Arif grinned when Holly perked up at the mention

of the sultan's overworked chefs and their daily menu plan. "If you think it was a job to cook four hundred sheep and goats every day, you can imagine what it was like when sherbet became the royal craving. Millions were spent just to bring snow down from Mount Olympus via camel caravan," he told his wide-eyed companion.

"Incredible!" she laughed. "I'm afraid that all this talk of food has made me ravenous."

Arif grinned in return. "Forgive me, Holly. I guess I'm guilty of dragging you away from your hotel before your breakfast could be brought up."

"You're forgiven if you can recommend a good inexpensive restaurant," she replied, smiling still.

Fifteen minutes later Arif led her through the crowded lanes of the Spice Market, its air pungent with the bittersweet aroma of dozens of exotic and familiar spices, and pushed open the door of a charming *lokanta*. The thick stone walls of the little tavern effectively blocked out the noisy din beyond, while its back windows opened unexpectedly onto a narrow courtyard where water trickled fitfully into a fountain covered with a thin sheet of ice. Holly sat back and savored the warmth wafting from the kitchen while Arif ordered their lunch.

She enjoyed each course of their long and leisurely meal, which began with a cucumber-and-yogurt salad followed by *hamur isi*, a hot rolled pastry filled with meat and spinach.

After the pastry course had been eaten, Arif informed her playfully, "The next dish was ordered especially for you: Circassian chicken."

"It's delicious!" Holly exclaimed a few minutes later when the chicken, cooked in a walnut puree and seasoned with pepper, had been served. "The more I hear about these Circassians, the more intrigued I become," she laughed.

After a dessert of rice pudding flavored with saffron, Holly sat back contentedly and watched Arif smoke a cigarette as she sipped at the last bit of coffee before her lips touched the gritty dregs.

Despite the increasing chill of the waning afternoon, they decided to forgo a taxi. They strolled in a companionable silence through the old town, crossed the Galata Bridge, where they'd begun their tour, and climbed the twisting street to the hotel.

When they stood at last in the red-carpeted hallway outside her room, the mood between them suddenly threatened to become stiff and constrained. There was an awkward silence for several seconds until Holly said at last in a quiet voice, "Thanks very much, Arif. I've had quite... quite a memorable day."

"Have you?" He lifted his fingers to negligently brush away a stray wisp of hair that had escaped her chignon, and she felt the warmth of his dark hand, the familiar exciting scent of cardamom and wool. She longed to have him leave his hand against her cheek, and her heart pounded with agonizing force at the remembrance of his sweetly sensual touch.

Wildly she sought to keep her reckless thoughts under control and grasped at the first conversational straw that leaped to mind. "Will... will you stay in Istanbul through the end of the week? You must be anxious to get back to Riadja."

At Holly's mention of his beloved ranch, his eyes darkened like black storm clouds. "There's much to do there, but my return can wait a little while longer. I had hoped to build several additional stalls and a new paddock with my Malmaison winnings, but I suppose I shall have to make do with a few less stalls." He shrugged indifferently.

Her cheeks flamed at his oblique reference to the fifteen hundred francs that the customs official in Edirne had pocketed from his envelope. And she recalled the five-hundred-franc bill that the man had slipped into the pocket of her parka. She had meant to return it to Arif immediately, but she had not seen him again after the incident. Instead she had placed it in an envelope at the train station and mailed it to him anonymously, in care of the Selimiye Barracks; evidently he had not yet received it.

Once again she sought to steer the conversation to more neutral ground. "Arif, I have to meet Rusty at the riding grounds at five to work Mandarin Lady, but I'm sure he'd be delighted to have you join us for dinner later."

"Thanks very much, but I've made other plans for the evening." He inclined his head curtly, and there was no hint of the teasing sparks of laughter that had lit his eyes earlier in the day. Once more his gaze was hard and arrogant.

Holly bridled at his change in attitude. "Forgive me for putting you on the spot, captain," she replied with a brittle air. "I'd almost forgotten what you told me at the British Embassy ball in Paris: you're searching for a wife. I understand that you must carry out your duties by day and reserve the nights for courting." The sarcasm in her words was unmistakable.

Arif's lips twisted in a hard sardonic slash. "I think we understand each other very well, Holly." And without another word he turned on his heel and disappeared down the hallway.

HOLLY'S SPURS dug lightly into Mandarin Lady's chestnut flanks, but the mare seemed to hesitate a little as she took the four-foot fence. Holly felt the telltale click of rear hooves against the wooden barrier; the jump had not been a clean one. Shaking her head with impatience, she reined the mare into a collected trot, and they moved in a slower rhythmic pace around the sawdust track. Holly glanced up at Rusty, sitting astride the inner fence rails with his battered gray Stetson pushed back on his grizzled head. He nodded sharply to indicate that they should take the same fence again.

Holly tightened her back muscles, pushed her calves against the mare's flanks and urged her into a canter. It seemed as though Mandarin Lady's initial impulsion was good that time, but once again in the takeoff for the jump there was a slight hesitation. This second time around, the wooden post was sent tumbling to the sawdust with a mortifying clunk.

Rusty's impassive mood of a moment earlier had vanished. He threw his battered Stetson down to the ground as Holly drew Mandarin Lady to a halt before him. "Damn it, gal! What's happened to your concentration? These jumps should be duck soup for the two of you."

Holly's brows knitted together in concern. "I'm

not sure, Rusty. I think she might still be tight from
that long train trip. Can that be it?''

He scratched his head. "I suppose we'll find out.
Let's do some light hack and flat work. Start out
with a cadenced walk and trot—we'll see if we can
elasticize her back and hind leg muscles some.''

Mare and rider went through their paces as directed, with Holly working in an occasional dressage half
pass to relieve the tedium. Finally after a half hour
Rusty ordered her to try the fence again.

The jump was a little smoother than the others;
still Holly had sensed the slightest hesitation on the
mare's part. Rusty's sharp eyes had picked it up, as
well.

"Shoot, I don't know who to point the finger at—
you or our Mandi-gal," her remarked to Holly as she
dismounted and loosened the girth. "But I guess
time'll tell.''

They were walking back to the stable area when a
voice called down from the stands. "Miss Holliford!"

She whirled around quickly, shocked to hear her
real name called out in the horse arena. A gray-
haired man of erect bearing descended the stairs from
the stands to the track and approached them. "Miss
Holliford, I am Adnan Memed. I know your father,
James, well.''

After they had shaken hands, Holly observed wryly, "I suppose it would be naive to think that your
showing up here at the Selimiye Barracks' riding
grounds was just a coincidence.''

Memed smiled urbanely. "The international business community is often a closely knit group. When James called and told me that his daughter would be visiting Istanbul, I told him I would be delighted to invite you to dinner. Won't the two of you join me this evening? Sadly, Istanbul's nightlife does not offer all that it might; still, the dinner and view from the Galata Tower are superb.''

Holly regarded the wealthy aristocratic-looking Turkish industrialist for a long moment. He was stamped of the same mold as her father and Alec Wright: elegant, urbane, witty, well informed. He was of that world that Holly had worked so hard to escape from, yet she knew she could not bury her head in the sand forever. She could not keep running. Besides, she knew that if she didn't accept, she and Rusty would probably spend an unsettled evening rehashing the problems with Mandarin Lady. An evening on the town would do them both good. With luck her mind would be diverted, as well, from thoughts of Arif Hakal and their senseless quarrel before they had parted at her hotel.

"Thanks very much, Mr. Memed. We'd be delighted to accept," she told him at last.

He smiled. "Good. I'll fetch you at the Pera Palas at nine o'clock.''

Holly observed him with narrowed eyes as he strode from the arena. She hadn't told him the name of the hotel, and she knew that there was no way her father could have known, either, since Rusty had made the reservations just as they'd left Paris. Or had he known? Was she being naive in thinking that her rich and strong-willed parents would let her escape their circle of influence without a fight?

THE ELEVATOR SLID SMOOTHLY UPWARD through the medieval stone tower, which had once been a prison, and deposited its occupants in a dark opulent dining room, its backdrop a breathtaking panoramic view of nighttime Istanbul.

The silk of Holly's lustrous blue green plaid skirt rustled against her legs as she followed the maître d' across the expanse of plush carpet. When she glanced around to see if Rusty was keeping up with her, he shot her a look from beneath his beetling eyebrows as if to question her wisdom in allowing them to be drawn into such a milieu. But her only response was a quick reassuring grin before she turned around once again with an air of cool self-composure.

A few moments later, when they were seated before an expanse of gleaming silver and snowy white damask and their host had inquired what they would have to drink, it was Rusty who ordered for both of them. "Make mine a bourbon on the rocks, and a glass of rosé for the lady in training," he said gruffly, looking highly uncomfortable in his navy blue serge suit.

Adnan Memed seemed momentarily nonplussed by the diminutive trainer's lack of social graces, and Holly had to quell the urge to laugh before turning to her host. "I had a few problems in my riding work-out this afternoon, Mr. Memed—"

"Call me Adnan, please," he interposed smoothly.

"Adnan," Holly repeated before continuing. "I

think Rusty would have preferred to see me retiring early this evening with a book on equine science and a glass of hot milk.''

"You're dead right," Rusty muttered, shooting her another cross look.

Thereafter the conversation turned to horsemanship, and Adnan drew her out cleverly on that subject, as well as on her own motivation for her involvement in the grueling competitive circuit. Holly was fully aware of the subtle cross-examination. She was well accustomed to the veiled curiosity of people who couldn't understand why a rich and lovely young heiress would willingly leave her posh life for such a demanding existence. Once again Holly was grateful that she was working and traveling under an alias, free of the hated Holliford name and reputation—except when individuals such as Alec or Adnan popped unexpectedly into her life.

Rusty's attitude improved miraculously after he had bitten into the succulent New York-cut steak that had been set before him. Holly's shrimp curry was excellent, as well; still, she found the cosmopolitan fare rather boring after the intriguing lunch she'd shared in the cozy unprepossessing *lokanta* with Arif. But she willed her thoughts away from him.

If this life of suave elegance and power born of moneyed influence was not hers, neither did she belong to the world of Arif Hakal's harsh enigmatic existence. Hadn't he made that all too plain to her? He would be only too happy to take her to his bed and cast her aside in the morning while he sought the woman of his dreams. The spoiled voluptuous Geneviève? The dark and lovely woman whom he'd embraced in the station?

Holly's dark musings were interrupted as Adnan Memed extended his hand and invited his young blond companion to dance. Adnan was an excellent dancer and expertly guided her through the steps of a fox-trot and slower rumba. After the small dance band had played the last number of the set and the lights dimmed over the polished floor, Holly brushed her hair back from her flushed cheeks and smiled. "Thanks very much, Adnan. I enjoyed that."

He smiled in return. "Thank you, Miss Holliford."

She regarded him levelly. "Please call me Holly; I prefer it—if you don't mind."

He inclined his head slightly. "Of course."

They were walking back to the table when the maître d' brushed past them and Holly found herself facing Arif Hakal with Geneviève Lamine on his arm, the two evidently having just arrived for dinner.

Arif's eyes flickered over her shoulder and settled briefly on the handsome cultured features of Adnan, also noting the man's possessive hold on Holly's arm. Holly found herself making the introductions rather hurriedly. To her surprise she saw that the two men seemed to take each other's measure, and the slightest spark of tension charged the space between them. Adnan said something in Turkish to Arif, but she did not hear the horseman's reply because Geneviève was addressing her.

"I see that you are wearing the same gown you wore to the embassy affair," the Tunisian remarked with an air of innocence, her amber eyes tilted cunningly.

"How sweet of you to notice, Geneviève." Holly stared down at the auburn-haired vixen with an icy regal smile, à la Alice Holliford, before turning her attention back to the two men. But their abrupt conversation had ended. She could not help but notice the smolder of black anger in Arif's gaze as he led his companion to their table, but she was totally mystified as to what could have passed between the two Turkish men.

Shortly thereafter, Adnan, Holly and Rusty left the elegant tower. To Holly's surprise, the trainer objected to their rather abrupt departure. He had mellowed considerably during the course of the evening and had insisted on finishing his snifter of Courvoisier and taking the last drag on the expensive Cuban cigar his host had presented to him earlier in the evening.

Ordinarily Holly might have laughed at this amusing turnabout, but her thoughts were too preoccupied with unanswered questions even to notice. Yet again she wondered what had passed between Adnan and Arif.

CHAPTER SIX

THE SELIMIYE BARRACKS, an immense square-sided structure with an open courtyard in the middle, housed the stables, track and grounds where the winter horse trials would take place. It was also the headquarters of the First Turkish Army.

Holly had risen just before daylight and walked down to Taksim Square, her eventual destination the army barracks. She'd caught the first Usküdar-bound bus of the morning, and it had traversed the long suspension bridge over the Bosporus in a gray freezing mist that showed no signs of letting up. The novelty of crossing from European Istanbul to its Asian shores via a twenty-minute bus ride had worn off quickly, and Holly's only concern that morning had been the physical condition of Mandarin Lady. She had worried about the mare on and off since their unsatisfactory workout the previous afternoon.

The possibility that the problem lay with the mare herself rather than with Holly's own lack of concentration or her tendency to nervous hands on the reins bothered her greatly. A little more self-discipline on her part could overcome those shortcomings, but an injury to Mandarin Lady would make their continuation in the European riding trials an uncertainty, if not an impossibility.

Holly clenched her fists angrily at the thought of returning to the United States penniless and defeated. She could imagine her parents' imperious "we told you so" and her father's insistence that she settle down after her "foolish little stunt."

Then her thoughts turned inevitably to Arif. While her family persisted in treating her as a child, the Turkish horseman had reminded her all too potently that she was not a child at all but a woman. She longed to test her mettle against him once more on the riding course to show him what she was capable of.

For all her competitive attitude, however, Holly could deny no longer her growing attraction for Arif Hakal. The powerful sexual chemistry between them had been like a quick-burning fuse igniting a firestorm of passion. The compelling physical need had at once engulfed and hidden the possibility that deeper feelings might lie beneath. Holly had come to realize those feelings and, more reluctantly, to acknowledge them.

She had found a bedrock of inner strength within him that she'd encountered in no other man. It had made him uncompromising, stubborn and strong willed. Yet countering that harshness were touching examples of his devotion to his family and their ranch on the distant Asian steppes. For a fleeting moment she envisioned herself sharing that life, hard and exciting; the long, unrelentingly cold winters and the lovely triumph of spring with the birth of the new foals.

Holly shook her head irritably as if to rid her brain

of such impossible thoughts, and she quickened her step past the wooden mansions and winter-bare gardens of Üsküdar. The freezing mist blowing inland from the sea stung her eyelids and cheeks, causing her to burrow her face more deeply into the collar of her burgundy parka.

But stubbornly her mind clung to the bronzed well-muscled image of Arif, his glinting black eyes in turn playful, angry, passionate. She couldn't admit to herself that she might be falling in love with him, a man who teased and toyed with her as if she were a green-eyed china doll that he could return to its box while he went on with the serious business of his life.

Arif had not deceived her on that point. She remembered the sardonic words he had flung as he'd left her before the door of her room: "I think we understand each other very well, Holly." But she hadn't understood at all. What mysterious "wifely" qualities could the voluptuous Geneviève possess that would make Arif court her so assiduously, Holly wondered, her musings by turn perplexed and angry.

MANDARIN LADY SNUFFLED LAZILY in her stall when Holly opened the door and came inside. The box had been mucked out and fresh hay strewn on the floor, and there was fresh water and feed, as well; the army personnel was doing a superb job of caring for the competition animals.

As she bent down to loosen the protective bandages that bound Mandi-girl's legs, Holly remembered Rusty's terse words of instruction. He'd advised her to gentle the mare, to ride her as easily as if they were both out for a morning's lark. He wanted no undue tension communicated to the pretty chestnut thoroughbred before the competition, which was now less than twenty-four hours in the future. Mindful of that advice, Holly led the horse out of her stall and away from the riding arena.

She swung up into the saddle and rode her along a bridle path that led to a dense copse skirting the barracks grounds. They rode at a light but steady pace for several miles. The brisk run, aimless and unpressured, served to relax both mare and rider, and Holly felt the cobwebs of confusion and uncertainty over the future gradually receding.

The path began to climb upward, and the mare took the ascent easily with her long graceful stride. Holly smiled in contentment to herself, feeling her confidence in herself and in the horse returning. The December chill was forgotten in the exertion of the ride, and she loosened the collar of her jacket so that the ends of the soft burgundy-and-gray jacquard scarf about her throat blew jauntily behind her, a dark contrast to the strands of burnished gold hair that she'd also permitted to tumble freely over her shoulders.

As it had the previous morning, the cold mist began to lift and Holly caught glimpses through the trees of long tables and rustic wooden shelters. She imagined the crowds of happy Sunday picnickers that must throng to the lovely woods in the summer months.

They crested the hill at last and Holly dismounted, holding the mare's reins lightly in her gloved hand. Her hand immediately tightened as Mandarin Lady's head lifted skittishly in response to something beyond a small grove of trees to their right. Holly half expected to see a shy deer or other forest animal rush by, but her ears soon picked up the unmistakable sound of horse's hooves, muffled slightly by the damp ground.

Thirty seconds later she found herself staring up beyond the familiar proud profile of black Sinjon into Arif Hakal's narrowed eyes as he rode slowly in her direction. Refusing to meet his questioning stare, she turned instead to give a reassuring pat to the nervous mare, whom she continued to walk. Arif dismounted, as well, and fell into step beside her.

"I see your late-night revelry hasn't kept you from your morning duties, Holly," he began without preamble.

"Naturally," she retorted. "What else did you expect?" She risked a sideways glance at him and saw him shrug expressively; then she caught the devilish black glint in his deep-set eyes.

"I would not have expected Memed to let you steal from his bed so early."

Holly stopped and turned to him, her eyes blazing their outrage. "You deserve to be slapped for that kind of cheap innuendo," she said with deceptive quietness, although her hands had tightened around the short riding crop she held in her free hand.

His eyes mocked her anger. "Why don't you try?"

Her green-crystal gaze bored into him for a long moment before she replied. "I suppose it isn't worth the effort."

She turned on her heel to stride away, but the curt command in his voice as he called her name brought her up short. Swiftly she turned to face him.

"We really have nothing to say to each other, Arif," she told him in a tone clipped and sharp edged as his own. Her pride would not let him see the pain his remarks had caused her.

"That's a strange way to talk for a woman who told me just yesterday afternoon that she'd spent a memorable day in my company." His voice and eyes mocked still, although she recognized the teasing glimmers lurking beneath the sharp mockery.

Holly's breath escaped in a painful little sigh. "That was nothing more than a dream, Arif. You above all should know that. We have no place in each other's life, do we?" The soft words were a challenge. "You've made that abundantly clear."

She caught a brief glimpse of his eyes before his thick dark lashes veiled their expression and his head inclined in curt agreement with her words. She thought she'd seen a jagged tracery of pain in their black depths, but she knew she had to be mistaken. He wished only to taunt her, to mock her, to use her.

His words were like chips of steel when he spoke again. "Nevertheless, we have unfinished business."

"What do you mean?" she demanded, her gaze suspicious.

"I refuse to discuss it out here. There's a *pastahane* down the hill a little way where we can talk."

Five minutes later they sat opposite each other in the unpretentious glass-walled pastry shop, a pot of tea and a plate of poppy-seed rolls on the small table between them. "Now," she demanded, "what unfinished business are you referring to?"

His eyes raked over her slowly before he answered. "A matter of five hundred francs." He pulled a neat-

ly folded envelope from the breast pocket of his
suede jacket. "It was in my box when I arrived at the
barracks this morning. You sent it, didn't you,
Holly?"

She blanched but said nothing.

When he spoke again, his words were quick, fierce,
angry. "I will not take money from you." He pulled
the bill from the envelope and held it out to her.

"It's yours," she shot back, ignoring the brightly
colored French bank note that he held out to her.

"No, Holly. You earned it," he replied bitingly,
tucking the bill inside the gray leather gloves that
she'd set on the table beside her. "I'm sure you'll put
it to good use, as the Edirne customs officer will."

"I had no idea the man would pocket that
money," she said quietly, her cheeks flushed.

Arif's shrug was almost indifferent. "It's one
more thing to learn. *Baksheesh* is an old ingrained
custom in this country. If an official is poorly paid,
he tries to find other ways to line his pockets. It's
become almost a game, and I happen to have been
caught—with your assistance." Once again a sardonic grin was in place on his features, amusement
and bitterness warring in his expression.

"I...." It was on the tip of her tongue to tell him
she was sorry, but her own stony pride would not
permit it. "I...think your talk about building up
Riadja is a facade. You'd just have used the money
to wine and dine Geneviève and to buy baubles for all
the women you're wooing," she told him, her voice
at once contemptuous and miserable.

"It's all the same in the end," he replied equably,

apparently unruffled by her gibe. He shrugged once more before regarding her with suddenly narrowed eyes. "Besides, what does it matter to you, Holly? Haven't you found a rich protector in Adnan Memed?" he demanded.

Holly forgot her own rising anger long enough to regard him curiously, surprised at the depth of bitterness in his voice. "You know Adnan well, then?"

Arif's answering laughter was harsh. "I know him only from his photographs in the newspaper. He's one of the wealthiest industrialists in Turkey. I thought you were running away from an arranged marriage in your own country, but perhaps I misjudged you, Holly. I'd imagined that you were hoping to find love, but I realize now that it's bigger game you're after. I suppose I should be congratulating you on your catch." The bitterness was cloaked in mockery.

The unintended irony of his words was almost too much to bear—that he should think her capable of marrying a man for his wealth and status when it was from precisely that kind of existence she had fled! But she swallowed the impulse to tell him the truth: that Adnan Memed was a friend of her father, who was himself richer than the Turkish industrialist. She wouldn't invoke the magical Holliford name just to prove she wasn't a gold digger. When she replied at last, it was simply to say, "I think you misjudge me, Arif. Adnan Memed means nothing to me. I met him only yesterday."

"Then I admire the speed with which he staked out his territory."

"Now what do you mean?" she demanded with impatience.

His right brow lifted quizzically, as if he did not quite believe her perplexity was genuine. After a moment he spoke again in a low voice that grated a little with remembered anger. "When we met in the Galata Tower last night, he told me in no uncertain terms that I was to keep away from you."

"What!" Holly gasped in surprise. "And what did you tell him?"

"What any self-respecting man would reply." Arif shrugged again, an inconsequential gesture belied by the flash of pride in his dark eyes. "I called him a meddling bastard."

Holly's light peals of laughter rang out in the deserted shop, startling both Arif and the sleepy-eyed waitress at the counter. Her green eyes sparkled with mirth as she imagined the scene in her own mind, and she tried to picture someone casually standing up to her father with such cool arrogance. Individuals such as Memed or James Holliford, surrounded by their devoted corps of yes-men, would not be used to a sharply challenging rebuff. Even her ex-fiancé, Stan Winthrop, who was on an equal social and financial footing with the Hollifords, had carefully deferred to the older man's power. Holly realized that Arif didn't give a damn about a man's wealth or influence, and she felt a new respect for him growing within her.

Arif had watched the play of emotions over Holly's features with narrowed eyes. "What do you find so amusing?" he demanded at last.

She shook her head helplessly, her eyes grown serious once more. "It would take a lifetime to explain," she replied, making a move to stand up from the table.

But his hand shot out, and she felt his strong fingers digging into her arm through the thick fabric of her parka. "I'm a patient man, Holly. Tell me."

She was more stubborn, however, and shook her head again. "I have to get the mare back to the stables. Rusty'll worry if he arrives and we're not there."

Arif stood up with her then and left several *kuru* coins on the table. Outside they remounted the patiently waiting horses and retraced their path up the hill.

As they crested it, they found the wintry mist had lifted completely, only to reveal a low mass of storm clouds. The Sea of Marmara extending far to the southwest was a forbidding gunmetal gray that reflected upward over the city, crowded on its seven hills. Crouched on one of them, the tawny fortress-like mass of Aya Sofya seemed an anchor for the ethereal minarets riding in dull silverpoint against the leaden sky.

Holly reined in Mandarin Lady and glanced over at Arif. "You must have a liking for immense vistas," she observed teasingly. "There was Eyüp yesterday and now this."

He laughed. "You're right, Holly. I ride up here frequently when I'm at Selimiye. It reminds me of home." He indicated the distant double ramparts of Topkapi, its conglomeration of rounded rooftops ris-

ing from four vast ꞈurtyards. "From here the palace
appears to be a seꞈ of nomads' tents. We Turks
haven't changed mu⸱h in a thousand years!" His
laughter was rich and for once devoid of any mockery or bitterness.

Holly was about to turn and urge the mare into a
brisk trot down the hill when Arif spoke again.
"Wait a moment. You haven't seen the rest of the
view—the real reason that I ride up here to
Çamlica." They brought their horses around until
their backs were toward the city across the narrow
channel, and Arif pointed through an opening in the
trees toward a wide empty expanse beyond the city
boundaries of Asian Istanbul. "You're looking at the
westernmost reach of the Anatolian plateau—the real
Turkey, as far as I'm concerned."

As Holly's eyes followed the wide sweep of his
arm, she felt a curious quickening in her blood. That
harsh untamed hinterland was his home: a thousand
miles to the east, where the plateau merged into rugged mountain, lay his family's ranch. Her lips twisted
with bitter laughter as she tried to envision the
luxury-loving Geneviève in that setting. But the
laughter died as quickly as it had bubbled up. The
draw was not the land or the hard life but the man
himself, that taut strength of his body and the surprising sensuality of his mouth, which could blot out
any other reality. Undoubtedly the spoiled heiress
had felt it as strongly as she herself had.

Arif, watching her expression, had misinterpreted
her laughter. "Perhaps you have to have been born
there to appreciate it. The land is not postcard pretty,

like a Swiss mountain or a stretch of white sand, but it has a wild arrogant beauty of its own.''

Her heart leaped to his as he uttered the stiff prideful words, and she longed to tell him that she well understood the subtle attraction of the craggy windblown plateau—so much like the man born of it. But he had wheeled away from her haughtily and urged the stallion into a loping canter down the long forested slope. Holly and the mare followed behind at a more collected pace.

When she rode into the stable area, Holly saw that Arif had turned the stallion over to a groom and was engaged in conversation with Rusty Wilkins. She had meant to ride past them, but her trainer's quick laconic greeting stopped her, and she brought Mandarin Lady around to face the two men.

''How'd things go this mornin', gal? Any problems?'' Rusty asked, his sharp eyes surveying mare and rider.

Holly shook her head quickly, her fair, somewhat tousled hair streaming in pretty abandon down her back. ''We followed your advice and took it easy. In fact we had a wonderful ride up to Çamlica.''

Holly felt the rosiness in her cheeks deepen as Arif's eyes played over her in teasing inquiry. Why did she have to use words such as ''memorable'' and ''wonderful'' to describe the moments spent with the Turkish captain? She dared not reveal her true feelings to him. Her own vulnerability was too fragile; she could not risk more pain caused by his coolly arrogant rebuffs.

Without another word she turned away and led the

mare to the stalls. She dismounted, handed the reins to a waiting groom and wandered inside the riding arena. Her eyes roved over the busy crowded track as she sat down in the first row of the wooden stands, but her thoughts were too preoccupied to focus on the disciplined intricate workouts of the international competitors.

Holly leaned back tiredly against the hard bench and closed her eyes, allowing her thoughts to play back in vivid detail the morning ride and her unexpected encounter with Arif. They had argued and accused, their stubborn tempers clashing like swords, but they'd laughed, as well.

How could she feel herself so powerfully drawn to a man with whom her relationship was like a tumultuous battle—first advancing and then retreating, their momentary truces undermined by new flare-ups of anger? Yet even as the question formed in her mind, she knew the answer: their clashes were stimulating, exciting. Just being in his presence made her feel more intensely alive than she'd ever felt in her life.

This sharpened awareness threatened to suffocate her, and she knew intuitively that she should avoid Arif Hakal at all costs. If she could not win his love, she would not risk losing his respect and her own pride, as well, by succumbing to the powerful attraction that flowed between them like a deep hidden spring.

In the horse trials at least he was forced to regard her as a professional equal. Perhaps by winning the event she could compel him to look beyond the isolated facets of her personality to the whole woman who possessed an inner strength of her own—caring, needing, ready to share both joy and pain.

Impatient with her idealistic musings, Holly opened her eyes. . . only to find Arif himself standing beside her with a quizzical smile on his lips. ''Welcome back to the real world, Holly,'' he laughed. ''I've been watching you for five minutes, sitting there solemnly as a sphinx. What were you thinking about?''

Her color deepened, and she drew back a little as he sat down on the bench beside her. ''Nothing you'd understand, Arif.''

''Why are you so secretive, Holly? Most women chatter like magpies until a man longs to beg them to shut up, but the only time you open your mouth is to lash me with your tongue,'' he observed with amusement.

''Then why are you so persistent?'' she shot back.

Arif lifted his hands palms upward in the expressive gesture of submission to fate. ''When a healthy male meets a beautiful female, logic sometimes takes a back seat.'' The smile that momentarily lit his eyes was full of boyish mischief, and Holly had to steel herself not to respond to it.

Instead she rejoined coldly, ''Aren't you pursuing a few too many women? This is the twentieth century, you know, and harems are no longer in vogue.''

His boyish smile faded to two subtle pinpoints of brightness in the velvety blackness of his eyes. ''You believe one woman is enough for a man?''

''If she's the right woman,'' she replied with a prideful little shrug.

"Holly." Her name was little more than a whisper on his lips, but the telltale depth of emotion in the spoken word washed over her like a powerful storm tide. With a shock she lifted her eyes to his and read the naked wanting there that seemed so much more than simple physical desire.

For an instant she felt as though they were completely alone in the vast indoor stadium, the shouts and pounding hooves in the sawdust arena a distant echo that did not touch them. Inevitably the moment was shattered by a voice calling out gaily in French, "*Bonjour, mes amis!* Arif, my darling, where is your stallion?"

Geneviève, outfitted in skin-hugging white jodhpurs and tight blouse, maneuvered the pretty gelding Bijou up to the fence and leaned across to kiss Arif deeply and intimately, her breasts crushed to his chest.

"Good morning, Geneviève," Holly greeted her coolly when the two drew apart at last. "Aren't you afraid you'll stain those lily-white breeches when you land backside in the mud?"

The woman shot her a glance from beneath her heavily mascaraed eyelashes. "If I were you, Holly MacKnight, I would be very careful whom I accuse of lying on her back." Then she turned with a petulant air to Arif. "Darling, when are you going to tire of your little escapade with this blond witch? I am getting impatient, you know!" she added archly.

Infuriated by the insinuation behind the woman's cheap double entendre, Holly turned and walked away from them both. Outside the arena she caught a glimpse of Tatiana Bulgakova and Kazan executing a series of tight figure eights in a small clearing between the buildings. Holly called to her friend, but the taut-lipped lieutenant was so intent on guiding the horse through the precise footwork that she did not even look up. Holly made a move to walk over to her, then thought better of it. Perhaps Tatiana had been warned to stay away from the two Americans who had befriended her. Holly had no wish to jeopardize the woman's position.

She was standing uncertainly in the middle of the stable yard when Rusty came up to her. "You look all wound up, gal. Why don't you go back to town for a while? I don't know what's been buggin' you lately, but you haven't been up to snuff," the trainer told her. "I suggest you get your head on straight for the competition tomorrow. That *is* what we're here for, if you'll remember."

"I know damn well why we're here, Rusty," she retorted irritably.

"Then you shouldn't mind a friendly little reminder."

"Friendly, hell!" she swore.

"The cussin's in my territory, Holly, and I'll thank you to leave it there," Rusty answered, his own short-fused temper beginning to rise.

"I'll swear if I feel like it!"

Rusty pulled out the straw he'd been sucking between his teeth and jabbed the air angrily with it. "Now if I were a mite taller and you were a mite shorter, I wouldn't think twice about puttin' you over my knee, gal. But maybe Cap'n Hakal'd be pleased to do the job."

"Why bring him into this?" she almost shouted. "And I'll thank you not to treat me like a child."

"Why not?" he shouted back. "You're actin' like one."

Holly stalked across the dried brown field, headed toward the bus station in Üsküdar. She'd had no final parting thrust to answer Rusty because he had been absolutely right about her childishly unreasonable behavior. It had been inexcusable to allow her seething resentment of Geneviève and Arif to explode against her well-meaning trainer.

As she walked briskly along the narrow two-lane road, a light freezing rain began to fall. The weather was a perfect complement to her bleak mood. She'd been walking along the roadway only a few minutes, however, when a car horn tooted without warning behind her and she turned quickly to peer down at the little red Fiat that had stopped beside her.

The right-hand window was rolled down, and Arif leaned across the passenger seat. "Get in, Holly," he commanded. "I'll drive you across town."

"No, thanks. I'll walk," she replied stubbornly. But as she continued her trek along the slick wet pavement, she was all too aware of the car, like a brilliant scarlet shadow, following slowly beside her. She was also aware of the gathering crescendo of blaring horns behind them as the cars, unable to pass because of the unending stream of traffic headed toward Selimiye, piled up in a snaking line.

"You'd better get in, Holly, because I intend to drive alongside until you do," he shouted over the cacophonous tooting of a dozen car horns.

Knowing full well that he was capable of doing just

that, Holly yanked open the door and slid into the seat.

Arif grinned at her surrender. "You're one incredibly stubborn woman, Holly."

She glared at him. "How could you bear to part from Geneviève?"

"It was not hard," he replied soberly.

Holly's expression was more curious than angry. "Have you proposed to her yet?"

"Proposed what?" His eyes were fixed on the wet pavement ahead of them.

"Marriage."

"No, I have not."

"But you intend to?"

"Of course."

Holly dug her fists into the soft gray corduroy of her slacks. "I despise her," she observed inconsequentially. "She thinks I'm your mistress."

"She thinks worse than that."

Her head swiveled to regard him, but his face was like a bronze mask, hard and expressionless. "What do you mean?" she asked.

"She thinks I'm in love with you." The tone, like his face, was devoid of emotion.

"Are you?" Her voice was as small and hushed as a child's, and the words seemed to hang on an invisible balance between them.

His staccato rapid-fire laughter erupted in the silence, but it was a bitter hollow sound. "Women!" he muttered wrathfully. "Don't ask questions that can have no happy answer, Holly. I can't allow you to complicate my life."

For a long moment there was no sound but the

rhythmical swishing of the wiper blades across the windshield.

"Life doesn't always follow a neat primrose-lined path," Holly said quietly into the stillness.

Arif's hands were tight on the steering wheel. "For me it must. Certain things in our lives are ordained."

"Marriage to Geneviève?" she asked incredulously.

"If not her, then another." He shrugged.

But why? She longed to scream the question but knew that she'd already asked too much. The conversation was beginning to tread on dangerous ground as it was.

As if in acknowledgment of her unspoken thoughts, Arif steered their talk to more practical matters. "Where shall I drop you?" he asked as he guided the small car onto the bridge.

She sighed. "At the bazaar, if you will. I suppose I should get my Christmas shopping done while I have the chance."

"Then you'll need me along to guide you through that rabbit warren of shops. There are more than four thousand, you know."

"It's really kind of you to offer, but I'll get along just fine," Holly told him.

"Kindness has nothing to do with it." He shot her a quick grin as he downshifted into first. "I simply want to be with you."

The lighthearted words sent a thrill of pleasure along her spine. She had no time to reflect on her feelings, however, because the little Fiat had surged ahead into the chaotic swirl of traffic on steep narrow streets and she was gripping the seat for dear life as he dodged in and out among pedestrians, donkey cars and smoke-belching buses. After a while she relaxed; Arif drove with the supreme confidence of a toreador dodging a herd of stampeding bulls—and seemed to be enjoying every minute of it.

Twenty minutes later he wedged the vehicle into an impossibly small parking space before finally turning to her with a triumphant grin. "Done!"

"Bravo! I'd have spent all day just finding the place," Holly laughed.

"I'll help you dicker, if you like, for your larger purchases. If you learn how to bargain with the merchants, you can save yourself hundreds."

She laughed again. "I don't need to worry about that. I've budgeted only thirty dollars total for everyone on my list! I'm not rich, you know."

"Yes, and life doesn't follow a neat primrose-lined path," he quoted her teasingly.

But as she laughed with him, Holly caught a brief glimpse of the expression in his eyes. Their indefinable, almost brooding light seemed to mock the lightheartedness of their repartee.

Quickly they got out of the car and made their way through the light curtain of rain to the steps of the Kapali Çarsi, or Covered Bazaar. Its maze of cobblestoned lanes led past a bewildering array of trading stalls, and Holly—for all her sophisticated urban upbringing—felt like a country bumpkin come to gawk at the splendors of this vast convoluted Oriental market, which offered everything imaginable.

Ornate copper and brass work gleamed from sidewalk displays, white alabaster statues stood demurely against eighteenth-century masterworks of Turkish rug weaving, while above their heads hung rows of soft leather and suede garments, which gave the stalls the distinctive odor of a tannery.

After a while the sensory explosion of colorful merchandise, thronging humanity and intriguing bazaar scents sorted itself out in her mind, and Holly began to shop with definite purpose. For Rusty she purchased an intricately carved pipe of porous white meerschaum stone and for her parents a small beaded prayer cap and pair of gilt slippers with turned-up toes, which she intended to send along with a curt note thanking them for the introduction to Adnan Memed. It still rankled her that the man had had the temerity to warn Arif away from her as if she were an underage child and the Turkish captain a clever pred-ator. Holly had more than a vague suspicion that the industrialist's behavior had been prompted by her father, but she could not very well accuse him of that in her Christmas wishes.

Her angry train of thought was dispelled, however, as Arif took her arm and led her to a display of chrome-plated *narghiles*. Amid shouts of laughter he demonstrated how Turkish men smoked from the water pipes, which they customarily rented for the afternoon in their favorite cafés. The *narghiles* in the bazaar were primarily for tourist consumption, it seemed.

Still laughing, they strolled on. Once again it was as if the conflicts and tensions between them had been suspended by tacit mutual agreement and they were free, for the moment at least, to share pleasure. They passed by the stalls featuring rich Bursa silks, and Holly paused to run her fingers lovingly over a flowing caftan with billowing sleeves. Its color was cinnabar, deep and vivid as an autumn sunset, and it was girded with an intricately patterned silk belt bordered with jade and black. The dress was gorgeous, an evocation of an Arabian Nights fantasy, but she passed it by at last, knowing she hadn't money enough for such whimsical finery.

Flowing silks were forgotten then as they stopped before a small vendor's cart that gave off a tantalizing aroma of roasting lamb from its charcoal spit. Arif bought two *sis kepab* threaded on long bamboo skewers, and they munched as they walked. More tantalizing aromas assailed them, and Holly found herself immersed in an exotic eating adventure. There were grape leaves stuffed with rice and pine nuts from one stall, Izmir dates from another and a sweet pastry-thin apricot confection called *pestil* from yet another.

"As you can see, we Turks are a race of eaters rather than drinkers," Arif informed her with a grin.

"Yes, I've noticed!" she laughed, licking the last bit of sticky-sweet apricot from her fingertips. "That's the most fascinating lunch on the run I've ever eaten." She interrupted herself as she spied a large tack shop ahead. "Arif, I've got one more gift to purchase. Would you mind if I run in there?"

"Why don't you go ahead? I have a few things to take care of myself. I'll meet you back here in twenty minutes, all right?"

She nodded quickly, staring after him as he threaded his way among the crowds. With his imposing height, broad shoulders and arrogant profile he seemed to tower over the rest of humanity in the crowded bazaar. With a little sigh she turned away and entered the tack shop with its neat rows of leather saddles and other exquisitely tooled riding equipment. She had meant to buy something special for her aunt, Jean Sims, the lovely Virginian who owned Mandarin Lady. Holly settled on a beautifully cast pair of brass horses in medieval garb and was about to pay for her purchases when she was struck by a clever idea.

Remembering the five-hundred-franc note that had been the beginning point for her argument with Arif that morning, Holly decided to put the sum to good use. Since he would not accept the return of the money, she would see that the stubborn Turkish captain was arrayed like a prince on horseback. Smiling conspiratorially to herself, Holly picked out a hand-sewn snaffle bridle in supple dark leather worked with silver threads, envisioning it against Sinjon's gleaming black neck. Swiftly she added a pair of fine leather gloves, platinum-bonded steel spurs and a scarlet-and-black saddle pad to the merchandise on the counter, giving the merchant Arif's name and the address of the Hakals' distant ranch, to which the items were to be posted.

Feeling rather pleased with herself at having so cleverly circumvented Arif's stubbornness, Holly met him a few minutes later and showed him the lovely brass figures she had purchased for the mare's owner.

As they walked out to the car, Arif turned to her and with rather uncustomary formality asked, "May I offer you tea or coffee?"

"Yes, I'd love it!" she exclaimed. "Do you have another charming *lokanta* in mind?"

"Actually, I thought we might go to my apartment."

Her startled gaze flew upward to meet his. "I'd no idea you had an apartment in Istanbul."

"It's been in the family for years," he explained. "One or another of us has used it fairly regularly when we've been in town for extended stays—schooling, business, my military duties."

The rain that had begun as they'd left the barracks several hours earlier had turned to a freezing mixture of snow and sleet, covering the rooftops and narrow lanes of the ancient sea town with a thin icy mantle. Traffic slowed to a crawl, and it was a half hour before they drew to a halt on a steep tree-lined street faced on either side with gray stone mansions.

"These magnificent old homes were converted into apartments before my grandfather was born," Arif explained as he led her up a wooden staircase and inserted a long key into the old-fashioned lock in the oak door at the top. "Both my great-grandfather and grandfather Hakal were advisers to the sultan's court at Dolmabahçe Palace, not far from here. They divided their time between the family lands in Kars and their duties here in Istanbul."

As they stepped inside, Holly stared around with fascination at the spacious high-ceilinged living room with its marble-fronted fireplace. It was flanked by two long French windows that opened onto narrow wrought-iron balconies. The room was an intriguingly eclectic blend of old and new. A few pieces of elaborately carved Georgian walnut were ranged about the perimeters of the space, while in the center a sleek leather sofa rested atop a much worn but still beautiful Turkish carpet. The walls picked up the same commingling of themes with prints of bold abstract expressionist art interspersed among elaborate Persian wall hangings.

Amused by the frank look of surprise on Holly's features Arif continued his monologue as he led her into the large but Spartan kitchen. "Until he retired a few years ago, my father was a member of parliament in Ankara. He was a little shocked when I decided to forgo politics as a career."

"You weren't interested in it?" Holly asked as she slipped out of her parka and watched him mix pulverized coffee and sugar in the small brass-embossed pot before adding water to it and putting it on the stove to boil.

"I was more interested in ranching and horses," Arif said quietly. "I suppose I get that from my mother's blood; she's a Kurd."

"What's that?"

Arif grinned. "I keep forgetting how little you know of Turkey. The Kurds are a small ethnic minority in the eastern mountains, with a language and culture of their own. Animosity between Turks and the Kurds spans centuries. In fact, there's an interesting story behind my parents' marriage. I'll tell you sometime."

"Why don't you tell me now?" Holly asked. Implicit in the question was the knowledge that there might not be another time for them, that this special afternoon was a brief stolen interlude in two lives that otherwise had no lasting connection.

"It's a simply tale, really. My father was—still is— a zealous Turkish patriot. A half century ago, after Turkey became a unified nation once again, the Kurds attempted a rebellion of their own and were put down. My father, an illustrious young M.P. at the time, decided he would help to ease the old flareup of animosity by making a symbolic gesture of his own: he married a Kurdish woman."

As he talked, Arif poured the boiled coffee into two small demitasses and they carried them into the living room. He went to the fireplace and flicked a lighted match into the pinecones and cedar kindling, staring down into the yellow flames that licked upward over the split logs in the grate.

Holly went to stand beside him, mulling over his little tale. "A symbolic gesture," she repeated at last. "You mean your father didn't love her?"

Arif's answering laughter was brittle, almost disdainful. "Holly, you are an impossibly naive woman. Romantic love does not exist outside of books; it cannot."

Her cheeks flushed angrily at his arrogant putdown. "I feel sorry for you if you believe that."

Arif set down his cup, opened a pack of cigarettes and savagely crumpled the paper before tossing it into the grate. "What about you, Holly?" he demanded. "After the European circuit is concluded, won't you be returning home to an arranged marriage, to the wealthy man whom your parents chose for you?''

"Never!" she replied vehemently. "Why do you think I'm so determined to win, Arif? It'll give me the momentary freedom to do as *I* choose with my life. Before all else, I prefer to be the mistress of my own destiny.''

"Destiny." He repeated the word moodily and took a long drag from his cigarette. "In Turkish we have a word for it—*kismet*, fate. Certain things are fated, preordained. We cannot change them.''

"Is that why you are so busily arranging your own marriage?" she flung at him sarcastically. "Another symbolic gesture?''

To her surprise then, he grinned, a rueful bitter expression that lent added harshness to the bronzed angular planes of his face. "No, Holly, I leave the idealism to my father. I am more of a pragmatist.''

"How can you be?" she demanded. "You use this word *kismet*, yet don't you believe each person is responsible for creating his own fate—day by day? Tomorrow everything could change!''

"You're right; it could. Tomorrow you could lose, Holly!" The words were clipped, brutal.

Inwardly she flinched at his callous mockery, though her eyes flashed pridefully. "I don't allow myself to think of losing. Perhaps it's you who'll lose the competition.''

"It doesn't matter...now." He shrugged, and the usually harmonious texture of his deep voice was roughened by some hidden depth of emotion.

"Now," she echoed softly. "You mean now that you plan to...to marry?"

His mouth twisted in a sardonic slash. "Congratulations, Holly. You've grown very astute in the short time I've known you."

Holly turned away from him with an angry sigh. "I still don't understand you, Arif."

"Nor do I understand you," he retorted. "Tell me this: if you were to lose in the riding competition, would you marry Adnan Memed?"

"Certainly not," she replied hotly. "Why must you persist in bringing his name up?"

"Because I saw you dancing in his arms. Because he tried to command me to stay away from you. If he means nothing to you, why were you with him?"

"I can't answer that, Arif," she replied stubbornly.

"I think you're as much of a pragmatist as I, Holly. You just won't admit it," he taunted her.

"I don't give a damn about money!" She turned around to glare at him her eyes like green vitriol.

"Indeed?" he countered almost lazily. "Then tell me this: if I were a poor man and I asked you to marry me, would you accept?"

"Is this a proposal, Arif?" The deceptive calmness of her voice was belied by a slight tremor.

"It is purely a hypothetical question."

She tossed her head defiantly so that a length of honey-blond hair cascaded forward over her shoulder. "I can't answer a hypothetical question."

"And if I were to say that I loved you?"

"Another of your hypothetical questions, Arif?" she retorted disdainfully.

Like burning coals his eyes glinted darkly at her taunt. But his hand, when he lifted it to her face, was gentle as he traced the outline of her mouth with his fingertips. "Don't ask more of me than I can give," he chided.

Her lips tingled deliciously at the remembered impression of his fingers; still she had to speak. "I can't be satisfied with half measures," she whispered softly.

"You want the primrose path?" he taunted.

"Don't mock me, Arif...."

But her bitter protest was swallowed as his mouth came down crushingly over hers in a demanding, deeply explorative kiss that blotted out all reason. With powerful feral grace he pulled her down beside him on the thick carpet before the fire. His dark fingers entwined in the golden mass of her hair before moving downward in slow sensual circles to her shoulders and the rounded curve of her breasts beneath the silky burgundy blouse.

"My God, Holly, you are so touchable," he whispered. "Yesterday morning when you came out of the hotel elevator you seemed a world apart from me—cool, elegant, a lovely mannequin. But now with your hair windblown and free," he murmured thickly, "I...."

He buried his head against her neck, the silky thickness of his mustache inflaming her fair skin with sensual delight. Her hands, like a gently inquisitive echo of his own, reached around to touch his soft jet black hair before caressing his neck and powerfully corded shoulders. As if they possessed a will of their own, her fingers loosened the buttons of his woolen plaid shirt and slipped inside to savor his animal warmth and the springy mat of dark hair covering his chest and flat hard abdomen.

She gasped with mingled fear and delight as Arif gently opened her blouse and bent to kiss her shoulders. He reached for the straps of her bra then and tugged them forward over her arms, his lips tracing a liquid film of desire over the softly vulnerable expanse of her fair neck and full breasts.

Holly's gasp became a low anguished moan of need as his mouth found the engorged fullness of her dark nipples. With impatient fingers he sought to undress her completely, lifting his head to whisper with rare tenderness, "Holly, if you were my Turkish wife I would christen you Melahat—beauty."

She heard not the tenderness of the words, however, but the subtle conditions they implied, and with a great effort she pushed him away. Never had she desired so deeply, but her aching vulnerability had temporarily blinded her to the harsh reality of their situation. "If!" she cried, struggling to cover her nakedness. "Always if—*if* I were to marry you, *if* you loved me, *if* I were your wife. What can you give me beyond those meaningless phrases?"

"Nothing at all."

"Nothing?" Holly's eyes glistened as if with tears, and her hands reached out tentatively to explore the tilted cheekbones of his face, the dark hollows beneath them and the silken black mustache that partially hid his mobile lips—as if to emblazon the tactile sense of him in her memory.

He stared down at her, steeling himself to ignore the gentle exploration of her fingers, and Holly saw the unwonted tenderness in his gaze fade irrevocably into a cold hard light.

At last he replied. "I can only give you the key to this apartment, if you choose to stay."

Holly withdrew her hand as if it had touched white-hot metal, and she sat up swiftly, running her fingers angrily through her tousled honey-blond mass of hair. "As your mistress?" she asked in a sharp bitter voice.

He said nothing.

"That *is* the meaning, isn't it?" she demanded. Her eyes glinted and sparked like dark fire opals, now green and gold in the flickering light from the grate.

As she stared up into his unyielding hard expression, something within her seemed to snap, and before she could stop herself the palm of her hand connected with his face in a sickening slap.

In an instant the room was filled with a taut charged silence broken only by the hiss and crackle of the burning logs; the sound was like a weak reverberating echo of an angry blow.

With lightning speed Arif's hands shot out to grip her arms, and he pulled her roughly to her feet. The dark fingers that had been capable of such maddeningly tender caresses now dug into her flesh as he shook her. His anger threatened to become a raging storm, but she was trapped by those powerful hands and fiercely blazing eyes. "Holly, do you think I brought you here today in order to seduce you?" he rasped. "Like some jaded caliph intent on sating himself with new untried flesh?" He shook her again as if she were a limp ragdoll.

"Yes!" she cried in a strangled voice. "Damn it, yes! Don't ever touch me again!"

The wincing look of pain that shot through his eyes was more intense than that caused by the physical slap she had hurtled at him so unexpectedly. He released his grip on her arms with such ferocious suddenness that she nearly fell backward.

Tears of hurt and rage stung her eyelids as she moved to gather up her parka and scarf.

Arif was about to speak again when the heavy chiming of the doorbell overrode his words. Then they heard a key turning in the old-fashioned lock, and a moment later a petite raven-haired woman stepped quietly into the apartment. Her quick glance darted from Holly to Arif and back to Holly again.

Holly recognized her immediately as the same lovely woman whom Arif had swept up into his arms when he'd arrived at the Istanbul train station, and she immediatiely assumed that the new arrival was another in Arif's "harem" who had been given the key to his apartment.

"Bonjour, mademoiselle," the woman addressed her quietly in French, her enormous dark eyes questioning.

The American girl was about to sweep past her to rush down the stairs when Arif's curt imperious voice, still with the power to command, brought her up short. "Holly!" He paused a moment as if to rein in his own rampaging emotions, and when he spoke again his tone had lost its grating edge. "I would like you to meet my sister, Leila."

Holly turned slowly to face the woman, her cheeks flushing to a dark red when she realized how very wrong her assumption had been. As she studied Leila, she recognized the family resemblance. Leila's enormous liquid black eyes were uncannily like her brother's, though in her small heart-shaped face they seemed rather too large and almost overpowering.

"Hello," Holly said at last in English, her breath escaping in a long sigh.

The woman turned sharply to face her brother after Holly had addressed her, and the two spoke to each other rapidly in their own language. To Holly's ears it seemed that Leila was flinging a series of questions at Arif, questions he answered with a lazy, almost detached air that seemed to anger his sister.

As the conversation trailed off, the woman's large expressive eyes glanced once more in Holly's direction, and she read with a sense of shock the animosity that gleamed in them.

Then as quietly as Leila had entered she left the apartment. Alone once again, Holly and Arif faced each other across the room.

"What was that all about?" Holly asked, her curiosity winning out over the last sharp edges of anger that still cut at her.

Arif lit another cigarette and inhaled deeply. "She was questioning me about you."

Holly's eyes narrowed. "Why?"

He shrugged. "Sisterly concern, I suppose. She wanted to know your nationality and background."

Holly wandered toward the French windows. "But she addressed me in French."

"Yes. She thought you were Geneviève."

Holly looked away sharply, her eyes taking in the deepening winter gloom that gripped the city. "Your marriage is a family affair, then," she observed at last, still not looking at him.

"It cannot be anything else."

The curt words seemed to drive an invisible wedge even more deeply between them.

After a while Arif spoke again. "Leila was shocked when I told her you were a penniless young American who hoped to win her fortune in the equestrian meets. My sister observed quite rightly that you have the regal bearing and beauty of a sultana. But I told her that the United States is a democratic country. Wealth cannot buy beauty."

Holly looked over at him, but the exhaled smoke from his cigarette had veiled his eyes so that she could not read their expression. "It can't buy happiness, either," she flung back at him.

Arif laughed sharply, although Holly was surprised to detect an undercurrent of sadness in the mocking sound.

"Come, Holly," he said at last. "I'll drive you back to your hotel."

She was about to move away from the window when her sharp eyes detected the pale familiar profile of a man who stood on the opposite street corner. Although he was half obscured by the freezing slantwise rain that had continued to fall without letup, Holly recognized him from the train. He was one of the men whom Tatiana Bulgakov had marked so sardonically as "tails." Despite the blazing warmth from the fireplace, Holly shivered. Could the man possibly think that Tatiana was here inside the apartment with her and Arif?

Arif noticed the involuntary hunching of her shoulders. "Are you all right, Holly?" he asked, a note of real concern in his voice.

Swiftly she turned away from the window. "Yes, of course. We had better go."

A few minutes later, as they climbed into the Fiat parked outside the gray apartment building, Holly could not resist another glance over her shoulder.

The man was still there on the corner, watching impassively as they drove away. Once again, a cold feeling gripped her. Her impulse was to turn and confide her concerns to Arif, but she quelled it. Arif had pressing concerns of his own—concerns that had nothing at all to do with Holly.

Despite the delight and sharing of their snatched moments together, their unquenchable attraction for each other was fated to come to an abrupt dead end. In Arif's words, *kismet* had decreed it.

Why, then, she demanded of herself, did she continue to care so deeply?

CHAPTER SEVEN

WINTER HAD TIGHTENED its uncustomarily harsh grip on Istanbul. The mixture of rain and snow that had fallen steadily since the previous afternoon had turned into a messy slush, deep and wet in some spots and brittle with a thin covering of ice in others.

Holly urged the mare into a light collected canter along the Selimiye bridle path, and they rode just long enough to unwind kinked muscles before turning to retrace their steps toward the barracks. Çamlica Hill was barely visible in the distance behind its deep gray shroud of mist and sleet.

As they approached the riding grounds once more, Holly directed Mandarin Lady toward the narrow clearing between the stables and indoor arena where she had seen Tatiana riding her handsome gray gelding the previous morning.

Holly exercised the mare briskly, using turns on the forehand and transitions from one pace to another as she led her through a series of loops, circles and large serpentines. Mandarin Lady's stride was rhythmical and precise, and on the flat work at least, Holly was aware of the powerful thrust of power coming from the animal's hindquarters. If she could maintain that impulsion in the more rigorous jump workouts, Holly would be able to breathe a little easier. She had not been able to shake the sensation that something was not quite right.

After a half hour of the exacting flat work, Holly dismounted to adjust her stirrups and walk the mare for a few minutes. But she straightened up quickly as she heard her name pronounced with a familiar light foreign inflection, and she whirled around.

Tatiana Bulgakov had come around the corner and stood in the cold shadows of the arena. With her hands thrust deep into the pockets of her oversized brown anorak, the lithe dark Russian lieutenant seemed even more diminutive than usual.

"Tatiana! Hello. I'm so glad to see you," Holly called cheerfully. As the woman stepped out of the shadows and Holly saw her face more clearly, she noticed that the lieutenant was wearing makeup. "You look so pretty today," she added impulsively.

Tatiana blushed and smiled a little at the compliment. "While we were on the train I took the liberty of looking through your fashion and beauty journals, so I learned a little how to use the makeup you so kindly gave me."

Holly's eyes took in the details of the woman's features now—the sweep of rosy blusher that at once brightened her rather sallow coloring and softened the sharpness of her facial bones, and the gray green smudge of shadow at the outer corners of her eyes. "You did a marvelous job—subtle but effective," Holly replied with an enthusiastic smile. "I'll give you those magazines to keep, if you like."

The lieutenant's tentative smile faded. "No, no!"

she demurred quickly, her voice dropping to an almost furtive whisper. "I could not."

Holly wondered then if Tatiana would have approached her if she hadn't been working in the half-concealed clearing between the buildings, out of sight of inquisitive eyes. Remembering the harsh visage of the Russian consular offical, Holly asked remorsefully, "Tatiana, did I get you into trouble by inviting you to our hotel? If so, I'm terribly sorry."

The Russian shook her head vigorously in denial. "It does not matter. I am not in their good graces anyway. Although," she added, her taut lips widening briefly in a rueful smile, "it did not help matters that the Pera Palas is next door to the American Consulate."

Holly looked shocked. "That never even occurred to me!"

"Please, Holly, don't feel guilty. You could not be expected to know the workings of the Soviet mind. Paranoia is a national pastime. We always seem to be looking over our shoulders, and over one another's shoulders!" Tatiana observed sardonically.

Wanting to shake off this gloomy train of thought, Holly smiled once again at her friend. "Have you had a chance to do much touring of Istanbul? I've found it intriguing."

"Is it the city you find intriguing or a certain Turkish captain?" the Russian countered solemnly.

It was Holly's turn to blush. "If you're referring to Arif Hakal, you're mistaken. He's set his sights on Geneviève Lamine."

Tatiana made a deprecatory gesture with her hand. "He is disdainful of the woman."

Holly glanced up swiftly. "How do you know that?"

Tatiana shrugged her shoulders beneath the hooded jacket. "I have seen the way he looks at her sometimes. Captain Hakal is a superb actor and extraordinarily charming, but I am not fooled by his act."

"Then why should he pretend?" she uttered rather more sharply than she had intended, her features paling. "If he doesn't care for her, then he cares for no one... except himself."

"You are a very harsh judge of character," Tatiana observed. "I would not have expected it of you."

A heavy silence fell between them, and Holly realized that despite their growing affection for each other their conversations were still apt to end up on rocky shoals.

Tatiana herself seemed to realize this, as well, and attempted to bring the conversation around to more neutral ground. "You asked me if I have seen the sights of Istanbul, but unfortunately I have not had the... opportunity. My tour has been limited to the eighteen rooms of the Soviet Consulate, each one with its framed photographs of comrades Lenin and Brezhnev." The Russian's tone was sardonic once more. "The view gets monotonous."

"Good Lord!" Holly exploded. "How do you stand it?"

Tatiana was impassive. "I put up with anything so long as I can ride." Before another awkward silence could intervene between the friends, Tatiana added with an attempt at brightness, "Besides, I have managed to see something of touristic interest—right here on the barracks grounds. And it should be of interest to you because I believe the woman is considered something of a heroine in the West."

"What do you mean?" Holly asked curiously.

"The famous nurse in the last century who cared for the British soldiers during the Crimean War—her headquarters were here. I believe her name was Florence Martingale."

"Nightingale, you mean," Holly corrected, suppressing the smile that rose to her lips at the Russian's confusion of the harness attachment with the nurse's name.

"Nightingale," Tatiana repeated carefully. "I will show you the room, if you like."

"I'd love it," Holly replied without hesitation.

The room, with its preserved desk, lamp and books, was at the top of a spiral staircase in one of the barracks' corner towers. After they had peeked inside past the nose of the bored security guard and were descending the stairs once again, Tatiana bent forward suddenly as if in pain.

"What is it?" Holly asked worriedly.

"It is my knee," the Russian woman muttered between clenched teeth, her face becoming pale beneath the new makeup. "The arthritis flares up when the weather grows extremely cold and damp, as it is now. I...I cannot bend it."

Holly took the woman's arm and slowly they descended step by step. When they reached the bottom of the stairway, Tatiana sat down and extended her leg stiffly. "Is there anything I can do?" Holly asked.

Tatiana shook her head. "I take aspirin, but it does not help much. You can imagine how difficult that makes it to ride."

Difficult! It would be impossible, Holly thought to herself, knowing full well the vital importance of knee contact against the horse's flanks.

Tatiana, reading the depth of anxiety in the American woman's eyes, seemed to drop her carefully maintained facade of control. "Holly, I am very much afraid," she confided softly, her normally bright quick eyes dulled by pain and apprehension. "If I fail in this competition, it will be the last one for me. They will send me back to Moscow, to a desk in army headquarters. I will become a paper pusher." Her small hands clenched around the traitorous knee. "I could not bear that—the thought of not riding again."

"But what will you do?" Holly asked helplessly, realizing for the first time how vitally important it was for the Russian equestrienne to place well in the event.

Tatiana's face grew grim. "I do not know, Holly. I do not know."

Outside once again, Holly gave Tatiana a leg up into the saddle of the waiting gelding before swinging up lithely onto her own mount's back. She rode behind the Russian, where she could not help but notice how the arthritic leg hung stiffly out of the stirrup. Yet again she wondered what would happen to the fiercely disciplined lieutenant, whose only ambition and love in life was to ride.

Rusty hailed the two women as they rode their mounts into the arena. As they returned her trainer's greeting, Holly saw that his sharp eyes had detected Tatiana's knee problem at one glance. And his speculative gaze continued to follow the figure of the tiny dark Russian woman as she trotted Kazan onto the sawdust-covered track.

Once Holly herself cantered onto the track, she attempted to block out all peripheral concerns from her mind in order to concentrate on the riding. Out of the corner of her eye she noticed the familiar profile of Arif astride Sinjon, but her only recognition was a curt nod.

Even that cursory glance was enough, however, to release a floodgate of remembrance: she recalled the sweet tide of passion he had aroused in her even though he was on the verge of committing his life to another. An unreasoning anger overwhelmed her as she thought back to his teasing persistence in seeking her out. Did he think her so weak that she would continue indulging in his teasing little games even though they both knew what the outcome had to be?

Angry then that she had let her concentration lapse so easily, Holly dug her heels into Mandarin Lady's flanks and with a determined expression on her face guided the mare toward the first low jump.

She had gathered her hair up that morning into a loose ponytail and tied it with a grosgrain ribbon that matched the deep green velour shirt tucked into her slim gray breeches. For all the set determination in her features, the swinging length of blond hair above the mare's flaxen tail gave the pair a jaunty look, and

Holly caught a glmpse of Arif's grin as he rode past them. But her only response was to frown the more fiercely.

In the final approach to the jump, Holly willed her hands to be steady and light on the reins, and her own position in the saddle was supple and fluid as Mandarin Lady leaped the rails. Made confident by the flawlessness of the execution, she guided Mandi-girl to a higher jump.

Despite the mare's perfectly balanced position for takeoff, with her head lowered and neck extended, Holly felt the almost indiscernible click of hesitation. She brought the mare around to take the same jump, but the second attempt was as ambiguous as the first: something wasn't quite right.

At once frustrated and perplexed by the mare's less than one hundred percent response, Holly cantered her toward a combination jump in which two fences were paired with a distance of twenty feet between them. Mandarin Lady took the first upright barrier with the now aggravatingly familiar click of hesitation, although her stride was extended and neat as she balanced for the second, more demanding jump—a wide spread. Despite Mandarin Lady's nice forward movement, Holly unbelievably felt the mare's rear legs buckling in the crucial takeoff stride.

A second later the terrified thoroughbred was crashing down atop the parallel poles, and Holly was catapulted onto the ground, her left ankle twisted beneath her. She lay stunned for a moment, but before she could pull herself shakily to her feet Arif was beside her. The soft rust-colored wool of his shirt brushed her face as he lifted her gently to her feet, and for a moment she clung to him—drinking in the strength of his encircling arms and feeling herself all too aware of the warmth and vitality that emanated from him.

Angered by her hungry, almost automatic response to what had been a simple good-Samaritan reaction on his part, Holly disentangled herself stiffly from the warm circle of his powerful arms.

Arif's hands still clutched her elbows as he bent down to her. "Holly, are you hurt?" he demanded.

She willed herself not to meet his gaze, afraid of what she might read there. "I'm perfectly all right," she replied sharply, brushing the sawdust and dirt from her clothes. "It's Mandarin Lady I'm concerned about."

Rusty reached the pair then, inquiring laconically, "You okay, gal? What the hell happened?"

"I'm not sure," Holly began.

But her reply was interrupted as one of the other equestrians rode up, leading the frightened mare with him. As he handed the reins to Holly, both Rusty and Arif bent to examine the mare's legs. Arif's dark fingers explored the rear leg tendons and joints expertly but gently, and once again Holly sensed his tremendous love and concern for animals.

When the two men straightened up at last, Arif's expression was unreadable. "There's a slight swelling around the stifle. It could be nothing; it could be...." He shrugged.

"Yeah," Rusty rejoined dourly. "The vet's been looking at her every day, and it's the same thing. Wait and see."

Engrossed as they were in the discussion of the possibilities, Rusty and Arif did not notice as Holly slowly backed away from them. Suddenly she wished to hear no more of what might be troubling the mare. She could not bear the idea that the animal might not be able to compete; so much of her own future was dependent on the outcome of the competition!

As she made her way toward the narrow bench-lined walkway between the stands and the track, Holly gradually became aware of a dull pain in her ankle—aware, too, that she was limping slightly to take the pressure from it.

Tears of frustration were beginning to well in her eyes when, without warning, she felt herself being swept up as a pair of hands grasped her waist and circled behind her knees.

"You lied to me," Arif observed calmly as Holly's startled gaze flew upward to meet his.

Despite the fact that she was cradled against his chest as he carried her toward the benches, Holly tried to stiffen her back with a prideful air. "I told you I was all right. Now put me down!"

Her demand was answered rather tardily when a minute later he set her down on a bench, bending forward at the same time to grasp gently the heel and toe of her scuffed riding boot.

When she realized what he intended to do, Holly cried out in alarm, "Please, you've done quite enough for me. Now leave me alone!"

Ignoring her alarmed protests, however, Arif stripped off her boot and woolen sock and rested her foot on his hard thigh as he examined the ankle with the same deft and gentle explorations he'd used with the mare.

Despite the dull throbbing pain in her ankle, Holly was shocked to feel the treacherous surge of pleasure spreading upward from some untapped depth as his fingers brushed her slim shapely calf and moved downward in a slow thorough examination of bone and muscle. For all the cool impersonality of his gentle probing, Holly found his touch to be exquisite.

She was called back to the cold reality of her situation, however, by his clipped speech. "Luckily nothing is broken. You've bruised the ankle a little, and it's already begun to swell." Before she could reply he had turned to one of the army privates who were doubling as grooms during the equestrian trials and spoke rapidly to him in Turkish.

A minute later the young private returned, flushed and panting from his run to the nearby first-aid station, and handed the captain what he had ordered.

Holly winced as Arif fixed the ice pack tightly in place around the bruise, but still she said nothing. A second later he had taken her in his arms once again, lifting her into the first row of benches in the stands and arranging the affected leg so that it rested in an elevated position on the wooden ledge.

"Now don't move it for two hours," Arif told her curtly.

"I'm not one of your subordinates. I'll not be ordered around by you," she flung at him, annoyed at her sudden position of dependency on him as well as at herself for the pleasure that had welled up at his touch.

"Yes, you will!" he countered roughly, leaning back against the narrow wooden ledge so that his dark questioning gaze could bore directly into her angry eyes. "Unless you don't give a damn about competing tomorrow."

"You know very well how much it means to me," she uttered between clenched teeth.

"Then you'd better follow orders," he replied equably.

Before she could respond he had swung his legs over the ledge and leaped agilely down onto the track, where another groom held the reins of his black stallion.

In the end, of course, Holly did precisely as she had been ordered, religiously keeping the foot elevated and relaxing as much as she could while her eyes surveyed the milling jumble of competitors on the field. Inevitably her attention was narrowed and focused on two riders only: Arif and Geneviève.

Holly had not looked for emotional involvements, had not wanted them. She had thought she wanted nothing more than to win. And now...there was Arif, dispassionate and hard, driven to marry a woman whom he did not love. And there was the woman he had chosen, Geneviève, who didn't seem to mind waiting, even though she guessed that Arif's feelings for Holly were more complex than simple sexual attraction. For the hundredth time Holly wondered at the depth of Arif's feelings and marveled at the woman's curious lack of pride.

For Holly herself knew that no matter how much she might love a man, she would give him up if she knew she could not have the whole of him—all of his love, his devotion, his commitment. Wasn't that what she already had done?

Shouts and happy excited voices from the track brought her mind back to focus on less troubling thoughts. The morning workout was over and a small group of riders had gathered at the portable lunch stand to quench their thirst with iced drinks and rehash their chances when the competition got under way. Arif's deep voice interposed among the others, and Holly heard him inviting the riders to his apartment that evening for a little pre-event celebration.

A few minutes later, after Holly had removed the ice pack and slipped her sock over the bruised ankle, which was only a little swollen now, she heard the heavy tread of boots on the wooden steps leading up from the track and lowered her head quickly to grab her own boot.

"Holly, you should have let me see that ankle again." Arif's deep chiding voice spoke down to the top of her head.

"Never mind. It's fine now," she murmured in reply as she pulled the boot gingerly over her foot.

"Did you hear my invitation to the others?" he inquired.

"Yes, I did." Holly still fussed with the boot, her face veiled by the mass of blond hair that she'd freed from its ponytail. "More duty, captain?" she asked tartly.

"My life isn't all duty." Annoyance ruffled the deep voice in response to her needling.

"Isn't it?" Her gaze swept upward, past the taut

muscled hardness of his thighs in the cream-colored riding breeches to his angry eyes.

For all their blackness, their expression was cold as an icy peak. "How could I ever have thought you to be soft and innocent?" The words were a harsh whisper. "You are the most bloody difficult woman I've ever known."

She stood up then, reeling slightly because of the still-tender bruise, but she coldly refused the supporting hand he extended to her. She dared not risk his touch again; its effect was too damnably potent! With an effort she drew herself up erectly. "Is that why you came up here—to insult me?"

He swore under his breath in Turkish at that. "Don't push me too far, Holly. I am not an unreasonable man. The reason I came up here," he began, controlling his temper with an effort, "is to ask if you would come this evening to the get-together in my apartment."

"No, thank you," she snapped.

He regarded her for a long moment, mockery gradually edging out the harsh cold light in his eyes. "There's a saying in English—something about safety in numbers. You won't have to worry that I'll try to seduce you, that you won't be able to resist my charm."

Holly recognized the words for what they were—a sharply harassing goad. Her eyes and cheeks blazed with hot angry color, and she held her fists clenched against her sides. Still she said nothing.

"Tell me, Holly," he continued in a deceptively quiet voice, "will I be blessed with another stinging rebuke from your hand?"

"You are an arrogant bastard!" She enunciated each word as if it were being chipped from stone. "You and Geneviève richly deserve each other."

Then she turned and strode away from him with as much dignity as her bruised ankle would permit.

THE WHITE-MARBLED FACADE of Dolmabahçe Palace stretched in two vast wings along the Bosporus shores. As Holly approached the edifice more closely she was struck by the contrast of its Oriental baroque splendor against the pure clarity of the snow mantling its grounds.

When her boot heel struck a patch of ice and she nearly lost her balance, Holly knew it had been foolish to leave the cozy warmth of the hotel. The fierce winter blizzard that had dogged the Paris-Istanbul Express for three days across the wide Eastern European plains had arrived in Turkey with a vengeance, and she should have burrowed down in comfort until it blew itself out. But the thought of remaining inside all afternoon had depressed her.

She and Rusty had lunched in the hotel dining room; neither one of them had been in a good mood after the debacle with Mandarin Lady that morning at the arena. Holly had had a sneaking suspicion, as well, that the trainer was as worried about Tatiana as he was about her. She had seen them talking intensely before one of the jumps, and she knew that the Russian had found yet another friend in Rusty Wilkins. While the thought pleased Holly, the gloomy parallel in the two riders' situation did not make for pleasant lunchtime conversation.

Holly had caught the bus for Dolmabahçe almost

on impulse. She'd remembered what Arif had told her about his grandfather and great-grandfather being advisers to the Ottoman sultans, and perhaps subconsciously she sought to find some connection with him. For all her blazing anger at the man, she still longed to learn more about him, to see beyond his icy facade.

The palace, built along European lines with one vast salon leading into another, was totally different from the courtyards and airy kiosks of Topkapi. Holly soon grew bored with the acres of oil paintings on the walls, the delicate Sèvres vases on the mantelpieces and the opulent crystal chandeliers glittering from the ceilings, so she decided to stroll along the old suburban neighborhood bordering the palace grounds.

She carefully avoided the street where she knew Arif's apartment to be and walked instead down a wider boulevard past the schoolyard of a girls lycée. Past the school was a café on the corner that looked warm and inviting, and Holly went inside. After ordering a cup of coffee and one of the flaky honey-pastry confections displayed in the glass case, she sank down with a grateful sigh before a windowside table.

She was just finishing her coffee when scores of young uniformed girls began to race along the sidewalk, and she realized that school was over for the day. She was so preoccupied with her own thoughts, however, that she didn't notice the small raven-haired woman who regarded her distinctive blond profile through the café window.

It was with quite a start then that Holly looked up for a moment later into the unsmiling features of Leila Hakal, who stood before her table.

"May I sit down, Miss MacKnight?" the woman asked abruptly.

"Yes, of course," Holly replied, once she'd recovered from her surprise.

As if reading the frank question in the American's expression, Leila explained, "I teach French and English at the lycée, and I was on my way home when I saw you in here. My husband and I don't live far from this corner."

"Arif didn't mention that you were married," Holly began, still uncertain how to respond to the woman, who so obviously disliked her.

"Didn't he? My husband is part of the historical team restoring the Dolmabahçe."

The two women lapsed into silence, regarding each other over the small round table.

"May I order you a coffee?" Holly asked, uncertain of the Turkish etiquette in such a situation.

"I did not come in here to make small talk with you and sip coffee, Miss MacKnight," Leila replied, her eyes like round dark saucers as she regarded Holly with an uncompromising stare.

"Then why *did* you come in here?" Holly asked curiously.

Leila shifted in her seat and waved the approaching waiter away with an impatient hand. "I'm not one for subtleties, Miss MacKnight, so I will get straight to the point. You must keep away from my brother."

Holly bridled at the woman's presumption, but she kept her temper under control. "I can't help wondering what business it is of yours," she replied softly.

"Our family is deeply devoted to one another, and their concerns are mine. Arif has not been the same man since he returned from Paris. His black moodiness and these quick-tempered rages are unlike him." Leila paused a moment before adding, "I can only assume that you are the cause."

Holly's eyebrows contracted thoughtfully. "Have you ever considered that his moods might be the result of contemplating marriage to a woman he doesn't love?"

The woman shook her head deprecatingly. "My brother knows what he has to do. Love does not enter into the picture But then—" she sighed with impatience "—what can you be expected to understand? You are of an entirely different world. What could you possibly have to offer him. . . except hurt? You must stay away from Arif."

Leila's words were like a sharp knife blade against her heart. "And if I choose not to?" Holly whispered.

"Then you are a selfish woman," Leila replied calmly.

Holly leaned forward across the table, her green eyes intense as they searched her companion's face. "Don't you think you're underestimating your brother by coming to me like this? From what I've seen, Arif is an immensely strong-willed man. It seems to me that he prides his duty over all else," she observed dryly.

"Yes, he does...or rather, he did," the dark-eyed woman conceded, "until now. I'd thought that once he'd had his fill of you or got you out of his system, things would progress as planned—"

"I'm not having an affair with Arif, if that's what you're insinuating," Holly interposed angrily.

Leila's liquid black eyes shone their disbelief. "Arif must return to Riadja with his bride, and you can never be that. He cannot risk losing what is most dear to him...to all of us."

"And what am I?" Holly demanded, her tone at once proud and angry.

"You are an interloper...a *gâvur*. You do not belong."

Long after Leila had risen from the table and left the café, her parting words seemed to linger in the air.

As HOLLY CLIMBED the wooden stairs leading to Arif Hakal's apartment, she heard the distant keening cry of a *muezzin* calling the faithful to the last prayers of the day. For an instant the mournful strains of the Islamic chant mingled with the hard-driving rhythms of contemporary pop music blaring from the apartment.

Holly had purposefully arrived late at the party, and as she pushed open the front door, which stood ajar, she saw that the large living room was overflowing with people. Along with a dozen of the international competitors, whom Holly recognized immediately, there were several Turks, evidently friends of the host. A few couples were dancing to the energetic music on the stereo, but most of the guests were ranged around the room in little conversational knots, laughing and talking loudly. Arif was nowhere in sight.

As Holly stared around the noisy, crowded, rather stuffy space, she could not help contrasting the scene with the still mood of charged intimacy when she and Arif had stood alone before the crackling fire. Anger, passion and other, unfathomable emotions had arced between them in the silence. The little contretemps had left them raw and hurt, yet filled with a need that could never be satisfied.

All of a sudden Holly wished desperately she had not come to the party. She still wasn't quite certain why she had come at all, unless it was to punish Leila somehow for her curt words of warning and accusation. But Holly realized that it was herself she was punishing by returning to the apartment with its poignant reminder of shared intimacy. Was she punishing Arif, as well, she wondered.

Holly had dressed in slim off-white slacks of worsted wool, paired with a simple black V-necked sweater. Her only jewelry was the teardrop diamond pendant on its slender golden chain and the matching diamond studs that gleamed beneath her sophisticated French-twist hairstyle. A "mannequin look," Arif had called it—distant, untouchable, cool.

She was still standing hesitantly in the doorway when the strapping blond Danish rider whom she recognized as the man who'd affably trod on her toes at the embassy affair saw her and pulled her into the party. *"Goddag,"* he greeted her jovially. "Better to arrive late than never, eh?'' he philosophized as he led her to the glass-walled liquor cabinet, where he evidently had set himself up as bartender for the evening.

Holly had thanked him for the brandy and soda that he'd splashed over ice for her and had turned to the center of the room when her eyes met the dark annoyed gaze of Leila, who had just come out of the kitchen with a tray of hot hors d'oeuvres in hand. Deliberately Leila turned her back on the tall willowy American and began speaking animatedly to a couple beside her.

Holly took two long nervous sips of her drink and immediately wished that she hadn't. She had begun to feel overly warm and claustrophobic in the crowded living room, and instinctively she moved to the relative coolness of a long hallway that led to the bedrooms. Relieved to escape the stale air of cigarette smoke that hung over the front section of the apartment, she wandered casually along the length of the hall.

There was a brass table lamp burning in the last room on the left, and Holly paused in the doorway. A fresh outdoor scent with a vague hint of spice emanated from the room. The familiar odors sent a treacherous thrill of pleasure up Holly's spine, and she knew that this was where Arif slept. The bed, with its inviting-looking fur throw, rested on a low carpeted platform. Along the far wall was a long low chest, its only adornment a horse in sculptured bronze—the complex workings of powerful straining muscles captured by the artist's hand.

Holly's eye was attracted then by a lighted glass étagère against the near wall, and she moved forward to examine with delight the small ancient urns and painted fragments of delicate Greek amphorae.

"Are you interested in archaeology?" The familiar resonance of the deep voice, amused and questioning, washed over her, and Holly turned slowly to face her host.

Although her face flushed carmine at the realization that she had invaded private terrain, Holly answered with cool temerity, "I was just wondering the same of you."

Arif moved forward to join her before the glass shelves. His strong dark fingers touched the ancient terra-cotta with an unwonted gentleness that reminded Holly of his softly probing fingers when he had explored her ankle and foot for injuries.

"I'm very much interested in Turkey's classical past," he said at last. "And fortunately it's a hobby that's easy to pursue, because these pieces can be bought very cheaply in the bazaar." He grinned as he looked across into Holly's eyes and read the interest there. "There is one catch, however."

"What's that?" Holly asked, curious.

"It is quite legal to buy these little remnants of antiquity, but it's strictly forbidden to take them out of Turkey—so the pieces are off bounds for tourists, unless they choose to remain in the country with their millennia-old treasures."

Holly smiled mischievously. "That reminds me of the old story about the monkey and the coconut. Do you know it?"

"No, I don't. Tell me," he commanded.

Holly noticed the subtle glints of laughter that now lit his eyes, and her heart twisted a little with pain as she realized that there would be no other times like this when they could share simple joys and laughter. The festering anger and suppressed passion of their uncertain relationship had eclipsed the sense of fun that had bubbled just beneath the surface. With a catch in her throat, she remembered the words he'd spoken to her in his train compartment. "So you can laugh and joke, Holly. I'm glad."

Realizing that his gaze was playing over her with curiosity, she plunged hurriedly into her story. "Well, they say that Malaysian hunters seeking monkeys for Western zoos used to trap them very easily by setting up a narrow barred enclosure with a ripe coconut inside. Evidently the local primates were inordinately fond of coconut meat, because they'd creep up to the barred cages and grab the fruit. They couldn't pull the coconut through the bars, of course, but stubbornly they wouldn't release their hold on their prize, either. The hunters would come by later and pick up their captives, still clutching the coconuts!"

Arif listened to the lighthearted tale with a rueful expression. "So the little monkeys had to choose between the coconuts and their freedom. One can't have both." He paused a moment. "You think that choosing life in Turkey would be like choosing the coconut over freedom; is that the moral?"

"No—that is I . . ." she spluttered.

It was his turn to grin mischievously at her confusion.

The silly playful moment, underscored with the same subtle tension that inevitably marked all their encounters, was interrupted as a thin Turkish woman whom Holly had never seen before stepped into the room.

As the two conversed briefly in their own tongue, Holly could not help but notice the way the woman's eyes sought Arif's with a furtive hungriness that seemed oddly out of keeping with her severely tailored herringbone suit and low practical pumps. The gaze with which Arif regarded the woman was very affectionate and kind, yet Holly sensed as she looked at him that it was reserved, as well.

"Holly," Arif addressed the American after a moment. "I'd like you to meet Dr. Ziya Aras. Ziya, Holly MacKnight is another of the competitors come to Istanbul."

A sardonic irony seemed to flash in the woman's sharp intelligent eyes as she extended her hand to the tall blond American next to Arif. "Another competitor? How charming." She smiled with the same touch of ironic humor that Holly had caught in her hazel eyes a second earlier.

Holly's reply was cut short by a sharp tap of high heels on the polished wooden hall floor, and a moment later Geneviève Lamine appeared in the doorway, looking like a sultry pouting Aphrodite in her gold silk jump suit. "Ah, here you are, *mon cher*. Did the ladies demand a bedroom tour?" she inquired archly.

Geneviève's amber eyes flicked with disdain over Holly before narrowing to regard Ziya Aras for a long moment. It was with a sense of shock that Holly realized the intent of Geneviève's stare. It was not Holly who was Geneviève's arch-rival for Arif's attentions, but Ziya!

"Shall we join the others in the living room?" Arif interposed smoothly.

"Yes, of course, darling," Geneviève replied as if she already were mistress of the manor, before turning on her heel and leading the others down the hall.

Ziya followed purposefully behind her, with Holly and Arif bringing up the rear.

Just as she was about to follow the other two women into the living room, Holly felt the light but firm pressure of Arif's hand on her arm. "Wasn't it the English dramatist William Congreve who once observed," Arif began, whispering against her hair, "I could never look long upon a monkey without very mortifying reflections."

Holly looked up at him swiftly over her shoulder and caught the darkly teasing lights in his eye. "Since you're so fond of old sayings, I have another one for you, Arif," she murmured in return. "It goes something to the effect that you can't have your coconut and eat it, too."

His sharp, somewhat rueful laughter rang out at her back as she made her way swiftly to the beige leather sofa before the fire. She did not miss the rankling look Leila had shot at her brother and his blond companion as they stood briefly together in the entrance to the living room.

Holly sank down into the comfortable leather with a sigh, pretending to follow the backgammon game in progress between a slender Japanese rider and a lanky bespectacled young Englishman.

As she nursed her brandy and soda and let her eyes wander about the room, she could not help but notice the adroit way in which Arif divided his attentions between Geneviève and Ziya. Holly could almost imagine that she was watching an English drawing-room comedy as the two female leads alternately preened and sulked before the arrogantly attractive protagonist. She might even have found it amusing if it weren't for the fact that she had a part in the little drama, as well, though she was completely mystified as to what her real role was. It was obvious that Leila regarded her as little more than a designing feckless interloper. She wondered if Arif shared his sister's feelings, if he was influenced by them.

Holly had decided that she'd had enough of the noisy celebratory mood of the party and was about to stand up when she was surprised to find Ziya Aras dropping down beside her on the sofa with a tired sigh.

"Well, Miss MacKnight, we haven't really had a chance to speak this evening," the woman began without preamble. "Someone mentioned you are from Philadelphia."

"That's right," Holly replied in a neutral tone. Once again she was struck by the woman's brisk efficient attitude and the sharpness in her hazel eyes. With her tightly bound hair and severe suit, Ziya had an air of austerity about her, and Holly could not imagine such a woman succumbing to Arif's virile attractions. Yet the expression in her eyes when she regarded him had been unmistakable.

"So," Ziya continued sharply. "I assume your mama and papa are underwriting your travels on the winter riding circuit. Rich American girls seem to have an affinity for horses."

Holly regarded her wryly. "I love horses, but I'm not rich. That's why I'm here—to make money."

"Forgive me, then, for the wrong assumption!" Ziya replied with a whinnying little laugh.

As the woman reached up to brush an invisible wisp of hair from her high forehead, Holly saw that the Turkish woman's only concession to femininity was her beautiful and graceful hands, which were impeccably manicured. "I believe Arif introduced you as a doctor," Holly remarked.

"That's right. I'm a plastic surgeon," Ziya replied. "My practice is here in the city."

"I see."

The little whinny of laughter sounded again. "No, I can see the question in your eyes, Miss Mac-Knight."

"Please call me Holly."

"Holly, then," she continued. "You are wondering what connection there can be between the busy surgeon and the Turkish captain. But it's very simple: we grew up together on neighboring lands in eastern Turkey."

"You must know him very well, then," Holly murmured.

"Yes. Arif has always been one to sow his wild oats, as they say, but he has grown to be an individual of great courage and kindness. Strong, too, both here—" Ziya gestured lyrically to her heart

"—and here." Her hand moved to indicate her own thin bicep beneath the wool twill of her jacket. "I haven't met another man to measure up to him."

"And so you wait," Holly put in softly. She noticed the fine wrinkle lines about the woman's eyes and mouth, the telltale streak of gray in the severe bun, and she guessed that Ziya was Arif's senior by one or two years.

The surgeon regarded Holly sharply, as if trying to discern any traces of mockery in her tone. "I have much to offer him," she said at last. "Not physical beauty, of course, but then I am a wealthy woman. I have a large home here on the Bosporus shores *and* a vacation villa on the Adriatic," she enumerated proudly on her fingers.

"How very fortunate for you," Holly countered dryly.

But Ziya had half turned on the sofa to regard Arif and Geneviève where they stood together near the French windows. She turned back as Leila addressed her, but Holly continued to regard Arif.

He seemed to sense her eyes upon him, and he deftly freed himself from Geneviève's possessive clutch to approach the sofa. Holly's heart skipped a beat as he held his hand out to her. "Come here, Holly. I haven't had a dance with you all evening."

A slow song began, and Holly slipped into his arms as if she belonged there. As they moved in languid rhythm to the music, Holly closed her eyes and allowed the delicious sensation of his nearness to wash over her—their thighs and hips molded together and his hands strong and warm pressed to the small of her back.

After a while she leaned back to look up into his face. "Aren't you worried that Geneviève and Ziya will get jealous?" she needled him lightly.

Holly felt the indifferent shrug of his wide shoulders beneath her hands before he answered. "They'll get over it."

"Women have no pride where you're concerned, do they?" Although her tone was light, Holly's eyes shone darkly as greenheart wood, hard and unyielding.

She felt a thrill of pleasure and fear as his hands slipped around to grip her waist while his thumbs languidly massaged her rib cage. Holly saw the slight flaring of his nostrils and once more was reminded of a stalking wolf.

"Then there is you, Holly," he whispered roughly at last, his eyes like devouring black holes that threatened to engulf her.

Shaken by the intensity of his gaze, Holly inclined her head again so that her temple rested lightly against his wide jaw. But after a moment she spoke again. "Arif, what is a...a *gâvur*?"

She felt the silent laughter rippling upward from his hard abdomen. "It is what you are, Holly."

Her head jerked back sharply. "What do you mean?"

"The term has come to mean 'foreigner' in our language, though its more classical meaning is...." He seemed to be searching for the right word.

The music had stopped, but neither one of them had noticed. Holly's neck was tight with tension as she leaned back to stare into his eyes. "The older meaning is what?" she demanded softly.

The feral grin leaped from his eyes to his lips, and Holly shivered as she imagined Arif's linkage to the past—the fierce Seljuk warriors of the Anatolian steppes.

"Infidel."

As he laughed aloud, his teeth gleamed whitely against the angular bronzed planes of his face....

Hours later, as she lay abed in her hotel room, eyes wide with sleeplessness, Holly recalled the string of jade beads that had lain before the photograph of Arif's parents in his train compartment. Then she remembered Leila's sharp words in the café. "He cannot risk losing what is most dear to him."

She fell into a troubled sleep at last, her mind awhirl with exotic images of ancient mosques and minarets. Running through her dreams like an accusing refrain was the single word: infidel.

CHAPTER EIGHT

HOLLY ADJUSTED the black velvet dome of her hard hat over her tightly coiled hair and tried to ignore the nervous flutter of fear in her stomach. So far things had gone superbly for her in the competition. She had placed second in the morning dressage trial, a scant five penalty points behind Arif, who was the front-runner going into the afternoon show-jumping meet. The arrogant Turk was still the competitor to beat!

Holly had worked the mare intensively on her tempo changes, flexion and pirouettes in canter, so she had been delighted but not unduly surprised to have scored so well in the dressage test of overall skill and obedience.

Her confidence was marred, however, by the sharp memory of the mare's buckling rear legs and their subsequent painful crash into the barrier during the previous morning's workout. As she observed the other competitors lined up ahead of her, all hoping to jump a perfect course in record time when their names and numbers were called to enter the inside field, Holly's thoughts returned to her conversation with Rusty a few minutes earlier.

"Take it easy," he'd advised. "With your second

place, you're goin' into the jumping strong. Don't jeopardize that."

The cautious note had been so unlike him. Normally the trainer would have been breathing fire into her before the jumping event, urging her to "go for it" and punctuating his enthusiasm with a loud war cry. She knew he was concerned about Mandarin Lady's performance, too. His mood that afternoon had been quiet, almost somber, and he had snapped out of it only when the conversation had turned to Tatiana Bulgakov.

"Her knee must be a lot better," Holly had observed. "At least it's well enough to have allowed her to score a very respectable fourth in the dressage."

Rusty had scratched his head sheepishly before confessing, "Yeah, well...actually I gave her some DMSO ointment to rub into her knee."

After a while Holly had asked him quietly, "You really care what happens to her, don't you, Rusty?"

But he'd kept his eyes stubbornly focused on the old Stetson in his hands. "I care about any rider who might have to give up what she loves best."

Holly had shivered involuntarily, though the physical response was less a reaction to the bitingly cold winds blowing outside the arena than to the trainer's words, which could be applied as easily to herself as to Tatiana.

Rusty had noticed the frown of concern on her face. "Cheer up, gal," he'd advised laconically. "This ain't no funeral for us yet."

Holly's attention was called back to the present as she heard Arif's name announced over the loudspeaker, and she maneuvered Mandarin Lady closer to the infield rails. As she saw him approach the judge's stand astride Sinjon to make the customary bow, Holly's pulse quickened.

Once again she had the overwhelming impression that stallion and rider were an extension of each other. Both animal and man exuded vitality and an unquenchable joy of living. Arif's proud composed features and his balanced poised carriage were matched by Sinjon's alertness and emotional drive.

The unique harmony between them was a result not only of superb horsemanship but of superb training, and Holly felt a sharp pang of disappointment that she would never see the family ranch at Riadja. She longed to see Arif on his home soil, to learn what lay beyond the hard length of sinew and muscle and bold arrogance.

She recalled the photograph of Arif and her together on the café balcony in Eyüp. She had tucked the photo into the mirror frame of the old-fashioned mahogany dresser in her hotel room, where she could look at it every day. The sharp black-and-white print had caught the essence of them in some indefinable way. At that precious moment in time at least there had been a connection between them, deep and bonding.

Now that tenuous but heartfelt bond could only be broken. Win or lose, Holly would be gone from his life while Arif was destined to return to Riadja... with his bride.

With a sigh she brought her thoughts to focus once more on the jump meet. Arif had completed the course flawlessly in near-record time. As Holly brought Mandarin Lady closer toward the gate through which she would enter the field after the next rider, she caught the grin of triumph on Arif's features. His powerful hand clapped Sinjon's neck in prideful joy before he dismounted, and Holly saw him give a short salute of victory to a group of people in the stands.

She glanced in that direction and recognized the angular features of Ziya Aras and the petite form of Leila, who stood with a slim man sporting a neatly trimmed goatee. The three waved back at Arif. *These are Arif's people,* Holly reflected miserably, *and his world.* She herself had no part in it, as Leila had reminded her so coldly.

The rider preceding her had finished, and Holly trotted the mare before the judges' stand as her name was announced. Her features were composed as she bowed formally. The stomach-twisting fear that gripped her was evident only in the taut whiteness about her compressed lips. Gently she stroked Mandarin Lady's flaxen mane and crooned encouragingly in her alert twitching ears.

Then the signal was given, and mare and rider hurtled themselves in a collected canter toward the first fence. The three-and-a-half-foot jumps were not great by competition standards, since the contest was more one of speed and style than anything else. Nevertheless, Holly was acutely aware of the mare's tension in her hindquarters, the hesitation in the crucial moment of takeoff when there should have been a great thrust of forward momentum.

A thin film of perspiration formed on Holly's upper lip as they went into each jump, and instinctively she leaned forward in the saddle a little more than was necessary, as if to take added weight from Mandarin Lady's troubled rear leg. Suddenly the six remaining fences on the course seemed to loom monstrously before them, and she became aware of nothing but her own tight emotional state and the animal's labored breathing.

She longed for the course to be completed; to her mind it felt as if they were moving in slow motion. Holly felt the exhaustion and trembling communicated upward from the chestnut haunches, yet the pretty thoroughbred continued to respond valiantly to her rider's leg commands.

Holly blinked back the stinging tears that threatened to blur her vision. Despite the mare's courageous last-ditch effort, she nicked the final two fences. It soon grew obvious to judges, onlookers and rider alike that this would be her last competition for quite some time. As Mandarin Lady limped from the field, Holly did not even bother to glance up at their time recorded on the flashing scoreboard. She knew it was over. A murmur of sympathy for the lovely competitor and her courageous mount seemed to swell outward from the stands, but Holly did not acknowledge it. Her back was ramrod stiff as she rode out of the arena. A frigid slantwise curtain of snow and sleet enveloped them as they crossed the wet grounds to the stable, but she seemed unaware of that, as well.

The stall was warm and fragrant with newly strewn

hay. Mechanically Holly went through the motions of removing the light saddle and gently sponging the mare's eyes, nose and dock. She picked up a body brush and with slow heavy hands began to wipe away the scurf and dried sweat from the mare's coat and mane. As her hands automatically went through the grooming chores, Holly cried. Mingled tears of frustration and sadness coursed down her cheeks, and impatiently she brushed them away with the back of her hand, despising her own weakness. So caught up was she in the turmoil of her own emotions that she did not notice the creak of the stall door behind her.

A second later she felt long supple fingers grasping her arm and whirling her around. She looked up briefly through her tears into Arif's hard chiseled features, and she had half turned from him when he caught her other arm.

"Holly," he whispered, his fingers almost gentle now as they kneaded her skin through the soft dark velvet of her riding jacket. "I'm sorry."

With a tremendous effort of will, Holly staunched the flow of tears. She would not display her weakness before this man, of all people. When she looked up at him at last, her eyes had the liquid-crystalline clarity of cut emeralds. She despised his sympathy, the kindly indifferent sympathy that he would extend to any failed equestrian in the meet!

"Isn't this what you predicted so mockingly in your apartment just a few days ago?" she whispered up at him bitterly. "You told me that I might lose today, and that's exactly what I've done. Now my fate is sealed. With all your talk about *kismet* . . . you were right about that, as well. Blind fate has decided my future. It should please you that your judgment is so bloody infallible!'' She spat out the angry sardonic words as her gaze held his unwaveringly.

Some destructive imp inside her noted with perverse delight the answering fury that rose in his eyes. ''Damn you, Holly,'' he muttered between clenched teeth, his fingers digging painfully into her arms. ''Don't punish me for something that's beyond our—''

The emotionally charged encounter was interrupted as Rusty burst into the stall, muttering in aggravation half to himself, ''I was afraid of this...damned afraid of this.'' He straightened up as he saw Arif and Holly. ''I think you were all too blamed accurate in guessing the diagnosis, cap'n,'' Rusty began testily, oblivious to the charged tension between his companions.

Holly leaned back against the stall partition, weary and emotionally spent. Her eyes automatically followed the men's examination of the mare.

Arif lifted Mandarin Lady's right rear foot to check for abscesses or bruises in the slender hope that something as simple as that might have caused her lameness on the jump course. But the foot was clean, as was the hock.

''I'm afraid I was right, Rusty,'' Arif observed quietly as he held the animal's stifle in a flexed position for several seconds before releasing it. ''The joint is inflamed. It's gonitis.''

A moment later the gray-haired veterinary surgeon arrived and after his own examination confirmed

Arif's diagnosis. "The inflammation has resulted from a sprain of the medial collateral ligament. Unfortunately these ligaments have a rather small blood supply and are very slow to heal. The mare will have to have complete stall rest for a month, with injections of phenylbutazone twice a day to prevent further inflammation."

As the terse professional words washed over her, Holly bit her lip painfully. She longed to scream or beat her fists on the flimsy wooden partition of the stall. Instead she whispered a curt stiff thank-you to the vet for his help.

After Rusty and Dr. Gaztep left the stall, Arif turned to Holly once again, but she did not give him the chance to speak.

"It's over," Holly enunciated dryly, the words a sharp contrast to the liquid green brilliance of her eyes. "Please...just go away," she whispered slowly, as if each word were being torn from her.

Arif hesitated for a moment, then turned and was gone.

HOLLY AND RUSTY watched the rest of the jump-course trials as spectators from the stands.

Tatiana Bulgakov would be the last competitor on the field that afternoon. The Americans watched carefully as she swung up into the deep girth of Kazan's back and eased her feet into the stirrups.

"That knee's botherin' her again," Rusty whispered in agitation to his companion. "See how she's sittin' a little off balance in the saddle to ease the pressure on it."

"So much for the DMSO," Holly whispered back somberly.

The trainer ran a nervous hand over his grizzled scalp. "Yeah. She's gonna have a hard enough time finishing the course, let alone placing among the top qualifiers." He shook his head. "It's a damn shame. She's a good horsewoman and one helluva plucky lady."

Holly felt the Russian woman's tension as keenly as if she herself were out on the course once again. Her fingers gripped the edge of the wooden bench, and she leaned forward as if her own healthy knees pressed against each other could communicate their strength to Kazan.

But Tatiana's position was as hopeless as Holly's had been, and her slow colorless finish brought forth only a smattering of unenthusiastic applause from the few spectators who'd remained to watch her complete the course.

Holly was waiting outside Kazan's stall for several minutes when she heard at last the muffled clop of hooves on the tamped-earth corridor and looked up to see the gray Hanoverian being led by his diminutive mistress. Holly's heart went out to the dispirited limping equestrienne, and impulsively she ran forward to hug her.

The two women clung together for a moment, then Tatiana drew back to look up at her tall blond friend. "I am so sorry that the mare is unwell," the Russian said softly, her gaze sympathetic.

"Tatiana, I'm sorry that *you* are unwell." Holly's own luminous green eyes grew dark with concern.

The lieutenant could only shake her head broken-ly. "Who would ever think that a person's own knee would play the traitor?"

Holly followed horse and rider into the stall and helped Tatiana pull the paddock sheet from the geld-ing's back. Then, as the Russian briskly massaged the animal's legs, Holly reached into the storage box for brush, comb and wisp. A moment later, as she was still rummaging through the grooming tools, her ears picked up the sound of rapid footsteps in the stable corridor.

"Tati-gal!" the familiar drawling voice called with uncharacteristic excitement from several feet away.

Surprised, Holly stood up quickly only to find her-self staring down over the four-foot stall partition onto Rusty Wilkins's grizzled head. He looked up at his rider, equally astonished.

"You sure get around fast," the trainer observed at last, his laconic words belied by the short gasps for breath interspersed between them. It was obvious he'd been running.

"So do you," Holly replied equably, the ghost of a smile beginning to brighten her troubled eyes. "And from the sound of your lovely little nickname for Tatiana, it seems that things have been progressing pretty rapidly under my nose without my even being aware of them!"

He rubbed his head sheepishly. "Never mind all that now," he replied with an aggrieved look.

Their interchange was interrupted as the tiny sub-ject of discussion came forward and looked over the partition ledge. "Hello, Rusty," Tatiana began gravely. "As you Americans would say, I think I am all washed away."

"Washed up, you mean," Rusty corrected automatically, before interrupting himself. "But what am I sayin'! You aren't washed up at all. That's what I was rushin' over here to tell you when I got distracted." He shot another dark look at Holly, who was grinning openly now, before speaking again. "The judges have just made a special announcement. They're postponin' the cross-country phase of the event for a week to ten days because of the foul weather. There's even talk of scratchin' today's first two trials altogether, which'd mean a whole new event!"

Both women's eyes widened in surprise at such an unprecedented action. "You're kidding," Holly murmured at last.

"Nope," Rusty replied, his quick eyes darting from Holly to the small dark Russian woman. "You know what this means, don't you, lieutenant?" he demanded at last before forging on without waiting for a reply. "With a week's worth of DMSO and hot-pad treatments for that bum knee and, with luck, a break in this cold snap, you'll be ready to pick up all those points you lagged behind in the show jump. You're one helluva cross-country competitor, as you proved in Paris—second only to that good-lookin' Turk and Holly!"

Tatiana's eyes lightened briefly at the enthusiasm in his voice, yet her reply was somber. "You are so good to encourage me, Rusty. Still, I fear that this delay can only be a temporary reprieve for me."

The feisty trainer slapped his hat against his thigh in frustration. "Now you just quit talkin' like a danged quitter," he railed loudly, obviously delighted at the opportunity to take up the cudgels again in the equestrian battle.

As the two began to talk animatedly, Holly let herself out of Kazan's stall and made her way down the long shadowy stable corridor, her thoughts revolving in slow aimless circles. The delay was like a gift from the gods for the plucky Russian lieutenant, but it made no difference at all for her. Holly MacKnight was indeed "washed up," she told herself ruefully. The mare's injury demanded a month of stall rest at least—too long and too late for anything at all. She and Rusty had no options left but to return to the States, broke and defeated.

Back at Mandarin Lady's stall she gave the mare an affectionate pat and rearranged the protective woolen blanket more snugly before reaching up to free her own hair from its tightly bound coils. Then she slipped into her heavy wraparound coat and went outside, fair head bent against the heavy mist of wet snow whirling about her.

She did not see the tall dark figure approaching from across the stable grounds until he loomed directly before her. "Arif!" she whispered in surprise, brushing away a wisp of gold hair that had blown across her lips.

Feathery bits of snow clung to his dark brows and lashes, but the faint licorice scent of his breath was warm and sweet on her face as he addressed her. "You can be an elusive woman when you want to be,

Holly. I've been looking for you. Have you heard the news?''

Her eyes sparkled with intensity. ''About the postponement? Yes, I've heard, but unfortunately it means nothing to me.''

She had taken a few steps away from him, but his voice compelled her to wait once again. ''Holly, will you have dinner with me tonight?''

She turned slowly toward him. ''Why, Arif? Tomorrow I'll be on a flight to New York. What more can we have to say to each other?''

''You're wrong, Holly,'' he told her softly as he reached out and cupped her chin with his gloved hand. ''There is much to talk of still.''

For a long moment she gazed into those sable-dark eyes. Had she imagined the concern, the caring, the naked need that she'd read there? Holly was on the verge of accepting his invitation when she glanced over his shoulder and saw the petite fur-clad figure of Leila approaching them. The woman's enormous eyes bored into hers with silent accusation, and like the echoes of a nightmare she heard the words reverberating inside her head: ''You are an interloper.... What could you possibly have to offer him...except hurt?''

Holly's troubled gaze returned to meet his. ''I'm sorry, Arif,'' she whispered, each word a painful effort, ''but I meant what I said. The interlude is over. You've got your life to live and I've...I've got to pick up the pieces of mine.''

Leila was beside them then, her small hand on Arif's sleeve. Holly turned and ran swiftly through the gathering darkness of the winter afternoon.

SHE STOOD BEFORE THE LONG WINDOW in her room, her gaze fixed on the cold white veil that clung to Istanbul's minarets and shrouded the pulsating vigor of the old city below. Holly had dressed for dinner in a heathery green sweater dress that heightened the slender loveliness of her figure, but she didn't really feel like going downstairs to the busy dining room.

She and Rusty had whiled away a few hours there over a pot of tea, discussing future plans. Rusty had decided to stay on in Istanbul for another week, to be with Tatiana. Holly hadn't attempted to change his mind. As far as she knew there had never been a woman in the trainer's life, and he had a right to whatever happiness he might find with Tatiana, even though the outcome might be as ill-fated as her own interlude with Arif.

She had come upstairs an hour ago and booked a reservation for one on the first New York-bound flight out of Istanbul in the morning. Holly imagined the exhausting transcontinental trip and then the switch to a smaller commuter jet for the last leg of the journey home to Philadelphia. She envisioned herself stepping into the wide marble foyer of the Holliford home with its moiré silk walls and delicate French Regency table, envisioned the expression on her parents' faces.

"I hadn't planned on a Christmas wedding," Alice Holliford would say to her daughter with lips compressed in cool annoyance, "but we shall have to make the best of it. Of course you shall have to call Stanley at once and apologize for your ridiculous irresponsible behavior."

Holly shivered as the minareted skyline before her appeared to fade, replaced in her vision by the shores of the Delaware River and the foursquare solidity of Independence Hall and Gloria Dei Church. In that moment she felt almost overwhelmed by a feeling of desolation, of loss.

A quick rap on the door brought her thoughts back sharply to the present, and she hurried across the spacious room to answer it. Fleetingly she wondered if Rusty had come to his senses after all and decided to fly home with her tomorrow.

In the instant she flung open the door, the unaccountable mood of coldness and loss vanished. Her heart raced as she stared up into Arif Hakal's lean bronzed face, its familiar harsh angularity sharpened by the tautness of his jaw.

Before she could compose her thoughts enough to address him, he was speaking in a low urgent voice. "I could not let you go like this, to have you walk out of my life as you promised to do this afternoon."

Holly fought back the surge of longing that rose within her. She could not risk letting him see how deeply his unexpected appearance had affected her. With a will she shuttered her face, carefully hiding the hurt, the anguish, the needing and wanting. She dropped her eyes, afraid of what their expressive depths might show.

"Come to dinner with me now," he whispered sharply, the words less an invitation than a command. "I have a proposal to make."

Her eyes flashed upward swiftly at that, angry that again he might be deliberately toying with her.

His teeth gleamed whitely against the dark bronze of his skin as he shot her a brief smile. "I knew I would break through that beautifully sculpted stone facade of yours, Holly. What I have to discuss is strictly business: a matter of horses."

"What do you mean?" she demanded, her expression mystified.

"Get your coat. We'll discuss it over dinner."

They descended a narrow stairway that opened onto a series of rooms with paneled walls and low vaulted ceilings. In one corner of the restaurant a group of Turks were singing Black Sea ballads while an old woman in a long bright skirt replenished their beer glasses.

As Arif pulled out Holly's chair for her, he whispered, "This place was opened by Russians fleeing the Bolshevik Revolution sixty-five years ago. They say that one of them was a ballerina from St. Petersburg. Perhaps that's her." Holly's eyes followed his as they regarded the old woman. She still retained an aura of grace despite her lined features and careworn expression, and Holly could almost envision her as a young prima donna on the stage.

"Whether the stories are true or not," Arif continued, "this little place has the best borscht and breaded veal cutlets in the city."

As they ate the delicious dinner, Arif regaled his companion with stories about old Istanbul. His conversation ranged from the exiled Russian noblemen who opened dance halls to the German spies who sipped cocktails from their hotel balconies while counting the Russian and English warships passing

through the Bosporus Strait. Then he told her a few
of the stories that had been told him by his grandfather.

Holly was intrigued by his amusing descriptions of
the inner workings of the Dolmabahçe Palace—the
steel doors on the sultan's harem and the secret windows from which the concubines could observe the
diplomatic intrigue and councils of war in the throne
room.

"I toured the palace a few days ago, but I guess I
missed all that," she laughed.

"What did you think of my grandfather's former
haunt?" Arif asked.

It as on the tip of Holly's tongue to tell him that it
had reminded her rather too much of her own home
in Philadelphia with its expensive bric-a-brac, but she
remembered her masquerade of being the down-at-
heels equestrienne. Instead she observed, "Pretty
fancy digs, but I think I prefer Topkapi Palace."

"Spoken like a true Turk," Arif grinned unexpectedly.

As the evening progressed, Holly found herself intrigued as much by the different facets of Arif's personality as by his witty well-informed conversation.
Although he could be very charming when he chose
to, she had more often felt the brunt of his brooding
darker side. It was as though he reserved the playacting for others, while for her he reserved...what?

Tonight, however, was a reminder of how delightful a companion he could be. She bit her lip, aware
that in less than twelve hours she would be affected
no more by Arif's changeable moods—the charm

blunted by arrogance and the dark wit intermingling with brooding anger.

He caught her nervous gesture, and his eyes were curious. "Have I said something wrong, Holly?"

She shook her head. "No. It's closer to the mark that you really haven't said anything at all." Nervously she twisted the stem of her empty wineglass. "Why did you invite me to dinner this evening? Why did you come to seek me out when I'd told you I couldn't see you again?"

Before he could reply, the old woman brought two cups of strong fragrant coffee and set them on the table.

Arif stirred his moodily for a long while before looking up into his companion's questioning green eyes. "Holly, I want you to come to Riadja with me."

Her heart skipped a beat, and she felt her mouth grow dry. At last she managed to ask, "Why?"

"There is a beautiful silver gray mare that I have been training. We call her Jinniyah. I think she would be perfect for you to ride," he observed simply.

Holly's gaze played over his features—the high tilted cheekbones and sensual lips, the strong jawline and black unfathomable eyes. She longed to touch him as she had that seemingly long-ago afternoon in his apartment. "Arif, I can only repeat what I asked you before," she replied, her voice soft yet demanding. "Why? To what point? Mandarin Lady is finished for the season. As am I . . . perhaps for good. There's no point . . . in anything," she concluded lamely.

Arif's eyes deepened in intensity. "You told me

once that you believed a person should make his own fate. You will have that chance now. The latest word from the event judges is that this morning's meet will be eliminated completely, and everyone will start over on an equal footing. You can compete again— this time with one of my ponies.''

Holly's lips were pursed as if to form yet another question, but Arif interrupted sardonically, ''Don't ask me why again, Holly. I swear that you try my patience as no woman has ever done. I'm suggesting this, Holly, because I care what happens to you. I want to help.''

She regarded him for a long time as if to discern what lay beyond this gesture of kindness. ''Arif,'' she replied, careful to keep her tone cool and objective, ''your parents are expecting you to bring home a bride, not a. . . a *gâvur*. Leila said—''

''I love my sister dearly,'' he cut her off, ''but she can be a meddling mother hen. I do not live my life to please her.'' There was a cutting edge to his voice.

''Then whom do you live it for?''

He threw his napkin down angrily on the table. ''Damn it, why does our every conversation have to turn into a debate! Will you come or not? I want you there, for a little while at least. I want you to see it. But then if you don't care to. . . .''

''Arif! I do care!'' Her jewellike eyes blazed into his. ''I want nothing more than to see Riadja, but I don't want to see either one of us hurt.''

''What do you think life is, Holly?'' he returned sharply. ''It is full of hurts, disappointments, loss. Yet we go on.''

"Life is compromise, too," she replied quietly.

"Some things cannot be compromised." The harsh clipped words brooked no argument, and a charged silence filled the air between them. After a long moment Arif expelled his breath in an audible sigh, though it was difficult to say if it was born of frustration or some nameless anger. "Will you come," he asked one final time, "to see Jinniyah at least?"

Holly would not meet his darkly demanding gaze. Her eyes wandered about the dim restaurant and focused on the men at the corner table, their voices still harmonizing in a mournful Oriental melody. It was a totally different world from any she had known—exotic, strange, almost frightening. Yet she found that she did not wish to break the bond, that tenuous connection she had made with Arif.

Tradition and duty had bound him to a fate that could not permit him to be a free man. She knew that, but she knew also that she loved him. Her heart was his, even if he could not accept it. She could not run away from that, no matter how certain the prospect of eventually having to give him up.

"Yes," she whispered at last, her eyes partially veiled by downcast lashes. "I'll come to Riadja."

CHAPTER NINE

THE TAXI MOVED CRABWISE along the ice-slicked avenue, bound for the gap in the medieval city walls that had been cut to make way for the wide thoroughfare leading to Yesilköy Airport. Holly and Arif sat side by side in the rear of the cab, close but not touching, each wrapped in private thoughts as they stared out over the freezing white mist that still gripped Istanbul.

Holly recalled the astonished look in Rusty's sharp eyes when she'd informed him of the slight change in plans: she would fly out of Istanbul as arranged, though her destination would not be New York but a fortresslike town high on a plateau above the eastern reaches of the Anatolian steppes. Holly had explained matter-of-factly that it was to be a business trip. If the mare Jinniyah proved suitable, then Holly would ride her in the competition with a percentage of the winnings to go to Captain Hakal.

Although the trainer had enthusiastically agreed to the plan, Holly knew he had not been fooled for one minute that the trip would be purely for business. She was deeply grateful that he had not lectured or harangued her or given dire warnings.

Holly would not confess her true feelings to anyone, least of all to the rugged Turkish captain beside her in the cab. It was imperative that they carry on the charade of a business deal—for both their sakes. For now at least it was enough that Arif had said he cared...cared what happened to her. How radically her ideas had changed in a few days! She had sworn haughtily to herself that she would have all of a man's love or else have none of it at all. Now she hadn't even the faintest prospect of that. Yet she had to be with him, to store up the memories of these few days.

Without ever having spoken the thought aloud, both Arif and Holly knew that in a sense they were entering forbidden territory. They knew it, but the smoldering flame of need that arced between them was more powerful than reason. Arif should have been accompanying the woman who was to be his wife. And Holly could never be that—she had been reminded achingly of the fact so many, many times. She shivered a little as she tried to imagine his parents' reaction to her appearance in their home. Would it be as apparent to them as it had been to Rusty Wilkins that she was hopelessly in love with their son?

Holly became aware that Arif's eyes were upon her, and she half turned on the cold leather seat to face him. His gaze was unreadable, though Holly sensed a fomenting of troubled emotion in their velvety depths. Was he already regretting the invitation he had extended to her?

She turned away from him to stare outside once again, and as the cab passed beneath the Cannon

Gate her gaze was drawn to the hundreds of tin-roofed shacks leaning as if for precarious support against the ancient stone walls. "Are they Gypsies?" she asked curiously.

Arif's gaze followed hers. "There is a long tradition of Gypsies encamping outside the city walls, but they are gone now. These people are Anatolian peasants who've migrated here with the hope of bettering their lives. We have a name for them—*gecekondu*, birds who came to roost during the night. The name has to do with another Turkish tradition. If a squatter can steal into an area by dark and have a roof erected over his head before morning when his presence is discovered, then he cannot be evicted. The shelter has become his home."

Holly repeated the strange word, her gaze focusing fleetingly on a beshawled woman outside one of the meager hovels. The woman's hands, gripping a short iron pick, were bright red as she attempted to break up the ice that had formed in a wooden washtub. Holly shook her head and looked back at Arif. "I hadn't realized what a sheltered life I've led," she sighed.

"Yes. It's a different world," he replied somberly.

Once again Holly was reminded of the vast differences in heritage that lay between them. How could love ever broach that?

THE DARK GRANITE WALLS of Erzurum rose out of the austere plain, its minarets like a hundred bristling spears against the sky as the twin-engined aircraft swooped low over them in its final approach to the landing field. Holly had needed no words of explanation to understand the city's long history as a fortress settlement. Her gaze took in the jagged sweep of volcanic ranges protecting it from north and south and the dark outflow of ancient lava that linked the mountains.

The air was bitterly cold but windless as they descended the portable aluminum stairway from the craft and hurried to the shelter of the small air terminal. Arif had explained earlier that because there were no flights to Kars they would rent a car and complete the last leg of the journey overland.

Since he'd warned that the arrangements might take quite some time, Holly decided to explore the town on her own. A steep lane crowded on either side by shops wound up to the ramparts, and Holly climbed it slowly with head bent in the collar of her parka and hands buried deeply into her pockets. As she surveyed the city from the crumbling Byzantine walls, she remembered Arif's description of the local weather: short burning summers and long, almost Siberian winters. As if in response to the bitter assault of the elements, the city seemed to hug the earth. It had a raw frontierlike quality that could not be softened by the more civilized aspect of modern Atatürk University and the gleaming tiled dome of Ulu Camii.

As she stared out over the fifteen-hundred-year-old city, Holly was filled with the same sense of excitement she'd experienced as the Paris-Istanbul Express crossed the border into Turkey several days before. Suddenly she was glad that she had come.

Her mood of ebullience warmed her as she descended once more into the heart of the city and entered the small café that adjoined the car rental agency. Arif hailed her from a windowside table, and she moved forward swiftly to join him.

"That was quick," she laughed as she shrugged out of her jacket and slipped into the wooden booth opposite him. "Where's our car?"

Arif shot her a rueful grin. "You Americans are incurable optimists. I've finished the paperwork, but they're still trying to dredge up something mechanically sound for us to drive. We'll probably be lucky to get a battered *araba* that did service in the Crimean War!"

"Sounds more exciting than an air-conditioned tour bus," Holly grinned in return.

Arif cocked his head curiously. "Are you always so adventurous?"

"As an equestrienne I'm used to taking chances," she replied lightly, her green eyes dancing with mischief. "I suppose I'm just a gambler at heart."

"Really?" His right brow shot upward inquisitively. "And just what are you gambling on?"

Before she could come up with a reply to that one, Arif was being hailed by a clerk from the agency. He rose swiftly and left her alone at the table. Holly was staring aimlessly out the café window, wondering at the faint challenge in Arif's tone, when her back suddenly went rigid with tension.

Past the stream of hurrying passersby and queued traffic at the intersection, Holly recognized an uncomfortably familiar profile hunched patiently against the cold. He was tall and fair but otherwise rather nondescript, and his gaze was fixed penetratingly on the busy café entrance. He was the same man whom she had seen in the square outside Arif's apartment.

Impulsively Holly stood up from the table, grabbed her parka and went outside. She crossed the narrow side street that fed into the main thoroughfare, pretending to focus her attention on the colorful window display in a corner dress shop, then stopped and stared past the fur-clad store mannequins through the adjoining plate-glass window that fronted the main street. Her heart thudded sickeningly as she saw the man pounce into action, dodging the never-ending stream of traffic as he sought to keep his prey in sight. For there was no question now in Holly's mind that the man was following her.

She moved swiftly down the block of storefronts, pausing at the end before a window filled with chocolates and rich sugar confections. Out of the corner of her eye she saw him moving forward with slow casual strides, as if he, too, were no more than an innocent window-shopper.

Holly went around the corner and slipped into the first doorway, her back pressed rigidly against the cold stone. She tried to quiet her jangling nerves by taking a few deep breaths, but her hands still trembled violently at her sides.

A moment later she heard quick heavy footsteps on the sidewalk, and her doorway was momentarily shadowed by the man's tall build as he hurried by. Before her courage could desert her, Holly slipped

out of her place of concealment and hurried to catch
up with her pursuer.

He continued at a half run, unaware that it was he
who was now being followed. At the corner he paused
in bafflement, and Holly chose that moment to grab
hold of his arm.

"Here I am," she taunted, as he whirled in astonishment to face her. "You were looking for me,
weren't you? I thought you were one of the Russians
detailed to keep an eye on Lieutenant Bulgakov, but I
see now that I was dreadfully wrong."

The man attempted to assume an air of puzzled innocence. "What're you talking about? Just because
we're a couple of Americans here in the same town,
you can't go assuming—"

"Why don't you save your story?" Holly interrupted angrily. "You can explain it to the Turkish
police after I've told them that you've been bothering
me."

"Now wait a minute, Miss Holliford," the man
addressed her with a conciliating attitude. "Let's be
reasonable about this. People who care deeply about
you have asked me to keep an eye out, you understand?" he murmured placatingly.

As she listened to his lower-east-side Philly accent,
the truth gradually began to dawn on her. She was
trembling again, not with fear but with rage.
"You've been hired by my father; he's had you
watch me since Paris," she whispered almost in disbelief, her eyes ablaze. "But don't *you* understand?
It's no one's business but my own what I choose to
do with my life."

He smiled unpleasantly. "You're a real innocent abroad, aren't you, Miss Holliford? Hasn't it dawned on you yet that this Hakal character you've been hanging around with is a gigolo? Do you think it's just a coincidence that all his lady friends happen to be wealthy aristocrats?"

"My father must have hired you for your brawn rather than brains," Holly shot back bitingly. "As far as Arif Hakal is concerned, I'm nothing but a penniless American whose fortune consists of five thousand miserable francs that I won at Malmaison."

"Taunt me all you want, Miss Holliford, but it won't matter. I guess it's always hard for a woman to find out that a man loves her not for herself but for her money," he informed her smugly.

"For the sake of a complete report, since I know my father will demand one," Holly replied with bitter sarcasm, "I'll tell you now that I'm traveling to Kars to visit the Hakal ranch. If I see your face again, it will be your word against mine. It would really be a shame to see you languishing in a Turkish prison for threatening a guest of a Turkish captain; I don't think they're pleasant places." Holly's demeanor was deadly serious as she paused to let her words sink in. "I suggest you get on the first plane for Philadelphia and don't look back."

To her surprise she saw him smile again. "That won't be necessary. Mr. Holliford should be arriving in the country this morning on a flight from New York. He'll be waiting for you when you get back to Istanbul." And he turned and walked away, a tuneless whistle marking his retreat.

Holly leaned back against the building, feeling curiously drained after the unexpected confrontation with this unknown man who had been shadowing her across Europe and Asia. It still shocked her to think that her father would attempt to manipulate her across a distance of six thousand miles. She thought of Alec Wright's surprise visit in Paris and Adnan Memed's arrogant confrontation with Arif in the Galata Tower.

Her thoughts returned once again to the shadowy bodyguard whom she would never have noticed at all if Tatiana Bulgakov's sharp eyes hadn't picked him out on the train. She dismissed the man's smug assertion that Arif Hakal was a gigolo. There had never been any talk of money between Arif and her, except.... Her cheeks burned at the memory of the sizable handful of bank notes that the Edirne customs official had pocketed from the captain's winnings, and Arif's casual comments later that the funds would have built a new paddock and stalls. She recalled, too, Ziya Aras's proud boast that she had much to offer the handsome Turkish captain.

Still, Holly laughed at the notion that Arif could be a sordid fortune hunter. Rather than unprincipled, he had seemed rather too full of principles and duty! If he had strict requirements in choosing a wife, they revolved around the need to find a woman who shared his heritage and could meld harmoniously into his life on the Asian steppes. *Not money,* she thought as she retraced her steps back to the café.

"I was afraid I'd lost you," Arif teased her when she rejoined him at the table.

"You won't get rid of me that easily," she replied rather more soberly than she'd intended.

"You are a very stubborn woman; I know that!" His dark, faintly quizzical gaze sought hers, but she would not look at him.

She longed to confide in him, to pass on the ridiculous allegations that the tall pale bodyguard had made, but she knew that in doing so she would have to unravel the tangled web of her own family affairs. She had no wish for him to find out about her father's humiliating attempts to control her life, or for him to learn of her anonymous charade as "Holly MacKnight." Suddenly her own playacting seemed so childish, so terribly pointless. How had she hoped to dream that she might escape the powerful web of Holliford influence?

She remembered her angry confrontation with the bodyguard and her curt threats. Holly guessed that he would not risk trouble with the police and probably was en route to Istanbul to report directly to his impatiently waiting employer. For the time being at least, Holly was free. She looked back at Arif. "Is the car ready?"

He smiled sardonically. "Yes, if you can call it that. Shall we go?" On the way he picked up a hamper from the café owner and handed it to Holly.

"What's this?" she demanded curiously.

"I thought we'd picnic along the way," he explained as he took her arm and led her across the busy square.

"Mmm, smells wonderful," she replied, lifting the corner of the basket to inspect the neatly wrapped food parcels that were tucked in between a thermos of coffee and a bottle of *raki*.

Her inspection was curtailed, however, as Arif drew her up short before the battered rusting hulk of a vintage Volkswagen Bug.

She stared at it in dismay. "My God," she observed wonderingly, "it looks like a reject from a demolition derby."

"What's that?" Arif asked. After she'd explained it to him, his expressive eyes glinted with amusement. "You mean they drive around in old wrecks and run into one another on purpose?"

"That's the gist of it," she assented.

"But why?" he demanded.

Holly shrugged helplessly. "Money, I suppose."

"Ah, yes, money," he replied, arranging the hamper in the back before assisting Holly into the passenger seat. A moment later, as he slid behind the wheel, he asked teasingly, "Isn't there a song lyric in English about money making the world go around?"

"That was love," Holly retorted dryly.

"Ah, yes, love," he repeated with a faint mocking air. "I'd forgotten I was traveling with an incurable romantic."

Don't taunt me, Holly longed to cry. *I've been taunted enough today about love and money.* Even as she recalled the guard's tawdry accusations, she envisioned the easy charm with which Arif had dealt with Geneviève and Ziya. Was it all a game to him? And where did she herself fit in?

THE TROUBLING THOUGHTS gradually receded from her mind as the lonely treacherous highway climbed northward past Artvin and the bleak plateau gave way to immense vistas of forests and mountain gorges cleft by a deep river basin, the Çoruh.

It was the wildest, most incredibly beautiful terrain Holly had ever seen. "How free it makes you feel," she murmured almost to herself.

"What did you say?" Arif asked, startled out of some reverie of his own.

"Nothing." She shook her head slowly. "It's just that I think I'm falling in love with your country."

Fleetingly his eyes left the twisting road surface to regard her. "Perhaps you can understand, then, why I feel so deeply a part of the land," he replied with quiet intensity.

A few minutes later they pulled off the road and climbed out of the car. Holly drank in the sweet pure mountain air that was clear and brittle as fine crystal. Beyond the easternmost range of peaks the clouds began to lift, gradually revealing a thin band of blue sky. Then a ray of sun broke through the rent in the cloud veil and illuminated the blindingly white peaks of ice and snow. "So much for the brutal Siberian winters," Holly teased. "That's the first bit of sunshine I've seen since I left Philadelphia!"

"It's nothing but a respite to lull the traveler into a sense of false security," Arif replied as he paced restlessly along the cliffs falling away to the silver bend of river far below. "The season has been exceptionally dry until now, but that will all end when the European storm front arrives behind us. In a week this highway will be muddy and impassable."

Holly shivered involuntarily at his calm prediction of a treacherous winter onslaught. "Won't people be trapped?" she asked, her voice suddenly sounding small and insignificant against that backdrop of arrogant grandeur.

Arif grinned, and she was reminded of the wolf, lean and intense as he stalked the land for survival. "Not the mountain people. They aren't bound by four wheels and a drive shaft. No, they use the more time-honored methods of conveyance—horse, shank mule, camel."

"Camel!" she repeated in surprise. Once more she was forcefully reminded that this was Asia, an ancient and—for her—an alien land.

He laughed at the look of shock in her eyes. "Climb back in the car and we'll have lunch. Some good Turkish food will revive your sense of adventure!"

The cramped interior of the Bug was soon filled with the enticing aromas of a spice market as they unwrapped the brown butcher paper from the food in the hamper. There was flat bread and cheese, cold vegetables cooked in olive oil and *cig köfte*, the spicy kebabs of meatballs with mashed chick peas.

As they ate, Arif talked once more with quiet intensity of the region's history. He explained that it had never been taken by conquerors in the Middle Ages, and Holly could readily understand why as she stared over the steep-sided gorges and rocky pine-covered slopes fit only for surefooted mountain animals.

After they had eaten, Arif poured a drop of *raki* into Holly's coffee before taking a quick swallow directly from the bottle and replacing it in the hamper. Holly sat back contentedly and stretched her legs as best she could in the tight space, then leaned one arm back against the bucket seat. "You come of a proud race, don't you?" she observed at last.

"How did you ever guess?" he retorted with a mocking grin. " 'Natural-born aristocrats' is what my father calls the Turks, since we've never been ruled or colonized by any other nation. But I should spare you that talk now; you'll soon hear more than enough of it after you've met my father."

His tone was affectionate, yet Holly sensed a faint sardonic twist to his words. Was there some old bone of contention between father and son, she wondered curiously. Once again a little ripple of apprehension sped up her back at the thought of meeting the Hakals. She could not help but wonder if they would be as openly antagonistic as their daughter had been. Her mind whirled with a hundred questions, but all she asked aloud was, "Do your parents speak English?"

"Yes, of course," Arif replied as he turned the ignition key and the underpowered engine chugged noisily to life. "Don't worry, Holly. They are wonderfully hospitable people."

She dropped her eyes in embarrassment to think that he had guessed her fears. Still, as they wound down through the mountain pass and approached once more the stony tableland of the Anatolian plateau, Holly felt as though a pair of eyes were boring into her—eyes that were enormous, dark and full of animosity.

Arif attempted to relieve the somber mood that had befallen his companion by distracting her with a lively lesson in the Turkish language. The patient teasing instruction soon had Holly laughing as her tongue tripped over the unfamiliar vowel sound, but she had a quick ear for it nonetheless.

"I think I'll get along with my three-word vocabulary very well," she said at last, laughing still. "As long as I can say hello, please and thank-you, I don't think I'll need much else. But heaven help me if I have to say goodbye! *Allahais*...." The word ended in a tangle upon her lips.

"*Allahaismarladik,*" Arif enunciated patiently yet again, grinning despite himself at the difficulty she was having with the mouthful. "Why don't you try this one instead: *güle güle*."

"Gew-lay gew-lay," she repeated carefully. "That's fun. What does it mean?"

"The same thing: goodbye. Only its more colloquial meaning is 'go smiling.' "

"What a lovely expression! *Güle güle*," she repeated softly.

The vast domed mountains that they now skirted cast deep shadows across the highway as the winter sun crept behind them. Though it was just two in the afternoon, it seemed more like dusk.

"How much longer until we arrive?" Holly asked.

"Another five or six hours," Arif replied. "When we arrive we'll take Jinniyah and her sire, Damudji, out for an evening ride if you like."

Business again, Holly murmured inwardly with a mingled feeling of sadness and frustration. The mare would be ridden and if all parties agreed she would be transported by rail back to Istanbul. Once again, money reared its ugly head. Had she deluded herself after all in thinking that this trip was more than simply business? Arif had watched Holly prove herself as a superb horsewoman in both the Paris meet and the first event of the Istanbul trials. If she were to compete successfully on the remainder of the circuit with a mare bred on his ranch, Riadja would be given added luster. The ugly thought crossed her mind that he might be coolly manipulating her; not for money, as her father's henchman had insinuated, but for her riding abilities. Had his admission of caring about her been a mere pretext?

Her suspicions were forgotten as she heard the car engine cough, sputter and die. "What's the matter?" she asked swiftly.

But Arif was already out of the vehicle and pulling up the rear hood with an angry hand. He swore furiously in Turkish, and Holly for once was happy that the language was incomprehensible to her. Once his initial fury had blown itself out somewhat, she asked more softly, "What's wrong with it?"

Her gaze followed the angry sweep of his hand over the battered innards of the engine. "This carburetor looks like it was rebuilt by a blind ape. They reused the old fuel lines and the rubber has started to disintegrate. If I see that rental agent again, I'll ring his bloody neck," he whispered tautly before slamming the hood down with savage force.

Though she knew his anger was not directed at her, Holly was nevertheless frightened by the steely menace in his harsh features. She hated to think what might happen if such rage had been directed at her. There was a wild fierceness about him that reminded her strangely of the magnificent but untamable terrain through which they'd just passed.

Without realizing it Holly backed away from him before speaking again. "Are we stranded?" she inquired with a pretense of calmness, her eyes sweeping over the austere horizon and the narrow black ribbon of highway that seemed to stretch into infinity.

"Someone will come along eventually." The new imprecations that rose to his lips were swallowed as he glimpsed the frightened look in Holly's eyes. "I'm used to surviving in the cold, but for a woman it's different."

Her fear was forgotten as she bridled at this insinuation of feminine weakness. "Don't be ridiculous!" she snapped. "It's no different at all. I've lived through cold before." The frigid wind blew across her face, making a mockery of her crisp bravado. She shivered as the bone-chilling gusts invaded her limbs.

"Have you, Holly?" He laughed harshly, noticing the telltale hunch of her shoulders against the bitter Siberian winds. "Not cold like this." His ebony gaze raked over her. "Come here," he ordered sharply.

Startled by the asperity of the command, she moved forward and stood before him, watching with perplexed eyes as he slowly unbuttoned his heavy suede jacket.

"Come here," he repeated. Although the words were spoken more softly, the familiar harshness still underlined them.

When she realized that he meant to shield her from the wind with his own body, Holly's pride bridled in spirited opposition. "No! I don't need either your protection or your warmth," she replied stubbornly. She refused to allow herself to be indebted to this man whom she already had found so damnably easy to love—despite the fact that logic and reason had told her it was foolishly futile to love him at all.

Arif shook his head slowly. "You're very much in need of both," he observed easily.

Her pride rebelled at the thought that she might be just another helplessly adoring pawn in his hands. "I'll jog around the car to keep my blood from freezing before I'll let you cradle me like a child," she flung at him.

He grinned mockingly at her hauteur. "You're like a rogue thoroughbred that's had its own way for too long. I think it's time you were tamed, Holly Mac-Knight."

His hand shot out and gripped her wrist. Then he pulled her to his hard body, and a second later she felt the thick woolen lining of his jacket enveloping her and his strong arms wound about her back.

Arif's warmth invaded her like a powerful soothing drug, and she became acutely aware of his beating heart and the clean exotic scent of him. There was no reality then but that of her thighs, stomach and breasts molded to his masculine form, all muscle and bone and uncompromising strength. The bitter cold and the fears she had experienced a moment earlier gave way to a slow flickering surge of desire, as the

simple instinct for survival joined an equally primitive force of physical need.

Holly felt that the loneliness and danger of the
stark landscape would be kept at bay as long as she
could feel Arif's arms wrapped around her, his cheek
bent to her fair windblown hair. They had stood that
way for several minutes, each reluctant to break the
primitive spell that bound them, when a distant
sound gradually invaded their hearing. Holly was at
once perplexed and startled as the barely discernible
rhythmic thud became punctuated with the melodi-
ous jingling of bells.

She was about to raise her head to look at Arif
with questioning eyes when she felt the low rumble of
laughter rippling upward from his diaphragm.
"What's so funny?" she demanded curiously.

"If my ears don't deceive me, Holly, rescue is on
the way from an unexpected source," he whispered
down to her, his eyes sparkling with laughter.

As the sound grew more deafening behind them,
Holly's face registered perplexed astonishment.
"Good grief, those are hooves—it sounds like a
thousand of them!" She imagined cattle thundering
on a Wyoming plain as the laconic weather-beaten
cowboys herded them toward new pastures. "Cattle
herdsmen?" she asked aloud.

"You're very astute, Holly," Arif grinned down at
her, "though I don't know if this is quite what you
imagined." He half turned then so that Holly had a
clear view beyond his right shoulder.

His deep laughter mingled with her gasp of astonishment as she regarded the swiftly moving scene of

cloaked figures astride camels and the scores of sheep and goats, bells madly jangling against their throats as they crossed the hard brown earth. "Who are they?" Holly asked at last, her arms tightening subconsciously about Arif's waist as if to seek protection from the approaching horde.

"Kurdish nomads," Arif replied succinctly, his gaze fixed not on her but on the whorls of dust kicked up by the galloping hooves.

"Your mother's people?" she asked in a hushed voice.

"Of the same blood," Arif acknowledged with a curt nod.

Holly had begun to speak again when the words were drowned by the nomads' approach and the mad barking of their dogs as they attempted to keep the herds tightly bunched. The riders came to an abrupt halt fifteen yards from the highway and silently regarded the stranded travelers. Then, after what had seemed an eternity to Holly, one of the men urged his animal forward onto the weathered asphalt and slowly approached them. The sharp clack of the camel's hooves against the road surface sounded unnaturally loud in Holly's ears, and she could not quite conceal the shiver of apprehension that swept over her.

Arif gave her shoulders a quick reassuring squeeze before releasing her and turning to face the man. The two spoke for several minutes, and it became apparent even to Holly's untutored ears that the harsh guttural intonations of the words had nothing in common with the softly voweled harmony of the Turkish language. They were speaking in Kurdish.

When Arif drew his forefinger across his throat in an all-too-descriptive gesture, Holly knew that he was making an impolite reference to the car rental agent in Erzurum. The nomad made a swift reply and laughed, revealing a row of strong tobacco-stained teeth above the gray stubble of his chin. He turned and repeated the little interchange to his fellow tribesmen, and a ghostly echo of his laughter rippled along the line of them.

Holly took advantage of the moment to whisper hurriedly to Arif, "What's going on?"

"We're in luck. He knows my mother's tribal lineage, and the two groups aren't at odds with each other," he explained.

"And if they had been?" Holly inquired soberly, still feeling quite apprehensive about this unexpected meeting with the wild-looking Kurds.

Arif grinned and raised his shoulders in an eloquent shrug. "Who knows? They might have left us here to our own fate."

"But we aren't going with them!" Holly countered in disbelief.

"What choice do we have?" Arif replied. "The little dead mouse will squeak no more, as our Kurdish host observed so wittily about the bloody car."

"Well, if I have any say in the matter, I think I'd prefer to stand guard over the mouse's corpse," Holly retorted dryly.

"You *don't* have any say. I've already accepted the headman's offer of hospitality, and as a dutiful Turkish wife you have no choice but to obey my wishes."

"Wife!" she blazed. "What the devil are you talking about, Arif?"

He gripped her shoulders fiercely, all traces of amusement erased from his harsh visage. "Listen to me well, Holly. In this part of the world no respectable woman would travel unchaperoned with a man not her husband. These people follow an ancient, carefully circumscribed moral code. If in their eyes that code is broken, they'll mete out punishment in their own fashion. I had to say it for your own protection."

Holly attempted to wriggle free of his viselike grip. "I'm sick to death of your trying to protect me!" she cried furiously. "You're...."

But her angry protests were cut short as Arif swooped her up into his arms and into the high boxy saddle atop a kneeling camel whose reins were patiently held by a young boy.

"Do I make myself clear?" Arif repeated as he took the reins and handed them to Holly. "For the duration of our stay with this Kurdish tribe, you are my wife!"

Before she could reply, he had thwacked the animal on the rump and its long legs unfolded in an ungainly rocking motion that caught her unawares and nearly pitched her forward over the beast's head. As the camel hurried forward to join its companions, Holly risked a quick glance over her shoulder. Arif stood in the roadway before the defunct automobile, his arms crossed stubbornly before him and his dark eyebrows drawn together in a brooding frown.

Despite her lingering anger, she was overcome by a

sharp fear that he would be left behind, and was greatly relieved when a moment later the boy rushed up with an animal for Arif. He removed their suitcases from the car and affixed them to the rear of the saddle before climbing easily onto the camel's back. When Holy turned around again, she found herself in the midst of the Kurdish women, who regarded her with forthright, unabashedly curious eyes.

Her discomfort at being the center of such avid curiosity was short-lived, however, as the caravan set off once again across the thin scrub of the plateau and her attention was focused completely on adjusting her balance to the camel's stiff lumbering gait.

The Asiatic winds blew ceaselessly over the dry tableland, but with the exertion of riding the unfamiliar animal Holly felt warmer than she had in the tiny automobile they had left abandoned by the roadside. Surprisingly quickly, Holly found herself adjusting to the gait and was even able to relax a little.

The men rode ahead, driving their large herd in a close wedge before them. Holly rode far behind with the women, their pace slowed by the enormous rolls that their mounts carried. When she glanced at them from time to time she caught a glimpse of bright colors beneath their darkly woven cloaks, and she felt her own curiosity growing. In the distance she could just pick out the figure of Arif astride one of the quicker animals. If he'd worn a woolen cloak rather than his well-tailored suede coat he would have been indistinguishable from the wild fierce Kurds with whom he rode.

As the caravan moved inexorably eastward, Holly

felt dwarfed by the immense vistas beckoning to them from the Asian horizon. The bleak austerity of the plateau was broken only rarely by the profile of a rammed-earth hut against the white haze of the distant Taurus mountains falling away to the south in ridges and domes. As her eyes absorbed the landscape with its occasional intrusion by Anatolian peasants, Holly came to appreciate the Turks' and the Persians' fascination with miniature art. In this vast terrain, men seemed dwarfed almost to insignificance: they were minuscule figures moving against a tremendous unchanging panorama.

Holly laughed to herself then at her philosophical musings, and she shook her head until her honey-blond hair streamed freely behind her in the wind. Much as she hated to admit it, she had begun to enjoy the ride tremendously. Arif and his insistence on their charade of man and wife be damned! For the moment at least, she felt incredibly free with neither past nor future to bind her: no jilted fiancé in Philadelphia; no angry manipulative father awaiting her return to Istanbul. She longed to banish, as well, the passionate aching love that had engulfed her, but her feelings for Arif had driven themselves too deeply within the core of her. The past and future of those twined emotions imprisoned her: the joy of loving him now and the searing pain of knowing that inevitably she would have to give him up. Aware of the Kurdish women's eyes upon her as she shook her head, Holly blinked back the hot tears that had welled up and set her features haughtily.

They rode on for hours. The sky had deepened to

bronze and umber and a few stars had begun to wink in the vast dome above their heads, but still they kept up the pace. It wasn't until a slender white crescent moon hung low in the night sky that the women caught up with the men, who'd already dismounted, put their flocks out to rest and pasture for the night and set the dogs to guard them.

One by one as the women rode up, they made curious clucking noises with their tongues and the camels would rock gently to their knees so their riders could dismount. Eager to exchange gossip and conversation after the long day of traveling, the women tossed their cloaks over the saddles and jabbered excitedly among themselves as they loosened the enormous rolls from the camels' backs.

Holly watched in fascination as vast sheets of leather, brightly woven carpets and iron cooking pots tumbled in neat array from the rolls. She attempted to imitate their clucking sound to her own beast, but he apparently was deaf to her command. Holly was beginning to feel rather discomfited by this state of affairs when the women suddenly ceased their happy jabberings and looked at her. They giggled briefly at her plight, though Holly sensed their laughter wasn't unkind. A young girl rushed over then and jerked on the animal's turquoise-studded bridle until he sank submissively to the ground.

After she had disengaged herself from the elaborate saddle, Holly turned around to find herself surrounded by a blaze of color. The Kurdish women, stately in bearing and nearly as tall as she, pressed forward, and she returned their fascinated stares measure for measure. They were dressed in incredibly colorful Gypsy fashion, with layers of flounced petticoats over silk bloomers and elaborate balloon sleeves flowing from their blouses. Their hair was dressed in pigtails, with beads and cowrie shells intricately woven into each braid.

A woman's silver bangles chimed noisily as she reached out to stroke Holly's long blond hair, and it was almost as if the sound were a signal for the others to begin a lively tactile exploration of their own. Hands reached out to her fair skin and to the down-filled parka, while other fingers admired the ribbed twill of her soft beige corduroy jeans and the fine leather of her boots. Holly feared that she would be drowned in a sea of bright silk and flowered cretonne, but the women backed off immediately at the sound of a curt male command. She recognized the voice of the gray-chinned man who had come forward to address Arif on the highway; evidently his word was law.

Holly was relieved to see Arif approaching her from the milling circle of camels. He grinned, and she couldn't help wondering if her feelings were written so blatantly across her face.

"Don't you like camels?" he asked with a mocking air.

"They're disgusting—long heads, little ears, tough-skinned lips. And they've got big flat feet!" Holly replied, annoyed with herself, yet half laughing at her own bitter tirade.

"But everything you mentioned represents an adaptation to desert life. They really are incredible animals. They have valvelike nostrils lined with hairs to protect them from flying sand, they don't need much water to survive and they can carry more than five hundred pounds on their backs. They might not be as attractive as a woman, but they're worth considerably more," he added, his dark eyes gleaming with mischief.

If it had been his intent to needle Holly with that remark, he more than succeeded. Her eyes flashed in return like emerald pinpoints in the darkness. "Is that so?" she answered swiftly. "Then maybe you should marry a female camel and be certain of getting good value for your money! And if she can jump a show course, you won't need Sinjon, either," she added tartly.

"I appreciate your emphasis on practicality," he replied with an equable air. "Perhaps you know my needs better than I myself do."

Holly sensed the subtle mockery in his even retort and, angered by it, continued her verbal sniping. "You could go on tour with your trained dromedary."

"Actually, that isn't quite accurate," he needled, catching the corner of his bottom lip between his teeth to keep from grinning. "Dromedaries are single-humped camels from Arabia. These double-humped creatures we've been riding today are called Bactrians; they're native to central Asia."

Holly regarded him in disbelief. "I don't give a damn!" she exploded at last.

He shrugged innocently. "You were the one who seemed to want to discuss the practical merits of camels."

"I don't care if I ever see another of these lumpy beasts. I came out here with you to talk horses, not camels," she informed him caustically.

"Ah, yes—Jinniyah. You would have ridden her tonight if fate hadn't intervened. Life has been throwing a lot of curves at you lately, hasn't it, Holly?" he observed with sardonic humor.

She looked up sharply at that gibe but decided to ignore it. "How far are we from Kars anyway?" she asked. "Do we walk the rest of the way?"

"You'd just be stubborn enough to try it, wouldn't you?" he demanded.

"What do you mean?" Her eyes widened in perplexity.

"Kars is thirty miles from here over the same kind of hostile terrain we crossd today. It's populated by nothing but eagles and gray wolves," Arif explained bluntly.

"Wolves?"

"Haven't you noticed the spiked collars around the necks of the Kurds' dogs? Possession of a sheep or goat is often hotly contested with a hungry pack of wolves."

Holly shuddered at the harsh matter-of-factness of his tone. "I had no idea we were so far from...civilization," she observed quietly. "Where will we stay tonight?"

"Here, of course."

"Here!" she echoed in disbelief. It was only then that she glanced about her and saw with a sense of shock that a village of sorts had materialized while she and Arif were engaging in their caustic battle of wits.

A half-dozen cone-shaped leather tents were ranged behind them, forming a pavilion where several bright fires leaped and flickered cozily against the darkness. She saw the women moving with efficiency and dispatch as they prepared the evening meal, and the scent of roasting kid wafted past her on the wind.

Holly whirled back to face Arif as he taunted her once again. "What's happened to that sense of adventure you were boasting of earlier today?"

She lifted her chin angrily before retorting, "I suppose it died with the 'mouse' back on Route 20."

"You're full of clever wit, aren't you, Holly?"

"No match for your cleverness, Arif," she mocked him. "I suppose this means we'll have to carry on the ridiculous charade of man and wife."

His hand shot out and he gripped her chin so forcefully that she almost cried out in pain. "I am sorry that the idea of being my wife is so repulsive to you, Holly," he muttered between clenched teeth, "but those are the ground rules that we agreed to."

"I never agreed to them," Holly shot back rebelliously.

"Nevertheless, you'll play by them." The words were a terse command.

"I dislike subterfuge," she replied, her green eyes raking his angry features.

"I'm sorry the world does not hold to your naive rules." He turned from her then and swiftly strode away.

Holly felt the tears of rage and frustration stinging her eyelids. *No, Arif,* she swore silently at his retreating back, *you don't understand. It's not the idea of*

being your wife that I hate—it's the painful irony of
having to pretend!

THE HEADMAN'S TENT was surprisingly large and
comfortable, which was a good thing, since all
twenty-five tribesmen from toothless grandmother to
the smallest infant had gathered inside to share a
feast in honor of their guests.

The roast kid and saffron rice, eaten with the fingers and washed down with a salted buttermilk-like
liquid called *ayran*, had been delicious. There was little conversation during the meal, and it was apparent
to Holly that everyone was as ravenous as she after a
long day's fast on their cross-country journey. Arif
had explained to her that the nomadic herdsmen had
left their mountain homeland a week earlier in search
of winter pasturage at lower altitudes for their flocks.
It was a lucky coincidence that the Kurds had crossed
their path at the highway and that they were traveling
in roughly the same direction.

Holly had leaned back against the rose cretonne
cushions and was idly tracing a pattern on the beautifully woven *kilim* upon which they sat when the
headman, Al-Carifni, made a quick gesture with his
hands. The women rose swiftly and cleared the com-
munal dining pots from the rug. Only then did he
clear his throat to speak. It was apparent that he was
directing a barrage of questions at Arif, who answered swiftly and with no lack of wit—if the smiles
on the Kurdish tribesmen's faces were any indication.

There was a break in the conversation as small
gourd cups filled with tea were passed around, and

Holly took advantage of the lull to ask Arif for a quick translation.

"They were praising my choice of a wife, as a matter of fact," Arif whispered back to her, his lips twisting briefly in an ironic grin. "They told me that they approve of mingling bloodlines, and they asked me if you were a Circassian."

"What did you tell them?" Holly inquired with narrowed eyes.

"I told them that you were."

"More subterfuge?" she whispered in return, her gaze silently condemning.

"These people are extremely devout Muslims. Why should I shock them by introducing a blond foreigner into their midst?" he replied with impatience.

"Infidel, don't you mean to say? *Gävur?*" Holly's eyes danced fire.

"Stop being such a bloody hellion," Arif whispered back with mounting impatience. "Neither have I told them that I'm a captain in the Turkish Army. These are fierce Kurdish patriots, and they have long volatile memories. They remember the Turks' brutal suppression of their independence movement fifty years ago as if it were yesterday. I don't want to take the chance that they'll slit both our throats and leave us as carrion for vultures."

"I'm sure that you're grossly exaggerating."

"Am I?" he replied evenly. "Remember, Holly, that these people are part of my heritage. I know them. There is a popular legend that the tribes of Kurdistan are descended from four hundred virgins who, while en route to Solomon's court, were ravaged by devils. They are a proud, wild highland race.''

Holly shivered as she recalled her own experience with Arif's brief outbursts of rage. In those moments she could easily have imagined him a spawn of the devil!

Al-Carifni interrupted their private conversation, and although she did not understand the words, Holly guessed that the testy headman was demanding a translation of the conversation that had passed between ''husband'' and ''wife.'' And when she heard their explosive fierce roar of approval, she knew Arif had told them that he'd explained to Holly the origins of the Kurdish race.

Once the samovar of tea and the after-dinner conversation had been exhausted, a few of the women pulled out musical instruments and began to pluck at them. One, the *saz*, was carved out of a single length of maple wood and plucked with a small implement that fitted the finger, while the other instrument, which Arif called a *ud*, closely resembled a Western guitar.

The music, with its repetitive atonal melody, sounded strange to Holly's ears, but evidently it struck a deep responsive chord in the other listeners, who by tacit agreement moved back to the farthest edges of the thick colorful carpet to make room for a dancer. Within a few minutes a graceful young girl clad in flowing shalvar trousers and a shirred silk bodice slipped into their midst and unselfconsciously began to dance, clicking out a swift rhythm with the pair of *kasik oyunu*, or castanets, fastened to her fingertips.

Holly recognized her as the same youngster who had hurried to her assistance early in the evening when the recalcitrant camel refused to kneel for her to dismount.

"Aren't the dancers required to wear veils?" she asked Arif in a low whisper.

"You are confusing Kurds with Turks. The Kurdish women have never worn the veil. They are surprisingly independent and often have a powerful say in community life."

As her gaze took in the mass of wavy jet black hair and the dark almond-shaped eyes, Holly turned to Arif again and whispered, "She is an incredibly lovely child!"

"She would be a child in your culture, Holly, but here she is already a woman," Arif whispered crisply. "She is betrothed to one of the tribesmen and will be married within the month. Her name is Carim, and Al-Carifni is her father."

Holly's expressive features registered shock. "Married! But she can't be more than thirteen."

"She's only young by your standards," Arif reminded her once again. His eyes played over her speculatively before he added, "Al-Carifni was curious, by the way, as to why our marriage hadn't yet produced any offspring."

"I'm sure you came up with some witty reply, captain," Holly retorted dryly.

His eyes gleamed with mischief as he raised his shoulders in an almost imperceptible shrug. "I told him that it was not for want of trying. Then our host wished us a fruitful night in his guest tent."

Holly's cheeks blushed scarlet at this badinage. It had not occurred to her until that moment that the logical progression of their masquerade as a married couple would be their sharing of the same bed!

"Damn you, Arif!" she swore at him under her breath. "As far as I'm concerned, the charade is over. I hope you have a comfortable night under the stars with the camels."

She rose swiftly from the rug and inclined her head graciously to their host before leaving the tent. As she left, she felt Arif's angry eyes boring into her back, but she didn't care what the others thought.

The air was sharp, clear and brutally cold after the close atmosphere of Al-Carifni's tent, but Holly drank it in gratefully. She drew the dark cloak that one of the Kurdish women had loaned her more tightly around her shoulders and glanced about the "pavilion" that only a few hours before had been nothing but open scrubland. Above, the sky was ablaze with stars, reminding her of diamonds scattered casually on a dark velvet cushion.

As she stared around her, Holly realized that she had no idea which tent she should go to. She started to walk across the clearing when a light touch on her arm caused her to whirl around and she found herself staring down into the dark friendly eyes of the young girl who had danced so beautifully in her father's tent.

"Hello," Holly said with a smile, wishing fervently that she'd asked Arif for a lesson in Kurdish.

The child Carim smiled in return and indicated with a graceful gesture of her arm that Holly should

follow her. Holly had thought that she was being led
to a place for her to sleep until the tent flap was
pushed aside and they stepped into a large enclosure
where several women sat companionably about a
rug, sewing and talking. Their voluble chatter ceased
momentarily as they regarded the newcomers in the
doorway; then it became apparent that they had
begun to tease Carim good-naturedly. The child
swept past them regally and led Holly to an open
chest filled with handwoven clothes and rugs.

Through intricate sign language Holly was finally
made to understand that the girl had woven all the
articles herself and that they formed part of her wedding trousseau. Holly shook her head in wonder-
ment, exclaiming to the girl after each item was
proudly displayed, "Beautiful!"

Although the word itself was incomprehensible,
the meaning was made abundantly clear by Holly's
eyes. After a while the girl reached out and delicately
touched Holly's gold knot earrings, enunciating carefully, "Boo-ti-ful."

The other women in the tent who'd been watching
the interchange interestedly erupted in gales of laughter at that, and an impish but pleased grin wreathed
Carim's pretty features.

On impulse Holly reached up and slipped the
pierced rings from her lobes. She placed them in the
girl's hand and closed her fist gently over them, indicating to her that they were a gift.

Carim's eyes widened in delight and she dropped
the regal pose of womanhood to race happily around
the tent, showing the women her precious baubles.

Then she came back around to the open chest, rummaged briefly in the bottom and triumphantly pulled out a pair of her own earrings. They seemed almost incongruously modern in their simplicity—two triangular-shaped wedges of jade, smoothed and polished to a high sheen. Carim lifted them and slipped the rings into Holly's earlobes.

The women swiftly gathered around and made soft clucking sounds of approval, gesturing from the earrings to Holly's eyes in delight at the close similarity in intensity of color.

Five minutes later the intriguing social visit was over, and Holly sat alone in the guest tent to which Carim had led her. The floor of the leather enclosure was covered with rugs, in the center of which were several quilts and blankets piled neatly with embroidered pillows. Folded at the base of the colorful bedroll was a white sheepskin rug, while next to it a small oil lamp flickered dimly. Arif's and Holly's suitcases had been set just inside the front opening.

Holly had pulled off her dusty clothing and slipped into a filmy white muslin nightgown with a gathered boat neck. It was a little too roomy, however, and persisted in slipping down over one shoulder. She brushed her hair with long vigorous strokes, feeling her stomach contract into a tight knot each time she heard the soft crunch of footsteps beyond the tent flap. Her nerves were on edge, and she expected Arif to stride into the enclosure at any moment—arrogant, scornful and mocking her modesty and her virtue.

But he never came, and the camp gradually subsided into a deep still silence. Holly, too, had begun to relax and feel her eyelids grow heavy with sleep when a bleating sound from the roped corral behind the tents intruded on the night's peacefulness. A moment later a low rumbling growl from one of the dog's throats mingled with the sheep's anxious cry.

Holly withdrew her hand from the brass knob of the oil lamp she had been about to extinguish and sat up erect on the bed's edge. A capricious draft of wind had found its way through the ventilation opening in the ceiling of the tent, and the lamp flickered a second before the air touched her bare shoulders with icy fingers. A cold shiver of apprehension racked her then as her alert ears picked up another, more distant sound.

It was a wild and melancholy howling, high-pitched keening notes interweaving and gliding past one another. Holly tried to tell herself that it was only the wind whipped to greater frenzy as the night deepened, but she remembered Arif's blunt description of gray wolves on the plateau stalking the herdsmen's flocks. She shivered uncontrollably as mingled feelings of fear, cold, desolation and loneliness swept over her.

A stealthy movement of the tent flap caused her to whirl around swiftly, and as she did so her foot brushed the burning oil lamp. She lunged to right the sooty glass cylinder, heedless of the loose neckline of her gown, which had fallen low over her left arm. When she looked to the doorway again, she saw that Arif stood just inside of it.

"I'm sorry, Holly," he muttered. "I thought you

would have been asleep by now." As if to belie his stiff apology, Arif's eyes slowly brushed her pale naked shoulders and precariously covered breasts like a smoldering fan of fire, and her own heightened senses leaped instinctively in response.

Gone were the coldness and desolation that had threatened to overwhelm her a moment earlier. He was here; no harm would come to her.

With great reluctance Arif tore his devouring gaze away from her and moved swiftly toward his duffel bag, which lay next to the bed beside Holly's more elegant gray leather luggage. "I came only to get extra clothing from my bag. You were right to chastise me earlier," he began curtly. "You must forgive me, as well, for dragging you into this situation in the first place." It was obvious that the apology had cost him a tremendous amount of effort. Holly guessed that he was accustomed to backing down to no one, and the fact that he was making the effort now touched her deeply.

When she replied, her voice was soft and filled with amusement. "Why apologize, Arif, for giving me a once-in-a-lifetime experience? I'm sure that fifty years from now I'll be telling my grandchildren how I traveled on camelback with Kurdish nomads!"

Arif glanced up at her swiftly, his gaze drawn to the sparkling pinpoints of laughter in her eyes. His lips, which had been drawn into a tautly compressed slash beneath the full black mustache, curved upward in a tentative grin, and he reached into his pocket and retrieved a large linen handkerchief. "You do, in fact, look like a woman of the steppes. With that smudge of soot on your cheek, I would have guessed that it was you who'd cooked the evening meal over the charcoal!'' he teased, laughing softly as he leaned forward and rubbed the handkerchief with a brisk motion over her cheek.

He caught sight of the polished jade triangles against her earlobes then, and with gentle fingers he pushed her hair back from her face. ''They *have* made you into a nomad's woman,'' he breathed, his thumbs lightly caressing the shadowed hollow of her throat. ''The stones match your eyes. . .those incredibly beautiful green eyes.''

A wicked rivulet of desire crept down her spine, threatening to ignite her entire body. The soft caress of his words and the strong sensual touch of his fingers against her skin were like an enkindling match. Her full lips half parted in anticipation and Arif did not disappoint her.

His mouth swooped down upon hers like an eagle devouring its prey, at once savage and swift. His tongue explored the moist inner flesh of her lip, then invaded the sweet well of her mouth. The kiss became demanding, invasive, an exquisite thrust of passion that left her breathless and trembling. She was frightened by its intensity, yet her own wantonly responsive mouth demanded more.

It was with a cold sense of shock that she realized he was pushing her away so violently that her head fell back against the embroidered cushions. ''No!'' he whispered, rising swiftly from his crouched stance beside the low bed. ''I must go now while I have some shred of will left. I will not have you accuse me of rape in the morning," he muttered with caustic bitterness. "Whether you choose to believe it or not, I am a man of honor."

He moved with feral grace across the enclosure, his virile body taut with leashed passion. His hand already had pushed open the tent flap and he would have stridden pridefully into the night, but her voice—husky with need—held him back.

"Arif. Don't leave me alone." She rose from the quilts and stood defiantly before the lamp, unaware that its flickering light cast her breasts and hips in exquisitely detailed outline beneath the filmy muslin of her gown.

The winter wind crept in through the gap in the tent opening, ruffling her hair and the gauzy hem of her gown and sliding upward along her bare limbs like icy tendrils. But she did not notice.

Arif stared at her as if transfixed, his eyes devouring every inch of her naked flesh silhouetted in the dim light.

Again she murmured his name. "Arif...I need you."

He let the tent flap fall closed and slowly he turned to face her. "Your lips are blue with cold," he taunted softly. "You don't need me. You crave my animal warmth."

She shook her head slowly, her eyes aglint with a somberly beautiful iridescence. "You stubborn idiot. I want...I need your love."

He crossed the thickly carpeted ground in two long strides, and his fingers dug with controlled savagery into her naked shoulders. "Holly, I want from you what no other woman can give me, but you are exquisite torture. We are both destined to be hurt."

"I'm willing to take that chance, Arif," she whispered up to him with passionate force.

"Damn it, Holly," he swore angrily, "my duty would have been so simple if you hadn't come into my life."

"But I *am* here, Arif." She lifted her hands to his face and gently traced his stubborn jawline.

"Yes, I know." His laughter was at once rueful and caressing. "Never have I been so burningly aware of a fact in my life."

His hands slid downward over her waist and thighs, cupping their fullness as he drew her roughly against his hard male body. "I am a dutiful man," he muttered hoarsely, his eyes boring into hers like chips of obsidian. "But I am, after all, a man before all else."

He reached up and ripped the flimsy gown from her body with one quick movement. Then he kissed her mouth, her hair, her closed eyelids, while his hands moved wantonly along her satiny trembling flesh. He cupped the engorged fullness of her breasts and lowered his mouth to them, drinking in their sweetness as if they were ripe melons.

Licking tongues of flame spread outward from her loins as he eased her down upon the bed. Swiftly he pulled off his own clothes until he stood naked before her, his muscular body gleaming in the dim light like a bronze sculpture of an ancient warrior. He lay down beside her, and her eyes drank in the splendid animal vitality of him.

With fingers at once shy and inquisitive she explored the rippling umber expanse of muscle and sinew, shuddering with mingled fear and delight as his head and shoulders rose above her. Instinctively she lifted her hips to his with sweetly aching need.

"Holly," he whispered, "you are passion, love...." He groaned with mingled despair and feral exultation. "You are life itself."

His lovemaking was at once gentle and savage, a powerful languorous rhythm that unlocked a depth of passion she had never known existed. Her body arched and curved beneath his like the inverted bells of the lotus. She felt her senses opening like the tropical flower, a slow unfolding of exquisite sweetness yearning toward fulfillment. Holly's fingers dug into Arif's powerfully corded back, and the tempo of their joined bodies became a swift joyous onrush of shared ecstasy. He lifted her hips and her hidden depths pulsated with heightened fire until she felt herself carried toward an explosion of fire-red sparks that left in its wake a deep contentment and blissful obliteration of logic and reason.

He lay down beside her, breathing huskily. Holly pressed her lips to his wide shoulder, reveling in the way her slender hip fit into the curve of his work-scarred palm. He caressed her with exquisite gentleness, as if she were an unschooled yearling, eager and uncertain, his fingers gliding easily along her perspiration-slicked body.

She lifted her head to regard him. "Arif, dearest, I love...."

But he pressed his fingers to her lips, which were

dark and swollen from the devouring hunger of his kisses. "Don't say it," he whispered almost harshly. "Morning will be here all too soon, and this night is best forgotten."

Her eyes gleamed like the polished jade in her ear-lobes. "I will never forget it."

"Nor will I." The words were wrenched from him as if they were a bitter curse.

A lurking gust of arctic wind crept into the tent and extinguished the flickering lamplight, but not before Holly had glimpsed the troubled depths underlying the passion that still smoldered in his wide dark eyes.

CHAPTER TEN

HOLLY LAY ON HER STOMACH like a child, fair hair tumbled over her face, which was burrowed deeply in the colorful mound of pillows. Distant shouts and a vaguely familiar bleating sound invaded her wakening senses, and she opened her eyes slowly. A shallow depression in the quilts marked the outline of where Arif had lain beside her. Reaching out to touch the spot, she found that it was still warm.

Memories of the previous night washed over her like a surging flood tide, and she became acutely aware of her nakedness beneath the warm protective nest of blankets. Slowly she rolled over, blinking her sleep-heavy eyes against the gray shaft of light that penetrated the shadowy interior of the tent.

Arif stood before the rolled-back doorway, his gaze fixed on some distant point beyond Holly's vision. He wore a faded pair of jeans slung low over his narrow hips and a pair of square-toed black boots, scuffed and comfortable-looking. His broad torso was bare, and Holly allowed her imagination to run rampant through the curling mat of black hairs that grew scrublike over the sinewy hardness of his chest and abdomen.

"Good morning," she called out at last, softly.

He turned away from the tent opening and came to stand beside the bed. "It's daylight already, and the Kurds will soon be on the move again. You had better get up."

Holly regarded him for a long moment in silence. His features were cold and shuttered, and she could not believe he was the same man who had loved and caressed her the night before, lifting her to sweet heights of ecstasy. She sat up, drawing the sheep's-wool throw modestly about her. She felt suddenly shy and vulnerable before this man who seemed almost a stranger. "Where do we go from here?" she asked quietly at last.

"Across the last thirty miles of barren plain to Kars."

Holly shook her head. "That's not what I meant, Arif."

He ran his fingers impatiently through his thick black hair and sat down on the edge of the bed, his eyes flickering over her almost angrily. "What do you want me to say, Holly? You know where we stood from the start. I have never lied to you."

"But, Arif, didn't last night change anything?"

"Nothing has changed." His answer was stark in its finality, almost brutal.

"What about the words you whispered to me last night?" The softly spoken question was underscored by the green sparks of defiance in her gaze. "All lies, Arif?"

"No!" The single word was a pained exclamation, as if torn from him against his will. He reached out and touched her cheek, gently brushing away the strands of burnished gold hair that tumbled across it. "I cannot marry for love, Holly MacKnight—you know that. But that will not stop me from loving."

"You refuse to consider marriage to me because I am a *gâvur*?" she challenged hurtfully.

To her surprise his lips twisted briefly in a bitter grin. "You've learned that one Turkish word so well that you are beginning to sound like a broken language-lesson tape that repeats itself endlessly. Your preoccupation with it is blinding you to the real truth. Religion has nothing to do with the matter." He stood up from the bed then, as if to signal an end to the conversation, and pulled on his shirt.

But stubbornly she would not drop it. "What, then?" she demanded.

He turned back from the tent opening to regard her. "It is pointless to discuss it with you. Nothing will change."

"But you love me?"

He was gone, however, not heeding or not hearing the desperate challenge she had flung at him. The tent flap stood ajar, ushering in an icy dawn wind that caused her to shudder with cold. She rose and dressed quickly.

Holly drank *ayran* from a leather flask that one of the Kurdish women had handed her and watched in fascination as the rugs and pillows were efficiently rolled into compact bundles. The tent in which she and Arif had so briefly shared love was the last to come down. The supporting reeds and stakes were pulled free, and the heavy brown rectangle of leather was rolled up with the rest. Within the span of five

minutes, the stony windswept tableland had reverted
to its natural state of empty desolation. Holly had to
choke back the tears that rose in her throat. Staring
out over the bleak unpopulated terrain, she found it
all too easy to imagine that the previous night had
never happened at all.

The long journey over the cold arid plateau was a
repetition of the previous day's adventure, with nothing but an occasional cultivated field or the tenuous
melody of a shepherd's pipe wafting on the wind to
break the gray monotony of the nomads' trek.

It was midafternoon by the time they reached the
environs of Kars, with its surrounding fields lying
brown and fallow and its granaries full to bursting
with wheat and barley. On the outskirts of one such
farm, Arif and Holly parted company with their Kurdish rescuers amid a dignified, highly formalized
leave-taking of handshakes and avowals of friendship. A third-class bus rumbled along soon afterward, and they completed the last leg of their journey
into town amid the cacophony of squawking chick-
ens, squalling babies and the blare of the driver's
radio.

Like Erzurum a few hundred miles to the west,
Kars was a frontier town, though the harshness was
relieved by its intriguing medieval picturesqueness.
Holly pressed her nose to the windowpane to catch a
better glimpse of the ancient Georgian fort that
seemed to guard the city still from its craggy heights
above the Kars River.

After he had cornered a young boy and sent him
running off on an errand, Arif led Holly into a bright

café with French bistrolike windows overlooking the street. While they waited for the tea and plate of *baklava* pastries to be served, a young peddler stopped in front of their table and offered to spray them with one of the many scents arrayed in tiny flacons in his box. Holly smiled a good-natured refusal, and he went off in search of other customers for his unique service.

"You know," Holly began, laughing still. "I get the feeling that if you sat in a Turkish café long enough, you'd be offered all the services you would ever need in this world—instant photos, shoe shines, flowers, magazines, even a spray of cologne. Amazing!"

Arif grinned at her astonishment, and Holly sensed that he had begun to relax. "Most women would be more annoyed than amused, but then you are not like most women, Holly!" He lifted the lukewarm cup of tea in front of him to his lips and tossed it back as if it were a shot of *raki*, his eyes never leaving her face.

He was about to say something more when they were approached yet again by another itinerant peddler, this one an old woman arrayed in colorful Gypsy attire. Her Paisley shawl was half draped over a small cage that held a pigeon.

He would have waved her away impatiently, but Holly extended her hand to his arm. She found something intriguing about the old Gypsy. "Wait, Arif. What service is she peddling?"

"The woman is a fortune-teller," he explained. "In exchange for a few grains of corn, her pigeon will choose colored slips of paper from which she can read the stars."

Holly grinned mischievously as she drew several *kuru* coins from the pocket of her jacket and slipped them into the old woman's palm. "This is one experience I can't pass up—having my fortune read by a Turkish Gypsy who has a pigeon for an assistant, no less! Will you please translate?"

Arif inclined his head in amusement. "Your wish is my command."

Once the woman realized she had a customer, she dropped her humble fawning manner and put on a serious, almost intense demeanor. She lifted a strand of Holly's hair and held it for a moment, then the colored bits of paper were laid out on the table, the corn was scattered, and mistress and pigeon set to work.

"There is a dark rugged-looking man in your life who will change it forever," Arif translated, his lips curving in a sardonic grin. "Don't these Gypsies ever add anything new to their repertoires?"

"I can do without your commentary," Holly chided laughingly. "What else does she say?"

"Another man awaits you in Istanbul with riches. He will dominate your life if you let him."

Holly stared at the old woman intently, and she felt goose bumps rising on her neck as she pictured her father's angry set features.

The pigeon picked up a blue strip, then a scrap of yellow.

"What else?" Holly demanded quietly, her gaze fixed on the old Gypsy's deep-set black eyes.

"There is much troubling you now, but you will win your heart's desire if you are clever and strong.

And, of course, the inevitable finishing touch," Arif concluded. "You will marry a rich man—the jilted fiancé in Philadelphia, perhaps?"

Suddenly his teasing rankled her. As the old Gypsy packed up the accoutrements of her trade and hobbled away, Holly leaned across the table and asked with cool flippancy, "Are you by any chance rich, Captain Hakal?"

His answering laughter was low and filled with gentle mockery. "I admire your tenacity, Holly MacKnight. You don't give up anything without a fight. In some ways we are very much alike."

Their thorny tête-à-tête was interrupted as a tall rangy man in rumpled wool trousers and what looked to be an army-surplus parka approached their table. "Captain Hakal?" he inquired, putting out his hand as Arif stood up. "I'm Bill Schneider, one of the Peace Corps docs working with Samsun Ezine. He got your message from the kid about wanting to borrow his jeep. He was tied up with a patient so he asked me to drop the keys off."

As the young American doctor talked, his eyes roamed again and again to Holly's features.

Arif made a curt introduction. "Dr. Schneider, this is Holly MacKnight."

Without waiting for an invitation, the American pulled up a chair and sat down, leaning his elbows on the table. "Hi, Holly. What brings a fellow American like you to these parts? Kars isn't exactly on the tourist track."

Holly gave him a friendly smile, immediately charmed by his engaging blue eyes and the unruly shock of brown hair that fell across his forehead, giving him a boyish look. "I've come to look at one of Captain Hakal's horses. We're both competitors in a riding event in Istanbul," she explained.

"That's just terrific," he replied, although Holly had the vague impression he hadn't heard a word she'd said. His eyes were roving over her eyes and lips, until she began to feel at once amused and discomfited by his almost hungry perusal.

"You...you must find it fascinating to work out here among the Anatolian peasants," she said at last to end the lengthening silence.

"'Fascinating' is the word, all right," he agreed. "Though we do get a little starved for female companionship."

Holly had to bite her lip to keep from smiling at the curious mixture of earnestness and blatant hunger in his open attractive features. When she happened to glance at Arif, though, it was quickly apparent he did not share her amusement. His brows were drawn together like black thunderclouds and his eyes blazed with ill-concealed animosity. Abruptly he stood up.

"I hate to interrupt your fascinating conversation, Dr. Schneider," he said sardonically, "but we're running a little behind schedule as it is. If you don't mind, I'll have the keys to the jeep now." He thrust his dark hand under the American's nose.

"Did you have to be so damned rude?" Holly asked five minutes later as she climbed into the battered jeep parked outside the café.

"Rude?" Arif repeated as he thrust the gear lever savagely into first. "I thought I was a model of civility. For two cents I'd have thrown him out of the place by the scruff of his mangy parka.''

"He was just trying to be friendly.''

"Friendly, hell!'' Arif growled. ''The bastard was raping you with his eyes.''

It dawned on Holly gradually that there could be only one reason for Arif's totally unreasonable animosity: he was jealous. She said nothing aloud, however; she was content to hug the thought to herself. How deeply did his feelings for her go, she couldn't help but wonder. Was that the extent of his caring— to resent another man's attentions to the woman whom he was barred from legitimately claiming for himself.

Arif turned from the paved highway onto a rutted dirt track that followed the twisting bed of the river. The jolting ride sent all the troubling thoughts from her mind. She glanced over at Arif, and to her surprise he grinned.

"Only twenty minutes more on this rough road,'' he laughed, ''but I swear to you that the view at the end will be worth it.''

A sense of excitement had infused him, and she could not help but be touched by it. She found herself leaning forward eagerly as the track began to climb upward away from the river.

At the summit Arif pulled on the emergency brake and hopped out of the jeep. Before Holly could push open the passenger door, Arif had flung it open and lifted her down to the ground. He kept one hand lightly about her waist while the other made a sweeping one-hundred-eighty-degree gesture. ''This is the

Hakal land, Holly. This is Riadja.'' There was a quiet exultation in the words.

As he spoke, Holly intuitively felt the atavistic impulse that stirred him. She knew that in a very real sense these wild highland moors were a part of him: the man beside her and the earth she stood upon were one. She moved away from him, slowly drinking in the vast distances and the silence that seemed underscored by the distant high keening of the wind.

To the south the gray slate roofs and minarets of Kars were just visible beyond a bend in the river. Westward in the direction of Europe the distant plateau stretched in a vast undulating wave of gray and ocher. Although the air smelled of winter, barren and swept clean, Holly caught the subtle lingering odor of aromatic grasses and short springing turf.

Arif had leaned back against the hood of the jeep and contentedly followed Holly's gaze. ''On the clear days in spring, after the air has been washed clean by the rain, you can see all the way to the Russian frontier fifty miles to the east,'' he told her.

She turned around to join him and he pointed over a slight rise toward a line of poplars, their bare branches like black filigree against the gray winter sky. ''You can just glimpse the house and stable grounds through the trees.''

She looked past his outstretched hand and with an effort quelled the nervous fluttering in her stomach. When she looked up again into his eyes, she smiled. ''Riadja is magnificent,'' she told him simply. ''It is all that I imagined it to be.''

Holly's heart contracted painfully as she regarded

the eager, almost boyish expression that suffused his
features. "I knew that you'd approve," he teased.
"In spirit at least I think you're a true horsewoman
of the steppes. Now get back into the jeep. You've
yet to see the best part of Riadja—the horses themselves."

As they crested the hill, Holly saw that the house
of gray stone and timber was magnificently situated
on a hillside. In summer she knew that the line of
poplars would shade it and protect it from the hot
winds blowing out of Asia.

A few minutes later they passed through an open
wooden corral gate and along a stone-lined track that
stopped a few hundred feet below the house. Beyond
the neat row of low stables to their right, the brown
pastureland dotted now with bales of hay fell in gentle folds toward the river far below.

Two little boys who had been sitting astride a paddock fence came rushing forward at the sound of the
jeep engine and threw themselves at Arif as he
climbed down onto the grassy field. "Arif Bey! Arif
Bey!" they shouted happily before rushing on in an
excited tangle of Turkish.

He ruffled the older boy's hair affectionately and
swept the younger, who appeared to be a bright
sturdy four-year-old, high up into the air. "These
handsome boys are the children of our chief hired
hand, Cemal Bayar," he explained swiftly before the
youngsters interrupted again with a series of excited
gesticulations.

As he squatted beside them to give him their full
attention—laughing uproariously a moment later
after they had related a particular incident—Holly re-

alized that he was a man who should have several children of his own. He was playful and easy mannered with them, yet she sensed immediately that he respected their simple childish opinions as much as he would respect and listen gravely to the thoughts of another adult. Holly couldn't help laughing ruefully to herself. Arif seemed to have as winning a way with children as he had with horses. . . and women.

He stood up and came to stand beside her, the laughter and enjoyment still sparkling in his eyes. "It's reassuring to know that nothing much changes in my periodic absences from Riadja. One of the mares got loose and they had to chase her several miles over the moors. One of the stable hands got drunk at a village fete and fell through the ice in a pond; luckily he managed to grab a low-growing branch and pull himself out. Now the boys tell me that the former rabble-rouser has become a teetotaler and goes to the mosque every evening."

Holly couldn't resist smiling with him. "I guess human nature isn't that different the world over."

He laughed, then caught himself up short. "Ah, forgive me, Holly; in my haste to find out what's been going on around here, I've neglected to make the introductions. This is Nihat and his little brother is Erim."

Holly shook the older boy's hand, then stooped down to Erim. *"Merhaba,"* she said shyly in Turkish. "Hello."

The boy rewarded her with an engaging grin and reached out to touch her hair before murmuring something incomprehensible to Arif.

"What does he say?" she asked curiously.

"He thinks your hair is like the sun. He's wondering if he might cut off a length and wrap it around his feet at night to keep him warm," Arif translated with a wicked grin.

"Tell him thanks for the compliment but I need the hair to keep me warm," she laughed in return.

A few minutes later, as they walked together up to the house, Arif remarked in a low voice, "Erim is an astute boy. Your hair *is* like the sun, especially when it is spread out on a pillow in the early morning. A sight like that would warm the cockles of the meanest heart!"

The intimate teasing words were like a seductive breeze wafting along her tautened nerve endings, and she became acutely aware of the pressure and warmth from his hand as he guided her up the wide flagstone path. It was the first reference he had made to the night they'd spent together in the nomads' tent. How was it that his light words and innocent touch could inflame her so? Especially when the rational part of her being insisted on reminding her that she had no right to need...to love him so deeply. He had told her that they were destined to hurt each other, yet being with him now at Riadja, all that she knew was a simple heartfelt joy. She wouldn't permit herself to think about leaving the ranch and returning to Istanbul—and to the Holliford name.

Her anguished thoughts were dispelled as an enormous dog came bounding around the far corner of the house and threw himself joyously at Arif. "This is Aslan," he explained as he rubbed the animal's head with an affectionate hand. "He's an Anatolian wolfhound, but he's named for another beast of the wilds—the lion.''

Regarding his tawny coat and lean sturdy body, Holly could understand why he was called Aslan. Like the Kurdish dogs, he wore a heavy spiked collar around his throat. "You have wolves here, as well?" she asked.

Arif shrugged. "This mountainous region is untamed for the most part. You will find wolves, bears, mountain lions, elk. It is a rugged but very beautiful wilderness. I think we love Riadja because of the hardships and dangers, rather than despite them," he told her pridefully.

In the wide front hallway of the house they were greeted by a gaunt woman with a weather-beaten face and sly gray eyes, whom Arif introduced as their housekeeper, Aggi, Bayar's wife. Holly regarded the woman with astonishment. Somehow she could not connect the laughing, sturdy young boys she'd just met outside with this middle-aged woman who apparently was their mother.

To the housekeeper's obsequiously murmured how-do-you-do, Holly replied in flawless Turkish, "Çok iyiyim, very well, thank you."

Aggi regarded the blond visitor with slightly narrowed eyes at that, while Arif grinned. "Beautifully spoken, Holly. You remembered our lessons!"

Holly smiled in return, a ridiculous warmth of pleasure spreading through her at his simple words of praise.

Arif led her past an airy deserted front parlor down a short passageway and pushed open a door that led into what appeared to be a library. The room was long and low with a Turkish divan, piled high with embroidered pillows, ranged beneath the windows. The far wall housed a crowded bookshelf lined with morocco-bound volumes, while before it was a low table piled with more books and magazines. There were several easy chairs set along the opposite wall, their stark whiteness offset by silk Persian wall hangings and several paintings. The room had a cozy lived-in feeling, and Holly guessed that the family spent most of their time within its confines when they weren't out working the ranch itself.

As they walked down the length of the room, she saw that there was a small alcove to the left of the bookcase. Behind the desk that filled the hidden space sat a woman, her head bent determinedly over what appeared to be ledger books.

At the sound of Arif's and Holly's approach, she removed her reading glasses and looked up swiftly.

"Mother, I've brought a guest home," Arif began without preamble. "She is Holly MacKnight, an American and fellow equestrian. Holly, my mother, Carana Hakal."

The woman rose from the desk and came forward to greet her son. As the two embraced briefly, Holly took in the woman's tall fine figure clad in a simple dark woolen skirt and sweater. Then Mrs. Hakal turned to their guest and extended her hand forthrightly. "Welcome to Riadja, Miss MacKnight. I hope you find its atmosphere as homelike as we do," she said in flawless English.

Her eyes were a clear light brown flecked with

gray, and the effect reminded Holly of chips of ice in a winter pond. Then Mrs. Hakal's gaze flickered downward briefly over the American's tall slender form, and Holly felt that she might have been a head of livestock on the selling block as the woman took in her eyes and hair, the shapely fingers with their rounded unpolished nails and the length of her legs and breadth of her hips.

Mrs. Hakal turned back to her son. "She is...?"

"Here on business," Arif interposed smoothly. "A matter of a horse."

"A horse?" she repeated in undisguised surprise.

Briefly Arif explained what had happened to Holly's mare, the delay in the competition trials and the tentative deal they had made regarding Jinniyah.

"That is all?"

"Yes."

In that last terse interchange between mother and son, Holly sensed a subtle clash of wills. In that moment the Hakals seemed very much alike, strong and stubborn and respectful of each other, yet refusing to back down. And Holly knew intuitively, as well, that the unspoken disagreement centered on herself and her unexpected appearance at Riadja.

She steeled herself against the undisguised animosity that she expected to fill Mrs. Hakal's gaze as it had Leila's. But the woman was more subtle and far less emotional than her daughter. All that Holly could read in those gray-flecked clear eyes was a certain hint of reserve as the woman said with polite cordiality, "Do sit down, Miss MacKnight. Aggi will be here shortly with the tea tray, and I'm sure you must be exhausted after your journey." Her eyes rested briefly on Holly's dusty cords, and the American had to steel herself not to brush at them self-consciously.

"Thanks very much," Holly replied with as much aplomb as she could muster. "Tea sounds wonderful."

She had just eased herself into one of the comfortable-looking leather chairs when the door swung open and Aggi came in carrying a polished tea service of English Georgian silver. Mrs. Hakal serenely poured the tea and passed around a plate of sugar cakes and rose-petal jam before sitting on the edge of the divan. She was about to speak to their guest when the door opened again, and they all turned to regard the tall stoop-shouldered man who stood there. Gray haired and distinguished-looking, with an aura of charisma about him, he was forced to lean for support on a cane.

Mrs. Hakal rose immediately and went to his side, "Riad, dear, Arif has come home and brought a guest with him. We were just about to sit down to tea."

"American, eh?" the man observed with a hearty laugh a moment later when Holly was introduced to him. "I have always liked the Americans, your President Franklin Roosevelt especially. He knew how to deal with Stalin at the Yalta conference after the war. The Russians, pah!" he observed contemptuously. "But then you must know, Miss MacKnight, how we feel about our neighbors to the east. Invaded by them four times in as many generations. How could we concentrate on the task of nation building in the last century when we had that lumbering giant of a bear to deal with!''

Holly leaned back in the leather chair and relaxed by degrees. As she sipped at the fragrant tea, she listened in fascination to his emotional monologue on the political ups and downs of Turkey. Beneath his well-practiced theatricality, she sensed a genuine friendliness extended to her, and she began to warm to the former member of parliament. Besides, she guessed instinctively that his timely arrival at the door had prevented his wife from launching into a cool cross-examination of their guest—an ordeal that Holly had not felt up to at all.

As she looked in Arif's direction, Holly saw the brief glance exchanged between mother and son. Then he rose and walked over to his father, clapping his hand gently on the older man's shoulder. "It's good to see you again, papa, but you must excuse Holly and me. I've promised to show her the horses. You wouldn't want to see her disappointed.''

"No, of course not,'' the elder Hakal assented. "Take her to the horses by all means. You know how I am when I get started on political issues!'' He laughed softly at his own foibles.

Arif picked up the teapot and refilled his father's cup. "We'll talk more at dinner. In the meantime, you should rest. You know what Sam said about your heart,'' he told his father almost curtly.

"That Ezine exaggerates,'' the old politician grumped.

"Nevertheless, you must not overexert yourself.'' Arif's tone was firm.

As she listened to this interchange, Holly had the distinct impression that the roles of father and son had been reversed, and that it was Arif who had assumed a protective attitude toward a clever but recalcitrant child.

A few minutes later they left the house, and Holly almost had to run in order to keep up with Arif's long impatient stride as they headed toward the stable area. "Your father is a charming man," she observed breathlessly at his side.

"Charming but stubborn," he replied sharply, not looking at her. "He is seventy-seven years old, yet he thinks himself still a vigorous man of fifty. He is totally unrealistic."

They walked in silence for a few minutes until Holly ventured at last, "You're more like your mother, I think."

His lips curved sardonically. "You could tell that in so short a time?" he demanded. After a moment he added reluctantly, "Yes, we are alike—we let nothing deflect us from our goals."

"She's upset that you brought me here, isn't she?" Holly observed softly. "She was expecting to be introduced to a...a prospective bride."

"Sometimes you are too astute for your own good, Holly," he retorted irritably. "You see too much. My mother and I understand each other, but she does not rule my life."

"She is a strong woman."

Arif grinned suddenly as he pulled open the low door leading into the stables. "So are you, Holly!" he teased.

Inside the dim horse barn they were greeted by the muffled stomping of hooves and the odor of dried grass and oat feed. Arif gave her a quick introduction to each of the animals and stopped by the last empty stall. "Come along; I want you to see my prize! He's being exercised now."

They went out through the rear stable door, which led to a large enclosed paddock. A frisky black colt ran about a vibrant, gracefully proportioned mare whom Holly immediately guessed must be Jinniyah.

Arif whistled lightly and both animals came toward him. Holly stood back and watched as he affectionately greeted the mare and colt before running his hands along their flanks and legs and lifting their hooves to examine them. Gentleness, cool expertise and a wealth of deep affection seemed to flow from his touch, and the animals more than responded in kind.

She was reminded of something that the ancient historian Xenophon had observed about training horses. It had been his belief that young horses should be trained so that they not only loved their riders but looked forward to the time they spent with them. It was evidently a philosophy that Arif Hakal lived every day of his life, and the results were more than apparent in the magnificent mounts his family was raising.

The stable door opened behind them, and a short square-built man with friendly eyes came out into the paddock. She immediately surmised that he was the chief hand, Cemal Bayar. Her guess was confirmed a moment later when Arif issued a curt order in Turk-

ish, and Cemal swiftly disappeared inside. He soon
returned with a leather saddle for the tall silver gray
mare.

As they waited for Jinniyah to be saddled, Arif
asked proudly, "Well, Holly, what do you think of
my stock?"

"Like the rest of Riadja, magnificent," she told
him. "The colt is strong and beautiful. What do you
call him?"

"Demir, which means 'iron' in Turkish. He will be
a proud one like his father, Sinjon."

Their conversation was interrupted as Cemal led
the mare over to them. Jinniyah was balanced, proud
and possessed a beautiful carriage. Holly lithely
swung astride the animal's back and trotted her
around the enclosure. Eager to see if the animal's
physical presence was matched by skill, Holly experi-
mented a little with subtle hand and leg commands.
The mare responded with obedient graceful precision.

Five minutes later she drew up before Arif, who
had saddled and mounted the handsome chestnut
stallion, Damudji. "She's a dream!" Holly told him
excitedly. "I must admit you are a magician with
horses. Jinniyah has been superbly schooled."

He grinned. "Did you expect anything less? Let's
go now; we'll explore some of Riadja on horseback
before it gets dark."

As they crossed the rolling fields and wide pastures, Holly had the heady sensation that she was
riding on the roof of the world. The cold winds
whipped incessantly about their heads, catching her

blond hair and trailing it out behind as if it were a silken gold banner. They rode for several miles, following broad ridges and dipping into protected valleys where clumps of hardy yellow columbine grew stubbornly before winter's inexorable advance. Only as the forbidding slate gray of evening deepened around them did they turn back at last.

As they slowed the horses to a walk, Holly turned to Arif and asked curiously, "Are Demir and Sinjon descendants of the handsome mare that's pictured in the book you lent me on the train?"

Arif looked over at her sharply. "So you did have time to look at the book, as well as examine the money in the envelope."

Holly felt her cheeks grow hot and was grateful that in the gathering gloom of the winter dusk he would not notice her blush. In contrast to her cheeks, her tone was decidedly cool. "Your behavior was every bit as reprehensible as mine!"

"Touché," he countered with a rough laugh. "But I did not bring you all this way to challenge you, Holly. Don't get so upset."

"Why *did* you bring me to Riadja?" she retorted.

He shrugged. "Because I am a selfish man. Why else? I wanted you to myself for a little while longer."

"Why?" she shot back with prickly anger. "To protect me from the Bill Schneiders of this world?"

Arif spat contemptuously into the dirt. "You are no fool, Holly. I know that. Idiots like him aren't for the likes of you. You will bide your time. Didn't the Gypsy tell you that you would marry a rich man?"

Holly shot him a wicked grin. "We should have

had your fortune read, as well, Arif. Perhaps she would have told you that you're destined to marry a rich woman."

"Not you, then, little hellion!" He dug his spurs into Damudji's flanks, and they galloped swiftly away toward the lights of Riadja.

She stared after him contemplatively, then reached down to pat the mare's neck. *Why,* she asked herself again. *Why do I have to love such an impossible man?*

THE LARGE AUSTERE BEDCHAMBER was bathed in the cold light of morning when Holly opened her eyes and gazed about in momentary perplexity. This morning's awakening was far different from that in the Kurdish tent. She had woken in that shadowy enclosure of piled quilts and rugs with a feeling of sated warmth.

But Holly had slept alone this past night. She attempted to burrow down more deeply into the crisp white sheets with their faint pleasant odor of rose of attar, but her thoughts began to dart about in active defiance of her relaxed limbs. With a sigh she rose from the bed and padded barefoot across the cold tiles to the window with its sweeping view of the countryside. The winter sun had risen over the eastern horizon, trailing faded pink fingers of light above the slowly massing clouds. It wouldn't be long now before winter snows gripped the high mountain ranch. She would have to leave soon to return to Istanbul.

As she splashed warm water over her face in the

small guest bath and ran a brush through her hair, Holly thought back to the previous night's dinner. Thanks to Riad Hakal's nonstop monologue, self-indulgent but witty and erudite, the family meal had not been the ordeal she had feared. Arif had said very little, seemingly content to let his father dominate the conversation while his thoughts roamed elsewhere. Although Carana Hakal had been as uncommunicative as her son, her speculative eyes had roved again and again in Holly's direction.

Holly had worn her favorite heathery-green sweater dress, a shade deeper than her eyes, and had slipped a pair of thick gold hoops into her lobes to replace the ones that she'd given to the lovely Kurdish child. She hadn't worn the triangular jade stones again since that last morning with the nomads; they were secreted away in the bottom of her brocade jewelry case like a precious souvenir from some long ago magical event, along with the photograph of Arif and herself together at Eyüp.

She'd been glad that she had taken so much care with her appearance, especially after the way Mrs. Hakal's gray brown gaze had flicked over her guest's dusty riding clothes with such a cool measuring air when they'd first met in the library. As the final finishing touch, Holly had gathered up her mass of soft blond hair into a tight chignon that was at once elegant and simple. She had noticed Arif's gaze flickering over the severe hairdo as they'd walked together into the dining room, but the expression in his eyes had been shuttered and somehow unfathomable.

Holly shook her head now as she stood before the

bathroom mirror, as if to banish those thoughts. She dressed quickly in her slim-legged gray cords and the cowl-necked burgundy sweater that nicely set off her fine winter-pale features.

Her boots echoed loudly on the wide stone staircase as she descended to the first floor, which seemed strangely deserted at that early-morning hour. Finding the dining room and front parlor empty, she hesitantly pushed open the door of the library and stepped inside. A small square of lamplight from the alcove desk spilled onto the rug before the bookshelves. Before she could decide whether to move forward to it, the squeaky wheels of an office chair sounded on the wooden floor and a moment later Mrs. Hakal's attractive but almost frowningly intent features peered around at her.

"Good morning," she greeted her guest crisply. "I hope you slept well. The rest of the family already has breakfasted, so I hope you won't mind helping yourself from the covered sideboard in the dining room."

Before Holly could say anything in reply, the woman had rolled back to her ledger books and she was left standing alone in the middle of the room with a curious feeling of letdown. Where was Arif, she wondered. Had he brought her a thousand miles only to abandon her so quickly?

Holly ate alone in the large dining room with its polished walnut appointments, intrigued by her first encounter with the typical Turkish breakfast of goat cheese, olives, bread and jam. She was just pouring a second cup of the excellent jasmine tea when Mrs.

Hakal entered the room and came to join her at the table.

"I hope you don't find the food too exotic a departure from what you're accustomed to," she said, the ghost of a smile about her lips.

"Not at all," Holly replied with a warning sparkle of defiance in her eyes. "Actually I prefer something substantial like this to the Kurds' morning brew of *ayran*."

To Holly's surprise, the woman uttered a sharp but hearty laugh. "I'd almost forgotten that you'd traveled with my countrymen for two days, Miss MacKnight. Perhaps I've judged you a little too hastily."

"Perhaps you have," Holly replied quietly, her gaze taking in more carefully now the woman's heavy knit sweater, long divided leather skirt and polished black boots. She appeared dressed for riding. After a moment Holly asked with a pretense of casualness, "Where is everyone?"

"You mean, where is Arif?" Mrs. Hakal replied quickly, puncturing the pretense. "He's completed the arrangements to have Jinniyah shipped to Istanbul, and now he's probably out digging postholes and repairing pasture fences." She reached out and poured herself a cup of tea from the pot before adding, "As I'm sure you've noticed, my son is a very physical man. When he has troubling things on his mind he takes refuge in hard work."

Holly's cheeks colored in response to the woman's coolly straightforward talk, but her tone was firm when she inquired, "What is troubling him?"

Carana Hakal's light eyes, impatient with subterfuge and innuendo, bored into Holly. "You're in love with Arif, aren't you? Oh, please don't try to deny it," she went on quickly as Holly opened her mouth to speak. "The sparks between you are like summer lightning. One would have to be blind not to see it."

Holly bit her lip, but she didn't look away from the older woman's penetrating gaze. After a moment she replied in a coolly controlled voice, "I can't see what business it is of yours."

"My dear, it is very much our business."

"Now you sound like Leila," Holly said with a frustrated sigh. "She regards me as if I were a poisonous snake."

Mrs. Hakal laughed gently. "My daughter gets a little carried away with her passions, though she means well. She wants what is best for all of us."

"But how can Arif's marriage to Geneviève Lamine or Ziya Aras effect that?" Holly countered impatiently.

Mrs. Hakal stood up from the table with characteristic abruptness, as if to signal an end to the conversation. "It's unfortunate that Arif can't be here to show you more of Riadja, but I'll be delighted to give you a tour. Would you care to come riding with me today?"

Holly had little desire to spend the day with this frank uncompromising woman who stood before her, but she knew she couldn't refuse the invitation without appearing childish. "Yes, of course," she replied with an air of resignation. "I'd like that very much."

CANTERING SIDE BY SIDE, the women rode in a north-easterly direction toward a low ring of mountains, their granite heights obscured by clouds. Holly glanced over at her companion from time to time and was forced to admit that the woman was as polished and natural a rider as her son. Then she caught Carana Hakal's measuring gaze upon her, and she could only conclude with a small inward smile that the woman was forced to admit the same about her.

Despite the new heaviness in her heart, Holly responded with a subtle sense of exultation to the wind-swept grandeur of the land. Once again she sensed Arif's deep devotion to it. What a magnificent heritage to have bequeathed from one generation to the next!

As they reined in the horses to guide them over a treacherously rocky patch of ground, Carana Hakal turned to her companion and began to talk. It was almost as if she'd divined Holly's thoughts when she remarked, "We have four thousand acres here. When Riad and I were married, the lands that were in our Turkish and Kurd families for generations were joined as one."

Holly hesitated only briefly before replying, knowing that the woman was not afraid of frankness. "Arif told me about the symbolic aspect of your marriage, Mrs. Hakal."

"Do I detect a subtle note of pity in your voice at such a political match?" the woman replied with a laugh. "Please don't waste such soft feelings on me! The union was as much my choice as it was his." Her tone was strong and prideful, reminding Holly once again of the son who seemed so much like her.

Not knowing quite how to respond to the woman's remarks, Holly asked instead, "Where are we riding to now?"

"To my father's village, on the very easternmost edge of the ranch where the foothills climb into the mountains," she replied, touching her spurs to the horse's flanks so that he leaped into a ground-eating gallop over the last stretch of flat land before the looming hills.

Holly followed suit, feeling delighted and vaguely fearful of meeting Arif's Kurdish grandfather.

The close-built village with its homes of sun-dried brick rose against a hillside that overlooked a distant valley. In the center was a small market square where the women in their brightly patterned petticoats gathered in colorful knots as they completed their shopping. In between her greetings to the villagers, Mrs. Hakal pointed out to Holly the various public buildings: a small mosque and public bath, the rustic schoolhouse and ancient cemetery.

They turned down a wide rutted lane and approached a low stone house with its herringbone pyramid of fuel stacked to the right of the front door. A moment later the door was opened and a tall fierce-looking man with a bristling gray mustache seemed to fill the wide entrance as he impassively watched the women's approach.

As she lifted her hand in greeting, Mrs. Hakal explained to Holly in a voice that was low and vibrant with love, "My father, Car Ishak. He is only a few years older than my husband."

A moment later they dismounted at his doorstep, and as father and daughter briefly embraced, Holly observed the man with no little fascination. Despite his age he still had the hardened sinews of the mountain people, and when he turned to regard her, the smile that smoldered in his wide dark eyes reminded her with an intense shock of Arif. The man was a reflection of Arif himself in forty years, strong, erect and proud. Holly's green eyes flashed a smile in return, and the wise old Kurdish chief tacitly acknowledged the intelligence and pride shining in their brilliant depths.

Ishak turned back to his daughter, who was busy pulling books, magazines and several dark round loaves of bread from her saddlebags. He glanced around at Holly again before saying something to Carana, who swiftly shook her head in negation. The old man said something else, and she shot him a look of exasperation.

Holly had little time to guess at the significance of their quick interchange because she was being ushered into the spacious house. A high divan ringed the whitewashed walls, which were devoid of decoration but for the stacks of books piled high on rustic wooden shelves. Ishak brought out a tray of bread, honey, cheese and yogurt and bade the women sit down.

As she ate, Holly was aware of a pleasant warmth that seemed to emanate from beneath the low table in the center of the room. Carana Hakal caught the American's curious gaze and said something laughingly to her father. Then she turned back to Holly. "I see you're curious about the home's heating system.

Here, let me show you." She stood up and lifted a corner of the table, then kicked back the rug beneath.

Holly stared in amazement down into the shallow depression that glowed hotly from the heaped logs.

"It's called a *tandir*," Carana explained.

"I'd call it the biggest charcoal brazier I've ever seen," Holly replied with a smile. "It seems quite efficient."

"It is," the woman laughed. "In the evening the whole family draws up their bedrolls in a circle around it, and believe me, they stay cozily warm. I have vivid memories of long winter nights spent round the *tandir*."

Holly regarded Carana with new interest. Somehow she couldn't connect the sophisticated well-educated woman before her with such a primitive background.

Thereafter the conversation ranged over a variety of topics, with Carana acting as interpreter. Time and again Holly was amazed not only by the old man's knowledge of events in the outside world but by the depth of his perception, as well.

It was midafternoon before they finally took their leave of the rugged isolated village. As the horses picked their way slowly down the rutted lane, Holly turned around in the saddle to glance at Ishak's home one last time. The old man stood in the doorway, arms crossed before his chest as he stared after them, and once more Holly was reminded forcefully of Arif.

The women followed a different route this time; it skirted the hills for several miles before cutting southwest across the rolling expanse of ranch land. Holly caught a glimpse in the distance of a strange conical-shaped structure and realized that Carana Hakal was making directly for it. After fifteen minutes of hard riding, they drew to a halt in front of the odd crumbling structure, which had been built of alternating blocks of pink and gray stone.

"What is it?" Holly asked curiously as they dismounted and left the horses to graze.

"An Armenian chapel—probably eight hundred years old. I thought you might enjoy seeing some of Riadja's archaeological remains," Carana flung back over her shoulder as she crossed the doorless entry.

Holly followed her inside and stared around in fascination at the crumbling remnant of the region's distant past. The ancient circular chapel had a sense of beauty and grace about it that she found enchanting. "It's lovely," she said aloud at last. "The more I see of Riadja the more astonished I become. It's like a little fiefdom out of the Middle Ages—ancient chapel, small village and all!"

She turned around to find Carana pouring tea from a thermos into the plastic cup lids. The woman handed one to Holly, and then they both sat down in the entryway of the chapel, gazes taking in the shifting skyscape of cloud and shadow over the rugged land.

"So," Carana asked at last, "what did you think of my father and his village?"

Holly smiled. "I was very impressed. Ishak reminds me very much of Arif."

That remark seemed to please the woman. "I've always felt the same," she replied quietly. "Arif is much closer to his grandfather too, than he is to Riad."

"Ishak is remarkably well educated for...."

"For a country bumpkin. Is that what you were going to say, Holly?" Carana laughed gently. "Education has always been of utmost importance to my father; he is totally self-taught in both Kurdish and Turkish. The thing he wanted most for his child was education, even if that child was a daughter! But then the Kurds have always been quite liberal when it comes to equality between the sexes. It was Riad who financed my education in Istanbul and London. Did you know that?" she added casually.

Holly looked over at her swiftly. "No, I didn't."

Carana smiled again. "That was all part of the elaborate marriage contract between the families."

"Did...did you love him?" Holly asked, shocked at her own effrontery even as the words were uttered.

But Carana didn't seem to mind the frank question. "I was grateful to him." She sighed then. "Riad married for idealistic reasons and I for practical ones. But the ultimate irony, of course, is that my husband has no head for business. He was a gifted statesman and an enormously successful politician, but when it came to his own investments.... He was always ready to listen to a friend's schemes—oil wells in the Adriatic that turned out to be dry, chromium mines outside of Diyarbakir that never panned out, and so forth," she concluded dryly.

Holly envisioned the woman bent over the ledger

books at her alcove desk, glasses perched on the end of her nose. "It's you who has held the ranch together, then."

"Arif and I have worked together to do it, but...." She seemed reluctant to continue. "Forgive me for going on so, Holly. May I call you that? Now why don't you tell me about yourself."

Holly felt discomfited at this rapid turnabout. "I...really, there's nothing to tell," she murmured in confusion.

Carana laughed and her eyes glinted briefly like a ray of sun striking a granite peak. "Arif has told me about your being a penniless American out to win fame and fortune in the European horse trials. But I'm sorry, my dear, I don't believe that for one minute!" There was neither rancor nor accusation in the woman's tone—nothing but rich amusement. "I've met scores of young women like you, when I was a student myself and later when my husband and I lived in Ankara. My dear Holly, breeding and advantage exude from your pores! Men never notice things like that—perhaps they're not catty enough or not oriented to small details—but you cannot fool another woman. My guess is that you're fleeing from a well-to-do existence and are out to prove something to yourself. Am I right?" The woman's eyes were sharply penetrating but not unkind.

Holly stared back at her, speechless. "Mrs. Hakal—"

"Oh, please call me Carana. I feel that we've come to know each other so well today, Holly," she interrupted, her tone at once ironic and genuinely friendly. "Don't worry, dear. Your secret is safe with me. It'll go no further than these walls." She glanced back with amusement into the deserted chapel.

"But Arif. . ." Holly managed to break in, feeling out of her depth with this amazingly frank and strong-willed woman.

"You must put him out of your mind," Carana replied with quiet force. "Rich or poor, you have no future with Arif. I know him."

"I will not accept that." Holly lifted her chin defiantly, and she thought she saw a glimmer of respect in the other woman's eyes.

"Arif is a man of unquenchable pride and spirit," Carana told her slowly. "It is what I admire about him most. You will accept it because *he* will insist on it."

Holly stood up angrily, her gaze fixed without seeing on the distant cloud-covered peaks.

Carana was speaking again, more softly now. "Look, Holly, I do not mean to be cruel. I've come to like you even. But I love my son, and I don't want to see him hurt by prolonging a hopeless relationship."

Holly turned around swiftly to face Carana, eyes ablaze like malachite. "I refuse to give up without at least knowing why I am being rejected. He says it has nothing to do with religion or heritage. What, then?"

Carana stood up then, and their eyes were nearly at a level. "Holly, you are a beautifully self-possessed young woman, so full of pride and vitality. You and Arif are too much alike! The truth is so simple and so ironic, but it is not for me to tell you. That is Arif's decision. Come, we'd better get back to the house now. We're having guests for dinner.''

Holly swung up onto the back of the bay gelding and spurred him into a headlong gallop across the empty plain. For the moment at least she wanted to obliterate all thought, to concentrate on nothing but the pounding of the horse's hooves and her own taut form moving in rhythmic harmony with its rippling back and flanks. But the images remained in her mind all the same: she envisioned Ishak's strong rugged features and the subtle approval she'd read in his dark eyes, but the image was swiftly replaced by Carana's cold honest appraisal. Was she adversary or friend? Holly shook her head in angry perplexity. Even as she struggled to come up with an answer to that, the conviction steadily grew within her that she could trust Carana. The woman was so like her son! Arif: his lean shadowed features leaped into clarity as Holly's thoughts turned to him. He was the enigma; his hidden feelings were the powerful unknown in the whole volatile equation.

Horse and rider rode into the stable yard lathered in sweat and drained of energy. Holly dismounted swiftly and handed the reins to Cemal. When she turned around, she saw that Carana had ridden her own mount equally hard and had pounded into the yard behind her. A moment later Carana came forward to her, and the two women faced each other, breathing heavily after the exertion of the ride.

The woman touched Holly's arm in a simple gesture of understanding. "That's good. Ride hard," she said between gasps of breath. "The sooner you get the frustration and fury out of your system, the sooner you will be able to face the inevitable. Accept the fact that you must give him up.''

''Don't underestimate me, Carana,'' Holly replied equably. ''I am strong.''

The handsome Kurdish woman smiled, and the expression was at once knowledgeable and a little sad. ''But my son is stronger. His mind is made up.''

''But not his heart!'' Holly flung back at her. Without waiting for a reply, she ran up the flagstone path to the house and pushed open the door into the front hallway.

There, unexpectedly, she found herself face to face with Arif. It was apparent that he'd just returned from a day of back-breaking labor on the ranch. Despite the cold outside, his faded blue work shirt was unbuttoned and a slow rivulet of sweat marked a passage through the dusty matted hairs on his chest. He smelled of clean earth and cold mountain air.

Coming upon him so unexpectedly, Holly felt the impact of his rugged maleness like a shock wave, and it was all she could do to keep from reaching out with her fingers and trailing a light passage along his sternum and stomach to the top of his belt buckle.

He sensed her response, reading it in the subtle flaring of her nostrils and in her eyes, which had darkened with need until they resembled jade stones. He moved closer to her, and she felt the heat emanating from his body like an arc of electricity drawing her to him. Slowly he reached up and caressed the side of her throat.

Holly savored the cool roughness of Arif's fingers

against her flushed skin, like sand rippling along velvet. She longed to feel the melting pressure of his long lean form against her own, and she would have lifted her hungry lips shamelessly to his. But the door behind them swung open, and they drew apart as swiftly as if a bolt of lightning had struck between them.

Carana came into the hall and regarded them a moment with her sharp gaze before addressing her son. "Hello, dear. You look as though you've had a hard day in the fields. Did Holly mention that we'd visited your Grandfather Ishak's village?"

Arif grinned at Holly. "I knew I could count on my mother to keep a guest entertained. How did you find the old man?"

Holly smiled in return. "Very much like you."

Arif threw back his head and laughed deeply. "So you find more Kurd in me than Turk? More wildness than civility? A tendency to fierce anger over cool diplomacy?" he teased her.

"Precisely," she retorted at once. "You're like the savagely proud wolf who brings down his prey without thinking of the consequences."

His lips tautened at that unexpected gibe, and mother and son exchanged quick glances. Then tension was broken then by Carana, who said crisply to him, "By the way, I'd almost forgotten to tell you. A package arrived from the Kapali Çarsi in Istanbul, and I put it in the hall closet."

"What?" he replied curiously, turning to open the closet door and pull out the large bulky parcel that was bound with brown paper and twine.

Holly and Carana watched with interest over his shoulder while he tore it open with quick deft fingers. A moment later an expression of mingled amusement and alarm crossed Holly's features as she recognized the bridle and gloves, steel spurs and lovely red-and-black saddle pad that she'd bought at the bazaar and posted to the ranch. She'd completely forgotten about her devious little purchase, but she said nothing now.

"This is superb tack, Arif. I'm glad you bought something for yourself for a change," Carana said approvingly as she headed for the stairs. "Now you must both excuse me while I change."

Arif waited until his mother had disappeared at the top of the staircase before turning slowly back to Holly, his eyes the brooding black of a horizon that presages a dangerous storm. Without warning his hand shot out and took her arm in a painful grip, and he dragged her headlong down the passageway to the library. Then he pulled her inside and slammed the door behind them.

Holly felt her heart thudding painfully in her chest as she stared up into his face, which blazed with dark rage. She willed herself not to show the fear that wound inside her, yet she found herself backing up step by step until her spine was pressed against the wall.

Arif grasped her arms and pressed them roughly to her sides, pinioning her helplessly. He leaned toward her until their faces were inches apart, and his warm breath rasped over her. "What the bloody hell are you trying to do?" he swore fiercely. "I do not accept expensive gifts from women, Holly. You will take the gear back to Istanbul with you. Do I make myself understood?'' The deceptive quiet of his voice was belied by the expression in his eyes with their glittering depths of controlled rage.

As she stared into them, Holly felt something within her snap, and a fomenting anger replaced the fear of a moment earlier. She refused to cower before his arrogant male dominance. ''Aren't you assuming an awful lot, Arif?'' she replied with an attempt at calmness, though her breasts rose and fell rapidly from the raging emotions that gripped her. ''How do you know the riding gear isn't a gift from one of the women whom you're wooing—Geneviève or Ziya? Perhaps the tack is Turkish bride price—something to sweeten the pot for the prospective groom!'' she flung at him sarcastically.

''Damn your insolence,'' he swore with a menacing softness that was much more frightening than bellowing rage. ''I know you bought it because I left you outside that very shop, and the date on the invoice is the same. Do you still deny it, Holly?'' His iron grip tightened on her arms.

Realizing that it would be at once ridiculous and futile to pretend no knowledge of the purchase, she replied at last in a decidedly mettlesome tone, ''Very well; I won't deny it. I bought the gear...but it was paid for with your money—with the five hundred francs that you were too damn stubborn to let me return to you!''

''That was a closed chapter between us,'' he muttered through clenched teeth.

"Not as far as I was concerned, Arif Hakal!"

"Damn it, you'll take the gear back."

"I will not. The gear is yours," she rejoined stubbornly.

His fingers began a slow kneading caress of her upper arms that was at once hurtful and curiously possessive, and his breath escaped in an angry sigh. "You are the most aggravatingly stubborn woman I have ever had the misfortune to...."

"To what?" she taunted in return. "Arif Hakal, you are an arro—"

But before she could complete the angry epithet, his mouth caught hers and smothered her protest with a punishing kiss that forced her head back and invaded her half-parted lips with ravishing intent. A shuddering sigh swept through her as she felt her tautened senses responding to the hotness of mingled anger and passion that ricocheted between them.

Arif crushed her to him, her breasts and loins melding to his until all else but the remembrance of the sweet joy of surrender was driven from her mind.

But the charged passion and intimacy of the moment was shattered as the library door swung open and Aggi's gaunt features popped around the corner, regarding them with sly eyes that grew avidly curious. Arif released Holly as if she were hot steel and in a low forceful voice muttered something to the housekeeper that sent her scurrying back to the kitchen. He turned then and went to stand before the long windows above the divan, his unfathomably dark eyes fixed on the eastern horizon. There was something remote and forbidding in his stance.

With an angry toss of her head, Holly slipped out of the library and made her way up the stairs to her own room. Her thoughts and emotions were in turmoil. It had been an absolutely ridiculous argument, blown out of all proportion, yet she sensed some deeper meaning behind it. She lifted shaking fingers to the lips that he'd ravished with such arrant demand. How could such anger have touched off such wanton passion?

As Holly entered the bedroom, her eye was caught by a large rectangular box that had been tossed casually onto the middle of the white crocheted spread. With quick steps she moved across the tiled floor and stared down at it for several long seconds, trying to imagine what was inside the box and who had brought it.

Unable to contain her curiosity any longer, Holly pulled the box to the edge of the bed, lifted off the cover and swiftly brushed aside the protective tissue. Then a surprised gasp escaped her lips as she lifted the exotic silk gown from its white tissue nest. Vivid shades of cinnabar and rust, jade and midnight black shimmered in the delicately patterned caftan as the light from the window caught it.

She recognized it immediately, of course, as the same gorgeous confection that she'd admired with such brief longing in the Istanbul bazaar. It didn't require much clever deduction on her part to figure out who had been the purchaser. Arif had been with her when she'd stopped to admire the lovely silk, and though she hadn't said a word aloud he must have guessed how much she longed to own such a vividly exotic creation. A little smile played about her lips as she reflected on his thoughtfulness.

Her tender amusement was short-lived, however, as she recalled the bitter argument that had impelled her to come upstairs in the first place. How dared he think she would accept such an expensive, highly personal gift after he had so stingingly rebuked her only five minutes earlier when the situation had been reversed! He, with his arrant pride, had been loath to accept anything from her hands. Well, she would show him whose pride was stronger!

Holly dropped the gown back into its box, then swept it from the bed and hurried downstairs, clutching the package angrily beneath her arm. She marched into the library, but he had gone. Undaunted, she hurried down the hall toward the kitchen and pushed open the swinging door.

Arif leaned against the counter, a bottle of dark ale raised to his lips, and his rugged form seemed to fill the low-ceilinged room as he turned to face the intruder. His eyes narrowed at the sight of her, so she could not be certain if what she had read in his expression was the subtle spark of amusement or a steely glint at facing battle once again.

Her heels clopped sharply on the tiles as she moved toward him, holding the box before her as if it were a shield. "May I ask what this was doing in my room?" she began without preamble.

He shrugged. "It is a gift—in celebration of Eastern Orthodox Christmas. Don't tell me you no longer believe in Saint Nicolai," he teased, his lips curving ironically.

"Saint Nick should be buying gifts for the trousseau of his bride, rather than for a blond interloper who is not wanted here at Riadja," she retorted softly.

Arif's hand swiftly grasped her wrist, causing the box to tumble open at their feet with an unexpected clattering sound. "*I* want you here. That is enough."

He released her hand, and they both bent at the same time to retrieve the box. As Holly replaced the dress carefully in the folds of tissue, her eye was caught by a string of beads sparkling on the kitchen floor. She recognized the finely crafted stones at once as the prayer beads that had lain before the photograph of Arif's parents in his train compartment.

"Arif," she asked in quiet perplexity, "why were these in the box with the dress?"

His dark work-roughened hand closed over hers around the beads. "I wanted you to have them," he said simply.

"Damn you!" she cried, standing up and pulling her hand from his. "How could you have the gall to give me such...such precious gifts—" she paused to swallow back the tears that threatened to well in her throat "—when you flung *my* gift back in my face! I won't keep either one of them!"

She attempted to shove the box into his arms, but instead his hands reached out to grab hold of her gently. "Wait, Holly," he said in a low coaxing voice, as if he were gentling a young foal. "This bitter squabbling has gone far enough. Shall we call a truce?" he asked, laughter glinting unmistakably in his eyes.

"What do you mean?" she replied suspiciously.

He chuckled aloud. "When I saw the riding gear and realized what you'd done, I flew into a rage—pretty irrationally, I must admit. Listen, Holly, I'll keep the gear if you will keep my gifts to you and wear them at dinner. For tonight at least, be my Turkish woman," he demanded softly.

Before she could reply, however, the back door to the kitchen had been flung open and Aggi hurried inside with another, younger woman in tow. Her companion was an attractive individual of about thirty, and although Holly had never seen her before, there seemed something vaguely familiar about her.

After smiling and greeting the two women, Holly turned to Arif and asked, "Who is she?"

"The mother of Nihat and Erim, the boys you met yesterday."

"No, no," she replied quickly. "I meant the younger woman."

Arif nodded his head. "That's whom I'm referring to, as well."

A second later the Bayar boys came tumbling into the kitchen, but Aggi immediately brought them up short with a tart command. Then she gave them each a bag of trash to carry outside, while she set the younger woman to work peeling vegetables.

Holly shook her head in confusion. "I'm afraid I don't understand at all," she said as they headed back down the passageway toward the front of the house.

Arif laughed. "It's very simple, really. When Aggi turned forty, she and Cemal had been married for twenty years. At that point it became obvious to her that she would never bear a child, and the thought bothered her. But Aggi is a crafty woman. She came up with a clever solution that would not only provide her with children but put her in a nice position of power, as well." He paused before adding, "Aggi convinced Cemal to take a second wife. That is the woman you just met, Fikriye."

"What!" Holly replied, shocked. "Is that legal?"

"What is legal in this country and what is traditional are two entirely different things. Half a century ago Atatürk swept away all the old laws that bound Turkey to the past, but it will take much more than fifty years to change custom among the peasants."

"A country with one foot in the past and one in the future," Holly observed softly as they climbed the stairs to the second floor. At the top she turned to face her companion. "Tell me, Arif," she asked, "where precisely do you stand?"

He lifted his hand to her face and lightly traced the finely sculpted bones of her cheeks. "It's difficult to say, Holly," he replied. "Sometimes I feel that I'm a man torn in two." His eyelids dropped like heavy curtains over his troubled gaze as he bent his face toward hers, and he would have kissed her then but for the fact that the door of his parents' bedroom had swung open. "I'll see you at dinner," he said, drawing back and turning to face his mother, who stood in the open doorway.

Holly inclined her head at both of them before turning and making her way swiftly down the long hall to her own room.

SHE SWIRLED BEFORE THE LONG MIRROR, pleased at the effect of the vividly hued caftan against her fair skin. The bodice formed a dipping vee that hinted subtly at the cleft in her breasts, while the long patterned belt, which she'd wound around her empire-style, emphasized their high full roundness. Holly had brushed her hair into a softly burnished mass that cascaded over her left shoulder and was caught back behind her right ear with a single ebony clip. Then she pulled out the triangular jade stones and affixed them to her lobes. There was an elemental quality about her reflection that intrigued her: cinnabar, jade and ebony contrasting with the ivory and gold of her features.

A few minutes later, as she descended the stairs to the first floor, Holly met Carana on the way up. The woman took in the transformation in Holly's appearance with interest. She reached out and delicately touched the triangular stone in her right earlobe. "I see that they have made a Kurdish woman of you after all," she observed, her gray-flecked eyes neither warm nor cold.

The woman's attitude of cool detachment rankled Holly, and she answered Carana's low remark in a low spirited tone. "I'll take a part of Turkey with me when I leave here, Carana, because the experience has affected me deeply. But I think that I'll also leave a very real part of myself here at Riadja; nothing that happens will change that."

She faced her Kurdish hostess with cool prideful grace, green eyes alight with passion and caring. Something in her serene, almost haughty attitude seemed to touch Carana then, and once again a strong measure of respect sparkled in her granite-flecked gaze.

The two women passed each other on the stairs without another word spoken between them, and as Holly stepped across the wide hallway she heard Riad Hakal's fine cultured voice raised in animated conversation in the front parlor.

Glancing about the room, Holly was surprised at the feeling of warmth that emanated from it. Gone was the cool airy empty feeling of the day. Flickering candlelight reflected off the oil paintings and small gilt-framed mosaics that decorated the walls while seeming to deepen the richness of the polished oak furniture. Several people strolled about, helping themselves to punch from a large crystal bowl or selecting tidbits from the artfully arranged assortment of canapés.

Since she did not see Arif, she went to join his father. Riad Hakal looked up in delight at her approach and broke off his conversation to introduce her to his friends. She shook hands politely with a lawyer and a local government official and their wives, all of whom spoke at least a smattering of English. Then she turned back to her host. "I met your father-in-law this morning," she began with a smile.

"Car Ishak. He's a good man," Hakal rejoined heartily. "He and I came of different culture and vastly different social backgrounds, but we shared two devotions—to the land and to our religious faith. Well, actually, it was three devotions," he amended with a chuckle. "We played backgammon together, as well. In fact it was over a board game that we hatched the plan to unite the Hakal and Ishak lands. Quite a scheme it was, too, enduring these forty years. And now....'' The old politician sighed. "But then, all of that isn't any of your worry, is it, Miss MacKnight? You are a guest here for a short time."

He launched into an amusing reminiscence about his parliamentary days, but Holly was only half listening. Once again she felt shut out, reminded of her status as an outsider—the temporary sojourner who could have no lasting place there. Riad Hakal's reminder had been totally unintentional and without the sharpness of her encounter with his wife and son, but the effect had been the same.

A gust of cold wind swept into the room as the front door was opened, and Holly turned to see Arif leading two more guests into the spacious parlor. He wore a short-sleeved burgundy polo shirt that emphasized the breadth of his shoulders and exposed the bronzed hardened sinews of his forearms. His beige trousers fit snugly over his muscled thighs, reminding Holly forcefully of the feral grace and strength that pulsated through him. On the surface he looked the modern country gentleman, engrossed in his ranch, his horses and his riding but beneath the exterior was an unquenchable animal vitality that linked him more intimately to the wildness of the land itself. It was that quality in him to which Holly's senses responded so alarmingly even now, across a room full of people.

As he came into the room, Arif looked up and caught her gaze. Swiftly then he came toward her, dark eyes smoldering as they swept down her figure in the richly hued silk caftan.

"Do you approve, m'lord?" she inquired teasingly. "I feel like one of those Circassian slave women made captive by Turkish warlords."

His eyes were aglint in the dim candlelight. "I do approve. If you were my captive, no amount of ransom would be great enough to set you free," he rejoined, the low words at once teasing and caressing.

The moment of charged intimacy was broken as his guests approached him, and he was reminded of his duties as host.

Holly smile cordially as she was introduced to a heavyset man with jovial eyes, Samsun Ezine, and the tall blue-eyed man with him whom she'd already met the day before in a Kars café. Briefly she exchanged greetings with Bill Schneider before Arif drew the young American doctor aside by the punch bowl to talk.

Holly was still wondering what they could have to discuss when Sam Ezine engaged her in conversation. "I think that you've met my niece," he began.

"Your niece?" Holly repeated, her brows drawn together in puzzlement. "Which one is she?"

"Oh, she's not here now. I meant that you met her in Istanbul," he corrected with a jovial chuckle. "She is Ziya Aras."

"Ah, yes. The plastic surgeon," Holly replied. "She's quite... quite an interesting person."

"Yes, indeed," he said happily. "We're all proud of her. Ziya has one of the most successful practices in Istanbul. She could return here to her native region and buy us all out." He laughed again. "All she needs now is to settle down and get married."

"Anyone particular in mind?" Holly asked innocently.

Dr. Ezine winked. "I think she's always been attracted to Arif, though I don't think he's ever regarded her as anything more than a sister. She and Leila are quite close, you know."

As he chuckled again, Holly couldn't help but wonder if that accounted at least in part for Leila's animosity toward her. Yet she hadn't reacted that way toward Geneviève, Holly remembered.

A moment later Carana Hakal stepped into the room and announced dinner. She wore a simple off-white gown of wool that contrasted attractively with her dark skin and eyes and the upswept salt-and-pepper hair. As she regarded the older woman Holly had to concede a grudging admiration for her. Carana was intelligent and proud with every bit as much breeding exuding from her pores as she had so astutely noticed in her American guest. Holly realized with a start that in other circumstances she and Carana would probably have become great friends, especially with their shared interest of horses and love of riding. But circumstances precluded that. Because they both loved Arif—in their vastly differing fashions—they were destined to be adversaries.

The meal was a simple but delicious one of lamb that had been roasted in an open pit and basted with a concoction of oils, lemon and spices. Holly was seated between Riad Hakal and Dr. Ezine at dinner, and she was grateful for their lively conversation, which necessitated little input from her. Her thoughts were free to roam, which they did uncomfortably, touching back on Samsun Ezine's reference to his niece's wealth and Arif's conversation with Bill Schneider. Whether by design or chance, Arif had been seated at the far end of the long table from her and she had only occasional glimpses of his profile. Suddenly she felt a pang of desolation, as if the night were already over and nothing but a memory. She was grateful when the meal ended and everyone retired once more to the front room for Turkish coffee and fruit.

Someone had switched on the stereo, with the music alternating between soft mournful Turkish music and the quieter strains of Gershwin. After she'd poured herself a small cup of the strong coffee, Holly turned around to find herself standing side by side with Bill Schneider.

"Hi!" he greeted her with a smile. "I haven't had much of a chance to see you this evening. I enjoy these get-togethers, but one thing I still haven't learned to appreciate is Turkish music."

Holly smiled in return. "It *is* strange, but it has a haunting quality, too. I think it might help if you saw someone dancing to it." She described to him the young Kurdish child Carim, who had danced in her father's tent, but once again she had the faint feeling that Bill wasn't really listening to what she was saying. She caught Arif looking in their direction once, but when he caught her gaze he turned to Samsun Ezine as if he hadn't even seen her.

"That sure is a beautiful dress," Bill was complimenting her as his eyes roved over the swell of her breasts.

"Thanks. It was a gift from Arif," she told him pointedly.

"Ah, I see," he replied, the charming grin a little crooked now. "I was hoping that we might get together once we're both back in Istanbul...."

Holly smiled gently to ease her refusal. "I really don't think so. I doubt if my riding schedule will leave me much free time." She briefly wondered what he meant by that reference to their both being in Istanbul at the same time, but her gaze was attracted to Arif's strong profile once again and she excused herself to walk over casually in his direction. Holly had the distinct impression that Arif was ignoring her, and the idea nettled her.

When she came up to Arif and Dr. Ezine they immediately lapsed into English in deference to her presence, and she soon forgot her annoyance with Arif as she became engrossed in the subject of their conversation. The two men were enthusiastically discussing Arif's plans to build a new and larger paddock.

"You know, Arif," Holly put in after a moment, "you might want to take advantage of that beautiful rolling pastureland on the north side of the stables. The reason I suggest it is that a paddock was built at Sims' Meadows that incorporated a hill, and it really paid off in terms of much greater endurance in the animals that were exercised there."

Both Arif and the doctor turned surprised but admiring glances in her direction. It was Samsun Ezine who spoke first, observing with a low chortle, "Now that is what I'd call a woman with true horse sense!"

Arif smiled, too, though Holly could not help but notice the subtle speculative glints that played in his expressive eyes. "Thank you, Holly," he said at last in a quiet voice. "That is an excellent suggestion."

Before they could talk further, Riad Hakal stood up from his corner chair and cried out jovially, "It's time for a Turkish dance now! No evening is complete without it," he added, his breath coming in short gasps from the exertion of having risen and made the energetic announcement.

As the guests drew back to the perimeters of the room, Arif and several other men gathered in the center. Holly watched in fascination as the men moved through a series of dances that ranged from a pavanelike rhythm, slow and stately, to a wild low-kicking fling that resembled a cossack show. Through it all her gaze was fixed on Arif's controlled muscular form. He danced as he rode—with grace, precision and self-discipline. One by one the men left the center of the floor until only Arif and one of the young lawyers from town stood there, silently confronting each other. Yet another performance began, and Riad explained to Holly, who now stood beside his chair, that it was called the dagger dance.

It was more mime than dance as the men took turns brandishing an imaginary knife in their hands, whipping it at each other's face with amazing rapidity. Holly quickly saw that the drama and beauty of the "dance" lay in the men's erect unflinching stance as they submitted to their adversary's attack.

The elder Hakal sighed with pleasure when the performance had ended. "That Arif has the honesty, courage and ruthlessness of a fighter, eh, Miss MacKnight?"

Holly politely smiled her acknowledgment of his proud remarks, while inwardly she shivered. Strong, ruthless, a man of duty. She thought back then to her conversation with Carana outside the Armenian chapel. Hadn't she essentially described her son in the same way, a man whose will must ultimately prevail?

Suddenly Holly felt trapped by the closed atmosphere of the room, and after excusing herself she hurried quickly outside to the front porch. The night air was brittle with frost, but she drank it in gratefully. Little by little she began to relax as her gaze roamed over the vast darkness beyond the tiny outpost of civilization that was the Hakals' home. A few stars twinkled brilliantly beneath the frieze of clouds moving eastward across the distant plain, and Holly realized with a sigh that her sojourn at Riadja must end all too quickly.

Her thoughts were interrupted by the sound of forceful footsteps on the porch at her back, and she turned to face Arif.

"Holly!" Her name was an impatient caress on his lips. "I was afraid that I wouldn't see you again this evening."

She looked up at him in surprise, but before she could utter a word he had swept her into his arms and his mouth was crushing down upon hers. The hungry lips and probing tongue bespoke a hard breathless urgency, almost of desperation.

Her mind's confused questioning was drowned then by the primitive needs of her woman's body, and she responded to him with reckless abandon. Her arms twined about his neck as his hands moved slowly upward from her waist in a long, agonizingly slow caress, as if his fingers sought to memorize every soft curve and delectable hollow. One hand pulled her closer to him while the other moved farther along her spine to the white softness of her neck beneath the thick honey-blond mane. His powerful fingers raked through her hair, then tightened about the strands and drew her head back with almost savage force. She felt herself bent backward over his encircling arm as his kiss became a brutal invasive quest that set her senses afire with mingled fear and longing.

The ravishing kiss grew gentler by degrees, as if the consuming force that had driven him was spent. She moaned softly as he drew his mouth from hers and his head slipped downward to the creamy mounds of her breasts, lips hovering but not touching as if he were steeling himself against their yearning sweetness.

He straightened slowly and let his arms fall away from her.

"Arif..." she whispered, her voice breathless with emotion.

But he would not let her continue. As he'd done once before, he lifted two fingers gently to her lips and pressed against them, forestalling the words he knew must inevitably arise there.

"I came out here to find you, Holly, to tell you that you will be leaving Riadja tomorrow." The words and tone were clipped, almost harsh, biting back any shred of emotion that might inadvertently reveal his emotions.

She stiffened. "When was this decided?" she asked, attempting to match his impersonal tone.

"Tonight. I talked with Schneider and arranged with him to get you a seat on the charter plane that he and several other medical personnel will be traveling on to return to Istanbul."

"I see." She turned from him to stare out into the bitterly cold dark night. So that had been the reason for his conversation with the American doctor! After a moment she asked, "And Jinniyah?"

"The mare will arrive a day later by train."

It had all been worked out so conveniently! She had received her curt notice of dismissal.

She raised her chin angrily, the gesture made to hide her shame at how she had melted so irresistibly in his embrace when all the time he had known it would soon be over for them. Damn his arrogance!

The taut silence between them lengthened. If he expected her to beg for his love, to beg for it not to be over, he had another think coming.

"Holly, damn it, say something at least!" he murmured with an explosive sigh, running impatient fingers through his hair.

She would not look at him, dared not risk having him see the desperately wounded pride and unvanquished love that still shone in her eyes. "It's best that I leave so soon," she whispered evenly, each word a struggle. "I have unfinished business in the city."

"What do you mean?"

She uttered a forced little laugh. "Don't you remember the Gypsy woman's prophecy?"

To her surprise, a breath of soft laughter escaped his lips. "I feel that I've known you a lifetime, Holly, yet in reality I know so little of you."

"Would it matter, anyway?" The words were at once a taunt and a challenge.

He shrugged with a pretense of indifference. "I suppose not."

"Then I suppose there's nothing more to be said." She moved swiftly toward the door, afraid her emotions might betray her. His eyes followed her as she turned to regard him from the dim pool of light that flooded the entryway—blond and beautiful, a prideful Western woman in alluring Oriental guise. "Good night, Arif. . . or should I say goodbye?"

She thought she heard a muffled curse exploding from his lips as she ran across the hall to the wide stone stairway.

CHAPTER ELEVEN

HOLLY STARED PAST THE WING TIP of the small chartered plane to the bleak emptiness of the land far below. There was nothing as far as the eye could see—a monochromatic tapestry lying cold and inert beneath the cruel blast of winter.

She sighed, thinking that the terrain was an apt mirror of her inner state. She felt drained of all emotion, empty and cold. Arif had warned her that they could only bring hurt to each other; why hadn't she listened? The frozen bitterness of her heart deepened as she thought back to that final embrace the night before, when their passion had dissolved into the cold indifference of strangers. He had severed the bond between them with the sharp precision of a surgeon's cut, neat and clean with no messy outpouring of apologies and recriminations. Yet she still bled inside. He had wounded her deeply, but she found herself still loving him. How could they meet again in Istanbul as indifferent strangers when her feelings had the power to betray her so easily?

Holly tried to blot out the painful memories, but they intruded again and again. Images of Arif and Riadja intermingled in her mind. Her last view of the ranch had been through the rear window of the jeep.

It had lain shadowed in the cold predawn light, surrounded by silence. She had not seen any of the Hakals again.

The hired hand Cemal had carried her luggage to the jeep and politely opened the passenger door. Once her limited Turkish vocabulary of "good morning" and "thank you" had been exhausted, the two had lapsed into a deep silence that had remained unbroken in the half hour drive to the Kars airfield. She couldn't help reflecting with bitter amusement that he must have been deeply grateful for the silence, since a man with two wives was apt to have little peace otherwise!

The image of Aggi and the browbeaten younger wife in the kitchen brought to mind an earlier scene when she'd angrily attempted to give back Arif's gifts. When she'd packed that morning, she had left the caftan neatly folded on the bed. But for some inexplicable reason she had kept the prayer beads. Throughout the long lonely drive down the mountain she had clutched them in her pocket like a talisman. The *tesbih* were her last link to Arif and Riadja, which she selfishly could not give up.

Holly's painful thoughts were interrupted as her companion in the adjoining seat touched her arm lightly. "Boy, you've been lost for two hours!" Bill Schneider remarked jokingly. "We'll be landing in the city in twenty minutes, but there's time for a cup of coffee from the thermos. What do you say?"

She looked up with a guilty start. "Sorry, Bill. I guess I've been lousy company. Coffee sounds wonderful!" Holly smiled warmly, hoping it would make up a little for her rudeness in ignoring him for the preceding two hours.

"Say, when we arrive in town, will you let me take you out for breakfast?"

"It's very sweet of you to invite me," Holly replied with a gentle shake of her head. "But I really have to get back to my hotel and see my trainer. He'll be anxious to find out how my trip went."

Bill grinned, his blue eyes as wide and guileless as a summer sky over Kansas. "Can't blame a man for trying," he teased lightly. "But I guess I just can't compete with that Turkish horseman. Man, I thought he'd break me in two just because I gave you a couple of admiring glances. He acted like he owned you. Are you two engaged or do you have some sort of understanding?"

Holly shook her head quickly, then turned to stare out the window again. No, she told herself bitterly. For her at least the understanding had come too late—that he could toss her aside so callously and deny his own feelings.

A pale watery sunshine was breaking through the morning haze by the time the plane touched down at Yesilköy Airport. As she hurried toward the taxi stand outside the busy terminal, Holly steeled herself not to think of her arrival at the same airport a few days before. The trip with Arif had held such sweet promise and had ended so coldly. Her feelings had been shattered like fragile crystal, yet she had no choice but to pick up the pieces and go on. No one but she herself would know how badly he had hurt her.

The mud-splattered cab hurtled at breakneck speed along the wet slushy streets of Istanbul. Most of the snow from the freak winter blizzard had melted, and the old city on the Bosporus had resumed its noisy tempo of living. Twenty minutes later, as the taxi darted into the narrow winding back streets of the European quarter, she felt a curious sense of claustrophobia. After the heady sweep of mountain and plain at Riadja, the rest of the world seemed somehow tawdry and small. Holly shook her head impatiently to rid herself of such thoughts, yet they persisted even as the cab screeched to a halt outside the Pera Palas.

As she entered the hotel, her eyes immediately picked out the tough diminutive form of Rusty Wilkins in a far corner. His smelly brier pipe was clamped between his teeth as he read a newspaper. With his old jeans and faded shirt and the haze of Bull Durham tobacco about his head, he looked ridiculously out of place in the old-fashioned splendor of the lobby. Holly felt a rush of affection for the grizzled ex-cowboy and hurried forward to greet him.

He glanced up at her approach and set aside his newspaper. "Hiya, Holly," the trainer greeted her laconically. "Did you get the mare?"

"She'll arrive tomorrow," Holly replied tersely as she sat down beside him on the faded damask sofa.

There was a long silence. Finally Rusty murmured, "Your old man is here."

A sigh of mingled frustration and anger escaped her lips. "I know," she replied simply.

Rusty sat up a little straighter at that unexpected

response. "What do you mean, you know?" he demanded, his sandy brows arching quizzically.

"I ran into one of my father's flunkies in Erzurum. The man had been tailing me all the way from Paris," Holly explained, bridling still at the memory.

Rusty took the pipe from his teeth, and his eyebrows lifted even farther until his features seemed a caricature of comical astonishment. "Well, I'll be damned," he swore softly. "You were bein' watched just like Tati Bulgakov."

"Exactly," Holly replied. "And all that time I had been pitying Tatiana her lack of freedom and privacy. Ironic, isn't it?" she added with a bitter little smile.

Rusty sighed in commiseration. "It's real tough, Holly, but you can't change it." After another silence he told her soberly, "Your old man has a suite of rooms over at the Istanbul Sheraton, and he's been sendin' that tall guy Rocky Stiles over a dozen times a day to find out if you got back yet. Your dad is damned anxious to see you."

"Well, he'll just have to wait a while longer," she shot back, her eyes darkening with anger at the prospect of the meeting between father and daughter.

She felt Rusty's gaze upon her and knew that he was itching to ask her a million questions. But, good friend that he was, he said nothing at all aloud. He would patiently bide his time until she was ready to confide in him. Tears of gratitude welled up in her throat, only to dissolve in confused feelings of anger and hurt as her thoughts turned to her father and to Arif. Like a child then she put her head on Rusty's shoulder and sobbed brokenly. "Damn them!" she cried half to herself. "Damn them both!"

Awkwardly he patted her arm, weathering the emotional storm with as much laconic stoicism as if he'd been caught in the middle of the Wyoming plain when a deluge broke: nothing for it but to sit and ride it out.

When the sobs had faded away at last into nothing but an occasional sniffle, Rusty smiled sympathetically. "Okay, kid, now that you've got it out of your system, what do you say we go into the dinin' room to get a bite to eat? This Turk food is really beginnin' to grow on me."

Holly managed a grin despite the shining wetness of her eyes. "Your stomach is like an alarm clock, Rusty," she teased. "It goes off every four hours on the button." Even as she teased him, though, Holly stood up with alacrity. She realized that she was starving, too, since she hadn't had anything to eat since dinner the previous night at the Hakals' home.

A few minutes later Holly and Rusty sat regarding each other over the crisp white tablecloth. Her eyes were red and swollen after her cry against Rusty's shoulder, but he forbore from teasing her about it.

"How is Tatiana?" Holly asked after a while. "Are you still prescribing DMSO?" she needled him lightly.

"Her knee's worse instead of better," Rusty replied, his lips drawn in a grim line. "And she gets more tense every day. She keeps expectin' to get the word anytime now to clear out and get back to Moscow."

"She must be miserable!" Holly replied.

"Hell, if they'd only give her until the spring. Then that bad knee of hers'd get better. Without that plaguey arthritis, she's a damn fine rider." Rusty pounded an angry fist on the tabletop.

"I know that, Rusty," she commiserated softly. "I respect and like Tatiana as much as you do." Fearing that she might have intruded too much into Rusty's personal feelings, Holly lapsed then into silence.

A moment later the waiter brought sandwiches and tea, and they ate without talking. Suddenly every subject seemed too thorny to broach, too peppered with the heat of emotion.

When she'd finished eating, Holly set her napkin on the table. "I suppose that I can't put it off any longer. I'm going to go and get ready for the big interview," she said with a drawn-out sigh as she rose from the table.

"Good luck, gal. Don't let him rile you," Rusty advised, twirling his empty teacup moodily before him.

THE TAXI HURTLED along the wide tree-lined avenue toward the elegant complex of international hotels and restaurants bordering Taksim Square. The twin towers of the Sheraton, Istanbul's newest and most luxurious hotel, rose like a gleaming modern sculpture above the leafless black branches in the park.

A stone-faced doorman in gray top hat and tails assisted her from the cab. *Leave it to dad to choose a place like this,* Holly reflected wryly as she swept past the attendant and into the plush lobby. The elevator climbed swiftly and silently to the penthouse suite that James Holliford had reserved. Holly stared with seeming absorption at the lighted numerals changing in rapid sequence and brushed back a stray wisp of hair with a nervous hand.

She had spent almost two hours in her room at the Pera Palas readying herself for this interview. Appalled at the sight of her tear-swollen features in the mirror, Holly had made cold compresses with ice wrapped in washcloths and had lain down across the bed, psychologically girding herself for the upcoming ordeal. She knew that he would attempt to intimidate her with the same manner that he'd honed to a knife-edged sharpness over thirty years. His business acumen and unparalleled ability to manipulate people had led him to build the family-owned Holliford City Bank into one of the richest and most powerful financial institutions in the United States. His technique was a quick but subtle offensive to put his adversaries off guard, followed by a relentless thrust and parry of carefully constructed logic to wear them down until they could come around to no viewpoint but his own. Her father was an iron-willed man; she would simply have to show that her own will was equally strong.

Satisfied at last that her face bore no further traces of a teary-eyed breakdown, Holly had showered quickly and spent a long time applying makeup and arranging her hair in a feminine but businesslike style. Then she'd gone through her wardrobe carefully before finally selecting a burgundy wool suit with a straight skirt and short jacket, which she paired with a softly patterned Chinese silk blouse. The womanly but no-nonsense look was rounded out with high-heeled pumps and a leather envelope bag. She wanted no weakness showing through the chinks in her haute couture armor. James Holliford would be forced to recognize that he was no longer dealing with a child.

Perhaps she owed a debt of gratitude to Arif for that at least. Though their relationship had been a raging battlefield of conflicting emotions and wills, Arif had always reminded her most forcefully that she was indeed a woman. Even now, with all her pent-up anger and hurt, her pulse could quicken with need at the thought of him!

The elevator door slid open soundlessly, and Holly found herself standing face to face with suite 1107. Taking a deep breath she stepped forward and pushed open the door. Before the dark Chippendale desk in the small anteroom sat her father's personal secretary, John Felson. Lounging in the chair adjacent to the desk was the tall pale-featured man— Rocky Stiles—who had shadowed her across much of Europe and Asia. He stood up quickly at her entrance, but she did not even deign him a glance.

The secretary stood up, as well, and came around the desk. "Miss Holliford, it is *so* good to see you again. We've *all* been anxiously awaiting your arrival."

Holly bridled at his fawning obsequious manner. *I'm home again,* she thought to herself with a bitter little laugh. But on the surface she was poised, cool, aloof. "Thank you, Mr. Felson. I'll go right in to see my father now, if you don't mind."

She brushed past the flustered secretary without giving him a chance to announce her arrival and stepped into the living room, carefully closing the door behind her.

James Holliford sat behind a walnut desk, which had been arranged catercorner to the window with its sweeping panoramic view of Istanbul's seven hills. He looked up swiftly at her entrance but continued dictating notes into a small machine before him.

Holly recognized his cool insistence on completing whatever business he was engaged in as one of his subtle power ploys. She circumvented it by walking forward coolly and addressing him even while he continued his monotone dictation. "Hello, dad."

He switched off the dictaphone and regarded her with slightly narrowed eyes as she approached. Holly avoided the low chairs and came around to perch on the edge of his desk. She smiled and leaned over to brush her lips against his gray temple.

He stood up and thrust his hands into the pockets of his impeccably tailored gray suit, staring down at his daughter's face with green eyes that were a paler, harder version of her own. "Hello, dear. It's good to see you. Your mother and I have been quite concerned about you, especially after this last escapade. Tell me, how was your expedition into the Turkish badlands?" he inquired with dry, almost brittle wit.

"Actually it was quite fascinating, dad. Our car broke down in the middle of nowhere, and we had to hitch a ride with a Kurdish caravan. I wouldn't have missed that experience for anything in the world," Holly added, smiling still.

The muscle in his cheek quivered slightly, and she knew that he had been angered and a little shocked by her airy words. But when he spoke his voice had not deviated from its crisp well-modulated timbre. "I did not appreciate your dismissing Rocky Stiles and threatening him with the police. He's a trusted employee of mine and he was doing an excellent job."

"As far as *you* were concerned," she replied evenly.

"I'm afraid that you've taken leave of your senses completely, Hortense. Do you realize that if you had been kidnapped, you would have been worth a fat ransom?"

Holly shivered at the thought of such a scenario, then quickly realized that he had meant to frighten her and put her off guard by his remarks. "But that didn't happen. Besides, even if it had, I'm sure you would have arranged to make some sort of political capital out of it," she retorted sharply.

He came forward until he stood directly in front of her, and Holly was forced to crane her neck upward to regard him. "I'm not an ogre, child. You are my daughter, and as such you are my first concern. We've digressed from the principal reason that I'm here in the first place."

"Which is?" she asked quietly.

"Your ill-advised affair. . .with this Hakal."

She lifted her chin pridefully. "I happen to be in love with Arif Hakal!" she replied without hesitation, surprising herself with the force and conviction in her voice.

Holliford's cool eyes bored deeply into hers. "And

are you naive enough to believe that he returns your love?''

"I think that's entirely my business, dad. Not yours.''

"Hasn't it dawned on you that he's interested not in you but in your inheritance?''

Holly couldn't refrain from giggling a little at that. "What inheritance! I thought that you and mother had disowned me the moment I walked out on my engagement to Stan Winthrop.''

Holliford scowled impatiently. "Damn it, Hortense, don't quibble. The Turk is a fortune hunter.''

"Arif doesn't know I'm a Holliford,'' she argued reasonably. "To him I'm the anonymous and quite poor Holly MacKnight.''

With breathtaking suddenness, Holliford switched his line of attack. "Has he asked you to marry him?''

"No!'' She stood up from the desk so that her eyes were at a level with his.

"And mightn't he have done so already if he *had* known your true identity?''

Nonplussed by this unexpected thrust, she could only reply weakly, "Dad, what's the purpose of this tiresome cross-examination?''

"I had hoped to be able to reason with you, but it's obvious that you're hopelessly besotted.'' His gaze was angry, cold, disapproving.

"I will not stand here and have you berate me as if I were a foolish child.'' Her clipped icy tone matched the coldness in his eyes, and they regarded each other stubbornly for several long seconds.

With a weary sigh he eased himself into the leather

swivel chair. "Sit down, girl." His eyes never wavered from hers and she perched once more on the edge of his desk. "How do you think I've spent these three days in Istanbul? Do you think I've been sightseeing and gambling at the Hilton casino?" His tone was clipped and sarcastic. "I'll tell you quite simply. I have been checking up on Hakal's financial situation."

"How dare you!"

But Holliford brushed aside her outrage with a sharp wave of his hand. "The man is on the verge of bankruptcy. He's incurred heavy debts—our research is a little murky there. We don't know if it's gambling or what precisely. But the point is that he's under tremendous pressure to repay them. He'll jump at matrimony with a rich woman because he needs the money to stay out of financial hot water. How much plainer can I put it?"

Holly bit her lip to keep it from quivering. "You make it all sound so tawdry."

"Isn't it?" he retorted swiftly. "If Hakal's intentions are so pure and honorable, then where is the engagement ring on your finger, my penniless Ms. MacKnight?" He paused to let the words sink in. "He's used you, and I'll wager that he's already tossed you aside. The man is totally without scruples or morals."

"You're vicious, dad," she whispered.

"Am I? I think not. The man is a cheap opportunist."

"You haven't proved that to me. I still love him," she retorted stubbornly.

"Damn it, Hortense," he said with unwonted

sharpness, "come to your senses. Forget this idiocy. You've already failed in the riding trials—"

"Not yet I haven't! I'll be competing again...with one of Arif's mares."

Realizing that he was getting nowhere with his arguments, Holliford shrugged. "I've brought some of your trunks from home. At least move into the Sheraton and out of that turn-of-the-century monstrosity where you and Wilkins are staying."

"No, thank you, dad. I'm quite happy there." She stood up and walked toward the door, then paused and turned around to face him. "Since you've come all this way, I hope you'll at least drive out to Selimiye to watch me compete in the three-day event. Maybe you'll have the satisfaction of seeing me fail, but maybe...just maybe I'll have the satisfaction of winning." And she swept out of the room and past Felson's desk without a backward glance.

Once she was safely inside the haven of the elevator, Holly leaned her throbbing temple against the cool metal wall. Her father's cold words of accusation were still reverberating endlessly in her head. "The man is totally without scruples...a cheap opportunist."

Then rising unbidden, as if in counterpoint to his sharp thrusts, was her own patchwork of remembrances: the night of the Parisian ball when Arif had coolly told her that he sought a wife who met his requirements; his charming drawing-room act with Geneviève and Ziya at his apartment; his own depiction of himself as a "practical man."

Holly thrust her clenched fist tightly against her mouth. "Oh, God," she murmured, "have I been duped completely?"

CHAPTER TWELVE

IT WAS A CLEAR DECEMBER AFTERNOON, sunny and almost warm after the long uninterrupted stretch of frigid weather. Holly had just taken the bus across to the Selimiye training grounds for the second time that day. In the morning she had checked on the stall-bound Mandarin Lady and found her resting comfortably. After patting her affectionately, Holly had made her way to Jinniyah's stall and saddled the silver gray Arabian for her morning workout. It had gone very well, and Holly was pleased.

Now this afternoon she planned to give her another light workout over jumps. As Holly brushed the mare's gleaming coat, Jinniyah leaned her head over the neighboring stall and playfully nudged Sinjon. Glancing over at the fine black stallion, Holly could not help but be reminded of Arif, and she wondered for the hundredth time if he would return to Istanbul for the competition.

Holly led Jinniyah from the stall, and once they were outside she swung up into the saddle. The sun felt deliciously warm on her back as she rode toward the arena, and she was glad that she'd shed her bulky parka. She felt relaxed and comfortable, clad in a slim pair of blue jeans and blue-and-green plaid shirt tied over a white T-shirt. Her hair had been caught back carelessly in a loose ponytail and she wore her oldest hacking boots. There would be plenty of time tomorrow for elegant cream-colored stocks and spit-polished gear. This afternoon she would concentrate purely on jumping.

Once again the workout had gone without a hitch, and Holly was whistling happily to herself an hour later as she led the mare back to her stall. For the first time since she'd left Paris, Holly felt that her chances of winning were excellent. Once again the idea of winning had become supremely important to her, and she realized that her feelings had been affected by her father's presence in the city. She vowed to prove him wrong...in this at least.

Once the mare was returned to her stall, Holly worked with brisk energy. After picking out Jinniyah's hooves and brushing them free of small stones, mud and other debris, she picked up the large body brush and began to run it over the mare's back and down her flanks with long smooth strokes until her coat gleamed brightly once more.

So engrossed was she in grooming Jinniyah and in talking gently in her ear to accustom the mare to the sound of her voice that Holly wasn't even aware the stall door at her back had been opened. When she turned around a moment later, she found herself face to face with Arif.

They stared at each other for a long moment. It was Holly who at last broke the silence. "So you've decided to return to Istanbul after all?" she observed, not quite able to keep the note of challenge from her voice.

"Like you, Holly, I have unfinished business here," he replied easily.

"To find the woman of your dreams?" she taunted him.

"That woman I had for all too short a time before I had to let her go from my life." There was none of the familiar sardonic mockery in his voice. In its place Holly sensed a strange hollowness.

"What a pity!" she retorted at last, with light mockery of her own.

"Not a pity, Holly, but a tragedy." His eyes shone with a darkly smoldering fire.

Suddenly she felt confused and afraid, as if the man who stood before her were a stranger, soft-spoken yet uncompromising. Holly pulled the curry comb through the brush with trembling fingers, unwilling to look at him. "Jinniyah is a fine mare," she said at last, as if to bring the conversation around to less personal terrain, "one of the finest that I've ever ridden."

"Good. Perhaps you'll win with her, Holly."

"Perhaps," she conceded slowly. "But I have so few illusions left."

"Isn't it better to have shared a dream for a little while, even if you're later forced to give it up, than never to have had the dream in the first place?" he asked with quiet force.

"Human emotion isn't a switch that can be turned on and off." She turned blazing green eyes on him. "What I feel now, I will always feel!"

"And you think I feel differently?" His voice was edged with hard anger.

"It doesn't matter what I think," she retorted with unwonted harshness. "As far as I'm concerned, you've already shown your true colors."

He swore softly under his breath. "Damn it, Holly, I can stand anything but your contempt! Do you insist that the words be spoken even though they will change nothing except to make us both more miserable?"

"What words?" she whispered.

"Three very simple ones: I love you." He repeated it with a slow soft vehemence, almost as if it were a curse that was bound to haunt him. "I will always love you, Holly."

She drew a slow shuddering breath. "I don't know, Arif. I no longer trust my own feelings. I've heard rumors about you . . . ugly rumors that you are a fortune hunter, an opportunist."

His eyes glinted with black anger. "Come with me, Holly," he commanded sharply, his dark hand imprisoning her slender wrist as he pulled her out of the mare's stall.

"Where are we going?" she demanded breathlessly, half running to keep up with his long purposeful stride.

"To talk," he flung at her. "It's time that you heard the whole story. I owe you that much at least."

THE ICE IN THE STONE FOUNTAIN had melted, and the clear water babbled like a mountain creek in spring. Holly and Arif faced each other over the small table in the Spice Market tavern that they'd dined in the week before. Had it been so short a time, Holly thought wonderingly. So much had occurred between them in the interim!

At that midafternoon hour they were the only patrons in the usually bustling *lokanta*, and the silence seemed to hang heavily between them. Arif glanced restlessly over the empty tables. "Where do I start?" he murmured, half to himself.

"How about starting at the beginning?" she replied, her eyes serious and watchful.

"I suppose it begins and ends with the land itself: Riadja." The small demitasse before him seemed as fragile as an eggshell as he cupped his strong dark fingers around it and stared down at the black residue of grounds in the bottom. Then he began to talk in a low voice. "Part of the marital agreement between my father's family and the Kurdish tribe of my grandfather Car Ishak involved a complicated yearly formula of payments with regard to the merger of the two landholdings. Because of an old Kurdish tribal law, their land could not be given outright. In a sense the Hakals were to pay a yearly bride price—initially grain and livestock—in order to keep the rights to the land that would devolve to me as the firstborn son and to my son after me."

Arif sighed and signaled the waiter for another cup of the strong unfiltered coffee before he began to speak again. "The matter became further entangled because, as I told you once before, the marriage between my parents was considered an important political symbol. More as a gesture than anything else, the

Turkish state was drawn into the complicated land-nuptials agreement as a kind of third-party guarantor—to lend added prestige to the union. Well, in the course of forty years much has changed with regard to the terms of the agreement. For one thing, as the Kurds themselves became more sophisticated, the yearly formula of payments began to be translated into money rather than products. The amount involved also became quite substantial." Arif broke off and rubbed the back of his neck. "Does any of this make sense to you, Holly?"

Her gaze was at once sympathetic and intense. She thought back to her conversation with Carana at the ruined chapel and the woman's subtle references to her husband's idealistic but improvident bent of mind. "I think I'm beginning to understand," Holly replied slowly. "But please go on."

Arif's breath was expelled in a frustrated sigh. "Until recently, my father insisted on handling the financial arrangements, and we assumed that the matter was being handled adequately. Unfortunately, we discovered a short time back that most of the profits he'd been working from were simply figures on paper, and the family had fallen in arrears to the amount of millions of Turkish lira. We received a notice from the state that unless the back payments were made, then land would revert to government ownership—on the basis of that 'symbolic' third-party-guarantor agreement made forty years ago! Riadja would be broken up."

"But the land had been in both families for generations! That would be a tragedy," Holly observed quietly, her eyes subtly mirroring the pain she read in Arif's dark gaze.

A sardonic smile briefly twisted his lips. "The final coup de grace is that my father took the last of the family's investment and put it in a chromium mine just east of Diyarbakir. My mother and I knew nothing of it until the ownership papers were signed. As with all his other schemes, he vows the mine will save Riadja, but at the same time I've taken steps of my own to see that the ranch is not lost to us."

Holly's gaze flickered over his lean, stubbornly set features, her eyes deepening in intensity until they were like polished greenstone. "Marriage to a rich woman," Holly completed for him. "Geneviève or Ziya."

"Precisely," Arif assented in a harsh sardonic voice. "To my parents' chagrin, I'd always been one to play the field—never interested in any woman for more than a very short while. I scoffed at the idea of love. Maybe it was a self-protective gesture because I knew that I'd never find a woman who not only was beautiful and intelligent but would be willing to share the rigors of my life at Riadja. So...I played. Then, of course, my mother realized that it was I who held the final trump card. Suddenly it became my solemn duty to use that well-practiced charm to snare a wealthy woman who would be more than willing to agree to certain financial terms—in exchange for marriage to me." The words were dry, self-mocking, and a grin once more suffused his features, though there was no mirth in his eyes.

"And you still intend to propose to one of them?"
Holly asked crisply.

"Yes, of course. It really doesn't matter which of
them it is to be. Only it must be done quickly; otherwise I might weaken and...."

"And what?"

Slowly he shook his head, eyes drinking her in with
an expression full at once of fierce pride and a deep
unquenchable sadness.

Her heart twisted with guilt and anger that she'd
allowed herself to be swayed by her father's accusations. Arif was a man of integrity and loyalty, and
she found herself loving him more deeply than she
could have thought possible. She would not give him
up without a fight!

"Arif," she began suddenly, green eyes narrowed
so that he might not read the glints of mischief
in their depths, "before you make any final deci-
sions, will you have dinner with me this evening?
I...I'd like to repay you for your family's hospitality at Riadja and for the loan of Jinniyah. Let
this be my planned evening from start to end. I'll
even pick you up at your apartment. What do you
say?"

A faint cloud of suspicion hovered in his eyes.
"What are you up to, Holly MacKnight?"

"Trust me, Arif. Is it a deal?" she asked, running
a nervous hand over her ponytail and tightening the
ends of her plaid shirt.

He nodded reluctantly. "Still the woman of mystery?" he teased her as she stood up from the table.
"Let me drive you back to the Pera Palas."

"No, no," she replied quickly. "I'm not headed there."

Before he could insist, she moved toward the front entrance of the little tavern. "I'll call for you at seven-thirty." And with a quick wave and a grin, she disappeared into the narrow crowded lanes of the Spice Market.

THE WINTER DUSK HAD FALLEN hours ago, but Arif hadn't bothered to switch on a lamp. The high-ceilinged living room was cold and dark, but he wasn't even aware of it. He stood moodily before the long French windows, staring out over the lamplit street below.

His thoughts were focused on a subject that had rarely been far from his mind in the preceding two weeks: the lithe blond American who had burst into his life like a ray of tropical sun. Even as he envisioned Holly in his mind, he was aware of the depth of his desire for her.

His attraction to the lovely foreigner was like a fever—consuming and without a cure. If he had taken her to his bed at once, perhaps that might have cured him. But that inevitably sweet, explosive surrender had come too late. By then he'd known already that he—the one always impervious to love—had fallen prey at last to the bloody emotion he'd mocked for so long.

The exquisitely painful irony was that he had found the one woman for whom he'd been searching subconsciously his whole life—a woman beautiful, prideful and strong. And he'd found her at the precise moment in time when she must be forbidden to him. He remembered the way she had approached Sam Ezine and himself at the party—cool and lovely in the exotic gown. Yet for all the delicacy of her beauty, she had a quick intelligent mind, and he realized that he undoubtedly would act upon her suggestion of utilizing one of the slopes in building the new paddock. He'd read in her eyes a deep-felt admiration for Riadja: she had an affinity for the land.

The fulfillment of his duty to marry—and thereby save Riadja—might have been one final postscript in a long meaningless series of interludes with the fairer sex... if it hadn't been for Holly.

His raging desire for her and the dawning realization of his love had begun to make a mockery of that duty. He envisioned the candlelit outline of her naked form in the Kurdish tent, the full sweetness of her breasts and the length of shapely leg. He muttered a bitter curse under his breath.

Arif knew that he had to propose quickly to Geneviève or Ziya—no matter which—because he knew that if he did not it would be Holly that he took to his marriage bed. In his heart and soul she was the true bride of Riadja, though in the harsh light of reality he knew that it could not be.

A low burst of affectionate laughter escaped his lips as he recalled Carana's description of the first meeting between her father and Holly. Car Ishak had wanted to know immediately if the green-eyed blond with the prideful bearing and beautiful intelligent gaze was Arif's woman. Even though Carana had denied it at once, the stubborn Kurd had insisted. "Nevertheless, she is the one for Arif."

Bravo, old Ishak, Arif mused to himself. *You saw in Holly the same qualities that I'd found.* Grandfather and grandson had always been so much alike!

But what did the old man's wisdom count for now? The union between Arif and Holly was never meant to be. He would, after all, put duty over love. Though the thought gripped at his heart like the tearing claws of an eagle, he could do nothing else.

For all his anguished thoughts before the dark window, Arif couldn't help but notice the long black limousine that had drawn to a stop beneath the streetlamp. He was still wondering which of his neighbors had access to such blatant accoutrements of power and wealth when a sharp rap at the front door caught his attention.

Striding swiftly across the room, he threw the door open, then stared down in perplexity at the gray-uniformed chauffeur who stood there.

"If you please, sir," the man addressed Arif politely. "The lady is waiting."

Arif continued to stare at the man as if he were some outlandish fantasy. "What the bloody hell is going on?" he demanded crossly.

But the chauffeur had turned around and retreated down the stairway, so that Arif had no choice but to follow behind him. Outside, the driver stood at attention by the curb and opened the rear door for him.

Arif stooped down and peered inside the opulent dark leather interior of the limousine. His eyes hardened with mingled shock and surprise as he took in Holly's smiling features and sumptuously clad form. Gone was the endearing ponytail and casual plaid shirt that had deepened the color of her incredibly green eyes. This womanly vision of elegance and wealth—large diamonds glinting in her earlobes above the sparkle of her silver-threaded gown and pale fox-fur coat—was an utter stranger to him.

"What masquerade is this?" he demanded, his voice harsh and edged with anger.

HOLLY'S HEART SKIPPED A BEAT as she regarded Arif. His lean hard jaw was set at a stubborn angle as his eyes raked over her in disbelief. His bronzed features were set off by the pale ivory of his shirt and the dark velvet of his well-cut dinner jacket.

"Haven't you ever read the fairy tale *Cinderella*?" she replied with a teasing smile. "Now climb in out of the cold, Arif, dearest. I've made our dinner reservations for eight."

He sank down into the plush leather and put his arm along the back of the seat. With one fingertip he lightly brushed her diamond-glittering earlobe, and the negligent touch of his warm fingers sent a thrill of pleasure down Holly's spine. But his eyes had not lost their hard obsidian edge. "Do you want to tell me what's going on, Miss MacKnight?"

"Arif, you kept me guessing for weeks as to your true motives. Surely you'll let me keep you guessing for a few hours," she retorted with a soft laugh.

He withdrew his hand and crossed his arms stubbornly over his chest, staring out into the lights and traffic beyond the tinted limousine windows, while Holly smiled conspiratorially to herself.

After she had left the Spice Market tavern earlier that day, Holly had gone straight to the Sheraton and her father's suite. She had crisply informed him that she'd changed her mind and would move into the luxurious hotel with him after all. Holliford had seemed a trifle suspicious of this abrupt change of heart, but he was an eminently practical man. To his mind, having her with him at the hotel was halfway toward winning the battle.

Afterward Holly had spent some time going through the clothes trunks that had been sent for her. Although she'd been appalled at the ridiculous extravagance of having the heavy trunks airfreighted to Istanbul, she was reluctantly forced to acknowledge her mother's master touch in the array of garments before her. It was obvious that the stubborn Alice Holliford regarded her daughter's sojourn in the cosmopolitan Turkish city not as a working visit but as a glittering social event.

Any other time Holly would have scoffed disdainfully, but that afternoon she'd felt only gratitude for her mother's misconception. It hadn't taken Holly long to select the long-sleeved floor-length gown of silver-threaded silk that clung to her slender but shapely body like a glove.

Everything in the trunks, from the furs and designer silks to the jewelry, bespoke wealth. Holly had been appalled by such displays in the past. But tonight she intended to use and flaunt it—if it would help her to win the man she loved.

Now, as the limousine turned smoothly onto the long drive leading to the Sheraton, Holly glanced once more at Arif. He had maintained a stubborn silence throughout the twenty-minute ride across town, but she smiled to herself once more as she caught the unguarded look of surprise on his features when the automobile drew to a stop before the ultra-modern hotel lobby.

He threw Holly a dark look. "May I ask what the devil we're doing here?"

"Dinner and dancing—simple as that," she grinned.

The view from the glassed-in terrace restaurant on the top floor was a three-hundred-sixty-degree panorama of an Arabian Nights dream—back-lit mosques and minarets like sculptured ivory tusks thrusting upward from the twinkling lights far below.

After the waiter had uncorked the bottle of Châteauneuf-du-Pape and poured it, Holly lifted her glass and chinked it against Arif's. "To Riadja," she murmured.

His eyes narrowed at the toast, but he lifted his glass and drank to it.

Arif showed himself remarkably disinclined to talk throughout the drawn-out and elegantly prepared meal, so Holly chatted lightly, touching on one subject and another.

Afterward they wandered into the Sultan Bar, where a small combo was playing slow romantic ballads. Holly held her hand out to Arif, and he drew her onto the small crowded dance floor. Her heartbeat quickened with agonized delight as he pulled her closer to him and their bodies molded briefly as if they were one. With one hand she reached up to caress the back of his neck and twine her fingers in the black hair. He groaned softly and his hands tightened on her slender waist as he savored the cool lavender scent of her and the feel of her rounded thighs through the clingy silk of her gown.

They drew apart slowly as the music ended and gazed at each other—the seductive smoky green of her eyes melting into the darkly raging fires that she read in his glance.

"I...I think we'd better talk," Holly said shakily at last.

The Harem annex to the Sultan Bar proved yet another evocation of Arabian Nights fantasies with its marble fountain, latticework window shades and sheepskin-covered couches ranged against the wall.

Holly sank down on one of the soft divans, kicked off her uncomfortable high heels and curled her legs beneath her. Arif sat down beside her, back straight and taut as he rested his elbows on his knees and stared moodily into the lighted fountain.

"Arif," she began tentatively, "have you ever heard of Holliford International Investments, Inc."

He shrugged indifferently. "I suppose I've seen the name mentioned a few times in business magazines. Why do you ask?"

Holly sighed. "You made your confession earlier today, Arif. Now I suppose it's my turn." He glanced up at her sharply, waiting for her to continue. "James Holliford is my father. And the life I ran away from was one of idle richness. I *was* engaged to be married to a wealthy man, as you'd guessed when we talked on the train, but the man my parents had chosen was selected not to make me more filthily rich than I already am but to carry on the Holliford financial empire. My full name is Hortense MacKnight Holliford.''

A bitter grin creased Arif's features at this totally unexpected revelation. ''So the Holly MacKnight of my dreams was nothing more than that—a beautiful wraith without substance.''

''No, Arif!'' she countered briefly. ''This glittering dramatic show was all designed to make a simple point: you can have the woman of your dreams *and* Riadja. You can live as you choose.''

Their conversation was interrupted as a dark waitress in sheer harem pants set down a glass of sherry and a shot of *raki* before them.

After she'd gone, Arif's fist tightened about the glass of clear liquid until Holly feared that he would crush it. ''As what, Holly? As your kept man—the sole male concubine in your cozy harem?'' His low taunting words burned with a smoldering anger.

She sat up straighter on the couch. ''Damn it, Arif. We love each other. What does it matter where the money comes from?''

''It matters to me,'' he whispered slowly, the words a faintly menacing hiss. With one hand he reached out and flicked the expensive silk of her gown. ''Do you think that this is part of the woman whom I fell in love with?''

''Arif, I haven't changed. I am still the same woman,'' she reasoned softly. ''All that's changed is that in addition to my love and caring I can give you everything else you need—the money to keep Riadja and to build it into a magnificent breeding ranch. I want to share that dream with you.''

"You've arranged it all so prettily in your mind, haven't you, Holly?" His eyes were like two burning coals. "But you have forgotten one thing: my pride. For duty's sake I was more than willing to marry a rich woman.''

"I *am* a rich woman.''

"You are the woman I love, Holly—fiercely and beyond all reason. I could never take money from you. Your money would destroy my pride and eventually our love. It is an impossibility.'' The words were curt, harsh, brooking no argument. As he stood up from the couch, she swiftly rose to her stockinged feet, as well.

"Nothing has changed, then," she said hollowly, the words reverberating with disbelief. "You still intend to marry Geneviève or Ziya?''

"Yes," he replied harshly.

Her eyes blazed with the brittle intensity of green vitriol. "Your raging pride is a curse.''

"Holly, I am sorry that we've had to hurt each other so deeply," he whispered down at her.

"Arif. . .'' she whispered helplessly in return.

For a brief second it was as if they tottered on the brink of a deep chasm, drawing them with inexorable force. She felt the heat emanating from his body, and he was agonizingly aware of the full thrust of her breasts against the thin silvery silk.

But before the short distance could be bridged,

Arif had turned away. He paused in the door, his caressing dark eyes at once fierce and illimitably sad. "Good night, Holly. And good luck tomorrow at the trials. I hope you win at least one of your heart's desires."

He was gone then, leaving Holly bereft and horribly alone.

As she stared out over the dark city, she was reminded of Carana Hakal's description of her son as "a man of unquenchable pride and spirit." She had warned Holly, "Rich or poor, you have no future with Arif."

Would that prophecy prove to be more telling than the droning words of the Gypsy in the Kars café?

CHAPTER THIRTEEN

THE GRUELING THREE DAYS of the riding event were curiously telescoped in Holly's mind: she had concentrated on nothing but the demands of each separate competition. The hours in her life were bound by endless stretches of waiting and tension at the riding grounds and long sleepless nights in her room at the Sheraton.

Over and over she had sought to come up with something that would resolve the impasse between her and Arif before he was lost to her forever. But increasingly she was afraid that he had been right: any shared future between them was an impossibility.

They hadn't spoken again since their emotionally charged confrontation at the hotel, except for the most cursory of greetings when they passed by each other at the riding grounds. The miserable irony of the situation was that the confidences they had shared had served to drive a wedge between them. Now they were more distant strangers than on that cold autumn morning at Malmaison when they had first met.

Holly longed simply to throw her arms around his neck and beg him to forget the demands of the rest of the world, but at the same time she recognized the futility, and the wrongness, of the wish. Arif was bound by his world, and she could not help but respect and love him even more deeply because of his commitment to it. That was yet another irony in the many that had seemed to mock their relationship from the start: the more deeply she loved him because of his devotion to Riadja, the greater was the pain at the thought of having to lose him.

Holly had ridden the first two events, the dressage and the show-jumping course, like an automaton. She'd allowed her lithe well-trained body to carry out the rigorous demands of the events while her thoughts were elsewhere. The unexpected result was that she was riding better than she'd ever ridden in her life. The focus of her thoughts on other matters unconsciously had served to relax her usually tense hands and limbs, so that the superb training of both mount and rider could successfully take over.

She had been surprised to see the official standings after the first two days of competition: Holly MacKnight in first place with Captain Arif Hakal running a distant second. A month ago the thought of being number one would have meant everything to her. Now she didn't really care at all. Besides, she acknowledged realistically that she could never really best the superb horseman of the steppes. Holly guessed that his thoughts, like hers, were focused on their last bitter conversation, and the thrill and the challenge of the riding competition no longer mattered to him. His future lay elsewhere.

THE FINAL DAY OF THE COMPETITION was brittle, cold and clear. It was Christmas Eve, but the customary round of merry well-wishing had been submerged in the tension surrounding the last, and most difficult, phase of the three-day event: the punishing cross-country run.

For once the situation was completely reversed, with Holly the cool calm practical one and Rusty Wilkins a taut bundle of nerves. It wasn't the young American rider he was concerned about, however, but the intense dark-haired Russian woman who'd managed to give a respectable if lackluster perform-ance in the first two phases of the three-day event. If Tatiana could just hold that sixth-place position in the final competition, she would probably get the go-ahead from her superiors to participate in the spring riding trials in Great Britain.

Rusty had informed Holly of all this with a quiet optimism that admitted no other possibility. For Tatiana's sake Holly hoped he was right. The other possibility—that of the Russian lieutenant being hustled back to Moscow in defeat—didn't even bear thinking of.

So engrossed was she in her thoughts of Rusty and Tatiana that Holly didn't see the gray Chrysler sedan until it loomed directly before her in the open grounds between the stables and the riding arena. She drew up short, smoothing down her hunter-green sweater and cream breeches. The prettily groomed Jinniyah, who was walking beside her on a long rein, stopped obediently, as well.

Rocky Stiles, her father's omnipresent guard, had

climbed out from behind the wheel of the luxury car and was opening the rear door as Holly drew to a halt before it. A moment later James Holliford and Adnan Memed emerged into the cold December sunshine.

"Good luck today, dear," Holliford greeted his daughter with a quick peck on the cheek. "I've become something of a fan of yours these past two days. I'm impressed. You're a real professional."

"Thanks, dad," she laughed in response. "Maybe if you'd seen me riding over these past six years you wouldn't be quite so shocked now by my professional status." Before Holliford could say anything in response, Holly turned to her father's friend and greeted the handsome Turkish industrialist.

"You are riding like a dream, Miss Holliford... er, Holly. I'm certain you'll maintain that incredible momentum today," Memed addressed her in his charmingly courtly manner.

"Thank you, Adnan." She gave him a warm smile in return, pleased not only by the compliment to her riding abilities but by his use of her preferred nickname.

Holly's attention was drawn to her father once again as he reached up to touch the mare with a gloved hand. "You and this horse are winners together, Hortense. Why don't you let me buy her for you as a Christmas present?" Holliford's pale green eyes regarded his daughter speculatively.

She was shocked by this unexpected turnabout in her father's feelings. Only a few short days before he'd called her a failure and had insisted that she return with him to Philadelphia immediately. Now it was apparent that he recognized Holly as a winner and would even be willing to help her.

The idea was at once touching and flattering, although Holly was fully aware of the dangers. She recognized that her father's generous offer was but another attempt to control the direction of her life, and she wanted no part of that. She took a deep breath before replying. "That's very generous of you to offer, dad, but I'll have to decline the gift. Jinniyah is Arif's, and the mare belongs in Turkey. Besides, Mandarin Lady's inflammation will be gone in a few weeks and she'll be as good as new."

"That's your damn pride talking, not common sense," Holliford countered swiftly, annoyed at Holly's refusal to accept his offer.

Father and daughter regarded each other in stubborn silence and the moment might have escalated into a full-blown acrimonious argument if the brisk sound of footsteps hadn't distracted them.

Holly's eyes widened in surprise as she turned to see Arif approaching them, his dark eyes and brooding features a somber contrast to the brilliant red of his competition sweater.

"Good morning, Holly." The greeting was clipped and bore no trace of emotion. Then he turned to his fellow Turk and extended a hand. "Memed," he remarked with equal curtness, "I believe we met once before." Arif's eyes reflected an unsettling blend of challenge and faint amusement.

The industrialist paused only a fraction of a second before accepting the hand of his self-possessed countryman. As she watched the little interchange, Holly was reminded of the men's previous encounter in the Galata Tower restaurant, and she had to quell the laughter that rose to her lips. It was apparent that Arif still did not give a damn about social status and power and whose toes he happened to tread upon in his own prideful advance.

Holly smoothly intervened with a light touch on Arif's arm. "I don't believe you've met my father. Captain Hakal, this is James Holliford."

Once again she had to stifle a mischievous grin as she noted the annoyance in her father's face. Despite the fact that James Holliford was a tall man, he was forced to crane his neck upward in order to look Arif Hakal eye to eye. Usually the situation was reversed and was an integral part of the American financier's subtle tactics of intimidation.

To make up for that initial disadvantage, Holliford addressed the Turkish captain in a voice of cool low arrogance. "I want to buy this mare, Hakal."

Arif grinned briefly at that. "Your offer is a compliment both to the mare and to the woman who rides her so beautifully, but Jinniyah is not for sale."

"Come now, Hakal," Holliford replied impatiently. "I happen to know that the money could come in handy to you, and I'm willing to pay handsomely for the animal." He named an amount that caused his daughter's eyes to widen in surprise.

The muscles along Arif's wide stubborn jawline tightened angrily at the American's none-too-subtle reference to his financial plight. With a tremendous effort of will, he controlled his anger and replied at last, "Once again, Mr. Holliford, I must decline."

There was a long taut silence, and then almost casually the American named an amount that was double his last offer. Arif shook his head in an attitude of curt, almost disdainful refusal that caused Holliford's own carefully contained emotions to rise dangerously. "Come now, captain," he began, his voice hard and smooth as polished diamond, "every man has his price. How much will you take?"

Arif crossed his arms over his chest in an arrogant manner and glowered darkly at the rich American businessman. "I see that you and your daughter are very much alike," he observed in a cold ringing tone that was like the clash of steel against rock. "Your wealth can buy much, Mr. Holliford, but it can't replace certain basic values of honor and pride. The sooner you understand that, the sooner you will understand me. Good day to you, sir." He turned then on his heels and strode toward the stalls.

Holly stared after him, eyes caressing the breadth of his arrogant shoulders. As she regarded his retreating form, she felt herself at once loving and hating him.

Her green eyes sparkled with tears as she swung up onto Jinniyah's back. "Damn you, Arif!" she swore beneath her breath. "How could you let your pride be stronger than our love?"

After bidding a quick goodbye to her father and his friend, she dug her heels into the mare's silver gray flanks, and Jinniyah moved swiftly toward the starting post of the grueling cross-country race. She was glad of one thing, though. Arif had not given in to her father and sold him the mare. Neither one of them would be James Holliford's pawns.

HOLLY PUSHED OPEN THE DOOR of the women's restroom and moved toward the row of white porcelain bowls. She smiled ruefully at her mud-splattered reflection in the mirror. The headlong three-mile gallop over rough and muddy open terrain had been every bit as taxing as she had expected it to be, and her own rather bedraggled appearance was proof of that.

Several riders had been thrown from their mounts during the tricky course, and Holly herself had had a couple of scares when even the surefooted Jinniyah had slipped and threatened to plunge knee first into the bog. But the plucky mare had regained her footing each time.

Almost from the outset there had been no question as to who would dominate the event. Spurred by a heady mixture of pride and suppressed fury, Arif had driven the stallion Sinjon as if he were a fire-eating war-horse. The plucky Jinniyah had followed gamely in the footsteps of her stablemate, but Holly and the mare had offered no serious rivalry to them.

But now, unlike that long-ago race at Malmaison, Holly was more than willing to concede Arif the victory. Though she might take the overall first place for total points in the three events, it was the polished Turkish horseman who had added the punch of excitement and grandeur to the new winter competition with his flawless performance on the dangerous and difficult course. The triumph was wholly his.

Holly's rueful smile dissolved in sadness as she moistened a paper towel and harshly rubbed the streaks of dirt from her cheeks. It was over now. Arif would retire to Riadja with a new bride, while Holly was left to covet her first-place ribbon. She couldn't even remember why it had been so vitally important to win, when all that she could feel inside was a growing sense of emptiness.

A moment later there was a sound of low hoarse sobbing, and Holly looked up quickly. Glancing along the row of stalls to the very last one, she glimpsed a pair of small black-booted feet and moved down the length of the tiled room. The low sobs grew a little louder.

Gingerly Holly pushed the stall door inward and peered around it. Immediately she recognized Tatiana Bulgakov's oversized brown anorak, for that was all she could see of her. The Russian's face was buried in her arms, and her small shoulders were heaving with uncontrollable sobs.

"My God, Tatiana! What is it?" Holly whispered sympathetically, kneeling down on the cold tiles and encircling the petite woman with her arms. For several long minutes she held her friend and soothingly brushed down her straight black hair as if she were a bereft child.

At last Tatiana straightened up and swallowed the last sob with a determined effort. Holly was shocked at her appearance. The Russian's thin features were awash in mud and tears, and there was a jagged cut along the side of her face where the blood had dried and caked. Holly took her hand firmly and led her out to the sink, where she moistened several towels with hot water and set about repairing Tatiana's battle scars.

"Do you want to talk about it?" Holly asked quietly, noticing the torn riding breeches and ripped sweater.

Tatiana shrugged. "Forgive me, Holly, for that childish outburst."

Holly shook the woman's shoulders gently. "I'm supposed to forgive you for showing human emotion?" she teased lightly. "You've learned to laugh, Tati, dear. Now I think it's about time you had a good cry!"

Tatiana smiled a little at that. "You are right, Holly. I have learned those things, though I think perhaps it is too late." Her sad eyes suddenly seemed to dominate her swollen pinched features. "I am certain that you can guess what happened. I was thrown from Kazan—and all my hopes for winning fell with me. I am now an also-was."

"You mean a has-been," Holly corrected automatically, her thoughts churning in wretched circles. "I guess what really matters is what happens now."

"That I do know." Tatiana gestured curtly with her head toward the high window above the radiator. "They are waiting out there to escort me to the airport."

Holly swiftly rose on tiptoe and peered out into the open yard where a small black sedan was parked. There was a driver behind the wheel and in the rear of the car she could just make out the profile of Viktor Kerensky, the consular official who had come to

Holly's room to fetch the lieutenant when they had first arrived in Istanbul. Even as she looked, Holly saw the familiar heavyset bulk of Tatiana's bodyguard approaching the car. He spoke to the other two men through the window before turning to face the arena side door. He leaned back against the car door, eyes never wavering.

Holly's heart leaped to her throat as she regarded the man. It was obvious that they were waiting for Tatiana to reappear so that they could whisk her away. She turned to face the petite lieutenant. "The choice now is entirely yours, Tatiana," she began slowly. "What do you want?"

The woman's eyes never wavered from her American friend's concerned features. "To be with Rusty," Tatiana replied with touching simplicity.

"You're certain about that?" Holly asked.

Tatiana nodded swiftly.

"You. . . you want to defect, then?"

The short length of black hair bobbed forward again. "Yes."

Holly's heart pounded so loudly now with fear that she was certain the men outside in front of the car could hear it. With an effort she brought her racing fears under control. "Wait right here, Tati, and don't even stick your nose outside until I can figure out what to do."

The two women hugged each other, then Holly let herself out into the deserted corridor. She had just glanced cautiously to the right when she felt a hand lightly touch her left shoulder. With a stifled gasp she whirled, only to find herself staring down into Rusty Wilkins's questioning features.

Holly leaned back against the wall and let out a long sigh of relief. "Thank God it's you! Tatiana is inside the restroom. She...she doesn't want to return to Moscow." Holly noticed that the trainer was observing her with a somber expression. In his hands were hot compresses and a first-aid kit. "You...you've already talked to her, then?" Holly whispered down at him. "You know that she doesn't want to return?"

"Yep," he replied laconically. "We had a long talk about it while I helped her off the field and stowed her in that bathroom. The only problem is— what the hell do we do now? This business is a tad out of my line."

Holly shivered. "Out of mine, too. Listen, Rusty, you keep her here while I try to figure out what to do."

"Sure thing," he agreed. "Just don't be all day about it. Those goons outside are going to get tired of holdin' up the show."

Holly headed swiftly toward the stable area without quite knowing why. Badly in need of advice as she was, she could think of only one person to turn to: Arif.

She raced down the long stall corridor and would never in her life have believed until that moment that she would be so relieved to hear Arif's and Geneviève's voices engaged in playful banter. The pretty Tunisian was perched astride the stall door and laughing down at the captain as Holly approached. As Geneviève flecked her amber cat's eyes in her American rival's direction, Holly couldn't help but notice the woman's impeccable riding apparel and perfect makeup. It was apparent that the intrepid Mademoiselle Lamine hadn't even bothered to put Bijou at the starting gate that morning. She had preferred the amused spectator's role as the other riders battled it out over the muddy treacherous course.

Geneviève was about to make some wittily contemptuous remark, but Holly neatly cut her off by calling out Arif's name. He came quickly to the stall door and curtly gestured for Geneviève to let him out. "What is it, Holly?" he demanded, his eyes sharp as he took in her breathless frightened appearance. Swiftly she whispered up to him Tatiana Bulgakov's plight. "What bloody madness!" he swore at last, raking his hands through his hair with an impatient gesture. "But let's see if we can outwit her pursuers."

As he moved to follow her down the corridor, Geneviève's sultry voice rang out at the backs. "Arif, *mon amour*, I am an indulgent woman, but my patience goes only so far. If you disappear now with her, it is the last you will see of me. I swear it!"

His glance over his shoulder was swift and disdainful, but he never paused as he followed Holly out of the dark stable. Beyond the low entrance they ran almost headlong into Leila and a pleasant-faced man who was quickly introduced as his sister's husband, Georg. As Arif's eyes took in his sister's petite form and dark features, he said quietly, "Holly, I have an idea. Would you please ask your father if we can borrow his automobile for the afternoon?"

"What?" Holly replied, perplexed.

"Go on, Holly! Have the driver park it in front of the Russians' car, then I want you to come and meet us at the side door of the arena."

Leila regarded her brother with confused, somewhat angry eyes and would have drawn away from him but for the fact that he'd taken her arm and her husband's in a tight grip that brooked no argument.

When she reached the Chrysler, Holly found that her father and Adnan were nowhere to be seen, but Rocky Stiles was behind the wheel, half dozing. She slipped in beside him and shook his arm. "I need the car, Rocky," she began peremptorily. "Let's go."

"But, Miss Holliford," he protested, "your father—"

"Dad won't mind at all," she retorted easily. "Besides, Mr. Stiles, I think you owe me one. Let's go."

He lifted his pale eyebrows but said nothing further as he turned the key in the ignition. Two minutes later he braked the car to a stop midway between the black sedan and the side door of the arena, just as Arif, Leila and Georg disappeared inside. "Come on, Rocky. I'm not sure what the plan is, but we may need you, as well."

Arif looked up as Holly and Rocky Stiles walked into the shadowy corridor. "Good, the more people the merrier," he murmured approvingly. "Now let's go."

He rapped sharply on the restroom door, and Rusty Wilkins peered cautiously around it. The trainer came out into the corridor, and Leila was bustled inside.

Holly went to join Arif, who stood back from the shadowy entrance regarding the waiting Russians. "Do you think it will work?" she whispered nervously.

Arif shrugged. "We have no choice but to try it. It just might work because they won't be expecting it."

A low murmur of surprise and approval at their backs deflected their attention from the disturbing scene outside, and Holly and Arif turned to regard the two dark petite women who had reentered the corridor from the restroom.

One was dressed in black riding boots, breeches and the familiar dark brown anorak, its hood pulled and knotted securely beneath the chin. The other wore a wraparound camel-colored coat with high-heeled burgundy boots and a stylish burgundy wool beret pulled low over her forehead.

They had emerged wearing the exact same apparel that they'd worn when they went in—with one simple difference. It was Leila who now wore the riding clothes and heavy jacket, while Tatiana was fitted out stylishly in the petite Turkish woman's clothing. They had exchanged not only clothing but identities, as well. The transformation was complete.

Glancing over at Arif, Holly saw his eyes narrow as he took in the appearance of the two women. "Excellent," he said at last in a low pleased voice, walking forward toward them. "Now I think we're ready for our cat-and-mouse game with the men outside."

Arif, Tatiana and Georg stood slightly back from the side entrance and watched in taut silence as the other four ran the few yards to the parked Chrysler.

There was a glimpse of the long brown parka and pulled-up hood as Leila disappeared into the rear seat, followed by Rusty Wilkins. A second later Holly and Rocky slipped into the front and the car squealed away from the open area. The black sedan revved its engine and followed in hot pursuit.

Arif turned and grinned engagingly down at the petite Russian woman at his side. "Well, lieutenant, I think our compatriots have taken the bait. Shall we drive on over to the American Consulate in the Fiat? I don't think you'll have to worry about shadowy tails any longer."

Tatiana managed a small but warm smile in return. "I cannot express to you what a remarkably wonderful feeling that is. Thank you, captain," she added simply.

HOLLY GLANCED NERVOUSLY AROUND past Leila's hooded head through the rear window of the car. The Russians were following closely, and it was apparent that they were determined not to let their quarry escape.

Leila turned around and risked a quick glance, as well. When she looked in Holly's direction again, the American girl was astonished to see Leila smiling. "Miss MacKnight," she said, enormous brown eyes alight with excitement, "I cannot wait to tell my father of this adventure. He will be proud of me... and Arif, too."

Holly's own smile was somewhat rueful; she wondered if Leila would be so amused by their little adventure if she knew that it had cost Arif's engagement to Geneviève Lamine.

Holly turned swiftly toward the front of the car, suddenly unable to bear looking at Leila's expressive eyes and dark features, which were so reminiscent of her brother's.

After a moment Rocky Stiles asked, "Where to now, Miss Holliford?"

She shrugged her shoulders indifferently. "It doesn't matter. To the Sheraton, I suppose, to return dad's car. He'll be furious as it is at the way I commandeered it."

As the car turned into the wide driveway leading to the hotel, the small black sedan that had been following so assiduously darted into the lane beside them and attempted to run the Americans' car into the shrubbery-lined border. After his initial surprise, Rocky warmed to the game and attempted some strong-arm tactics of his own, so that the two automobiles ricocheted drunkenly off each other in a crazy zigzag almost to the front doors of the hotel.

Driven by desperation, the two men in the front seat of the black sedan jumped out as the Chrysler came to a halt and brandished a pair of revolvers at the occupants in the back seat.

Rusty jumped out, followed by Leila, who threw back the hood of the brown jacket as she stepped out onto the sidewalk. "I think there is a law against the attempted kidnap of Turkish citizens," she said sharply, eyeing the men confronting her.

They turned in confusion to look for further in-structions from their boss, and a moment later Kerensky stepped out onto the curb. "Please forgive the misunderstanding," the official said in a smooth dry voice that was remarkably devoid of emotion. He turned then, and his sharp gray eyes raked the interior of the Chrysler until they met Holly's gaze.

"Hello, Mr. Kerensky," she greeted him with a mischievous smile as she slid across the seat and stepped out onto the sidewalk. "So nice to see you again."

The Russian's only reply was a steely glare. He had just turned to climb into his own car when a taxi pulled up and James Holliford emerged from it.

Holliford's gaze took in the burly Russian guards just putting away their guns and the satisfied looks on the faces of his daughter and her diminutive trainer. "Hortense! Wilkins!" he began curtly. "May I ask why you took my car and driver and what the devil is going on here?"

Holly linked her arm through his. "It's a long story, dad. I think Rocky should drive Rusty and Leila over to the American Consulate. In the meantime I'll treat you to lunch out of my winnings, and I'll explain everything."

Holliford's eyes narrowed. "What choice do I have? It looks as though you're suddenly calling the shots."

"Only as far as my own life goes," she retorted quietly. "I'm rather a different person from the one who ran away from Philadelphia six weeks ago."

Holliford smiled wryly. "Yes. I can see that."

She stepped into the lobby with him, willing herself

not to think of Arif and the others at the consulate.
Holly felt curiously spent after the little drama that
had occurred. She couldn't yet steel herself to under-
go another when she was forced to tell Arif goodbye
for the last time. That would have to wait.

CHAPTER FOURTEEN

THE BEDSIDE PHONE rang shrilly. Holly groped for it in the darkness and lifted the receiver.

"Hello?" she mumbled sleepily.

Her trainer's familiar drawl crackled over the receiver to her. "Mornin', Holly," he began brightly. "Can you make it over here to the American Consulate right quick? We're in need of your services."

"Rusty! What time is it?"

"Seven," he replied at once. "Try to make it by eight. Okay, gal?"

"Rusty...." She had been about to make a sharp retort, but the line clicked into silence as he hung up. She replaced the phone on its cradle and rolled over onto her back with a sigh, wondering what that had been all about. She was tempted to burrow back down beneath the covers, but she couldn't let Rusty down now. She willed herself not to think of her own future looming so emptily before her.

Holly recalled her lunchtime conversation with her father the previous afternoon and the new look of respect in his eyes. She knew she'd won a great tactical victory as far as her father was concerned: he had acknowledged her as a woman with the right to forge her own destiny. He would no longer interfere.

The bitter irony, of course, was that the life and the destiny she would have chosen were denied to her by the one man who had loved her as no other man would ever love her again. Arif had put his pride before their love, and now they both were to suffer for it.

Holly threw back the covers and padded barefoot to the bathroom, hoping a hot shower would ease the dull aching of her exhausted emotions. But as her soaped hands slid languidly along her wet breasts and thighs, she recalled the pressure of Arif's warm capable touch arousing her to joy, and she knew she would never exorcise the memory of that dark sensuality and the fiercely tender love that had flared between them.

A SLEEPY-EYED GUARD unlocked the wrought-iron gate and ushered Holly into the dark consulate. In the foyer an immense pine tree aglitter with tinsel and shiny glass ornaments reminded her with a shock that it was Christmas Day. The guard gestured toward a narrow stairway at the end of the hall, indicating that she was to make her way past the rows of closed office doors to a small suite on the second floor.

As she headed toward the dimly lit staircase she drew her fringed challis shawl closer around her. She climbed slowly, her footsteps muffled by the deep carpet.

At the top she drew in her breath as she glimpsed the familiar dark rugged profile before a second-story hall window. Arif's hands were thrust into the pockets of his gray corduroy suit pants as he stared out into the consulate gardens, his brows drawn together in a thoughtful attitude. He turned swiftly at her approach and straightened the black knit tie at his throat.

She stopped several feet shy of him and raised her chin to keep it from quivering. The mere sight of him was like a devastating blow that left her weak and unsteady. She quelled the urge to run toward him— he was not hers to claim.

"Arif, what are you doing here?" she asked, keeping her voice low and cool with an effort.

When he saw that she meant to approach no closer, he came forward with slow easy grace. His dark eyes gleamed like fire against a nighttime sky as he stared down at her, but she sensed a hidden mischievousness in their depths. "I'm here for the same reason you are, Holly—a small matter of a wedding ceremony."

"Wedding?" she repeated uncertainly.

"Yes. American marriages require two witnesses in order to be legal, don't they?"

"Of course," Holly replied, once again keeping her voice steady and even only with great effort. She turned her head swiftly toward the window to keep from meeting his gaze. For one insane moment she had thought Arif was making a reference to a wedding of their own rather than to Rusty's and Tatiana's. Now she could not let him read the pain and disappointment in her eyes.

As she flung her head, the jade stone against her earlobe caught the morning light, and Arif raised his hand to it. His dark fingertips brushed her jawline and the edge of her cheek as he pushed back her honey-colored hair to regard the stone. His innocent but sensual touch was like a caressing breeze, and unable to bear the exquisite wanting that it aroused, she reached up to push his hand away.

But as she did so, the flowered shawl fell away to reveal the jade *kisbeh* wound in triple strands about her slender wrist. Arif caught her arm with strong but gentle fingers and slowly lifted it.

"You wear my heritage beautifully," he whispered in a slow caressing voice. Then he raised her palm to his lips and gently kissed it.

Holly struggled to pull her hand away, but he held it firmly imprisoned. She shook her head, eyes glistening with tears until they resembled the darkly luminous Turkish jade that she wore.

"Arif, no! I can't bear any more of this!" she cried, cursing herself inwardly for having kept the jade. She had wanted to keep a part of him with her, but she knew the remembrance would only serve to make the loss more painful. "You...you shouldn't have come here this morning. Or else I shouldn't have. It's wrong for us to be near each other when we could so easily—"

"We are here because our friends asked us to be," he broke in as she attempted to turn back toward the stairway.

Her head whipped around at that. "Pardon me, Captain Hakal. I forgot your precious adherence to duty," she said angrily, all the old hurts torn open once again.

To her surprise he laughed, a rich harmonious

sound that held neither bitterness nor mockery. "You will always be the high-tempered mare, won't you? Quick to bridling anger...but equally quick to love."

She stopped her struggle to free her wrist from his viselike grip and stared up at him with eyes that raged and sparkled like a deep mountain pool in sunlight. "That's something you'll never know again, Arif!" she whispered softly.

He inclined his head in an attitude of mock defeat, eyes filled with subtle glints of mischief.

A door opened behind them and a round cheerful face above a black collar peeped at them. "They're here," he called back into the room. "We can proceed now."

Rusty and Tatiana stood before the consul's desk, their features at once solemn and radiating happiness. The trainer grinned sheepishly in Holly's direction, then turned back quickly as the beaming minister cleared his throat.

As he intoned the traditional words—"for richer or poorer...in sickness and in health"—Holly could not hold back the sad envy that threatened to suffocate her and engulf the genuine happiness she felt for her friends. The fleeting stir of envy was supplanted then by anger. She glanced in Arif's direction, only to find that his eyes were upon her, regarding her with a deep measuring gaze. When he caught her glance, Holly saw his lips curve slightly in a grin, and she wondered in aggravation what he had to be so happy about.

A few minutes later the short ceremony was over,

the bride was kissed and a bottle of champagne was opened.

Holly lifted her glass to Rusty's with a teasing grin. "For an old cowpoke, you moved mighty fast on this one."

"Well," he drawled with a grin, "you know how it goes. I figured that marryin' her right away would for sure keep her out of the clutches of that old bulldog who was tailin' her from place to place."

"Well, you should be grateful for that old bulldog," she laughed. "If it weren't for him, a confirmed old bachelor like you might never have taken the plunge."

Rusty grinned. "I expect you're right about that."

There was a lull as both their thoughts turned to more serious matters.

"What will you and Tatiana do now, Rusty?" she asked at last.

He shrugged. "Find a nice horse ranch in the States and work like the dickens. Even though Tati is in safe hands now, I still think it'd be better to get her out of this atmosphere."

Holly sighed. "I'm sure you're right."

Rusty looked up at her sharply. "But what'll you do without a trainer? You ain't goin' back to Philly with your old man, I hope?"

"I honestly don't know, Rusty."

Arif came up then to extend his congratulations, and Holly took advantage of the opportunity to slip out of the room after giving a quick hug to Tatiana. Downstairs she hurried along the deserted halls past the unlit Christmas tree and let herself out onto the street.

The morning air was crisp and clear as she made her way along the narrow sidewalk. Fruit hucksters and pastry vendors worked busily to set up their stalls as early-morning commuters whipped along the cobbled lane.

Holly glanced into the Pera Palas as she strolled past, the old-fashioned splendor of its lobby bringing to mind a patchwork of memories: her first night in Istanbul and waiting with Tatiana for the creaking iron-caged elevator; Arif's unexpected appearance at her bedroom door that next morning; their journey to Riadja.... Her eyes filmed with tears, and a second later her high heel caught on an uneven stone in the sidewalk.

She might have fallen but for the strong hand that reached out to catch her arm. Holly turned around to thank her rescuer, but the words died on her lips when she saw that it was Arif.

Though she regarded him coldly, he ignored her chilly mood. "Fine day for a wedding, don't you think, Holly?" he remarked conversationally as he fell into step beside her, keeping a firm grip on her arm.

"I suppose so," she replied coolly, her eyes roving over the colorful street scene of morning vendors and shoppers. "Now if you'll excuse me, I have to get a cab back to the Sheraton."

"What's the rush?" he asked innocently.

"I've work to do. My trainer just quit and I've got a lame mare on my hands," she retorted crisply. "Now if you will excuse me...." Holly attempted to free her arm, but she found herself being pulled around to face Arif squarely.

"It's difficult to talk to you, Holly, when you're trying to rush pell-mell along a crowded sidewalk," he said impatiently.

"What can we possibly have to talk about, Arif?"

He shrugged, and a wicked playful gleam lit up his dark features. "I suppose that I'm next in line as groom, since Rusty passed this on to me." He reached into his pocket and retrieved a lacy garter, which he dangled in front of her nose.

"How very charming," Holly observed dryly.

"Indeed," he retorted, his voice soft and underscored with amusement. "In fact, I've decided on the woman I'm going to marry."

"Oh, really?" Holly replied with a sarcastic lilt. "And am I supposed to beg to know the name of the lucky woman? It shouldn't be too difficult a matter of deduction. Or was Geneviève's little scene yesterday at the stable merely an act?"

Arif grinned. "As you once noted, Holly, some women have little pride where I'm concerned."

"That should contrast nicely with your overweening arrogance," she shot back tartly.

Arif threw back his head and laughed. "Hellion!" he swore softly.

Before she had time to fling out another angry gibe, he had signaled for a taxi and bundled her into the back seat, climbing in beside her. He gave curt orders in Turkish to the driver, and the cab leaped into the din of traffic.

After five minutes Holly protested. "This is *not* the way to the Sheraton. I resent being kidnapped like this."

Arif shrugged easily. "You left something behind at my home. I wished to return it to you."

"What do you mean?" she demanded suspiciously.

His only reply was a mocking grin.

Within another five minutes the taxi had pulled to an abrupt halt before his building, and Arif thrust a wad of *lira* notes into the driver's hand before leading Holly up the stairs to his apartment.

Once inside he strode to the fireplace and threw a match atop the cedar kindling in the grate. The fire crackled to life and reflected off the decanter of wine and two crystal glasses set on the low coffee table before it.

Holly marched behind him and set her hands angrily on her hips. "Okay, Arif. You've got me here; now tell me what it was that I left behind!"

He lifted the lid from the box on the sofa and pulled out the silken caftan she'd worn only once before. Then he held it out to her.

She shook her head proudly. "It's not mine, Arif. Save it for your wife."

His brows drew together as if he were concentrating deeply, although the somber expression on his face was belied by the dark laughter in his eyes. "Perhaps you're right, after all," he said slowly. "It is appropriate only for the bride of Riadja."

"Then I have no further business here." She moved toward the door, but he blocked her way. Slowly he reached up and pulled the shawl from her shoulders, and deftly his fingers unfastened the top buttons of her ivory shirt dress. He paused then and held the caftan out to her.

"Here, Holly," he said, the rich timbre of his voice deepened by some new well of emotion. "Put it on."

"What. . . what do you mean?" she stammered.

"Holly, I am asking you to marry me."

"But, Arif. . . what has happened to change your mind?" she asked, her voice softly incredulous.

Arif grinned and lifted caressing fingers to her face, tracing the pretty line of her questioning lips and the luminous softness of her cheeks. "The hand of fate intervened," he teased. "Remember I told you of my father's unwise investments and his latest venture in a Diyarbakir chromium mine?"

Holly nodded, green eyes transfixed on his teasing dark gaze.

"Well," he continued, "his partner struck a mother lode. The mine has made rich men of them both overnight. My mother telegraphed the news yesterday. Riadja is saved by a stroke of fate."

"You beast!" Holly retorted. "You've been leading me along all morning, though I suppose I deserved it after the turnabout I played on you as the rich American heiress," she chuckled. Then her gaze grew serious once again. "Arif, this means that you. . . are a free man, then."

"Yes, Holly. Free to marry the woman of my choosing. . . free to marry the woman whom I love and cherish. If you will accept."

"I thought you'd never ask," she laughed softly, her eyes radiant as she lifted her face to his. Her lips parted joyously to the sweetly demanding invasion of his kiss.

HOURS LATER they lay arm in arm before the dying embers in the grate, a soft throw pulled over their entwined limbs.

"You see, Arif," Holly teased, her voice sated with love and happiness, "the Gypsy woman in the café was right after all. I was destined to marry a rich man."

"Ah, yes, I'd forgotten," he laughed against her fragrant hair. "The dark stranger destined to change your life forever. Perhaps we should seek out the old woman again."

"Why?" She turned her head on the pillow to look at him.

"To have her tell us how long it is before we can expect our first heir to Riadja."

"Wretch!" Holly cried out in mock dismay. "She found you a bride. Can't we work out the rest on our own?"

What readers say about SUPERROMANCE

"Bravo! Your SUPERROMANCE [is]...super!"
R.V.,* Montgomery, Illinois

"I am impatiently awaiting
the next SUPERROMANCE."
J.D., Sandusky, Ohio

"Delightful...great."
C.B., Fort Wayne, Indiana

"Terrific love stories. Just
keep them coming!"
M.G., Toronto, Ontario

*Names available on request.